KING ELIJAH

THE ZEMIRAN CHRONICLES

2

D.L. BLADE

SOCIAL MEDIA

To learn more about D.L. Blade and her books, click the link to visit:

Goodreads:

@D_L_Blade

TikTok:

@authordlblade

Facebook:

@dlblade

Instagram:

@booksbydlblade

Pinterest:

@DLBlade

YouTube:

@DLBlade

Newsletter:

www.linktr.ee/dlblade

AUTHOR'S NOTE

Full content warnings can be found on my website:
www.dlblade.com

NEWICK
COUNTRY OF MYLORIA
HEYERBERG
MYLORIAN SEA
WHITESTONE MOUNTAIN
ZEMIRAN SEA
COUNTRY OF ZEMIRA
TERTH

I

ELIJAH

The Palace

The lilac-gray ceiling was now a blank slate of nothingness. Ornate art once lined the chamber walls—each piece more repulsive than the last. The gaudy art had been designed by one of the former king's craftsmen. Elijah's dark brows drew together at the memory of a home he once had, a place reminding him of his father. When Elijah was crowned the King of Zemira two years ago, he set out to make the palace his own, erasing any trace of that man's shadow.

Turning to the side of his pillow, he rolled off his mattress and sauntered to the floor-length mirror by his wooden armoire. He gazed at the image staring back at him.

Dark shadows were smeared under his deep blue eyes, and his disheveled, unruly black hair reminded him that he hadn't slept in days. Magic stirred inside him, seeding a dark sense of foreboding—the unseen danger clutched at his chest. It was a heightened awareness that something was drawing closer.

The hollow sound of horses' hooves echoed off the pavement through the palace courtyard.

It wasn't morning yet; he had barely shut his eyes.

Something's wrong, Elijah thought, *especially at this hour of the night.*

He placed his thick black robe on, tightening the belt around his waist.

Before reaching the door, Liam stormed in without even a knock to warn him. His iron-gray hair glinted against his rich brown skin within the darkness of the room, reflecting the faintest light from the wood torches outside Elijah's window.

Liam Cadigan was younger than Elijah by a few years, but Liam had gone gray at the early age of twenty. If it weren't for his smooth, unblemished skin, one would think he was too old to be King Elijah's head of the royal guard.

"Stay in your room, Your Majesty," Liam said hastily, pressing his hand firmly against Elijah's broad chest to move him further back into the room. He turned his head to look over his shoulder through the entrance of the doorway.

"Someone has breached the wall." Liam unsheathed his sword and held it out in front of him, as if the intruder would come charging into the king's chamber at any moment.

Elijah's brows knitted tightly together. "Breached the wall?"

How the hell did that happen? the king thought.

At least a hundred men guarded the palace. It would be impossible for anyone to get close enough to the gates before being struck down. The drawbridge was the only other entrance aside from the underground tunnel that led to the dungeon.

"What about the guards at the front gates?" Elijah asked, looking at him pointedly.

"Four men down," he replied sharply.

Elijah furrowed his brow. "Dead?" he asked, rushing past Liam despite the guard's order. "Lock down the castle. If someone is inside, we can trap them before they can escape. I'll get my hands on whoever thought they could break into my palace and walk out of here alive!"

Liam threw his hands up. "Before they kill you, you mean?"

A glint of irritation crossed Elijah's features. "Liam, you underestimate me. I am *not* my father," he reminded him. "You think this is the first time someone from my kingdom has tried to assassinate me? I'll not run and hide as he did."

Liam straightened his red tunic and bowed his head. "Of course, sir. What would you like to do?"

A devious smile crept up Elijah's lips. He turned to face the corner of his room where his sword lay across the table. "See who's still standing, and have them block each entrance. Even the ones that don't face the city."

Liam gave him a curt nod. "Yes, Your Majesty," he said, leaving Elijah alone in the chamber.

He had meant what he said; Elijah was no stranger to the feeling of his own people trying to kill him. When he became King of Zemira, his focus had been on bringing peace to the people, and thus far, he had seen remarkable success. Magical creatures and humans now lived side by side once again. Most of the rebels had surrendered because they no longer believed the royal family was a threat to them. The beginning of Elijah's rule represented a fundamental change in the fabric of the kingdom for most people. Law and order were the governing principles as he worked to keep his people safe.

However, Elijah wasn't naïve enough to ignore the darkness that had always followed him. Not every Zemiran felt free, and he was an easy target for their ire. They would rather blame one man than tease apart the many threads of their society and history that kept them feeling uneasy. He could manage their misguided anger, though. It was only when that simmering resentment pushed his own people to try and take his life that he let himself feel unfairly judged.

Elijah never wanted to be the villain, yet that was exactly how they saw him.

Quietly, he crept through the doorway and into the hall.

He stopped, listening to the faint sound of someone coming up the main stairs. The king swallowed, feeling a sudden tightness in his chest. Several of the assassination attempts on King Elijah occurred in the city but were always stopped by his guards before any harm could befall him. A break-in inside the palace was brave.

Or stupid, he thought.

A dark shadow dashed from one room to the other, catching his eye. Elijah stilled, holding his sword out, and began to summon his power. The delicate tingle of the mist left his fingers, trailing down the baseboards. The black smoke crept into the room that the intruder had snuck into, feeling for their presence.

"I would suggest you come out now, or I'll end your pathetic life in your poor attempt to take mine," Elijah warned, waiting for a response that didn't come. "Or," he began again, "I can draw you out and cast you to the dungeon. It has been too long since I've had a prisoner to torture. I hope my skills haven't gotten rusty."

He wondered if the intruder was human—or something else.

Right at that thought, a throwing star flew from the darkness toward him. He dodged the sharp blade right before it hit his chest.

Elijah blinked. "Well, that wasn't very nice. I can't even see you. Let us play fair, shall we?"

The floor creaked as the hooded intruder stepped into the hall. The shadow at the far end was tall and willowy. It was clear to Elijah that the assassin was a woman.

Elijah's eyes narrowed as she took a step closer to him.

Oh, so brave! Elijah thought with admiration.

"How about you surrender what weapons you have left before I—"

She ran toward him at full speed while unsheathing the sword at her hip. The blade came straight at Elijah with deadly intent.

He raised his hands, allowing the dark smoke to move forward, but she dodged the attack skillfully before the magic took hold of her. She leapt at lightning speed, sword held high overhead as her boots found purchase on the wall, using it to kick off and come down on Elijah from above. Elijah was forced to bend backward to avoid the blow. The assassin barreled down on him, but the blade missed Elijah's throat—if only by an inch. The sharp sting of the blade caught on his arm, and a line of red appeared on his skin, but it was only a scratch. Nothing could deter Elijah from bringing up his own weapon and slashing at the hooded killer. It was far from a lethal blow, but he felt the blade bite into the flesh of the assassin's arm, causing her to stumble. Her sword clattered on the floor, and she let out a loud yelp of pain.

Elijah had expected to see the assassin reach for her fallen sword, but instead, her face turned up to look at him. The momentary distraction was enough, and Elijah was caught by surprise as she lashed out. A black bootheel smashed into Elijah's chest, sending him flying across the hall.

The force from that kick was unlike any human he had ever encountered.

She's unnaturally strong, he thought.

Before Elijah could clamber to his feet, his legs became tangled in the folds of his robe that had fallen open when he slammed into the ground. Before he could react, the assassin was on him. The boot's heel was coming for him once more—that time aimed at his face—but Elijah was able to reach up and grab her leg before it made contact. With one hand wrapped around her leg, the assassin was trapped in an awkward position, allowing Elijah to use his other hand to release his magic. It poured from his fingers and reached for the killer, grabbing her by the throat and squeezing. Elijah wanted to see the life choked out of her, but she jerked her foot out of Elijah's grasp and stumbled backward, out of reach. The assassin coughed a few times, trying to purge the smoke still clinging to her throat, and Elijah couldn't suppress a hungry smile at its sound. He had always relished the feeling he got right before he was about to make the final blow.

Elijah stepped forward. "I can make it quick if you'd like," he said. "Tell me who sent you."

He began to slowly ease the magic so the woman could speak, but the coughing continued.

"Tell me who sent you!" Elijah repeated. "Now!"

The assassin stopped trying to pry Elijah's power away but instead reached inside her cloak, pulling out a golden gem.

A *Newick* gem.

Elijah's sight honed in on the unnatural light bouncing off the gem. The bright golden hue suddenly lit the hallway, releasing its magical power. As Elijah shielded his eyes from the blinding light, the intruder slammed her shoulder into Elijah's chest, sending them both crashing to the floor.

The gem slipped out of the assassin's grasp, soaring through the air, and landed in one of the open bedrooms. They both reached for each other, trying to get better leverage on their opponent. The length of the assassin's body pressed him into the floor. The killer was strong and fierce but, as a woman, much smaller than the king. Using his weight, Elijah heaved himself up, flipping them to reverse the position, and grabbed the intruder's arm while turning her body toward him. He forcefully bent the arm up behind her back at a curved angle, subduing her with the threat of a dislocated shoulder.

The fingers of his other hand dug into the rough fabric of the woman's cloak, yanking back the hood to finally reveal her face. But when Elijah saw what had been shrouded in shadow, he went still. The unexpected sight of delicate features and large, bright blue eyes blindsided him.

The woman's hair was as white as the freshly fallen snow. Her eyes shined like sapphire-blue diamonds, and her lips were colored in a vibrant shade of rose.

He reached out, and she flinched away, going completely still. Elijah set his lips in a hard line before pulling back her long strands of hair to the side to reveal her ears.

The assassin was an elf. A *beautiful* elf.

Her body went rigid as she looked into Elijah's eyes. The beginning of a smile crept across his face, but it was short-lived. The elf snapped her head forward, closing the distance between them, and collided her forehead with his nose with a *crack*. Elijah couldn't stop himself from flinching back in pain, blood slowly seeping from his nostrils. He released his hold on her just enough for her to twist out of his grasp. She produced a small dagger from within the folds of her cloak, thrusting it toward him, but Elijah managed to catch her wrist before she struck a blow.

His fingers squeezed and twisted her delicate wrist until she released the dagger, dropping it to the floor. Elijah shoved her hard, and she slammed back onto the stone floor. He brought his focus to bear on keeping her pinned beneath him. She was lithe, attempting to use her slight frame to slip out from under him, but he squeezed his knees together to where they bracketed her hips and pushed her wrists into the floor, keeping her still. He grabbed the belt from his robe and quickly lashed her wrists together, further restraining her movements.

"Is that all the weapons you have?" he asked with a smile tugging on the side of his lip. "Or do I need to search under your clothes?"

Her lips parted, and she took a few heavy breaths. The Elven woman's eyes dimmed right before she flashed her teeth at him in a hateful snarl. "Such pathetic threats from an incompetent king," she said. "You are crushing my hips."

He squeezed harder, grinding into her until she winced. "You were saying?" he said, but they were quickly interrupted by the remaining guards, led by Liam, running down the hall toward them.

Elijah crawled off her but kept her bound wrists in a tight grip. He kept his eyes carefully on the woman before turning to Liam. "Search that bedroom for a yellow gem," Elijah told his guard while two men roughly gripped each of the elf woman's arms, making her stand on her feet. "And I demand to know how she got into the palace without being seen!"

She tried to wrench free from the guards' hold, but it was to no avail.

The woman defiantly lifted her head and turned away, avoiding his eyes.

Elijah reached out, gripped her jaw, and forced her to look at him. His features darkened, and he knew she felt his power as her breathing turned ragged. "You come into my palace, kill my men, and try to kill me? The king?" he said, his brows pulling together. "I should snap your neck right here in the hall or run my sword through your chest and let the courtyard ravens feed on your corpse."

She wriggled again, but the guards kept her in place.

A tiny smile pulled at the side of her lips. "Hmm. Interesting choice of a weapon to kill someone when you have magic," the woman said, raising one of her brows. "Perhaps you're not as scary as all the tales I've heard."

Oh, Elijah thought, *she is going to be fun.*

He straightened his back. "Put her in the dungeon. I will see to her once I get a good night's sleep," he said, turning to Liam once more as he handed off the gem to the king.

"Is that a Newick gem?" Liam asked.

Elijah didn't answer, only swirled the magical gem in his palm. His eyes set to the Elven assassin who had turned her nose up. He could see the fear in her eyes despite her false bravado.

"How many guards are left, Liam?" Elijah asked without looking at his guard—his eyes on only hers, afraid that she would disappear if he were to blink.

"The guards who protect the front gates are down. We will need Aiden and his men to stay inside the palace walls until we can replace them. There is not enough defense to protect you from this happening again."

"This," Elijah said through his teeth, gripping the stone tightly, "will never happen again!"

Elijah pocketed the gem and relaxed his shoulders.

"How do you know that's a Newick gem, Your Majesty?" Liam asked, that time avoiding the king's eyes.

A smile flickered across Elijah's face. "Because I felt its power moments before you marched into my room."

The truth was, he had felt its power for weeks now but was unsure what it was exactly. The assassin must have been hiding in the city long before the attack.

Liam stepped next to the king, his hand lying loosely on the sword at his hip. "And what of the elf woman, sir?"

Elijah's smile broadened, glancing back at his new prisoner. She swallowed at the predatory look on his face. "Tomorrow, we start our interrogation, of course." He stepped toward her, reaching out to run his hands through her long white hair. "And you, little elf, will tell me everything."

2

NOLA

Credale

Nola tightened the ornate shawl around her body as a brisk chill swept across the ship.

"Do you—" Lincoln started jovially, his teeth clattering from the cold.

Before he finished the question, Kitten held up her palm. "It's not as if we're going to say, 'No,' Captain," Kitten said. "I will!" A smile broadened her lips as she looked back at Boots. "Absolutely, aye."

"I will," Boots echoed warmly.

The two held hands and kept their eyes locked. Mazie leaned into Nola and nudged her with a shoulder.

"I'm not going to cry," Mazie said. Her pixie, Bay, perched on her shoulder and fluttered her wings in empathy. "I don't cry at weddings."

Nola turned to Mazie as her usually stoic friend leaned back against the chair. Mazie donned a bright red dress for the ceremony that complemented her deep ebony skin and flowed softly down her ankles. It wasn't her usual all-black and skin-tight attire. Nola found the outfit stunning on her, except for the scowl painted across Mazie's lips and a barely noticeable tear falling down her cheek.

"Oh, Mazie, stop pretending you're void of feeling."

"I am," she said distastefully. Nola did her level best not to smirk.

Their attention turned back to the front, where the ceremony was concluding. "I now pronounce you Pirate and Pirate," Lincoln said. "Woman, kiss your first mate."

The crew leapt to their feet, shouting congratulations, throwing up their hats, and raising their glasses.

Boots pulled Kitten in and then wrapped his arm around her waist. Then he dipped her back and passionately kissed her on the lips.

Lincoln didn't see a second of it, though. His eyes were on Nola like they always were, and a soft glow of affection surrounded him. She looked up at her captain, their eyes meeting, and he mouthed, "I love you," so only she would see.

The sea splashed hard against the ship, causing it to rock, and the crew planted their feet on the deck to keep their chairs from falling over.

Seagulls migrated overhead, and the sound of the city bells chimed. They only had a few hours before they needed to move the ship away from the dock to allow the city supply vessels to come through.

The town of Credale was one of the smaller cities in Zemira, south of the capital, Terth. They were at least two hours by ship from the palace, and though the crew had discussed docking near the castle for a few nights, there was a winter storm passing through, and they didn't want to get trapped in it.

Nola clambered to her feet. When she turned around, Kitten stood there, a vision in her enchanting black wedding dress with a radiant smile across her face.

"Thank you," Kitten said softly, her eyes glistening. "You really have been one of a kind."

Kitten hadn't stopped thanking her since they left the Shadow Land; at least, that was the name they had called it. It was the last and final world they had ventured to with the Kroneon. The world that, if it were not for quick thinking on both Nola and Mazie's part, would have consumed them all.

"Leaving the pirate life is nothing I ever thought I'd do," Kitten said. "But it's for the best." Nola looked down as Kitten placed her hand affectionately on her belly. "She's already kicking."

"You think it's a girl?" Nola asked her.

Kitten nodded. "I can already sense her fearless heart."

Boots staggered over and pulled Nola in for a warm hug, squeezing her so tight the air left her lungs for a moment. "Take care of the crew," Boots said, setting her back down. The look on his face was one they had all seen in each other's eyes since narrowly escaping the Shadow Land two weeks ago—genuine fear.

"We're safe, Boots," Nola reminded him. "We aren't going back. Ever."

Boots nodded and turned to his new bride. Kitten smiled and held out her hand for him to take.

"I'm hungry as a whale, love. Let's eat!" she said.

Boots walked hand in hand with Kitten, and they stepped off the Sybil Curse's ladder, turning around one last time while standing on the gangplank. They both wiped away the tears falling down their cheeks, waved goodbye, and walked together toward their new beginning in the city.

Lincoln watched his longtime friends for a moment, and then his beautiful green eyes gleamed as he turned to look into Nola's.

It had been strange between them the last two weeks. Well, it was strange for all of them. Nola and the crew had sailed, eaten, and laughed together for two years, facing the dangers of the waters and the other worlds again and again, but they had almost died in the Shadow Land. Every single one of them came within inches of violent death. The creature who chased them out of their land had nearly latched on to Kitten, knocking her to the ground as the portal opened and causing her to land hard on her belly. She had realized she was pregnant by then, and her every thought was about her unborn child's life. It was too close.

After they escaped and closed the portal, Lincoln locked the Kroneon up so no one could ever touch it again. Kitten and Boots decided it was best to leave the pirate life, at least on the ship, for the safety of their family.

Three days after they closed that portal, Boots knelt before Kitten. His hushed proposal was made clear when he held up the very ring the crew had stolen from Queen Aliyana, the fierce ruler of the Land of the Banshees. The wedding, though, wasn't what they expected.

Hill staggered over and straightened up his suit.

It is strange, Nola thought, *seeing him dressed up with his hair nicely styled and slicked back over his head.*

Hill's leg had been injured on their journey, and though he wouldn't match Boots with a peg leg, it was enough for him to leave too.

A wedding and four fewer crew members to follow.

Nola recounted the decision that had been made a week prior.

"I'll take care of him, Lincoln," Ardley had promised after they had escaped the Shadow Land, helping Hill to sit on the nearest chest. "Hill has had it rough, and I think it's time we hang up our pirate swords."

The tipsy pirate raised his sobered, pain-filled eyes to his captain and offered a weak smile. "Aye, Captain. I am no longer of use to you; I am broken beyond repair," Hill had said with sadness choking his voice.

Lincoln took a breath and then walked to Hill, placing his hand on his shoulder. "Hill, you are an unbreakable force that I am honored to have had on my ship. You cannot be replaced, mate. You'll heal, and you'll walk tall once again." Lincoln smiled and turned to Ardley.

"Matey?"

"Yes, Captain?" Ardley replied.

"You have my blessing to depart from Sybil Curse and take care of our dear Mr. Hill for as long as it takes." Lincoln winked and clapped a hand on Ardley's shoulder.

Ardley swallowed the tears welling up and clasped Lincoln's arm. "Thank you, Captain Lincoln. Thank you." He sniffled quietly.

Nola's thoughts drew back to the present. The conversation about Kitten and Boots leaving wasn't surprising to her, but Hill and Ardley had planned to stay behind as well—she hadn't expected that.

Lincoln turned to Nola and placed his hand on her cheek, caressing his thumb along the softness of her tanned skin. "We need to head further east as soon as we can. Zemiran waters are freezing this time of year. We won't make it past the reef before hitting the ice."

She gave him a curt nod. "I agree."

Ardley helped Hill to a chair and gave him a mug of water. He turned to his mates, smiled, and said, "Now that the stuffy formalities are over, let us celebrate like the pirate bastards we are!"

A cheer rose as Ardley played a tune on his psaltery, and the crew sang shanties until the moon shone brightly overhead, bathing the sea in a silver hue.

3

ELIJAH

The Palace

"King Elijah!" The muffled sound of his name behind his tall chamber door jolted his body into sudden awareness.

It had been three days since his violent encounter with the female assassin and three days since he locked her away in his dungeon for interrogation. Her face, mingled with the haunting dreams of his own death, gave him another night of restlessness.

The elf woman had refused to speak with either him or his guards. Each night, Elijah had gone down there, hoping she would share with him who had hired her, but her lips pressed together, staying quiet. Her stubbornness was beginning to agitate him.

Elijah turned to look out the window. The sheer curtains had been pulled back and tied off at the sides, allowing him to see the sun that hadn't fully risen yet. Vast clouds stretched over the

Zemiran Sea's horizon, casting out the morning sunrise against the cerulean sky.

It is barely even dawn, he thought, grumbling under his breath as his eyes adjusted to his dimly lit room.

A hard knock thumped at the door moments later when he didn't respond to the shout that came from the hall.

Elijah took a deep breath, willing his body to relax as he slowly released it. He hadn't slept easily for a single night since she'd come. His Elven assassin—the unknown stranger who refused to divulge her secrets—had consumed his mind. The memories of everything that had happened weighed on him every time he tried to sleep. He struggled to decipher what her presence might mean for his future, what kind of threat she truly represented. At night, his mind was gripped by the fear he had worked tirelessly to suppress during the day. It crept through his body and mind with long, grasping fingers, making him feel exhausted and constantly on edge. He needed to get something useful out of the elf, and soon.

Just the thought of her dragged a low growl from his throat. It wasn't only her motivations or how she had snuck in undetected that worried him but how she was carrying a Newick gem in the first place. His mind had latched onto the mystery of her existence. It refused to let go, causing thousands of questions to flood his every thought.

The Newick gems belonged to his family, his true bloodline. He may not have met his people face to face, but he refused to believe that they would betray him like that. An elf would never have been freely given the gem, let alone an elf with questionable motives. There was no chance that they had simply handed it over.

She had to have stolen it, he reasoned.

Since Elijah became king, he had learned many things about the Newick witches that his father hadn't shared with him. From his newfound knowledge, he learned more about his birth mother, Gal. She wasn't only a sorceress—she was a commoner who lived in the small village of Heyerberg on the other side of Whitestone Mountain. But that entire land wasn't ruled by royalty. They were people who governed themselves, forming small covens throughout their country of Myloria.

Almost all the people held magic, and since the beginning of the Zemiran battle twenty years ago, they had refused to help. Even knowing that the Zemirans had lost their sight of magic for over twenty years, the call for help went unanswered. The covens chose to abstain from being involved in Matthias's war against magic, fearing he would use his hate-filled wrath against them if they tried.

The Newick covens were cowards, he thought to himself, reminded that though they shared the same blood, they were not family and never would be.

Naturally, Elijah had been tempted to travel north to Heyerberg on more than one occasion to meet Gal's family and discover a part of the ancestry he never knew. The desire was nestled safely deep in the back of Elijah's mind since he first learned about his birth mother.

Would they accept him? Would they blame him for what happened to his mother, even though he was a baby? Could they separate him from his father, who held the pillow over her face until she slipped away?

Elijah's thoughts went back to the assassin, not wanting to think about the mother he lost any longer.

It was clear how carefully crafted the elf's moves were—skillfully trained, strong, and undoubtedly brave. The woman had also known where he slept and, more worryingly, how to get inside the palace. Someone had to have given her the information on the castle and his location, which meant there was possibly another spy within his kingdom.

Nothing she had done so far was predictable, and he was sure she didn't believe she would ever get caught. Her fate now would only lead to execution.

No matter how beautiful she is, he thought, *I must be willing to kill her.*

Elijah tried to focus on his suspicions about her and unravel whatever plot she was attempting to execute, but his mind kept wandering. The image of her long, soft white hair and delicate features distracted him. He thought about how smooth her skin was wherever her clothes were rucked up enough for his fingers to find purchase during their fight. He found himself unconsciously running his fingers across the cool sheets beneath him. His body remembered how she felt, small yet strong, while he had pinned her to the ground.

Hot rage flushed his cheeks—*why had he not killed her?*

Elijah had planned to inflict the same swift punishment he would have dealt to anyone who was deemed a threat to his kingdom. However, the moment he pulled off that cloak, her appearance stunned him into silence. A minor lapse in judgment he would not allow to happen again.

The pounding on the door continued, pulling Elijah's thoughts back to the present.

"Is the palace on fire, Liam?" Elijah yelled through the closed door.

Silence.

"Uh...um, no," Liam said.

"Gods Almighty," Elijah groaned quietly. "Then go away."

Elijah pulled the thick wool comforter over his head when Liam knocked again, not as loud as before.

"No fire, but we do have another inconvenience."

King Elijah almost growled in frustration, tossed the blankets back until he was only partly covered, and stared at the ceiling. He was prepared to get up from the bed and the restless feeling that clung to it. He would grit his teeth, go out there, and deal with the situation at hand. Ruling his kingdom was the only thing in his life that mattered anymore.

Elijah hadn't felt like himself for the past two weeks, and it was starting to scare him. He had spent a lifetime being the first to wake up and train with Liam before most people had emerged from their rooms for the day. But now, he couldn't sleep and had become withdrawn from his normal routines. He thrashed in his bed, tossing and turning throughout the night. Constantly haunted by the images of the thousands of ways he could fail and the innumerable threats that chased him. What little sleep he did get was far from restful, like he was slowly being sapped of his strength.

Exhaustion had sunk deep into his bones. It was even beginning to affect his interactions with every other person in his life. The palace staff, the people in his city, even his own friends and advisors—he had lost his patience with all of them. It was as if something had snapped inside of him three days ago. He had fought the elf, pulled off her hood, and looked into those sapphire eyes. Now something about him was profoundly, fundamentally changed. He didn't know what it meant, and that frustration threatened to overwhelm him.

"What is it, Liam?" he said before throwing his long legs over the mattress and pulling his robe off from the back of his headboard.

He swung open the door and stared back at Liam, who stood with his arms crossed over his chest, his muscles flexing against his coat. He also looked exhausted.

A smile tugged at Elijah's lips. "You look like you're having a bad morning."

"It's the damn elf girl," he said, sounding more exhausted than agitated. "We tried to feed her, but—"

Elijah rolled his eyes and held up his hand. "Give me five minutes, please," he told Liam and shut the door in his face, turning on his heel to freshen up in his washroom.

Elijah quickly bathed and put on clean clothes: black trousers, a dark gray tunic with gold threading down the center, and his thick leather boots. He wet his hair with warm water, combing it back to keep it from his eyes, then rubbed between his eyebrows a few times before splashing water over his face and dabbing it dry with a clean towel. Elijah almost felt revived by the cooling effects of the water. He looked at his reflection in the mirror, noting the dark circles that remained. He walked out and picked up his sword from the table next to the window.

You must be willing to kill her, he repeated in his mind before placing his sword in his sheath and leaving his chamber.

Elijah pushed open the kitchen doors, and the aroma of freshly baked bread hit his senses, causing a rumble in his belly.

The heat of the oven brought a calming warmth to the spacious kitchen. Elijah removed his cloak and placed it behind the dining chair. The castle's cook, Ella, had her back to him, tending to the stove.

"Good morning, Ella," he said, watching her slightly jump, as if she hadn't known he was right behind her.

Ella turned her head and placed one foot behind the other, bending her knees to answer back with a tiny curtsy. She waved her hand toward a tray in the middle of the rolling island.

"I've made you eggs with two biscuits, Your Majesty," she said. "They're fresh out of the oven, so give it a few minutes before chowing down."

Elijah walked over to the steaming plate of food and picked a biscuit from the basket, feeling the heat sting his fingers. He scrunched his face playfully, causing Ella to giggle at his reaction.

Ella was an elderly woman with silver hair, round hips, and kind eyes. She had worked for the royal family in the kitchen since Elijah was five years old. He always regarded her as a motherly figure amongst the palace staff.

She tossed him a napkin before saying, "As I said, Your Majesty. You're going to burn that tongue of yours."

He gave her a flirtatious smile and winked. She blushed and turned away to go about her kitchen duties. Elijah took a bite of the cooling biscuit, relishing in the savory taste of the dough. Noting the time, he took the half-eaten biscuit and wrapped it in the napkin.

The eggs will have to wait, he thought. *I have a stubborn elf to spar with.*

"Thank you for the food, Ella. I have to address some business, but keep those eggs warm for me." After she gave him a nod, Elijah turned on his heel and walked out of the warm kitchen.

The long corridor leading to the dungeon had once carried the scent of elf blood. Since then, it had been cleaned and sanitized, leaving a pleasant aroma of soap and freshly painted brick.

Elijah wasn't opposed to killing criminals—those deemed a threat—but he wasn't a monster like his father. That despicable king had taken innocent lives for his own entertainment and twisted ambitions.

He stepped in front of the cell where the woman was held and peered inside.

The small bed in the corner was empty, neat, and made with military precision. The elf sat on the floor beside the bed, her body curling in on itself and her weight pressed back against the mattress. It was a position that would make most people look small and frightened. Elijah didn't think that the assassin was capable of that level of fear.

Her head wasn't buried between her knees, arms wrapped around them as if to comfort herself. Instead, she held her face to his, chin tilted proudly, with no fear, to look into his eyes. It was impossible to discern that she was a woman currently wavering on the dangerous line between life and death. The elf regarded Elijah with a stern, set expression and waited for him to speak.

The longer she glared at him, unflinching, the more anger he felt curling through his body. His jaw was tight, and the veins in his neck bulged; he could feel it. A hot wave of something like shame flashed through him. It had been a long time since someone thought they had the right to look at him with that kind of defiance, and he didn't care for it. It was clear the elf needed a lesson in how much respect was due to a king.

"I'm not hungry," she finally said, "if that is what you're here for." Her eyes turned to the half-eaten biscuit in his hand.

The pallor of her face was gone—the part of her that appeared fragile was a façade. However, it was clear she was hungry, starving, even.

Elijah tilted his head to the side, studying her.

"Eventually, you *will* need to eat," he said. "I need you alive so you can share all your dirty secrets with me." He bit into his biscuit, swallowing a bite. "And this is mine, by the way."

One more bite finished the biscuit off, and Elijah brushed his palms together, the tiny crumbs hitting the floor.

"If you think intimidation will work, *Elijah,*" she said, not addressing him as King, "you'll have to work much harder than that. You see, I'm perfectly content with dying. I'm fine staying down here for months as you starve me to death."

His upper lip twitched before he stomped forward, pressing his forehead against the bars of the cell. "I'm willing to negotiate your freedom, little elf," he said, watching her huff out a laugh while holding her smug expression. "If we can come to an amicable agreement about what I need to know, that is." The lack of control of his wrath stirred his magic inside his bones, threatening to escape. "We can end this ridiculous feud and stop whatever war your leader is trying to create by having me dead. I don't want to hurt you." He lifted his chin, taking a tiny step back. "Tell me what

I need to know, and then I will consider releasing you from this cell."

She cocked her head, her dry lips turning down into a frown, but her silence seemed like she was considering his deal.

"Is this about politics?" he asked, waiting once again for her to answer.

"Politics?" she repeated, as if the word were poison on her tongue.

Elijah narrowed his eyes at her. "It's always about politics. Our world has nine other kingdoms, and we are not alike. Most of my assassination attempts were from my own people. I would have noticed you in the streets." He flashed her a crooked smile. "So, that only tells me you come from somewhere else." Elijah paused again before asking, "Who sent you?"

The corners of her mouth tugged upward, her eyes daring to challenge him. "Like I said..." She stretched out her legs and bent her elbows, placing her hands behind her head as she leaned against the back cell wall. "I'm fine right here"—she paused for a long moment—"until I die."

Elijah pinched the bridge of his nose. "Don't be a fool!" His voice came out harsh and venomous. "You being a woman does not save you from my punishments. I will treat you like any other prisoner I've kept down here."

She pursed her lips. "Can't wait," she sneered.

As Elijah studied her, she shifted under his gaze. His presence made her uncomfortable; he could tell. The elf was trying once again to appear brave.

Amusement sparked in his eyes. "You don't fear death?" he asked. "To be tortured so ruthlessly that you beg for it all to stop?"

She remained silent for a moment, time seeming to slow down around them. The elf then stood up, moving toward Elijah slowly and deliberately, reaching the bars of her cell and gripping them with long, feminine fingers. Her gaze was unwavering and intense, and Elijah forced himself to tear his eyes away for a second.

When he glanced back, something had changed. The elf's eyes were shining with unshed tears. Her expression remained firm, but he saw the effort to control whatever emotion the woman had been struck with. He hadn't realized how close they were standing until he felt her shaky breath brush across his face. Elijah took a deep, steadying breath himself, but then he caught her scent, which did nothing but make him unsteady. She smelled like the ocean breeze pulling off the water and through the trees.

Intoxicating.

Elijah felt his lips part on instinct as he leaned even closer to her. He brought his own hands up to rest on the bars. Their fingers now touched, but neither seemed willing to move away.

He searched her deep, blue eyes and saw a woman who never belonged in a cage. She was a warrior through and through, and her need to roam the land was the most fundamental building block of her existence.

"My name is Janelle," she said surprisingly but with a baleful stare.

The assassin giving her name was a bit of a shock to Elijah. He truly believed he would have had to torture the name out of her.

"I tell you this," she continued, taking another step closer to the cell bars until her forehead pressed against them, "because I want you to think about my name when you inflict whatever pain you have planned to get the answers that I will never tell." Her head tilted to the side, continuing to bait him. "And then when you eventually kill me, because you will, I hope you hear that name in your dreams until it haunts you for the rest of your pathetic existence." The elf's face twisted in disgust.

Elijah slammed his fist against the iron bars, causing her to jump back, her body freezing in place like a statue, arms raised in a defensive position.

But before he could reply, he regained his composure, allowing a smile to tug at his lips.

"You think if I kill you, I will have trouble sleeping at night?" he said in a flat tone but found his fingers curling into a fist again at his side, his own doubts laid loosely on his tongue.

She shrugged, finally relaxing, and lifted her chin again in defiance.

"You don't think my people prepared me for this?" she asked. "My being caught?" Her lips flattened into a grimace. "If you believe that because you have me locked in a cell, you're suddenly safe. Well, then, you have no idea what is still coming for you."

Elijah pondered. If she worked for someone, they would, without a doubt, send another if she failed. Whoever sent her wanted the King of Zemira dead, and no bars in a dungeon would stop that from happening.

The king stepped back and looked her over. The only information he had was that she was Elven, her name was Janelle, and she had a Newick gem in her possession.

And she's incredibly stubborn and pigheaded, he thought to himself.

Hopefully, the information he did have was enough for now, but he would send his men throughout the kingdom to find any answers that may be hidden.

"King Elijah," Liam said from behind him, drawing the king to look over his shoulder before his eyes drew back to Janelle's.

She winked.

The nerve, he thought.

"Yes, Liam, I'm a bit busy at the moment." His eyes never left hers.

"It's Aiden, sir. He's entered the gate," he said. Elijah watched her stir at the sound of that name. He furrowed his brow, confused by her reaction, but put it aside in his mind.

Elijah straightened his tunic, willing himself to break their gaze. "Send him down."

"He's with the brigade, Your Majesty. Do you want them all down here?"

Elijah glanced down the hall, watching the lanterns flicker as the footsteps sounded above in the ballroom. "Fine, have the warriors stay put. I'll be up shortly."

Liam turned on his heel and headed back upstairs. Elijah heard a click from the steel door at the front.

He slowly turned back to the cell, his fingers linking around the iron bars once more.

"I have worked tirelessly to keep this kingdom safe, *assassin,*" he said through clenched teeth. "War is in the past, and I expect to keep it that way." He licked his bottom lip as he watched her bare her teeth. "Are you here to start a war with my people and me?"

Janelle narrowed her eyes at him and opened her mouth to speak, but nothing came out, as if she struggled with her own doubts. Elijah cocked his head slightly to the right, and his lip turned up again, sinister and void of kindness. Black smoke trailed from his hand through the cell bars, climbing up her pants. She jumped back and smacked at it, but her hand only went through the dark mist.

"I will say, I do find you fascinating, Janelle," he said. "Kind of like a new little toy of mine." He flicked his wrist, the smoke taking hold of her, causing her knees to buckle and fall to the hard, stone floor.

Janelle's eyes grew wide as the smoke reached her throat. He slowly squeezed his hand. Her hands gripped at the smoky fingers that latched around her neck and cut off her airway. He eased the pressure, but only enough for her to let out a heavy groan, and her eyes glared into his in defiance once again.

"Under normal circumstances, I would never lay a hand on a lady." He felt her satin-smooth skin through his magic, causing an unexpected flip in his stomach. "But you—"

"You still won't!" Elijah heard a shout from behind—Aiden.

The black-haired elf and head of the Elven warriors stood tall, almost towering over Elijah, with his arms crossed over his broad chest.

"Aiden," Elijah said, facing him while still holding on to his magic.

"Let her go," Aiden said, his voice rough.

Elijah's face grew hard. "I told you to wait in the ballroom."

King Elijah felt the fury run through him again. His irritation at the peace in his kingdom being threatened frayed at his control. The magic only fueled his anger further, making it harder to come down from his wrath.

"You will let go of her throat," Aiden continued. "You are hurting her!"

Elijah didn't release his hold but instead tightened his grip. Janelle gasped, moaned in pain, and pressed her back against the brick wall.

"Well, if she would stop behaving like a petulant child, I wouldn't have to do this."

Aiden unsheathed his sword and quickly turned to him, holding his other hand up, but before releasing his magic, Aiden pressed the blade to the king's throat.

Elijah's eyes turned dark, the black smoke seeping from his other hand, reaching toward his warrior. "Aiden, be very careful about what you do next," he warned. "This is madness!"

Aiden stepped forward, watching Elijah's magic climb up his own body, wrap around his arm, and up his neck.

"I have no intention of killing you, my friend," Aiden exclaimed, trying to move back from the magic himself, but it hovered over his throat, threatening to squeeze. "But that girl in there cannot die."

Elijah regarded Aiden's pleading expression, dropped his magic, and stepped back, the sword only grazing against his throat. Janelle coughed repeatedly from behind him, but he didn't turn toward her again.

"And why is that?" Elijah asked as the darkness within him quieted.

"Because," Aiden said. "She's my sister."

4

ELIJAH

The heated debate echoed loudly off the ballroom walls.

"Dammit, Elijah, are you even listening to me?" Aiden's eyes were etched with raw pain as the desperation in his voice drove nails into Elijah's heart.

Elijah wasn't the heartless monster many believed he was. However, he still had his pride—a duty to defend himself and his kingdom. He was sure Aiden wouldn't be thinking clearly, so he had to choose his words carefully, or he would surely lose one of their kingdom's greatest warriors—and his best friend.

"That's my sister down there. My family," Aiden continued, lacing his fingers together into a tight knot, waiting for Elijah to respond.

Elijah did consider his plea, but he had to think about his kingdom first. If he showed favors or weakness, he would lose the trust of his people. Word had already spread throughout the kingdom of the failed assassination and the captured elf who did it. They would now look to him for the next course of action. Public execution? Life imprisonment? Or would he consider mercy?

He cleared his throat. "You saved my life once. After my father shot me on that ship, I was on the brink of death. If it were not for the Fae water that you gave me...I would, no doubt, have died that night. I will forever be grateful to you. You know that." He leaned forward and tapped his fingers against the table, sucking in a deep, calming breath. "But my order still stands," he said. "A deadly assassin is still a deadly assassin."

Pain flickered in Aiden's eyes—Elijah had to shut it out.

Elijah watched as a rush of color touched the elf's cheeks. "I demand you release her from that cell!" Aiden jumped to his feet, his tall figure towering over the king. His eyes turned from desperation to anguished sadness. "Please, Elijah."

Aiden would not give up on his sister, Elijah thought. *Never; I must get through to him somehow.*

Elijah leaned back, running his hands calmly down his tunic. "I don't care that she shares your blood." Each word he spoke slammed into his chest like a heavy brick, his doubts crushing deeper and deeper until he had to remind himself to breathe. "Four men, Aiden. Four of my men are dead because of her; she is not leaving that cell until she opens that stubborn mouth of hers."

Aiden's lip twitched, a snarl of rage slowly forming.

The elf clenched his hands into fists and stepped forward. Valkanon, the most loyal member of his brigade, quickly jumped forward, gripped his elbow, and pulled him back. "Don't be a fool," said Valkanon, who had been standing silently behind him. "There are wise ways to do this, and committing treason is not one of them."

Elijah wondered if Aiden was going to let the situation go. Janelle may be his sister, but Aiden respected Valkanon. He had hoped Aiden would understand where he came from and why he couldn't give her special treatment after the crime she committed. However, he would consider cooperation on her part to reduce the severity of her punishment.

"I'll tell you what," Elijah said. "If she agrees to tell me who hired her, I will forgive her crime, and then she can leave my palace in exile. On this, Aiden, I give you my word." He pressed his lips into a thin line, watching to see if Aiden would accept his offer. "Listen, my friend. Unmasking the coward who gave the order is far more important than an elf rotting inside my dungeon."

Well, not entirely, he thought.

Elijah knew Aiden wasn't a fool. No crime could go unpunished. In the past, Elijah tortured his prisoners with his magic, causing them to suffer until their secrets were revealed. Janelle wasn't innocent, despite what Aiden claimed to know about her. She would answer his questions, and Aiden would stand aside.

Aiden peered down at Valkanon's fingers, still wrapped around his elbow. When his lip lifted to show his teeth, Valkanon released his hold and stepped back.

"Don't think I'll forgive you for the death of my family member just because you helped to free my people," Aiden said. "Please, Elijah, I ask you—give me ten minutes with her! Let me convince Janelle to speak. My sister is a fool. She always was outspoken and reckless."

Elijah tilted his head and smiled. If he played his cards right, she might not have to confess anything under the pain of torture. Aiden knew her, understood her past, and he had enough to go on to find out her connections. It would just be more difficult without her cooperation.

"Tell me about your sister," Elijah said. "I've learned much about your people, and this is the first I've learned that Hagmar had another child."

"She—" Aiden began, and then he cut himself off to look over his shoulder at the rest of the warriors standing at ease, forming rank against the back wall.

Elijah looked to Aiden and then to the elves. He lifted his hand, dismissing them to take their leave. Whatever Aiden was about to share, the elf didn't want the rest of his brigade to know about it.

As Valkanon backed up to follow them, Elijah said, "Not you, Valkanon. Stay."

Valkanon stood silent with his arms at his sides again and lifted his chin, his hands hooked behind his back.

Aiden cleared his throat and ran a hand through his jet-black hair.

"After hiding the Kroneon on Crotona Island for the queen, my father died, not knowing that my mother was pregnant. Janelle and I were almost eleven years apart, but we grew very close in the short time we were together. I helped to protect both her and my mother in her final days. That was, until Queen Cassia exiled me to live with the trolls. Janelle was furious with Cassia, and my brigade advised her to retire to the Eastland Forest, more for her protection than the queen's. When the queen finally did release me, Valkanon was able to inform me that Nelle had fled. This was before the war with the pirates, so he believed I would never be free of Cassia. Nelle would have escaped right after she turned fifteen."

So that means she's now twenty-one, Elijah silently reasoned. *Old enough to be punished, and I'll not feel guilty about it.*

Elijah considered what Aiden had said. She was still young; if she were a trained assassin, then brainwashing her as a naïve teenage girl to revolt against a king would have been the perfect time to start. Whoever was responsible for his assassination attempt used Janelle as a weapon. There was no reason for Janelle to have a personal vendetta against him. He had no quarrel with the Newick witches or the elves. He had to show compassion to that young woman in his cell because she didn't know any better. If she had, she had been led wrongly.

"This is what I've decided, Aiden, given what you have told me," Elijah said, running his hand down his face. He moved his neck from side to side to ease the tension that had built up. He still felt exhausted, and the stress of the day had only drained him more. "If you go against my will, you will no longer be allowed to cross my palace walls. Do you understand?"

Elijah's last question was delivered kindly and carefully, the words of a king in the presence of a friend. Aiden nodded but kept his hand on his sword in the sheath. Elijah assumed that Aiden was ready to fight for his sister's freedom if he gave the wrong answer.

"I will show mercy to Janelle and grant her freedom from sitting in her own filth inside my dungeon. But she'll not be allowed to leave my palace gates. She will remain here until I find the answers as to why she tried to kill me and why she had a Newick gem. Most likely, your sister stole that gem to use against me. I need to find out why. You can cooperate in this process by helping me find some answers. The sooner I know, the sooner I can release her to your care."

Aiden nodded, and though the Elven warrior had always been loyal and brave, there was genuine fear in his eyes. A fear that made him feel uneasy.

"And what of Nelle—Janelle?" Aiden asked. "Where will she sleep?"

Elijah leaned back in his chair, tapping his fingers rhythmically against the wooden tabletop.

"Aiden, would you like to stay here at the palace and ensure I don't kill her?" Elijah asked with a slight smirk on his lips. He realized he was stepping on dangerous ground—Aiden would most likely slit his throat while he slept.

"Yes, Your Majesty."

Elijah nodded. "Very well," he said. "Janelle will sleep in my mother's old garden room a few doors from mine, and you and Valkanon will sleep in the two apartments near the ballroom." The king stood and placed his own hand on the sword at his hip. "I have many eyes on this kingdom, Aiden. There are still many here who hate your kind, so listen carefully. You are under no circumstances to see your sister unless I permit you. You will continue to serve my guard until I find enough soldiers to replace the guards from the gate...the ones your sister slaughtered three nights ago, may I remind you." Elijah gritted his teeth.

Aiden blinked. "Of course," he said. "Thank you, King Elijah."

Aiden bowed his head and exited the royal hall with Valkanon, joining his brigade in the hallway. Elijah turned to Liam as he came back into the room.

"Her name is Janelle," he told Liam. "You are to bring her to the Garden Room. Have the ladies-in-waiting run a bath and clean her. Then she is to wear the pretty red dress hanging in the far back closet that once belonged to one of my father's mistresses. I expect her back in the dining hall for supper at six."

"You—" Liam started and looked around the empty room as if he were looking for something or someone. "Sir, you want to have the staff bathe her, dress her, and have her dine with you? The woman who tried to kill you? This seems reckless."

A wide smile grew on Elijah's lips. "I need to gain Janelle's trust, Liam. She is still a prisoner, but we will not treat her like an animal in my kingdom. I haven't forgotten what she has done, though. Trust me on that."

"Yes, sir. As you wish," Liam said and rushed out of the room.

Elijah strolled across the hall and over to the window that faced the city.

The townsfolk below the hill the castle sat on bustled about, moving through the thick snow and sheets of ice. Now dormant, the once blossoming trees faded to almost nothing as the winter cold approached. Vast quantities of slick ice covered the sea like glass, making it nearly impossible to sail through, but the city didn't stop. They didn't hide away in the winter months. Their kingdom had been without magic—without beauty—for twenty years. Even though the cold chill of short days and long nights had come, they would press forward. All would readily survive it, knowing it could be so much worse.

Elijah turned back to the ballroom, slowly placing his arms in his thick wool coat. He wrapped it tightly around his waist before taking a seat on his brass throne. The former Prince Elijah, sworn to never be like his father, had decisions to make that his kingdom could not understand. Now, as the king, he knew they questioned whether history would repeat itself. He was determined to prove to them it wouldn't.

That alluring yet infuriating Elven assassin would need to be broken piece by piece until she gave up the rest of her secrets.

5

ELIJAH

The day had flitted by quickly, Elijah doing anything and everything he could to divert himself from the inevitable.

"Why does it feel as though you're holding back?" Liam asked. "A king never loses, Your Majesty."

Elijah threw his sword on the floor and placed his hand against the column of the training room, trying to catch his breath. "I'm a bit distracted if you haven't noticed," Elijah said, stretching out his back and rolling his soft, sheer sleeves up to his elbows. "You almost sliced off my arm."

His guard sighed. "King Elijah, our practice usually ends with me lying on my back and your magic and sword at my throat." Elijah's face tightened, causing the muscles in his jaw to twitch. Liam tensed. "Honestly, Your Majesty, I thought you'd be able to block it."

The blunt apology wasn't well received.

Elijah cursed Liam silently, turning his attention away to the open window.

After Elijah became king, he named Liam as the head of his guard. The king questioned if it was the right decision. Liam was tough as nails, both in his muscular physique and his ability to make difficult decisions for the protection of the kingdom. However, it wasn't lost on Elijah that he had once worked for King Matthias, his father. Liam was never asked to do the unthinkable to the subjects of Zemira. Still, his loyalty was unwavering, and it begged the question, would he have? He was loyal to the royal family, willing to defend the kingdom as if he had ruled it himself. Eventually, that loyalty proved to Elijah that Liam would be the right man for the job.

At the time, Elijah wasn't ready to make Aiden the captain of the guard. The elf was too occupied leading his own people—the Elven warriors included—settling them back on Zemiran land. He trusted Aiden more than any man in the kingdom, and he was sure that Aiden would have said yes if he had asked. Aiden could have traded in his sword for a high rank at the king's side, but it would have drawn a line between him and his own kind. It was better to focus on his people so that he could rebuild the trust between the elves and humans after their banishment.

"Are you fucking kidding me with this ridiculous dress?" Janelle shouted from the doorway, drawing both of their eyes to meet her enraged face. Her arms folded across her chest before she turned up her dainty nose.

Elijah gave her a cocky smile, taking her all in.

"You're finally dressed like a lady and not a filthy rat," he said humorously, watching as she gathered up the train of the dress. It was layer upon layer of fabric, hanging heavy around her legs and preventing her from walking forward. He could see the fury in her eyes, but Elijah found it delightful.

A tiny strand of her white hair had escaped her high bun and fell over her right eye. The red silk dress was stiff and formal, creating a striking contrast to her curves and exposing miles of soft, porcelain skin. Her eyes glittered like hundreds of tiny blue zircons, and he found it painstakingly difficult to tear his eyes away.

She was breathtakingly beautiful; he couldn't deny that. However, even the most exquisite flower from the Zemiran forest could be deadlier than a thousand daggers.

Elijah didn't try to hide his amused expression, watching the rage that ran through her and flushed her skin. Her rose-colored lips were set in a thin line, and he could see her untamed hatred as sharp as a knife in her eyes. Elijah had no doubt that if he could read her thoughts, he'd see the wheels turning as she plotted his violent demise. He thought being captured would be humiliating enough, let alone having to walk the castle dressed like a primped-up noblewoman. Which is precisely what he had in mind when he sent the dress to her.

If she wants to be a royal pain in the ass, so will I, he mused.

"A bit overdressed, though. Don't you think?" Elijah taunted, waving Liam away for the evening.

He watched Janelle's features shift at the mocking tone of his voice. The twitch on her lip from annoyance only caused his heart to thump harder in his chest.

Elijah swallowed, hating the woman and finding her so utterly fascinating that he couldn't shut her face out of his thoughts.

What is it about her? he thought.

"Come," he said. "Your dinner is getting cold."

He walked in front of her, hearing her stomp her heels loudly behind him. She winced with every roll of her ankle, trying to keep herself from falling. At least that answered one of his questions: despite her prestigious background, she didn't flee to family wealth when Aiden was banished. It was clear she was a warrior to her very core.

Aiden stood from his chair as they entered the dining hall.

She stilled, refusing to walk any further.

Blasted woman, Elijah cursed in his thoughts, her defiance making his temper flare.

Elijah turned around, closed the distance between them in one smooth stride, and wrapped his hands around her waist. He pulled her warm, tight body close to his chest, lifted her weight, and threw her over his shoulder. One of his arms had to press across her thighs to keep her still.

"What the fuck are you doing? Put me down," she shouted, slamming her fist against his back as he walked forward.

A heavy sigh came from Aiden, who waited at the dining table. "Is that really necessary?" Aiden asked. "A little kindness won't hurt you, Elijah."

Her sharp nails dug into his neck, sending a wave of pain exploding throughout his body. He winced, grunting under his breath before dropping Janelle down on the hard floor next to the table.

"Kindness?" Elijah said, watching her stumble over her heels, her butt hitting the tile floor. She craned her neck to look at him with furious indignation, but he refused to help her back up. "This, right here, is the least I can do. She did hurl a throwing star at my face." He glanced back up at Aiden, who only bit his tongue before running to his sister's aid.

"Are you trying to get yourself killed, Nelle?" he said, extending a hand.

She brushed out the dress before meeting her brother's eyes and taking his hand. She didn't appear pleased to see Aiden—more annoyed or ashamed.

Interesting, Elijah thought.

"I'd rather sleep in that dungeon than wear this ridiculous dress, brother. That pompous king is making me wear this to humiliate me," she said, turning to Elijah again. "I want to take it off and burn it."

Elijah bit his bottom lip. "Mmm," he hummed. "That sounds like quite the party. I'll wait," he said, smiling so big it reached his eyes that time.

He leaned back slightly, looking at her with smug self-satisfaction as he blatantly sized her up. Elijah had intended to make her angry; this had quickly become his greatest source of amusement. Still, he found himself distracted by the sight of her, her body stunning him silent, and making him drink in every curve and the softness of her features. It stoked a fire in him that he didn't remember ever starting.

It felt as if time stood still, right before a butter knife flew toward Elijah's nose. He had been so caught up in a gaze that he had barely caught the handle in time.

"Well," he said calmly, placing the utensil back on the table with an air of nonchalance. He focused on appearing calm, but he felt himself shaking with anger. He swallowed thickly, trying to choke back the wrath coursing through him before he lashed out and did something he would immediately regret.

"Ella!" He looked up as his cook walked into the dining hall, carrying a tray of wine and water.

"Yes, sir," she said, her gaze bouncing back and forth between the three of them.

Elijah lifted his glass and sipped his water before placing it back down in front of him, the action doing very little to quell the anger boiling within him. "Please remove all of the butter knives from the table," he said. "Maybe the forks too."

Ella nodded quickly, hustling over to the table as instructed. Elijah kept his eyes on Janelle, who lowered her hands to her side and looked disappointed that she was unsuccessful in her second attempt to bait him.

"What in the stars are you doing, Nelle?!" Aiden cried. She still refused to make eye contact with him.

Elijah leaned back and calmly gestured for her to sit. He was almost tempted to make her eat on the floor.

"Now that we have gotten that out of the way," Elijah said. "Sit."

The staff opened the back double doors from the kitchen, spreading out in the dining hall and placing a wide array of food and drinks on the table.

Elijah observed as Aiden pulled out a chair next to him and gestured for her to sit. He drummed his fingers against the table while she took one last glance at him and sat where Aiden had suggested. Janelle's eyes turned down, only staring at her brother's hand. Elijah narrowed his eyes, wishing so badly he knew what was going through her mind.

"Nelle," Aiden said. "I thought you had died."

Elijah's ears perked up to listen.

"The Fae told me trolls ate you," she said, rocking her head from side to side as if in disbelief at seeing him sitting at the royal palace's dining table. "There was no reason for me to come back." She reached out and placed her hand in his. "I heard you were alive and back in Zemira, but I didn't know you sold yourself to the royal family. Working for *him*!"

Her eyes rose to look at Elijah with an accusatory glare.

Him, he fumed in his mind as his temper flared. *Why would she say it like that?*

The way she said that word almost sounded as if she knew Elijah, or at least the fictional version she was given from wherever she had come from.

She retracted her hand and reached for a warm dinner roll at the table, biting into it like a grown man and gnawing at it with her mouth partly open.

Gods, he thought.

Janelle acted nothing like the women in his kingdom. She was crass and uncultured.

"I was told you fled the Eastland Forest, but you had most likely died out in the sea," Aiden said.

She cut into her soufflé, took a bite, and then placed her spoon on the table. Elijah watched her every move from the corner of his eye.

"After that bitch banished you to the Woodlands, I had to leave. It was no longer safe for me there."

Elijah's curiosity clawed at his insides as he opened his ears to listen more closely. All it would take was one mistake from her lips, and she might very well reveal her secrets.

"Except I didn't die," Aiden said. "Cassia released me two years ago, and I joined forces with some pirates and a siren to save this very kingdom. Surely you heard the stories—"

"Yes," she said, her eyes then turning to Elijah. He cocked his head curiously, watching her eyes bore into his. "I heard the stories about what Elijah and that crew did, but I didn't know you were among them, and I most certainly didn't know you'd been working for Matthias's son since then."

Her accusation sounded like poison coming from her lips. Elijah had to remind himself that she didn't try to kill someone off the streets. She tried to kill the king, which meant treason—war. Under those circumstances, she wasn't Aiden's sister—she was an enemy of the crown, an enemy even to her brother, regardless of blood ties.

"You know, Aiden," Janelle started, placing her napkin back on the table, "I think I'll eat in my room." Elijah slammed his hand hard on the table as she began to stand, rattling the plates.

She flinched.

"Sit. Down!" Elijah shouted, his words echoing off the walls. "You'll eat here with me." He slammed his hand on the table again. "Aiden, you may go now."

"Elijah!"

"Go," Elijah said, softening his tone. He was losing control again; his temper started to crack and seep into his vision. His magic roiled underneath his skin, wanting to punish.

Aiden gave the king a nod and leaned forward, lowering his voice, but Elijah could still hear the faint whispers. "I'll not be able to protect you from the king," Aiden warned. "Do you understand what you have done?"

Her expression was unreadable.

"We are both not the same as we were back then," she said, her voice growing louder. "You'll blindly work for the royal family who has done nothing but destroy this kingdom and our species. You think that little coward at the end of this table is any different from his father?" Janelle turned her gaze from her brother and stared at Elijah. "You can torture or humiliate me all you want, you stupid little man. But if you think killing me will save you, you are more foolish than I thought."

She rose to her feet, wrinkling her nose before she stepped to the side of the table. She attempted to move past Elijah, but he reached out, gripping hard at her wrist.

"Janelle, love," he said, swallowing back his temper as she twisted her body to face him. "Do I have to tie you to the chair?"

They locked eyes before she yanked her wrist away. "You place your hands on me again, *Elijah*, and you will soon find out where Aiden's loyalty really lies."

The corner of Elijah's mouth turned up as she left the dining hall, her feet stomping hard against the tile floor.

Elijah couldn't believe he had let her go after such disrespect. He should've thrown her over his knee, hiked up that ridiculous dress to reveal her smooth skin, and then spanked her for her defiance until she was as red as the fabric. He made a mental note to create another humiliation for Janelle when he saw her again.

Aiden bit his bottom lip and leaned back against his chair with a sigh. "She is," he started, "exactly how I remember her."

6

JANELLE

Janelle kept her eyes locked on Elijah as he entered the Garden Room. His stance was easy, but he rested his hand on the pommel of his sword all the same, as if he expected her to attack again the moment he let his guard down.

And I plan to, she thought.

"Have I no privacy?" Janelle asked, throwing her hands out. "Do you see any weapons on me? I am basically defenseless—"

Elijah huffed, walking further into the room. "Defenseless?" he repeated, his hand dropping from his weapon. "Oh, I wouldn't say that. I've seen you fight without any weapons at your disposal." His low and steady tone made the hairs on her pale skin stand up straight.

Elijah was like a predator, body quiet and controlled, waiting to strike at the first sign of weakness.

"How did you learn to fight like that, anyhow? Is there an Elven colony I'm not aware of where you practice throwing insults when you run out of throwing stars?"

She smirked. Janelle had known that Elijah was a calculating, intelligent man from the start. She saw his tactical edge. He didn't seem to speak without reason, and it was unlikely that he was asking her questions for the sake of it. She made a mental note to carefully choose her words, ensuring she didn't let anything slip.

However, Janelle wasn't fooled by his handsome face and the occasional softness in his eyes. She knew he was an evil man. Her teacher, Kora, had warned her about his true nature. The son of King Matthias Delamere, who laced his love of violence with the magical power born only to a Newick witch. He enjoyed causing pain more than anything; he would rape, maim, and murder for fun. She wouldn't let herself be deceived.

Elijah is despicable, she reminded herself.

Her eyes narrowed at the king as he sat on the chair in the corner of the room. It didn't slip past her that he had chosen the most defensible seat possible, positioned with his back to the wall.

"Tell me, Janelle," he started again, his handsome features carefully arranged in an unreadable mask. "How is it that an elf, whose supposed purpose in life is to protect others, could become an assassin? And not any assassin; an assassin bent on destroying a kingdom that only cares about bringing peace to the world?"

She gritted her teeth, feeling a torrent of hot, angry blood rush through her veins. "Peace?" she said. "Does genocide and rape bring you peace?"

Elijah's face grew hard as stone, and Janelle felt a tingling prick across the back of her neck. There was a sudden tension in the room, like the crackle of lightning in the air before a thunderstorm.

"Rape?" he said the word with utter disgust. "It sounds as if someone has been manipulating you, assassin. Picking just the right words to stoke your hatred. Have I killed before? Of course, I've slaughtered many of my enemies, and I would kill thousands more to keep my people safe. But I never, not one day in my life, considered killing an innocent. Nor have I ever forced a woman. I prefer fucking someone whose face is full of ecstasy while they look into my eyes. *Not* terror. Any man in my kingdom caught doing something like that would swiftly find themselves lacking their favorite appendage as a punishment." Elijah's jaw was clenched, and his eyes glittered with barely controlled rage as he leaned closer to her.

Janelle's lips parted, and she felt her breath quicken as she waited for him to continue, confusion about what he had told her flooding her mind. Maybe Kora had been wrong or had lied to her. He seemed flushed with anger at the thought of it all, appearing completely sincere. Or perhaps, he was telling her what she wanted to hear.

"I'm not my father," he growled in a deep voice, "and I don't share his deplorable values, despite any brainwashing you've received to the contrary. My only priority for my kingdom, and the one thing I work for above all else, is peace. The sooner you realize that, the better."

Elijah let out a sigh, and Janelle could see his mask slip enough to reveal his clearly felt weariness. The shock of how exhausted he looked struck Janelle to her core. His tone felt sincere and almost sounded like the truth. She forced herself to harden her heart against him despite her growing desire to believe his lies.

"I am not the same man as I once was," he said. "If this is about—"

"Save your breath," she said. "Zemiran royals are all the same." She stood up from her bed, trying to regain some sense of control. The horrible red dress was long gone. As soon as Janelle returned to her room, she tore the wretched thing from her body and tossed it out the window. Her slim, brown pants and black shirt were back on, and she felt more like herself than she had in days. "If you expect fear or obedience from me, you have another thing coming, *King*," she sneered. "I have no intention of revealing anything about myself or my mission. Whatever tortures you have planned will be a waste of time." She took a few steps toward him, bracketing him with her arms as she leaned her weight on his chair and moved close enough to feel his hot breath on her face. "You might as well kill me and get it over with."

King Elijah smirked, and she wanted to smack the amusement from his face.

"If I were you," she continued, "I'd begin by locking down your kingdom. The next one to come for your life, as I have clearly failed, won't stop at you and your guards. They'll rip this entire kingdom apart and kill anyone who gets in the way."

Elijah's eyes changed from blue to black in an instant. He sprang forward, grabbing her by her shirt and jerking her so close that her breasts were pressed into his muscular chest.

Joined from hips to shoulder, Elijah's grip was tight on her as he marched her backward, only stopping when her legs hit the bed. A quick shove sent her sprawling backward, and before she could blink, she found herself lying on her back, looking up at him. His expression was fierce as he placed one knee on either side of her body, squeezing her tight and pinning her to the mattress. It made her breath hitch, lips part, and voice fall utterly speechless as she stared back at the man she thought she hated.

There were rumors about how handsome the King of Zemira was, but she hadn't expected them to be this true. And, more importantly, she hadn't expected her own body to respond to him like it had, to go soft and supple in his hands, despite all the terrible things she knew. Or at least thought she knew.

He hovered over her, face full of rage and fury, in a comfortable position to take her life. Despite that, fear and desire coursed through her in equal portions. For all her bravado, she wasn't ready to die. But she also didn't think she was prepared to explore the part of herself that wanted to believe all his claims of righteousness. No matter where she let her thoughts travel, it was undeniable that her body felt tuned to the monster's body pressing into her.

Elijah hovered over her, and the room seemed to still. The only sound was the ragged breathing of the two as they stared at each other. Janelle was almost startled when Elijah finally moved his hand, and she found herself both frightened and wanting. He smoothed his fingers over her hair, his touch feather-light, and then traced over the hinge of her jaw. She felt her heart thud when his hand turned firm. He gripped her jaw, pressing the pad of his thumb into her chin to hold her still, just barely grazing her bottom lip. Her mouth unconsciously opened further as if inviting Elijah to slide inside. She had no idea what she was doing. She was losing control over herself to him, her enemy.

"It's best you try not to fight me," he said in a low, dangerous voice. "You will stay right where you are until I'm finished with you."

Janelle's mind grasped wildly until it seized on her anger and hatred, overpowering the part that wanted to let her body melt into him. "Fuck you!" she snapped but instantly regretted her words as his eyes turned dark again. It wasn't only the look of menace; his power was taking hold of him. The energy that swept between them caused every hair on her body to stand straight. It felt as if her own Elven powers were starting to surrender to his dark magic deep within.

"Don't do this, Janelle." His voice was like a purr to her ears, almost desperate. "Becoming my enemy would be a foolish thing to do."

Elijah shut his eyes and sucked in a deep breath. When his eyes opened again, the beautiful blue from his irises returned.

"If you fear whoever sent you," he started, his voice calmer and more controlled, "I can protect you from them."

She blinked but knew she couldn't look away with his grip tightly against her chin. It didn't hurt, but she couldn't free herself. She slowly closed her eyes, holding back the tears that threatened to spill down her face.

Janelle knew she would be doomed either way. If Elijah weren't dead by sundown on the fifteenth day, the punishment her people would give would make her wish Elijah had killed her himself. It didn't matter if she wanted to do it. If she didn't, she faced a fate far worse than death.

Elijah eased up on her body but didn't release her. He leaned down, placing his lips near her ear.

"I can be your ally, love. Or I can be your villain," he said, and his breath felt like fire against her skin. It caused every muscle in her body to stiffen. The thought of it was terrifying, even though she did her best to hide it. Janelle wasn't a fool. She knew what he could do to her, and no one would stop him.

I will never show my fear, she reminded herself. *Never.*

Janelle opened her eyes and glared back. "If that is true, you really *are* exactly like your father," she said, right before his hand slid down and gripped her throat. He didn't squeeze, only held it in a tight warning.

Janelle's training kicked in. Her hand lashed out, fisting his shirt, then she pulled him close enough to crack her skull against his forehead.

He winced, rolling off her before she bolted for the door. She only made it to the end of the mattress before he reached out and grabbed her by the neck, yanking her back until her shoulders hit the bed again.

Elijah pulled a knife from the sheath at his hip and pressed it against her neck, hard enough to feel its sharpness but not hard enough to draw blood. Janelle was pinned under the king's thighs once again, but the feeling of the blade was enough to keep her from struggling. She only stared at him with fierce defiance, trying to ignore the heat of her body where he pinned her down, the sensation developing between her legs. She swallowed down the painful lump in her throat.

Elijah didn't smile or appear to find pleasure in her fear or pain. If anything, he looked as if he felt sorry for her or regretted his decision to lash out.

He pulled back the knife and placed it back into his sheath. Janelle's heart hammered in her chest, the rush of blood creating a thunderous roar in her ears.

She honestly thought it was the end of her.

"A warning," he said. "I hope whoever has sent you trained you to endure torture, for your sake. Because that is all that I have left."

He rolled off her body and planted his feet on the floor next to the bed. He turned, looking back at her, still lying on her back while straightening his shirt.

"Tomorrow, we will begin. Whether you offer up information freely or not will be your choice. Pain will be waiting, and Wayland will not be kind or gentle with you. No matter how beautiful you are."

7

ELIJAH

Elijah didn't know Wayland's real name. As a young child, he had seen the massive man come and go whenever his father had brought in new prisoners, requesting questionable and rather vile services.

When Elijah became king, he sought him out, but only when he believed it was justified. The 'Reaper,' they had called him, the very essence of death itself. He towered over most men, three times Elijah's size. He had seen prisoners confess their wrongs just at the sight of him. That was the reason he had chosen someone like that. Elijah's desperate hope was that Janelle would be frightened into giving up her secrets before the torture could even begin.

I hope I've not underestimated her, he thought.

Elijah winced at the thought of what was about to happen. The idea of hurting her made him feel physically ill. But he had an obligation to protect his people. A threat to the king was a threat to all Zemira, and it was his duty to get to the bottom of whatever plot she was spearheading.

The guards had placed Janelle back in the dungeon but in the farthest cell—a very different type of room. A reclining steel chair sat in the center, with thick metal clamps for the victims' wrists and a tray of instruments at hand. Long iron chains hung loosely from the ceiling. The floor was marked with rust-colored stains, and no matter how many times Elijah had it cleaned, the evidence of all the blood spilled there would never be washed away.

Janelle's head hung low. She had been strapped into the steel chair, and a filthy rag shoved into her mouth. This was to keep her from choking on her tongue...and from biting. Elijah placed his finger gingerly under her jaw and tilted her head up to make eye contact with him. She tried to wrench free of the clamps, chewing at the gag in her mouth and looking up at him with a mixture of rage and terror. Elijah had to force himself to tear his gaze away before he weakened and changed his mind.

Then inhumanly heavy steps echoed through the dungeon.

Elijah looked up at Wayland when he entered the room, constantly surprised that the man was so massive that his head grazed the ceiling.

The man didn't speak; only his dark brown eyes met Elijah's for a moment before turning to Janelle.

Elijah reached out and placed his hand carefully on his wrist. Wayland slowly turned, and with a whisper, he said, "No blood, Reaper. Don't leave scars."

Wayland gave one nod and trudged forward. Janelle wiggled again and tried to scream, but the gag around her mouth muffled her cries.

The Reaper looked down at the tray of instruments and shrugged. Everything there would slice skin, break a bone, and shed her blood. Torture wasn't precisely a low-risk activity for the victim; regardless of what the outcome was, there would always be scars. Instead, he set the tray next to the cell door and grabbed the rag lying under the instruments, then headed to the back of the room. He unhooked the bronze jar from a water barrel and filled it to the brim with water.

"Who hired you?" Elijah asked as Wayland returned, hooked his free hand to the chair, and tilted it back until her legs bent back in an arc and her feet barely grazed the floor.

Janelle's eyes narrowed at him, and she shook her head.

Wayland turned to the king, and Elijah nodded for him to continue.

The large man walked behind her, removed her gag, then placed the rag over her entire face, holding it tight behind her head with one strong hand. Janelle began to struggle and scream with rage beneath the fabric, twisting more viciously in the chair. Wayland then began to pour the water slowly over the rag. Slight gasps and gurgles left her lips before she went silent. All but the desperate slap of her bare feet thrashing against the chair's clamps. He couldn't do this. Not to a woman. Not to Aiden's sister.

Elijah held up his hand for Wayland to stop. He removed the rag, and Janelle repeatedly gasped for air, choking and coughing.

After a moment, she lifted her head slowly and smirked. "That's all you've got?"

Elijah pressed his lips tightly together and bit down hard on his lip, trying to control his temper to not march himself over to her and—

He broke free of their gaze and remembered something else.

A smile crept on his lips. "Wayland," he said, craning his neck to look into his dark eyes. "Thank you for your time, but I think I have another way."

Wayland, still not speaking, gave the king a nod and left the cell.

Elijah strode to her and placed his hand over her lips where she had bitten down on her own skin. He felt his heart sink at the sight of her face.

Blood was drawn, even though she had done it to herself when her animal instincts had taken over, thrashing and fighting in the face of death. It wasn't Wayland's fault. It was Elijah's.

Janelle cocked her head. Water and blood dripped down her chin onto Elijah's hand as she took in the sight of him. Elijah knew he looked pale and strained. Disgust was evident in his expression. He disliked torture, let alone a twisted kind like what he had ordered Wayland to do.

"Maybe you aren't like your father after all," she said with a tiny tear threatening to fall down her cheek. "You seemed to care what happened to me just then."

There was an unusual softness to her voice, but it wasn't a compliment. The elf, who usually looked vibrant and fierce, now seemed resigned to her fate. Shoulders slumped, ready for it all to be over. It made him wonder what had really motivated her to come there. She didn't look like a fanatic anymore; she looked like someone who had lost all hope. Perhaps whoever had sent her had forced her hand, promising her a fate worse than death if she failed.

Elijah knelt and placed his hands on her legs, tilting his head to the side. He ran his palms slowly up her thighs until she gasped, looking at him in horror. "Don't worry, I told you I don't do *that*," he said, "but I will be violating you in *other* ways."

Elijah removed the Voleric pendant from his pocket. He gripped it in a tight fist, closing his eyes and projecting his power into her mind. Her body vibrated under the hand he still had on one of her legs. For a short moment, she resisted, and he felt something strange. It was like magic of her own seeped into him. Obviously, he had known about Elven light, but it didn't feel like typical elf magic. It was as if she was vibrating in perfect time with his own power. Like they were matched. She kept trying to push him away, but she was weak, and soon she slumped forward, lost in her own dream.

Elijah looked around in her dark space, vivid images parading around him from her mind's dream state.

The grass began to grow. Bright, lush green covered the ground. In the distance, a spacious, towering village stood. The homes and buildings reached high above the trees, casting dark shadows over the open field within its stone-covered walls.

Elijah spent most of his life in Zemira, never venturing far enough to see the other countries or meet their rulers if there were any. He would have no idea where that place was. The people coming and going inside the town were not dressed as royalty, but they didn't appear poor either.

Little children ran outside one of the gated homes. Their pointed ears showed, and magic radiated from their fingertips.

Was this a Fae or Elven village? Elijah wondered.

They laughed and played while Janelle sat by a tree at the far end of what looked like a garden. Her hair shone brightly in the beaming sun. She smiled as the children surrounded her, but her eyes went dark as she spotted Elijah. The children disappeared as quickly as they manifested themselves in her dream. She dropped the book she had been reading and trudged forward.

"What is this?!" she asked, pointing around as bits and pieces of her dream fell apart.

"You tell me," he replied, looking around with her.

She pressed her lips together.

Elijah smirked, stepping around her. "This," he said, gesturing his hands around, "is your dream state. I know it's scary at first, but you will give me what I need to know if you relax. And unfortunately for you, you will not be able to shut me out."

Janelle stepped back, but he reached out, gripping softly onto her fingers, and pulled her in. He held her there, using his other hand to run down her bright white hair.

Elijah leaned in and kissed her gently against the cheek, feeling her body go rigid against his touch. When he removed his lips from her skin, he whispered, "Who sent you?" Her head shook. "Where is this place?"

Janelle tried to move from him, but he gripped harder.

"Where are we?" He looked around again.

A low voice in the distance called for her, drawing his attention to look up.

The voice belonged to a tall, brunette man in a long black cloak who hurried toward them. Unlike the children, he didn't look like Elven or Fae. His almond-shaped eyes were azure blue, and his warm honey skin glowed like clouds from a Zemiran sunset. There was something about him that was profoundly masculine. The way he held himself coiled in tightly controlled strength, like a jungle cat. His sharp jawline was covered in dark scruff, and he had wavy hair that looked permanently messy, like someone had run their fingers through it. Elijah assumed he was about the same age as himself by the man's smooth and undamaged skin.

"Who is that man?" he asked.

"How are you seeing this?" she asked, moving back again; Elijah let her go that time.

"Because your subconscious wants to tell me everything, but you know your life is at risk if you do. I can ask you all the questions I want here, and your desires will always be known."

She shook her head. "I can't!" she shouted.

"Janelle, baby, get inside," the man said.

A hint of jealousy ripped through him when the man placed his hand on her waist, pulling her into his broad chest. Though it was only a memory, he felt the urge to tear them apart.

"We need to prepare you for your journey." He held out his hand, but she wouldn't take it. Her eyes closed tightly as if fighting Elijah's power.

"Wake up!" she shouted at herself, but Elijah stayed focused, wielding his power through the pendant.

The man's hand remained outstretched. Elijah observed gray smoke curling out of his fingers, sliding up her body and twining around her wrist. Elijah jumped forward, trying to stop the assault, but the unknown stranger held her firm with his power.

He's a sorcerer, Elijah noted, analyzing the power the man wielded.

Anger contorted the man's face before he said, "Kill King Elijah, then find me those despicable pirates of the Sybil Curse...and get me my Kroneon back!"

Janelle moved her head from side to side, trying to shake the images away from her mind and Elijah's eyes. She struggled to move away from the man's grip but couldn't free herself.

With every pull from his hand, her body lit up, letting out a bright light of power.

"You need to stop, Janelle. It will sense your magic," the man said, touching her face as if to calm her, but she yanked away from him. She was afraid of the blue-eyed man whose possessive hold drove Elijah to explode with rage inside his mind.

"Janelle, stop!" he cried again as the sun around them dimmed, and a shadow covered the land. The shadow moved, but not with any objects. It moved as an entity of its own.

"Elijah, get us out of here!" she cried, her fingers prying at the man's hold.

The shadow screeched, moving quickly through the field before it manifested into a solid form. The eyes turned red, and the mouth opened wide. As Janelle's white light pulled from her body, the earth vibrated under their feet. The creature sucked it out of her and into its mouth, growing in size as the light magic was consumed and flickered into darkness.

"Please, get us out!" she cried again; her voice wracked with desperation.

Elijah quickly dropped the pendant, their eyes both opening back to the cell he locked her in.

He gently wiped away the tears that poured down her damp cheeks. Hurt sparkled in her eyes at what he had done to her. Even if he fought it with all his might, his gaze could not leave hers.

Elijah stood and stepped back, trying to wrap his mind around what he had just witnessed. "Janelle," he said, and she looked up, "there's something that you and I need to discuss."

8

ELIJAH

Janelle and Aiden sat quietly at a corner table inside Elijah's chamber. Elijah paced the room, glancing over his shoulder once he stopped at his bed.

"How could this have happened?" Elijah asked, breaking the silence that weighed heavily between all three of them. He gave Janelle a sideways glance, watching her stir uncomfortably.

Her confession caused his stomach to tighten. None of what she shared was what he expected, though he didn't know exactly what he thought he would learn in her dreams.

Janelle had been living in the country of Myloria, in a small town called Newick, where the witches first formed their coven. The city was right outside Heyerberg, where Elijah was born. She had been there with the Newick witches since leaving the Eastland Forest.

The witches lived peacefully until a creature appeared, wreaking havoc on their people. The Shadow Creature, they called it. A monster that hid within the woods, blending in as the shadow of the trees until magic drew it closer to their village. This monster wasn't like the creatures born of the land.

According to Janelle, the Sybil Curse crew used the Kroneon to open a portal, letting in a creature that didn't belong in their world. It not only killed its victims, but it sucked their powers from them, growing stronger with each life it took.

Elijah looked down, seeing Janelle's cheeks turn bright red as if shame or fear of what was to come had consumed her.

"I've seen it, Elijah," she said, meeting his eyes. "It is almost impossible to detect. That *thing* blends within the shadows of everything around it. All we know is that it solidifies once it has fed. The witches' magic on that land has helped it become something more. Once that stolen power fades from the creature, it becomes a shadow once more until it's ready to feed again. It constantly hides, never staying in the same place for too long, endlessly searching for magic to consume."

"With a land of sorcerers," Elijah started, "how have they not been able to kill it by now?"

Elijah let his own power flare to life inside him, just a little, taking comfort in the warm curl of it in his chest. Surely there was some mistake, some error on the part of the sorcerers. No creature was powerful enough to escape capture for that long. How would he be able to protect his people if it traveled to Zemira?

"Sure, the people are strong," she said. "Most of them are Newick witches, wielding their power with every strike of their sword. However, in the last few weeks, we have seen that they're not strong enough. Too many have died at the hands of the Shadow Creature; without *your* men, *your* soldiers, they fear their entire kind will be wiped out and—"

"It is only a matter of time before it comes here next," Elijah finished. "For the magic of *our* land."

She nodded. "The man you saw in my dream is Kieran—the coven leader. He wants your soldiers to help him, and he knows you'll not give them up without a fight. If you're dead, he can take your throne and command your battalion to follow him. With enough of your men, they have a fighting chance of killing that...*thing*." She glanced at Aiden. "Kieran will sacrifice every Elven warrior before sending his own. He's lost too many to that creature. They won't survive without yours."

Elijah flicked his tongue. "He cannot simply take my throne or my warriors upon my death."

"Sure, he can," Aiden said. "You have no heir, Elijah. The law states that the people choose their king upon your death if you cannot pass it down to your blood or have someone else in the line of succession. If Kieran can prove he will protect your people, why would he not seize that opportunity?"

"Sending an assassin instead of doing it himself protects him from treason or retaliation," Janelle added. "I cannot be traced back to him. No one would believe elves and fairies live among the Newick witches." She glanced at her brother. "He will use whatever power he has to send that monster back to where it came from or destroy it; he doesn't care who dies in the crossfire."

Elijah thought of the pirate crew and their newest crew member, Nola. He had entrusted the Kroneon to her, and she now held the ability to send that creature back to its own world. He would need her help. It wasn't just the Zemirans who were in danger; it was also the crew of the Sybil Curse—his *other* family.

"You seem so certain it was the crew who did this," Aiden said. "We are not blind to the fact that creatures from other worlds have crossed over into ours throughout the centuries on this planet. That shadow could have been here for who knows how long."

"Their oracle saw it happen three weeks ago," she said. "It was then that Kieran realized the Kroneon had never been destroyed after Matthias died. The oracle *saw* the portal open and the crew jumping out of it, leaving the Realm of Shadows. The crew thought they had repelled the creature after it attacked them, but it fooled them by attaching itself to the shadow of the ship that waited on the other side, passing through undetected and seeking out easier prey. The pirates don't even know they did it. Regardless of whether it was an accident, Kieran will not forgive what they have done. Too many of his people have died in the last few weeks, and who knows how many more since I've been here."

"The Newick witches have oracles now?" Elijah said, a bitter frown pulling at his lips. Even he realized his words were far from the point.

Elijah pressed back the guilt sweeping over him as his shame was drowned out by the nerves rattling violently inside his stomach. He rotated his shoulders backward, trying to ease the tension that had built up since he saw inside her dream.

"I should not have given Nola the Kroneon. I was a fool."

Aiden stood from the chair. "You couldn't have known—"

"No?" Elijah clicked his tongue. "I have never trusted anyone but myself my entire life. But no, I hand off the most powerful weapon on this planet to a siren and a crew of unpredictable pirates." His face hardened. "Now a country of witches holds me responsible for the deaths of their people and for ripping them from their power." Elijah turned and folded his arms across his chest. "If that happened to my people, I probably would have sent an assassin to those responsible, too." He ran his hand through his dark hair. "It is only a matter of time before that creature I saw in Janelle's dream comes for us on our own soil once it has finished with Myloria."

The Kroneon was a delicate and powerful weapon he foolishly let a crew of pirates sail out to the sea with instead of returning it to the rightful creators—the Newick witches. Every single drop of blood shed by the shadow was his fault.

Elijah traced his fingers along the edges of his jaw, thinking about everything the elf woman had told him so far. Being kept in the dark the last three weeks since the creature arrived at Myloria had agitated him. It wasn't his country, but the honorable thing would have been to send out a warning to neighboring lands. Janelle explained that once the witches learned about the creature, the Newick coven used their magic to draw it toward their land, hoping they could kill it themselves before it wreaked havoc on the surrounding towns.

By then, it was too late. It stayed, leaving bodies in the streets each night and hiding within their forests, just waiting for someone to wander out alone.

They foolishly gave that creature a taste of their power; now it needed more.

"Janelle," he called. Her eyes turned up to look back at him. "Why did you agree to do this? Kill me, that is? Those are not your people. What does Kieran have on you?"

Janelle paused to take a steadying breath, and Elijah drew his gaze to her mouth. Her bruised lip trembled just slightly, as if she were gathering her thoughts to continue. When she let her breath out, Elijah felt something in him settle. Nothing about the situation had changed, but the ever-present tug between him and the elf was somehow grounding. Her bright, intelligent eyes looked up and bore into him.

"Kieran knows me, Elijah," she sighed. "The village of Newick was a safe haven for so many who could escape Zemira after your father banished magic, and I became one of them years later. Like all the others, that coven took me in and made me feel like I belonged. Like I was safe." Her gaze drifted down to where she rubbed her fingers together in small circles. Elijah felt her drift away as if parts of her were experiencing it all again: the hunger and fear, suddenly replaced by a sense of family. "I was adrift at sea, and suddenly I had a home. Of course, I wanted to believe whatever they told me. I wanted to make them proud. I already hated Matthias for his part in destroying my people; it didn't take much of a push for them to make me hate you, too."

Elijah was struck by just how much chaos the girl had survived. Her tone shifted to something hard when she continued. He felt the barriers between them build back up.

"Kieran trained me to be faster, stronger, and ready to kill for him, and he demanded my loyalty in the process. There's nothing about me that he doesn't know. He knows that I would sacrifice anything in the world to save Aiden from his magic, and he wasn't afraid to take advantage of that."

Janelle's eyes flashed with a quiet rage at the memory. Elijah could hear the choke of emotion in her as much as she tried to hide it. "Two weeks," she said. "I have two weeks to kill the King of Zemira, and if I fail—"

Aiden's hand reached toward her in comfort, but she flinched away from him. Her arms slid around her own waist as she seemed to fall in on herself. There was still fear in her eyes, but it was more than that. She looked side to side, rabbit-quick, because she still hid something.

Her gaze grew distant as she avoided Elijah's eyes. He could almost feel the shame curling around her—shame for allowing Elijah so deeply into her thoughts.

But why? he wondered. *If there was a creature devouring powers from one city to the next, why would they plot murder before they even considered warning the rest of the world?*

He was missing something. All the subterfuge, all the fleeting looks of fear, and Janelle's refusal to truly open up to him...She was holding something back. Elijah just needed to find the right combination of words to get her tough exterior to crack. He was tantalizingly close, and the frustration of it was beginning to drive him mad.

"Would they even listen to us?" Aiden suggested, drawing both their eyes to his. "We can agree to fight with them to take out that monster. We could send it back to its world. No one would have to die; we work together until it is dead."

"He sent your sister to kill me, Aiden, or have you forgotten?" Elijah reminded him. "You want me to make peace with my enemy? I'd rather sit back and watch it devour every single one of those damn witches while we prepare for the fight on our own land." He turned from them again and placed his hand against the wall. "You're completely out of your mind if you believe I would *ever* help that man."

Aiden shook his head. He put his hands on his knees, pushing up from the table and beginning to pace across the small chamber. "It may be the only way," Aiden added. "If we can convince him that we would fight alongside their people, that we could help send that creature back to where it came from or kill it—we don't have to go to war."

"I may have deserved a bit of punishment for my part in all this, but what about the four men he made her kill to get inside the palace?" Elijah asked. "Am I to forget that blood was shed *inside* the palace gates? Regardless of my sins, no one touches my people or me."

Aiden blinked, and Janelle looked away to the floor.

"Yes," he said. "That is precisely what I'm suggesting. Forgive me, but we are still rebuilding after the battle that solidified your reign. I can travel to their land and—"

"No," Janelle said quickly. "Kieran does not make treaties with kings. He takes. You will be dead the moment he sees you and your ship on their shore. You are not to go there, Aiden. Ever!"

Elijah watched Aiden's eyes turn dark. He would do anything to protect his sister, but he agreed with Janelle for once. Going onto Mylorian land and charging into the village of Newick without proper protection and a solid, carefully constructed plan would be more idiotic than what the pirate crew had done.

"How much longer did you say before he sends someone else?" he asked her. "Since you failed to cut off my head." A smile curled upon his lips.

"He may have already sent another," Janelle replied.

"Alright," he said. "I will call for Lincoln to return to Zemira. In the meantime, you will continue to stay here at the palace under my protection." He turned to Aiden. "Your job is to make sure she does not leave that room!"

"I'm a prisoner again?" she asked, aghast, jumping to her feet.

"For now," he sighed heavily. "I still don't trust you fully, little elf. For all I know, everything you just shared is tactical. So, you will take your ass back up to that room until I know it's safe for my people—and for you." He held her eyes with his.

Her lips pressed together, and Elijah knew she fought hard to control her tongue, but she remained silent.

Aiden reached out. "Let's go," he said. She placed her hand in his and let him pull her gently to her feet. An angry scowl covered her face as she turned to sneer at Elijah before they left. It was a face he had seen her make countless times, but that time, she paused. Their eyes locked again, and her practiced sneer began to falter. There was a softness in her gaze as she looked at Elijah for just a moment. Something like regret filled her eyes. Elijah felt his lips part, felt his body subconsciously lean toward her, into the pull of her soft expression. But then her mask of anger snapped back into place. The moment was over, and Aiden led her to her room.

⸻

Elijah pulled out the Voleric pendant, placing it at the center of his palm. Branches danced in the wind surrounding the docks, the sound of ice sheets cracking from the moving sea below.

He had no idea where the Sybil Curse was, whether they were in their world or another. If the oracle witnessed the Shadow Crea-ture escaping through the portal, would she have seen their attack?

Or worse—their deaths? Surely Janelle would have said something about their demise.

His mind centered on Lincoln, interlinking their bond through the magical device. Whatever was happening on the ship, Lincoln was elated. Elijah hadn't seen his brother, and the pendant was the only way they had been able to communicate for the last two years.

He shivered at the coldness surrounding him. The Voleric pendant had always been somewhat of a mystery. The magic gave him the sense of being trapped in a dream. A dream where he saw everything from the outside, not experiencing it from within. Not until recently could he feel his own magic becoming a part of it. The more he used it, the less he used his own magic to harness its power. The more it *became* his power. He could feel, smell, and touch it as if the stone were reality itself.

Lincoln? Elijah said in his mind. *What are you doing?*

He inhaled the scent of the ocean waves, feeling himself rock as if he were on the ship himself. There was no light, only darkness, which meant they had to be close to Zemira and not in another region of the world.

Soft hands touched Elijah's, and when he pushed his power further and further into Lincoln's consciousness, those hands trailed up his neck and then slowly down his chest. They rubbed into his firm flesh and traced the curves of his body. His blood warmed, moving southward, and he stiffened at the touch. Elijah groaned, realizing he was interrupting something he shouldn't have.

Lincoln, he called again, adjusting himself between the legs. *I know you're a little occupied with Nola at the moment, and I kind of don't want her to stop, but I need you to gently push her aside, so we can speak. I can feel her hands still on me.*

Elijah couldn't help himself. The trace of Nola's fingers made him picture Janelle. How she would look, her face a mixture of pleasure and indignation as he trailed his fingertips over her skin and between her legs. Nola's feminine touch stroked his length through Lincoln's mind. He imagined it was Janelle's long fingers wrapping around him with a firm grip, making him throb with need as she moved. Elijah could see her blue eyes staring at him through heavy lashes with a naked hunger; her plush lips opened as her breath came quickly. All from the pleasure of touching him. Giving herself to him.

Fuck. Elijah tried to shake the image from his mind. *Don't be a fool*, he scolded himself, wincing as his erection pulsed hot between his legs and willing it to go down. He pulled himself away from Lincoln's consciousness and waited for a few seconds to regain his composure before reaching out again.

Blackness circled him as parts of the ship began to manifest itself. Lincoln had one hand behind his head, lying naked on his bed with Nola's arm slung over his chest and one leg tucked between his thighs.

"Eyes on me, brother," Lincoln said through the bond as Elijah found himself taking in the sight of Nola's naked body.

Elijah broke out of his reverie and chuckled. "Sorry to interrupt, but we have a problem," he said, shaking the image of her out of his thoughts.

Lincoln's brows pulled together. "What is it?"

Elijah heard footsteps above their deck, and memories returned from the last time they saw each other. It felt like a distant dream, and his chest ached a little. He willed himself back to the present.

"Do you still have the Kroneon?" he asked, desperation seeping into his tone. "Please, please tell me you still have it."

Lincoln nodded. "Of course, we still have it. It's locked in the chest in the weapon room," he said, growing concerned. "Why?"

"When did you use it last?" Elijah asked.

Lincoln looked confused. "Why do you ask?"

"During your little adventure with the Kroneon, you let something into our world. A shadow."

Lincoln quickly withdrew the arm he had wrapped possessively around Nola, almost knocking her off the mattress, and stood quickly to his feet. Nola shot an annoyed look up at Lincoln before realizing that he was talking with someone who wasn't there. She sat on the bed and tilted her head to listen.

"Shit. We barely made it out of that land alive! We actually agreed to stop using the Kroneon after that. It terrified Kitten and Boots so much that they no longer sail with us. Hill got injured, and Ardley agreed to tend to his wounds on land. We just, three days ago, dropped them fifty miles from Zemira. Kitten is pregnant, Elijah. They didn't want to risk losing their child to the dangers of the other worlds."

Elijah felt a tug at his chest, but he didn't have time to focus on them. He was losing their connection.

He gave Lincoln a rundown on what was happening in Myloria, specifically in the town of Newick with the covens.

"We can discuss more when you get here," Elijah said with haste. "Time to come home."

"We're only a day out because of this blasted weather," Lincoln said, "Expect us to dock by dinnertime tomorrow night."

Elijah severed the connection as his powers drained. He had been using the Voleric more times than he was used to lately.

"See you soon," he said to the wind. "See you soon."

9

LINCOLN

After the Voleric's power fell away, Lincoln sat back down on the bed. He opened his eyes to Nola standing over him, stroking his hair with the tips of her fingers.

"What happened?" she asked, cupping her palm over his cheek. "Lincoln, what's going on?" He could hear the rise of panic in her voice, and it brought him fully back to wakefulness.

Lincoln leaned forward and wrapped his arm around her protectively, his own fear swelling in his chest. "We fucked up; that's what happened."

Nola's eyes narrowed as Lincoln tried to find the words to explain without frightening her.

"The Shadow Land," he started, and her eyes immediately went wide.

"What about the Shadow Land?"

"We let something in," he said, looking above deck. "Fuck. We need to get Mazie to turn the ship around."

Her lips pressed in a hard line, and she stepped back, shaking her head.

Lincoln rolled off the bed and grabbed his trousers, slipping on his clothes. She followed him, quickly getting dressed and reaching for her sword to sheath at her hip.

"We closed the portal," she said. "I don't understand."

"Not until after a shadow slipped through. It was so dark when we returned to that shore. We couldn't have seen it escape through the portal with us."

She ran her hand through her thick, long strands, taking a few heavy breaths.

"Is it in Zemira?" Nola asked. "Are Elijah and Aiden okay?"

Lincoln shook his head. "There's another country north of Zemira. Elijah's birthplace. The monster must have felt the power of the sorcerers who resided there and headed their way. It's been devouring their magic and killing scores of people for the last few weeks."

She let out a heavy gasp. "Then we have to stop it," she said. "This is our fault, Lincoln. We must make it right. The Kroneon—it can send it back!"

Lincoln cocked his head and gave her a small smile. "Always so eager to fight, but we have no plan."

"Then we make a plan. This is our fault and our responsibility. A shadow is precisely what that thing is—a shadow. It almost killed us! It injured Hill, and in that battle, I was the only magical creature for it to feed upon. The only way to drive a sword through its chest is to solidify it."

"Then we feed it magic."

Her face hardened. "From me?" she asked. The pain and fear in her eyes skewered him. He couldn't believe she would think for a second that he was capable of doing something like that. He could never use her as bait. The pain of the moment washed over him, and it was more than a minute before he could collect himself enough to speak.

"No, Nola," he stammered. "I could never..." He kept looking at her, his own expression pained to match hers. When he spoke again, his voice was quieter, more fragile than she had ever heard before. "Do you really think I would put you in danger like that?"

Nola stared back at him, taking in the sudden shift in his body language. She visibly softened and took a step toward him. The moment her face hit his chest, his arms came up, as if on instinct, wrapping themselves around her slender shoulders to hold her. He was squeezing her too tightly, but he didn't care.

After a moment, they both pulled back enough to look each other in the eye. That brief, inconsequential moment had shaken them both more deeply than either of them would admit. Lincoln brought his hand up to caress Nola's face. His fingers were light, almost worshipful, as he grazed over her soft skin. She felt like something fragile and precious that he must protect at all costs. She always would for the rest of his life. He could only hope that she understood that.

"I could never put you in harm's way," he said, voice still quiet. "I don't have it in me."

Nola seemed soothed by his words, and she pressed her cheek into his tender touch. "Then what will we do?" she asked.

"We go to Elijah, and we figure this out together as a family. For now, we make sure that the Kroneon is safely locked where we stored it away, and we turn this ship around and head to Zemira, where Elijah will be waiting for us."

Nola nodded, but her eyes still looked wary and scared. "Okay," she said. "Let's go home."

10

JANELLE

Janelle lay calmly on the bed in the Garden Room, staring up at the ceiling. She had plotted every scenario on how to escape. When she was strapped to that chair, Janelle felt helpless; she wasn't the same after Elijah had used magic to invade her mind. As much as she tried to push him out of her dream state, he was stronger. He trapped her mind and memories in a cage she so desperately attempted to claw herself out of. He had seen some of her innermost secrets.

Was it enough? she wondered. *Was it enough for him to stop asking questions?*

She reminded herself her silence was to protect her brother and her future.

Janelle also knew that she had nowhere to go. If she went back to Kieran, she would lose her freedom again but to a man who *would* hurt her. One thing was certain about Elijah; he was nothing like the monster she was told about. The coven warned her that Elijah would beat, rape, and bind her to a life of pain if she were to get caught. But he hadn't. He wasn't gentle by any means, but he never hurt her. Not like *that*.

She ran her hand down her face and looked out the window to the sea. The cold air seeped through the glass and the iron bars; she could taste forbidden freedom—a life she would never have again. Behind the closed doors of Elijah's palace or in the bed of her enemy, she was still a prisoner. One who could run from her fate to gain her freedom, but by doing that, she would risk Aiden's life—the only family she had left.

Janelle sat bolt upright as the bedroom door swung open. Elijah stood under the door frame, leaning against the wooden casing with his arms folded across his chest.

"What is it?" she asked, a little agitation in her tone. She had given Elijah the answers he wanted, but the asshole still locked her up.

Elijah stood silent, staring at her with that unnerving gaze, making something twist in her gut. "The crew will be here tomorrow night," he said in a low, calming voice. "Once the Kroneon is in my hands, we will be in more danger than we already are. It will only be a matter of time before the sorcerers come for it here."

"What are we supposed to do with it then?" she asked. "We can't keep the weapon. It belongs to the coven. Not—"

"I know," Elijah said, cutting her off. He shifted on his heel and leaned back against the wall. "There is a heavy storm coming through, which can buy us some time. We need to prepare my kingdom, but we cannot venture outside our land to bring it to Kieran. Not yet."

She nodded.

"The crew will stay here for a few days, and then we can orchestrate a plan to get this weapon back to him without them killing us first."

She nodded again. It was the right thing to do. It didn't belong to the crew or the Zemiran king. If anyone could send that creature back, it was Kieran. But Kieran still wanted Elijah dead and to take claim over his military. They had to think like Kieran to pull off any plan they used against him.

"I need you to be safe, Janelle," he said. Her lips parted, wondering why he even cared about her safety. "You won't be returning to that man."

She opened her mouth to speak but couldn't find her words.

"Janelle," he said, stepping toward her. "Were you really going to kill me?"

What a stupid question, she thought.

"Elijah, I'm pretty good at what I do; I was just a little distracted." She cleared her throat. "Of course, I was going to kill you."

A small smile edged his lips. "Why were you distracted?"

I am not going to answer that and feed his ego, she thought. She knew what he was doing.

"If you're fishing for a compliment, you will not get one from me. Your magic was more powerful than they had warned me it would be, that's all. It caught me off guard." Her chin turned up, trying to appear braver than she felt. "The Newick gem was my only hope of taking you down, but—"

"But you gave up?"

She turned fully around and scowled at him. "Gave up?"

Now he was agitating her even further.

"Well," he said, raising a brow. "You didn't seem to put up much of a fight once I was on top of you." He gave her a cocky smile. "Grinding my hips into yours."

Her jaw dropped in shock, but she snapped it shut immediately.

"Are you saying I don't know how to defend myself?"

Elijah smiled again and moved away from the door frame, moving into the room with slow, easy steps. His body was loose as if daring her to try something.

"I saw a little taste of that power of yours. You could have used your magic. But you didn't."

"My magic is unpredictable," she said quickly as she took a slow, steady step backward.

It was the truth. Janelle's powers were not a toy she played with whenever she wanted, unlike Elijah, who used his magic as if he needed it to breathe.

Elijah's handsome stare as he stepped forward into her space caused her stomach to flip. She was a warrior, always poised and ready to fight. Elijah seemed to excel at making her feel wrong-footed, and it was beginning to wear on her.

Is he trying to provoke me? she questioned.

"I mean...if you say so," he replied. "I guess I'm only curious about what your teacher taught you. Aiden shared that he trained you well with the sword as a child, but what else can you do?"

Elijah was mere inches from her now. He seemed to curve himself to match her stance. She didn't miss the way he tilted his head down to look her in the eyes or the warm feeling of his breath as it danced over her skin. The twisting in her stomach moved up until she almost felt too strangled to speak. Janelle blinked a few times, willing herself to focus.

"Why are you asking me this?"

Elijah sighed, reaching one hand up to run one finger loosely through a stray curl of her hair. "Janelle, I'm grateful you shared with me what you did, though I gave you no other choice in the matter. But I have little patience for those who harm my people, including the guards you so heartlessly killed in my courtyard."

His touch was still featherlight, a counterpoint to the steel in his voice and the tightly controlled fury on his face.

Of course, he shows this other side of him again, she thought. *Now that Aiden is not here to protect me.*

Truthfully, the memory of the lives she took felt like a stab to the chest. At the time, it felt justified, as her mission was to kill the king at any cost, but it still didn't sit well with her. Janelle took no pleasure in killing innocent people.

"I said I was sorry," she tried to control the tremble in her voice and ignore the hot prick of tears behind her eyes. "I can't take back what I did, but I had no—"

"Choice?" he interrupted, spitting the word out with disgust. "Yeah, you keep saying that. You have a choice now, though, right? I'm doing my best to keep this kingdom safe, including those who give their lives to protect me within these walls. Because you failed, Kieran may come for you, and more blood will be shed on my grounds. I want to see how you can fight because if anyone else steps foot inside those gates, I may not be able to protect you. You have made it very clear how easy it is to get inside." He leaned into the small space between them, the movement menacing and enticing at the same time. "How did you get inside, by the way?" His voice was a low growl, barely loud enough for her to hear. "I've been turning it over in my head, but I cannot figure it out. The front gate was locked, secured by guards, and you stabbed each of them in the back."

Janelle leaned away from him, ignoring the pull she felt to close the rest of the distance between them. She crossed her arms and cocked her head to the side, hiding in the familiar stance and letting his question go unanswered. No one else would be punished for her choices, and there was no way she would reveal her accomplice to the king.

"Why do you care if I live or die?" she asked.

"Because," he said, "you are the little sister of my closest friend."

She raised a brow and frowned at Elijah's answer and the sincerity in his voice. Yes, Aiden worked for him, but she had never thought how close they might be. Not just allies but friends. *Close* friends. The thought of it made something in her shift with discomfort.

Elijah stepped back from her abruptly, creating a large gap between them. She shivered at the cold air that rushed in to fill the space. His voice was back to its normal level, and she knew that the strange moment between them was over.

"Pick a weapon," he said, pulling his tunic up to expose a small dagger and a sword in their sheaths, "and then show me how you'll defend yourself with it!"

Janelle felt hot and cold, tugging in every direction with the constant game he seemed to take so much pleasure in. It irked her, and she found herself wanting to give him nothing unless she absolutely had to. She turned around, ignoring him entirely and placing both hands on the windowsill. "No," she said. "I'm not going to fight you."

She felt the air ripple as the dagger flew toward her, and her instincts kicked in before she had any choice in the matter. She whirled around, her hand coming out to catch the dagger before it pierced the back of her skull. The tip of the blade was inches from between her eyes, with her hand clutched on the hilt, holding it steady.

"You bastard," she said, dropping the dagger on the floor at her feet with a clatter. "What if I was too slow?"

Elijah smirked and walked across the room, bent his knees, and picked up the dagger, swirling the sharp blade in circles on his palm. "But you weren't," he said casually. "I must say, I'm quite impressed. Aiden is the only one I have seen use such precision and speed, aside from myself."

She felt her nostrils flare as thinly suppressed anger coursed through her. "You're an asshole. You know that?"

Elijah chuckled. "I've been told."

He placed the dagger back in the sheath.

"I'll send Ella up here to bring you some tea to help you sleep," he said before turning on his heel and leaving the room.

What was that all about? she wondered, realizing she was a prisoner once again as she heard the lock of the door click.

All Janelle desired was to lie down on the soft silk pillows and erase everything that had happened in the last week. Her heart still pounded in her chest, and she felt a slight tremble in her hands. The constant, sudden surges of adrenaline made her feel worn thin. Elijah hadn't intended to kill her; she knew that. With one threat down, the fear of death was still an ever-present part of her existence.

The only safety she had left was Aiden. She had to convince him to escape with her, to flee from Zemira and the Newick people. She failed her mission, which meant Kieran would come to collect her, and she would pay the price with her own life. The Shadow Creature wasn't the world's only threat. Kieran would undoubtedly come for the Zemiran soldiers himself. He would kill more men than she had to to get inside, and she wasn't going to be waiting for him when he did.

II

Elijah

Elijah watched the lights go out in Janelle's room, comforted at knowing she was safe enough behind a locked door while he was away from the palace.

She's well protected, he thought, reassuring himself a few more times before leaving the palace gates with Liam at his side as his personal guard.

The city looked on edge as they walked the streets. The judgmental looks and wary faces made him feel unwelcomed, especially by the other magical residents in the town. It didn't matter if he promised his people peace two years ago when he took the crown; he was still the villain in many of their eyes.

For years, Queen Cassia had brainwashed the Fae into hating humans, especially those with powers. That ideology wouldn't simply vanish. Many of the village folk kept their distance from the magical beings to protect themselves, and they had a right to do so.

Elijah stepped into the tavern and spotted Annabelle at the bar. Her yellow wings were spread wide before she turned, eyeing the king at the doorway.

"Shit!" she screamed, bolting for the back door while the rest of the patrons watched. Elijah's hands came out, releasing a wave of power that blasted through the tavern and toward the back. The rest of the drunken folk scurried out as his power latched onto her legs, yanking hard and pulling her to the ground.

Elijah ambled her way, his black cloak flowing gracefully behind him. She tried to stand, but he gripped her hair, pulling her to her feet. "It's been a while, Annabelle," he said. "I think it's time we have a little chat."

As he dragged the fairy out the back door of the now-empty tavern, she attempted to pull at his hair, but her struggling only amused him.

Annabelle was stunning, even when she was pissed off. Especially when she was pissed off. Her green eyes shone with ragged rage, her blue hair framing her peach-colored skin—a feisty, petite Fae with the curves of an hourglass.

She clawed at his face, fighting like a wild cat trapped in a snare. He rolled his eyes at her as if he cared enough to let her go. Elijah wouldn't release her until she gave him what he wanted—he'd not back down or show mercy.

They rounded the corner of the bar and entered a dirty alleyway. Elijah pushed her face against the wall, holding her hands behind her back and trapping her wings down. The obscure corner would conceal his magic. If she didn't scream, no one would see them.

"Come on now, Annabelle. You were much more willing the last time I was behind you."

She turned her head, shooting him a sneer. "Last time, you cherished my body and took me to the peak." She looked back to the wall, but he gripped her jaw from behind and turned her around. "I know why you're here now, *Your Majesty.*"

Of course, she does, Elijah thought. *But how willingly will she cooperate, and how far will I have to go to make her if she doesn't?*

The fabric of her bodice was stretched to the point of tearing as her chest heaved, trying to wrench out of Elijah's hold and fly away. She was strong for a fairy. Elijah's magic slid from his fingers to gain more control of her.

She froze.

"Are you going to tell me what I need to know, or do I have to hurt you?" He gritted his teeth close to her neck, allowing his magic to encircle her, slowly forcing the air from her lungs. "I don't want to hurt you."

Annabelle squealed, her skin turning dark red, like the color of wine.

When she opened her mouth to speak, he eased his power, giving her back the oxygen she needed.

She coughed a few times before saying, "I'm done with you, good-for-nothing. You're cloaked in the pretend shroud of a king to confuse us, but you know what you really are?" she said through clenched teeth.

His face grew hard.

She continued as if purposely trying to provoke him. "A dimwit that challenges sensibilities. You shouldn't be the king. You should be an errand boy, made to clean all the filth from here to the mountains until your body aches with the pain your lineage made me go through. You vile animal, piece of shit!"

His power slammed back into her, choking out the very breath she cursed him with.

Annabelle's hands latched onto the black smoke around her neck, trying to free herself. Her wings came up, fluttering wildly to escape. However, her still body followed Elijah as he stepped even closer until their chests touched. He leaned in, removing his power, and placed his forearm against her collarbone. She couldn't match his strength, which was more than enough for the moment.

"You have quite a filthy mouth on you," he said. "Let's use that nasty little tongue of yours and tell me about Janelle." He smiled. "You helped her get inside my palace, didn't you?"

Annabelle pushed back against his arm, but her wings started slowing down.

There was a degree of disappointment in him. He quite enjoyed the little fairy's fight.

"Shh!" Elijah whispered into her ear, brushing her blue hair behind her ear lobe. Her sparkling green eyes dimmed slightly but still looked like two perfect emeralds shining in the sunlight.

The fire and energy written in them were truly unique and what drew him to her when they first met.

She was trapped against the wall this time instead of between his body and the sheets. He reminded himself that Annabelle became his enemy once he pieced together her connection to the assassin.

Annabelle lifted her hand, trying to slap him, but he caught her wrist. He then took his other hand and slammed her aggressively against the wall again, even harder.

Anger built up inside his chest so strongly that he could no longer contain the dark beast that writhed in his soul. "Now," he said, his eyes turning black. "Tell me what I need to know."

12

AIDEN

Aiden looked up as Elijah came into the tavern.

What is he doing here? he asked himself, looking to Valkanon. They quietly placed their mugs on the table and kept their heads down, their hoods covering their hair and ears.

"King Elijah in the city is never good," Aiden said.

"We need to get out of here," Valkanon said as they watched Annabelle flee to the door, Elijah shooting out his magic toward her. "Now!"

"No," Aiden said. "I need to find out what's going on. You can stay here. Make sure his man, Liam, doesn't follow."

Valkanon gave him a nod and slipped to the front of the tavern with the rest of the patrons who fled the establishment. At the same time, Aiden moved to the back door, watching Elijah drag Annabelle into the alley. It was hard to resist the urge to help her as Elijah assaulted and inflicted pain on the fairy woman, but if he were to get caught, Elijah would lock him away. Instead, he focused on trying to hear their conversation and figure out what Elijah wanted from her.

"Now," he said. "Tell me what I need to know."

Aiden's elf senses honed in on their voices, and he could hear the fairy's answer as clearly as if he were standing in that alley next to her.

"Fine," she said. "I told her where the tunnel was, okay? She's my friend, and she needed my help. I gave her a home for the last two weeks. I took care of her as she shared the horrors of her life in Myloria. So, yes, I drew out the layout of your castle so she knew where to find you. But I only did it to save her life. If you only knew—"

"Knew. What?" Elijah hissed out through gritted teeth.

A loud sob ripped through the air in response. "The result of what would happen if Janelle failed to kill you, Your Majesty. Kieran controls her. She owes her existence to him. And he wouldn't hesitate to give her a cruel, painful death if she failed him. You don't understand how dangerous he is."

"I think I fully understand the danger of the man who wants me dead." Elijah leaned his weight into Annabelle. His voice was low and dangerous, and he wasn't backing off. "You're hiding something. You're both hiding something, and I'm guessing it's something that I need to protect my people from. Now tell. Me. The truth."

A keening noise escaped Annabelle's chest, and Aiden could almost see the twisted pain on her face. She was scared, petrified even, but Elijah wasn't known to show empathy when getting answers by violent means.

"He's making hybrids!" she shouted, finally revealing the secret.

Aiden and Elijah, a wall between them, both froze.

"Hybrids?" When Elijah spoke, he was breathless, like the word had punched him in the chest. Aiden felt much the same, a sense of horror flooding his body.

Hybrids were forbidden. They had been for as long as anyone could remember. Nola was one of the only hybrids that Aiden knew to exist, and they had been lucky that she turned out to be as uncomplicated as she was.

Mixed magic was unpredictable and incredibly dangerous. Anyone who thought they could play with the building blocks of existence for their own gain must be completely mad.

"He's breeding elves and witches to create hybrid children. They're strong, fast, vicious, and grow at incredible speed. Kieran's uncle started breeding them twenty-two years ago when your father went to war with magic. They needed something stronger than a sorcerer's power to protect them from the king's threat. Kieran continued his uncle's experiments after he died and hasn't stopped. If someone were so inclined, those hybrids could make a very dangerous army."

Elijah looked away in disgust. "And what is Janelle's role in all this? What does Kieran want from her?" he hissed.

Annabelle looked pained as she spoke. "Kieran is in love with her, or at least the idea of her and her magic. He plans to marry her, breed with her, and raise his own children to be more powerful than any of us could imagine. His own personal assassins to target your kingdom and anything else that gets in his way." Annabelle licked her lips nervously, her voice dropping before she continued. "If Janelle doesn't return with your head, that will be her fate.

She'll spend the rest of her life as a prisoner, forced to propagate his obscenities."

She sagged forward when Elijah suddenly released her weight. He turned his back to her, shoulders hunched in anger, and Aiden could see the pain written all over his king's face. Aiden was shocked by the expression. It was almost as if Elijah truly cared about what would happen to Janelle.

Slowly, Elijah turned around to face Annabelle again. "If that's truly what Kieran wants from her, he'll do it whether she kills me or not."

Aiden felt fear and anger wrap around his heart like a clenched fist. His sister wasn't safe in Zemira. He couldn't protect her behind palace walls, and neither could Elijah. Something would have to be done.

His mind ran a mile a minute, and it was only in an instant that he was resolved to go to Myloria and kill Kieran himself. The Shadow Creature, too, if that was what needed to be done. Anything to protect Janelle.

Aiden knew he wasn't thinking clearly, but he had no other choice.

13

JANELLE

Janelle's eyes were closed, but the noise in the streets outside the palace walls kept her awake. Her mind drifted once again to how to get out of there. Elijah now knew everything; well, almost everything. Not the one thing that, if it were to reach her brother, would cause her to lose her only family. The moment he learned what Kieran was doing and what he had planned, Aiden would no doubt travel for days just to cut off the head of the man who would soon steal her future.

Janelle rolled out of bed and lit a small torch protruding from the wall by the washroom, moving to the back of the room where the garden and fountain lined the walls. She placed her hand against one of the plants, running her fingers over to the purple buds dangling in the corner: Shy Bloom Daisies.

"Well," she said, eyeing one of the most poisonous plants in Zemira, "isn't he an idiot."

Shy Bloom Daisies were not deadly, but they could knock out a grown man for days.

Just enough time to get Aiden and flee this country, she thought.

She smiled to herself, plucking three buds from the plant, careful not to press too hard where the juices would leak into her skin.

Over by the fountain was a watering can. Janelle gently scooped up some of the water from the fountain into the can and dropped the flower buds inside. Then she rushed to the sink and dripped soap on her fingers, scrubbing them in case she missed any of the flower's residue. She took a twig from one of the dry branches on a vine, cracked it off, and then stuck it into the can. She crushed the purple buds until they broke open in the water, releasing the poison.

After mixing it thoroughly, she poured the liquid into a cup, using the stick to pick out all the remaining leaves and petals. All that was left was poison-filled water.

Now, she thought, *how to get the guard outside my door to drink it?*

She glanced out the window, looking to the forest on the other end of the main square, and wondered where Aiden was. The Elven warriors guarded the gates again, but she hadn't recognized any of the men from Aiden's battalion.

If Janelle asked her brother to flee with her, he would without question. They always protected each other. If Aiden was hidden from Kieran, Kieran would have no leverage to force her hand.

She and her brother could do this. They could escape and take care of themselves. No one else cared enough about their safety. Janelle wouldn't become a prisoner locked behind anyone's door again.

A knock at the door startled her.

Janelle hadn't cleaned up the soaked buds on the counter.

Shit! she cursed in her mind.

Janelle backed up, nearly knocking the poisonous water onto the floor while trying to shield the mess she had made with her body.

Elijah entered the room, and her heart pounded so hard against her chest that it reached her throat.

Why is he not in bed? she thought.

Elijah wrinkled his brows as he stalked forward, his jaw set. His hand came out to take hold of her wrist, but she moved to the side. Then, without thinking of the consequences, she raised her hand and slapped him hard across the cheek.

Her eyes went wide at what she had just done to the king. She scrambled backward until her back hit the wall.

Elijah blinked, his hand coming up to his cheek. She watched as his throat bobbed, his face shocked, and the room seemed to kaleidoscope in and out of focus. Elijah seemed to take up every inch of space in it, every breath of air, until he was the only thing she could see.

Her body thrummed at the thought of his presence, but her rational fear fought its way through her bizarre, physical reaction. Every fiber of her mind screamed at her to bolt for the door.

"You've got quite some strength in those skinny arms of yours," he finally said. His wicked blue eyes glared up at hers, causing every hair on her body to stand straight.

"I thought you were going to grab me," she said, attempting to step back even more, but she could not budge.

"I was!" He straightened his back, his lips pressed tightly together, breathing heavily through his nostrils.

A thin smile tugged on her lips. "Well, then"—Janelle swallowed as she lifted her chin—"I hope that hurt."

She didn't care how angry he looked then. Her natural fire was coming back to her through the fear. Janelle was sick of being pushed around by him.

But then his beautiful, haunting eyes fell on her, and she shifted nervously. He had a way of leaving her breathless and, even worse, wordless in a way that no one else had ever managed. Something about the deep blue of his eyes and the crease of his dimples when he looked at her angrily. It made heat build low in her belly.

Don't let yourself fall apart for a pretty face, she scolded herself. *You're not some vapid princess.*

She needed to turn her head away from his penetrating stare; all it did was cause her to lose focus on everything she had planned out in her head before he came into the room.

"You lied to me," he said, suddenly moving forward. He didn't touch her that time, only placed his palms flush to the wall on each side of her head, boxing her in. He looked down, her eyes immediately flicking to his lips as he ran his tongue over them, making them glint with moisture in the soft light.

"Did I?" she said, looking back up to meet his stone-cold gaze.

He leaned in further, face still stony and unmoving, but his hips were pinning hers and slowly easing her legs wider around him. Their bodies were flush, every inch, creating some unexpected sensations. The most obvious one was something firm digging into the crease of her soft hip.

Is he really aroused right now? she thought.

"Please, Elijah," she said, glancing down, "put that thing away." She tried to make herself sound derisive and disinterested, but she was sure it came out more hitched and breathy.

Maybe she was just a wilting princess, after all.

For a moment, she thought about grabbing the watering can full of poison and throwing its contents in his smug face. That would render *him* helpless for once.

Elijah's lips curled up as he slid his hand between them, his knuckles grazing over the sensitive crease at the top of her thigh as he grabbed hold and adjusted himself. He moved just slightly, leaning back until their hips were not quite touching. "Sorry, darling. I had a beautiful, blue-haired fairy in my arms earlier tonight behind a tavern. The memory is proving to be distracting."

Annabelle? she wondered.

Something sharp and hot rushed through her at the image. *Jealousy? It couldn't be.* She hated the prick with every fiber of her being. Why should she care if he mounted some Fae over a pile of garbage before he came into the room?

Wait, did he fuck Annabelle to get her to confess? she then wondered.

"What did she tell you?" Janelle asked. Annabelle was her friend, but loyalties only go so far when your life is in the hands of a magical king.

"You know very well what she told me," he said but didn't look angry. He looked sad, upset even.

"How did you know about Annabelle?" she asked.

Elijah smirked. "I don't know why I didn't connect the pieces right away. You lived in the Eastland Forest, and so did she. It wasn't news that Annabelle had been a frequent visitor to the palace when I first became king. And to this day, she is the only woman I brought inside my bedroom. Annabelle knew the castle's layout and exactly where I slept. She also knew her way around the underground tunnel that leads right to that tavern." He bit his bottom lip, his nostrils flaring. For a moment, Janelle thought he would lash out at her.

"Two weeks you were in the city?" he started again. That time, his voice came out more controlled, even though she could tell he was fighting through his temper as his blue eyes darkened. "You were in Zemira for two fucking weeks." He eased up, creating a small space between them. "I was right as to why I've lost so much sleep lately. That Newick gem was within reach, calling to me, right outside these palace walls as you studied the layout on how to reach me without being seen."

He dropped his hands and stepped back. His face grew serious, and all his previous playfulness drained from the room.

"Why didn't you tell me?" he asked. "Hybrids? How is that even possible?"

"It was never impossible. Our species has always been forbidden to mix bloodlines, because of the possibility of unpredictable magic. But it was never *impossible*."

"And you?" he said, his voice taking on a softer tone. "You're going to be forced to create them with that man from your dream?"

She nodded.

No reason to hide it now, she thought.

"I knew if I told you or Aiden, he would get hurt. Elijah, I know what Aiden would do if he found out I would be forced to marry a man and bear his children. He would leave this place on a hero mission without thinking of the repercussions."

Elijah shook his head. "I would never allow that to happen. I told you before. I will protect both of you."

A long silence stretched out between them. "I don't believe you care enough," she said.

She waited for his response, her heart thumping so hard she felt it in her ears. She wanted him to care, but she didn't believe he was capable of it.

Elijah didn't answer, and she felt that his silence spoke volumes. She tried to shake the fog of strange arousal from her mind and focus on what was real. His steely gaze, his muscular chest and masculine scent, the feeling of being small and protected whenever he towered over her. Janelle reminded herself those were nothing but distractions—Elijah was still the enemy.

One of them, at least.

She placed her hands on his chest, light but firm, and pushed him farther away from her. "I want you to leave, Elijah," she said firmly, trying to convince herself more than him to leave the room.

He stepped back and stared into her eyes intently, his silence making her feel more uneasy.

"I'll leave, but you need to get some sleep. The pirates will be arriving tomorrow, and I need to get this house in order. I'll send for you when it's time for breakfast." He turned and walked back to the exit, leaving an emptiness in the air around her.

Elijah placed his hand on the door before leaving and turned around. "Oh, and Janelle," he said. "Please don't touch my daisies." A smile crept on his lips. "I would hate for the poison to seep into your bloodstream through your fingers and make you defenseless against your enemies."

She kept her eyes locked on his, refusing to blink and too afraid to address the obvious.

Elijah had quickly fallen into the habit of walking a thin line between making her feel alive with desire while hinting at threats to her virtue. She didn't believe he would do it, not one bit, but that contradiction was starting to make her question herself. How could her body be so drawn to someone that her mind was telling her was a threat? But still, when he turned that dark, hooded gaze on her from the doorway, she felt something in her hum with pleasure at being the focus of it.

"That is three times now you have tried to kill me," he said. "I would hate to have to tie you to that bed from here on out."

14

ELIJAH

The ship had docked shortly before sunset. Thankfully, the winter storm had died down just enough to allow the Sybil Curse to sail through the ice-covered water. Janelle had been in the study most of the day, spending her time with books and humming to herself. The boredom of being locked inside a castle—every hour, every day—seemed to be taking its toll on her. Elijah sent his staff to prepare the guest rooms and put together supper upon the crew's arrival. After checking to see that Janelle was sufficiently preoccupied with the massive shelves of books, Elijah walked over to meet Liam.

"They're here, Your Majesty," Liam said, his brigade lining up behind them. "I spotted their dragon flying overhead. I've already sent a few of my men to escort them to the castle. But—" He swallowed. "Sir, I think we may have a problem."

"The dragon?" Elijah asked.

"No, sir. It's Aiden."

"Aiden?"

"There's news from his warriors that they saw him and Valkanon disappear north through the woods early this morning before sunrise. He didn't show up to train the new guards this morning."

Elijah stilled.

"And we learned moments ago he was at the tavern last night; around the time we were—"

Elijah slammed his hand against the table, rattling the wood, before hearing something drop behind him. Janelle stood at the room's door frame with two books now at her feet.

"He...he what?" She shook her head, backing up.

"Liam, take care of it," Elijah said, still trying to calm the rage that Aiden would be so reckless as to travel to Myloria, let alone with only one of his men.

Janelle bolted toward the hall, but Liam took hold of her, wrapping his arms around her waist to pull her in. Her head came back, attempting to crash against his skull, but he dodged the assault, bending her arm back to subdue her.

"Easy, Janelle. Don't do anything stupid," Elijah heard his guard say in her ear.

Janelle was a skilled fighter, but she had no advantage over Liam's size and training.

"Get your hands off me, Liam. Or I swear I'll—"

"Elijah," a calm, soothing voice called from the other end of the room.

Elijah turned, seeing Nola standing with a large travel bag at her feet. She only eyed Elijah for a second before turning her attention to Liam, wrestling with Janelle at the far end of the room.

"Did we interrupt something?" she asked as Lincoln and Mazie stepped up behind her.

The little pixie hovered over Mazie's shoulder and then zipped into the room.

"Nothing we can't handle," Elijah said, giving Nola a wink. "It's good to see you."

"What?" Lincoln said. "No hug?" He held out his arms.

Elijah smirked, but before sauntering over to them, he looked over his shoulder to see Liam finally subduing Janelle to the point where she stopped moving. Another guard grabbed her elbow to help her stand straight.

Elijah held up a hand. "Give me just a moment," he said. "Make yourself at home. Supper will be out shortly."

As Elijah turned toward Janelle, Nola's eyes narrowed at him. He realized she wouldn't like what was about to happen, but he had to deal with it, or he would have bigger problems than Nola's judgmental glare.

"Janelle, love, I need you to get back to your room. Library time is over," he said calmly, reaching out only to have her slap his hand away.

"Aiden is traveling to Myloria, isn't he?" she asked.

Elijah paused and looked at Liam before saying, "We're ninety percent sure."

Her legs buckled, and Liam had to catch her from falling. Janelle looked like she had been punched in the gut, her body doubling forward with the shock. Liam's arms held her up, but it only reminded her of her captivity and made her struggle against his hold once again.

"They'll take him and use him against me! Then Kieran will kill him," she said. "I have to leave and save my brother!" There was an edge of hysteria creeping into her voice. She looked like a desperate, trapped animal, ready to gnaw off its own leg to escape.

Elijah watched her struggle and claw to free herself from Liam. Her eyes glistened with heavy tears, and her pale skin was flushed with emotion. Once again, it was all his fault. He should have been more careful. If anything happened to Aiden, he would never forgive himself.

"Liam, put her in her room," he said calmly, his voice deliberately cold. The last thing he needed was for Janelle to see his own weakness in the face of her fear.

"Elijah, please! He will die the moment any of those sorcerers spot him in Newick! Stop being a fucking coward and do something about it!" Janelle screamed as Liam pulled her away.

The only thing they could do now was set out to help Aiden, but venturing past Whitestone Mountain without a solid plan was just as reckless as what Aiden was doing.

When he turned, Nola stood behind him with her arms folded across her chest. "Yes, Nola," he said, watching her face scrunch up.

"Is she a prisoner here?" she asked.

He sighed heavily and walked past her, not answering her question. Elijah had dealt with enough sass from Janelle; he didn't need it from her too.

His eyes turned to Lincoln standing behind her. "It's good to see you," Elijah said. They didn't hug; he wasn't sure they would ever have that kind of relationship, but Lincoln tipped his tricorn hat and Elijah turned to Mazie.

"No hug from me either, Your Majesty," Mazie said. "That's alright. You might have to with Bay, though. She weirdly likes you."

"You named her Bay?" he asked, remembering the stories of her sister who died years ago.

Mazie shrugged. "It seemed fitting, given how Bay always wanted wings. Now she can live through a pixie." She looked up at her little friend. "Queen Cassia never gave her a name. I think it suits her."

Bay zipped over and perched on Elijah's shoulder, tapping his ear.

"Yes, Bay?" Elijah said.

He felt a soft touch on his earlobe when she leaned onto it, giving him a tiny kiss.

Her delicate wings buzzed, and she flew back up, heading over to Mazie again.

"I'll bring out the wine and rum—"

Lincoln held out his hand. "No rum, please. I think we tapped out on rum when we had our last night with our mates. Wine is perfect."

"I thought your crew looked a little small," Elijah said. "What happened to the others?"

"Long story, brother. We will share it over dinner, and I can share with you what we know about those creatures from the Shadow Land."

Elijah glanced over his shoulder again where Nola stood, her face still firm, judging him.

"But I will let the two of you catch up first," Lincoln said, gesturing to Mazie to move forward to the kitchen table.

Elijah gestured for Nola to follow, heading into his study while Lincoln and Mazie made themselves at home in the dining room.

"Care to explain what I saw earlier?" Nola asked as they sank into the couch by the bookshelves.

Elijah let out a weary sigh. "It's a long story, so I'll tell you the short version. *That* wildcat you saw with Liam is Aiden's sister, Janelle. She was hired to kill me by the Newick coven leader in Myloria. She's my little guest, nice and cozy until we get Aiden back and get to the bottom of this assassination plot."

"Get him back?" Nola frowned.

"He went to kill the man that sent her," Elijah said in a casual tone, "Kieran, a powerful sorcerer who wants me dead and plans to breed a race of dangerous, hybrid warriors."

Elijah glanced around to avoid her eyes, one leg propped over his knee. Then he absently picked at his fingernails to clean them. "I was planning on telling you all this at dinner."

Nola's face wore various expressions of shock and annoyance.

"Elijah," Nola started to scold, "you can keep your arrogant, nothing-bothers-me bullshit for your subjects. You're skimming over the important parts, like why are you keeping Aiden's own sister prisoner?"

"Spare me the judgment," Elijah huffed.

"No, I won't. I know you, and I know that monster tone is a cover-up for how you're already judging yourself, but I don't care. You obviously know this is wrong. I do not for one second believe you don't feel something for that girl and what you're doing to her. Or do you need a reminder of who you really are?" She stared at him, lancing him with her stern gaze and making Elijah's stomach flutter with nerves. Not many things could make him feel small and childlike, but Nola's disappointment was one of them.

But he was king, and he would not be shamed. "Who am I, then?" he asked in a challenge.

Nola let the tension ebb from her body and leaned back. Her face turned kind and compassionate, and somehow that made Elijah feel more shameful. "You are not the same man you were when I first met you," she said with a sigh, "and you're not a kidnapper."

"She's a prisoner," he spat angrily, "not a victim. Don't pretend to waltz in here and understand what's going on. A powerful sorcerer wants me dead, and she is the living, breathing instrument of his violence. My people need to be kept safe from her and the enemy she serves!"

Tension hung in the air between them. Elijah slumped back onto the couch, rubbing one hand over his face as a wave of exhaustion hit him.

When he continued, his voice was soft again. "He's abusing Janelle, Nola. Kieran saved her life so that they could brainwash her. It didn't take much for him to convince her she was doing the right thing by coming here to kill me. If she returns without evidence of my death, he will keep her under lock and key. He'll use her to breed his hybrid children, and he doesn't care how much pain he causes her in the process. I won't let it happen. I'm protecting her by keeping her here, not punishing her. Regardless of how she sees it." He finished with a snort.

He watched as Nola's jaw dropped. Obviously, he had left out some of the salient details the first time.

"I know we got off on the wrong foot two years ago, but there is always a reason for everything I do," Elijah said. "Aiden has left for, what we assume, a hero mission to avenge his sister. If I don't keep her safe, she will be off herself, putting her and our kingdom at risk."

Nola drummed her slender fingers against the couch's armrest, staring at the floor. "Then go with her," she said.

Elijah shook his head.

"Stop shaking your head at me, Elijah. You know I'm right. The water is too frozen to travel by ship; we barely made it to the docks. It won't be safe to travel until this ill weather dies down and it warms up enough to melt some of that ice and snow. But you need to go with her, or she won't survive the journey by horse. Janelle doesn't seem like the kind of girl who will take well to her imprisonment and just wait here for the news of his demise by your enemy. Go with her."

That idea had crossed Elijah's mind. Janelle would kill anyone in the kingdom to get her freedom, especially now that Aiden was gone. But if she were to leave, the safest thing for her, and their best chance of getting Aiden back, was to help her. True, she had traveled alone when she ventured to Zemira, but the weather then was nothing like the storm coming in now. It was too dangerous.

"Let's have a drink, catch up, and I'll think about it," he said.

Elijah extended a beckoning hand to help her to her feet.

"And thank you," he said as her hand touched the doorknob. He felt his mask of strength and confidence slip just a little so that she could see the real him.

"For what?"

"For reminding me of who I want to be, even though I struggle to be him most of the time," he said before pulling his mask back up.

Her smile was faint, but she stood on her tippy toes and kissed him gently on the cheek. "You *are* him, dear Elijah," she said. "You just tend to forget."

Supper with the crew reminded Elijah of the last time they broke bread. An inebriated crew, Mazie's wild tongue spouting foul insults at everyone. He didn't know the others as much, but he felt a sense of sadness for Lincoln that parts of his family were now gone from the ship.

Lincoln shared more details about their visit to the Shadow Land, what happened, and why they chose to leave. As angry as he was at the crew for having let that creature into their world, it was a mistake, and Lincoln would be paying for that with his guilt for the rest of his life.

Once the laughter settled, they created their plan. Elijah would take Janelle to rescue her brother, hoping to catch him before reaching Newick. Then in two days, the crew would set sail, floating idly on the other end of the mountain, close to the shoreline. Elijah knew it was risky, but something about the potential course of action was setting him at ease.

Traveling with a thousand soldiers, a dragon, and a pirate ship would only get them killed before they reached the city.

"The plan will work, Lincoln," Elijah said as the help cleared the dining table. "Or at least I think it will, as long as there are no surprises."

"We just have to be vigilant," Mazie added as Bay snuggled up to sleep at the crease of her neck. "It's not as if we haven't faced worse situations." Mazie yawned and reached up, scooping Bay into her palm and pressing her close to her chest to keep her warm. "Goodnight, mates. Tomorrow, we'll make this plan a reality." She scooped up a midnight snack and winked. "I've been dying to kick someone's ass."

Lincoln draped his arm over Nola's shoulder, not caring if everyone watched. He leaned in, kissing her gently on the forehead. Then gently ran his fingers down one of the silver streaks within her brown and purple hair. "Time to sleep ourselves," Lincoln said. "It's about time we got a good night's rest. The last few weeks have been daunting."

Elijah nodded and leaned back into his chair. "I put the two of you in the farthest room from mine."

"Excellent." Lincoln winked at Nola, holding out his hand for her to take and leaving Elijah alone to think.

The castle servants spread out, helping the crew to their rooms, while Ella hurried to the last bottle of wine to top him off.

"You look as if you need another," she said.

Elijah looked up. "Always taking care of me," he said, taking a slow sip of his wine. "Has anyone checked on Janelle?"

"I did personally, Your Majesty."

He waited for her to tell him more.

"She's been crying," she said. "Don't be a fool and go up there. She hates you at the moment."

His lip turned up. "At least she's consistent."

Elijah dismissed the staff and picked up his last glass of wine for the night. The morning would change everything, and he prayed to the Gods he and Janelle wouldn't kill each other before they reached Myloria.

15

ELIJAH

Janelle's arms folded defiantly as King Elijah wrapped a rope tightly around her wrist, then attached the other end to his. He channeled his magic into the fibers, hardening them into a steel-like quality that couldn't be cut.

"Is that really necessary?" she asked with a trace of bitterness in her tone.

Elijah flashed her a humorous smile. "Well, I can't have you running from me or trying to kill me again," he said.

"You have the Newick gem back. I'd be a fool to fight against your magic," she said. "I only want my brother safe. That's all—"

It didn't take much to convince her about the plan, but he was sure that she would set out herself without him if the rope connecting them were to be severed.

"No, you want to take down Kieran yourself." He sized her up. "It is the only thing I like about you. Besides, you're still my prisoner because you thought throwing a weapon at my face would somehow get you on my good side." He gripped his large satchel of traveling supplies and threw it over his shoulder. "And now you're my travel guide," he added.

"You're an idiot to try to storm into that city without your soldiers," Janelle said.

"They *are* coming," he reminded her, "just a few days behind. And you will be surprised as to what my magic can do. I won't risk the crew's lives or my fighters unless I can see with my own eyes what we're dealing with. They'll be ready when I send for them; Liam is already gathering half my soldiers to ensure Zemira is not left without defense. The plan is not to get caught before we find Aiden." A smile pulled at his lips. "You know your way around that land more than I do. The two of us can fight them together if we must—"

"May I remind you it is not the coven that is deemed the only threat," she said.

"Right, that shadow thing," he said. "I haven't forgotten."

Elijah couldn't stop thinking about that unknown creature. If they could reach Kieran before he used the coven to attack them and take Janelle, they would perhaps have a chance at reaching peace to fight that thing together. Maybe it would be enough to bargain for her freedom.

But peace would be replaced by blood if he so much as touches Janelle or the Zemiran soldiers, he said in his mind. *And Aiden too.*

"Elijah, are you sure you can't take some of us?" Lincoln asked. "Even traveling up that mountain is madness."

"We have packed enough supplies to help us get there," Elijah said. "We'll be fine. What I need is in two days: the Zemiran soldiers by the top of the mountain and your ship waiting idly outside the Mylorian docks. I'll call for you when it's safe." He tapped his pocket where he held the Voleric pendant.

"The horses are ready," Liam said.

"Everything else ready?" Elijah asked him, and Liam responded with a curt nod. Elijah turned to Lincoln. "Wait to feel my power, then ready the ships. I don't want you on their land. Not yet."

Nola stepped forward, leaning in to kiss Elijah on the cheek. "Be safe." She turned to Janelle. "Try not to kill him, please."

Janelle let a small smile slip, but a scowl immediately replaced it when Elijah yanked her forward.

"We'll see you at the port," Nola said, raising her voice. "If you need us sooner, I'll use my siren call to send any creature on this land to save you."

Elijah dragged Janelle away but was careful to keep her from falling. He hooked his foot in the stirrup and swung up onto the horse's back.

"We aren't sharing that horse, are we?" she asked as he reached out to help her up.

"As I said, you're still my prisoner." Janelle rolled her eyes as he pulled her up and settled her on the saddle between his legs. "Don't look too excited," he added before leaning forward. "I know you're scared." She turned to look him in the eyes. "And I swear to the stars, I will risk my own life to save Aiden if I have to."

Janelle's features softened. She gave him a subtle nod before Elijah kicked his heels, and they set out for Whitestone Mountain.

16

AIDEN

The storm had raged through the mountain range for most of the day, but the wind had finally slowed to a steady howl around dusk. Aiden was confident they wouldn't get far through the muddy terrain.

"It's too dangerous, Valkanon," Aiden said. "We won't make it through."

Valkanon stopped suddenly, looking up at the skies. "What do you suggest, then?" he asked him. "If we don't make it up the mountain, we'll be sleeping down here all night, and I have the keen sense we won't make it up much farther once the height of the snow reaches two feet."

"Let us hope the storm moves east by midnight," Aiden said.

Aiden ran his hand through his black hair and turned to Valkanon. It was foolish not to bring along their brigade, but he couldn't risk their plan getting back to Elijah—he would have never let him go. Aiden already felt guilty for bringing Valkanon.

Aiden glanced around the ground at the foot of Whitestone Mountain. "Alright. We'll camp here, but we need to set up the tents now while the wind is not as fierce," Aiden suggested. "That mud will collapse if we attempt to climb right now, so it's best to wait and rest."

Climbing up a mountain to enter Myloria in the dead of winter—what was I thinking? Aiden thought.

Aiden had to make Kieran listen. What he had to negotiate was far greater than Janelle's life. He had to be certain the sorcerer would take the bait. If not, he would have to kill him, and war would be inevitable.

After the elves had set up their tents and tied off the horses to the trees, they settled in, creating a fire to keep warm. They had packed enough blankets and food for the journey, but they still didn't know what was ahead.

Aiden pulled out several wool blankets while Valkanon gathered more wood for the fire.

Once they were warm enough, Valkanon closed his eyes, and Aiden took the first watch. He turned and placed his hand on the sword his father had given him before he passed away, running his finger over the black stone on the hilt. Aiden closed his eyes and reminded himself why he was doing it all. His sister would never return to Kieran, and he would do whatever it took to make sure of it.

When dawn broke over the horizon, Aiden was the first to leave the tent, searching the area for anything out of the ordinary.

Aiden said a silent thanks to the Gods that the ground was hard again. It would make it easier for the horses to move on. He stretched out his back and looked to the skies. The clouds forming above were a light shade of gray—they had to move before the snow fell again.

He stepped back inside the tent. "Valkanon," Aiden called, tapping his friend on the shoulder to wake him. "We need to start moving."

Valkanon's eyes opened, and they darted around wildly in a panic. He grabbed his sword, swinging it up, but Aiden caught it by the blade, the sharp iron digging into his skin. Blood dripped down Aiden's arm and onto the ground.

He winced but kept his body still as Valkanon slowly realized what was happening around him. The older elf hadn't slept well since the war with the Fae two years ago. He was plagued with nightmares and vivid flashbacks. They had lost many friends that day, and he had been on edge ever since. Aiden had tried to calm his mate and heal the fear that no warrior should face. Still, Valkanon was older, weakened spiritually, and too stubborn to stop fighting for Zemira.

"Easy, friend. It's only me," Aiden said soothingly, then placed his hand on Valkanon's shoulder. "Time to pack up and go. We need to get to the other side of the mountain. Once there, the town of Newick is not far—perhaps a day."

Valkanon dropped his sword and looked around, rubbing his eyes. "The air feels thick," he observed.

Aiden nodded because he felt it too.

They quickly packed the horses and began to move toward the mountain. The blustering wind howled loudly in his ears, the moans blending into something else. Something *alive*. There was an eerie sense of an entity within the woods that previous night; he felt it as if it were next to him. The presence kept him awake for hours before he succumbed to sleep. He had noticed the air restricting his breaths when his eyes opened to the sunrise. For a small moment, it felt as if his magic was being snuffed out, trying to rip itself from his body.

A tiny snowflake hit Aiden's pointed nose as they crested along the narrow, treacherous path. He pulled his hood over his head to keep his ears warm. The trail was wide enough for their horses, but they knew they were entering dangerous territory.

His horse, Nalla, shook her head and took a step back. "Nalla, hang in there, girl." He threw his voice so that Valkanon could hear. "We need to get around the bend, where the mountain has blocked most of the snow blowing in."

They trotted forward, resisting each gust of cold wind that sent an icy chill against Aiden's cheeks.

As the sun rose through the breaks of the clouds, the trees created dark shadows along the path. Aiden's eyes narrowed as a thin shadow moved swiftly, growing against the cliffside next to them.

The shadow slinked past him again, that time from behind. Aiden's eyes struggled to adjust to the sudden darkness around them. He thought it was his imagination until the shadow shifted against the sunlight, opposite of the trees' shadows.

"That is no shadow of the trees," he whispered. An icy prick from fear stung the back of his neck. The stories Janelle had shared about the Shadow Creature were etched in his mind. But those were nothing compared to seeing it with his own eyes.

Nalla jumped forward, sidestepping the dark creature as it slithered between them. The mere movements from the shadow wracked utter fear through his body. He took a long, shallow breath, feeling his heartbeat thud, but remained steady.

The shadow moved so fast, like a wild beast, causing both horses to rear back, Valkanon's horse kicking up his front legs.

In a blink, it rushed by them again. That time, a cold chill shivered over Aiden's skin that wasn't from the elements. The shadow hovered longer near the path, as if it watched and observed its new prey while slithering along the trail. After a second, it blended into the snow, disappearing within the vast forest.

"We're slipping, Aiden!" Valkanon cried as his horse bucked again against the sleek ice.

Aiden turned just in time to see Valkanon's horse hit the ground hard, one leg snapping at the knee and sounding like the crack of a tree falling. His friend was jerked forward, thrown over his horse's head, and hit the ground with a cry. The force of the impact threw Valkanon close to the edge of the trail.

"Valkanon!" he shouted.

The path is narrower now, he thought, panicking. *He's going over the edge.*

Suddenly, the shadow moved again. That time, Aiden saw something that caused every hair on his pale skin to stand straight. It was no longer a black, translucent aura, but its form knitted together into a large body with scale-like wings behind it. The monster reached out, clawing at the elf's chest with its bright red eyes bearing into him.

One more glint of those eerie eyes shone in the darkness before the creature disappeared within the trees near the steep, white cliff.

"What the fuck?" Aiden said, looking for Valkanon, but instead saw his wounded horse thrashing, trying to right itself. Aiden jumped off Nalla, running to his friend's aid, but Valkanon was caught on a rock, hanging dangerously over the cliff's edge.

One of the horse's legs clipped the thick mud that was holding Valkanon in place, and then they were both slipping, falling down the cliff.

"No!" Aiden shouted, diving forward.

Valkanon's horse plummeted, disappearing into the trees below with a cry that was cut short. Aiden watched Valkanon slip even further, his arm stretching forward and reaching out to capture his wrist.

Aiden gripped tightly to his friend, but he was too heavy. He was slipping down the icy mud as well. Valkanon's legs kicked frantically, causing Aiden to struggle to hold on.

"You need to stop moving, so I can pull you up!" Aiden slid forward, his chest hanging in empty air. He was going down with him.

As he attempted to grip both hands around Valkanon's wrist, the shadow moved swiftly again, hovering over the Elven warriors. Aiden felt the creature at his back, rough prickles traveling up his neck like sharp thorns.

Power vibrated against Aiden's chest, the magical light pulling from his body. He fought it with everything he had, feeling his power waning with every moment the creature latched on to him.

Valkanon blinked, and Aiden watched a tear roll down his cheek. "Fight it with your father's sword, Aiden," Valkanon said, trying to pry Aiden's fingers from his wrist. "Let me fall so that you can fight it!"

Aiden edged closer to the cliffside, gripping a rock to avoid sliding down with him.

He shook his head, feeling his own life pass before his eyes as magic drained from him. Valkanon wrapped his fingers over Aiden's hand, digging his nails into his skin.

"Don't," Aiden pleaded desperately. "I can save you. Stop digging into my fingers."

Time stood still, his friend's eyes growing dim as if he had lost the fight in them.

Valkanon shook his head and whispered, "Fight it, Aiden. Fight it, and save your sister's life."

With one kick off the cliffside, Valkanon's wrist tore free from Aiden's grip.

Valkanon was quiet as he fell. Aiden felt like he was in a dream; one minute, his friend's wrist was in his hand, and the next, he was gone. It happened so fast, and the only evidence was the echo of a faint cry when Valkanon hit the trees. Aiden knew that it was a sound that would haunt him for the rest of his life.

He let out a pained scream and slammed his fist onto an ice-covered rock, splitting his skin at his knuckles. His body welcomed the pain as punishment for letting his friend fall. For allowing Valkanon to follow him to Myloria in the first place. As the searing pain pulsated on his hand, the haunting sense of danger once again lurked behind him. He flipped around, throwing his hands out and releasing his light as the shadow came crashing down on him.

He felt pure rage rushing through his veins, hurling him toward the monster. It was less translucent now, almost in a solid form. It reached out toward Aiden with a malicious howl, but the elf released his magic just as it grabbed him. It hit the creature in a wave, making it shriek so loudly that the snow cracked on the mountaintop, falling down the trail.

It let go, dropping Aiden down on his back. After clambering to his feet, he swiped up his sword from the snow and charged forward—wielding his sword in one hand and his power in the other. He swung his sword down with one slice through the darkness, hitting the snow beneath. The cries from the beast rang out, shaking the mountain until the ground cracked beneath Aiden's feet and snow fell from the trees. The creature shifted back into a mist-like form and fled into the forest.

Aiden kept his sword out front, feeling the burn at his palms. He was ready to attack if it came back. When he no longer felt its presence and finally felt the crisp, thin air again, he fell to his knees and wept for the friend he couldn't save.

Heavy, painful grief filled his heart as he stared down at where his friend had fallen. He attempted to simmer the adrenaline surging through him while heavy tears poured down his cheeks.

Aiden withdrew his sword, keeping it flush with his hip for a beat before dropping it at the side of the mountain. He dragged himself back until he hit the rocks. Aiden lowered his head between his knees, his long hair draping over his legs.

How could the crew be so foolish as to let something like that into our world? he thought.

What Janelle shared about the Shadow Creature and what Elijah had seen in her dreams, was nothing like what he had just witnessed. That shadow was the first monster that had truly terrified him, and it would come back for his magic.

I'm never going to make it, he wept bitterly. *I'm going to die before I reach shelter.*

17

AIDEN

Aiden's heart felt like it had been burned to ashes, and the embers of his grief seared at the bottom of his chest. As he climbed up the mountain path, tears fell like biting icicles down his cheeks and neck. Valkanon didn't only lose his life to that creature, but he sacrificed his life to save Aiden from falling with him. The man who stood by his side through his banishment to the Woodlands and even helped raise him after his father passed—was dead.

Why did I agree for him to come with me? he questioned repeatedly as he reached the top of the mountain. He tortured himself with every trudge through the snow. Every bite of the cold against his skin punished him for believing revenge against the man who threatened his sister was more important than the lives he risked. All that death just to follow through with his vengeance.

Beyond the trail, smoke rose from a wooden cottage—the first sign of life he had seen since they left the central city near the palace. He loosened the gritty reins from the saddle and kicked his heels against Nalla's sides to move forward.

Not knowing what to expect, Aiden kept his eyes on the land around him, surveying the old and barren town being awoken by the sun rising above the trees. A wooden tavern at the end of the road caught his eye. A few carriages were lined up across the storefront—the tavern lights brightly lit with torches encased in glass.

It is never too early for a drink, he thought. Anything to drown out the pain and guilt that clutched so hard at his chest that he could barely breathe.

Tired, hungry, and frozen from the bitter cold, Aiden had to get inside to warm up and rest. He rubbed his hands together vigorously, feeling the temporary heat touch his skin. Checking his sword one last time at the sheath, he reminded himself to be ready to defend his life if the people in that town didn't welcome strangers.

After tying off Nalla to a tree, he glanced around once more. "Hang in there, beauty. I'll be back out shortly," he whispered in her ear.

Once he opened the tavern doors, he immediately felt the warmth of the fire, and the scent of roasted coffee beans hung in the air. He cast a glance at the patrons drinking at their tables, then over to the bar.

A few men looked over their shoulders as Aiden, being massively tall and strapped with weapons, maneuvered in and out of the tables until he reached the counter.

The barmaid turned her eyes up from below the counter and greeted him with a warm smile. "Hmm," she said, sizing Aiden up. "You don't see many elves coming through these parts." She pulled out a mug and placed it in front of her. "What would you like, handsome? Coffee, tea." Her smile grew wide. "A beer?"

The woman is incredibly beautiful, he thought. Light, tiny freckles sprinkled under her eyes like specks of sand and across her pointed nose. Her hair was a dark shade of auburn, her lips red like fine wine, and her bright emerald-colored irises were almost painful to look away from. Her braided hair fell over her shoulder, the lock so thick it covered one of her breasts. His eyes dropped to her slender frame that curved like an hourglass against her thin shirt, exposing her tiny waist.

Aiden's lip turned up, finally finding his voice to speak. "A water would be fine," he said, watching her raise a brow. "And a coffee with a splash of bourbon."

She flattened her smile and looked over her shoulder. "Water and booze, coming up." The woman reached for the mug, scooping it back up before ladling out some water from one of the barrels under the countertop, then turned to the kettle.

"Is that enough?" Aiden asked, tossing ten brass coins on the counter.

She turned back and glanced down, sifting her fingers through the coins. "It's more than enough, stranger," she said. "This might even cover for one of the tavern ladies to show you upstairs and help you relax." The barmaid winked at him. "You look like you could use it. So, so serious." The red-haired woman leaned forward, placed the drinks on the counter, and smirked. "By the way, they're all staring at you."

Aiden gave her a quizzical look.

She folded her arms against her chest, flashing another smile, but it was barely noticeable that time. "You might want to unsheathe that sword of yours, elf."

"What?" he asked, turning around to face three slovenly dressed men, all holding weapons and matching grimaces on their faces.

He casually brought his water to his lips and then placed it beside him. All three had hair the color of tar with bright, beady blue eyes and darkly tanned skin. Triplets, it seemed. All three stood with their mouths agape; their breath smelt of hard liquor.

Great, he thought. *Three drunken brothers, looking to fight at seven in the morning.*

Aiden growled under his breath and inhaled sharply. "Men, I don't want any trouble—"

One of the men—the slightly taller one—threw out his fist, but Aiden caught it quickly in his large palm, pulling his elbow down to twist the drunk man's wrist, holding it there as he watched him wince from the pain.

"I would think carefully about what you little boys plan to do next," Aiden warned, squeezing ever tighter until he felt the satisfying crack of his attacker's bones. The man yelped, stumbling back until he hit the chair behind him, then stumbling over it. His head cracked against the floor; his screeching moans echoed against the walls. The second one, with a well-shaped jaw, pulled a sword from his hip, and then the third brother, a small pistol.

The one with the pistol barreled toward Aiden, but he lifted his leg to his chest, slamming his heel against the man's collarbone. The blow sent him flying back against another table, knocking over one of the patrons. Aiden wielded his sword over his head, slicing against the other man's chest as a warning the moment he leapt forward—not deep enough to pierce his skin.

Aiden didn't want to kill them—they were sloshed and acting like fools. It was clear that the townspeople didn't welcome strangers, or perhaps it was because he was an elf.

"That's enough!" the barmaid said with an edge to her voice that caused the men to stagger back, glancing at each other as if the brawl had never happened. She turned to Aiden and smiled. "Well, that was exciting and quite embarrassing for those men, too." Her shoulders sagged as her smile faded. "You look like you've not eaten in days, elf. Do you need a place to stay tonight?"

What in the—Aiden's thoughts stopped themselves as he watched the three men patch up the wounds he inflicted, the first one rubbing his wrist. Not an ounce of concern read across her face as she gathered empty bottles on the counter and placed them in the basin.

"Fuck," he said aloud, breathing in sharply. He realized he had ruined his plan to stay unnoticed. There were ways to subdue his enemy without causing such a stir, and he entirely failed at that.

"Don't mind them," she said. "They're the village idiots." She leaned forward, placing her hand near her mouth to whisper. "They think elves are rubbish in a can of waste and piss." The woman pulled off her apron and placed it on the counter. "Come on, let's clean you up." She snapped her fingers and gestured to the bar.

Aiden's brows pinched together as the man who held the pistol placed it back in his holster and came around the bar as if he, too, worked there.

Aiden kept his feet planted on the floor, refusing to move.

The redhead's lips tightened as she glared at him. "What are you doing?" she asked. "Come on, now, they'll be fine. Grab that stronger drink and follow me."

Aiden glanced at the men once more. All three immediately looked away, most likely realizing that fighting a six-foot-seven Elven warrior had been dimwitted and careless. The man with the broken wrist hovered in the corner, using his other hand to hold it together.

Aiden followed the woman to a hallway at the back of the bar. She bent down, gripping a latch on the floor.

"I'm Tegan," she said, her lips turning up into a genuine smile that caused her dimples to appear.

Her vibrant beauty caught his breath. "Uh, Aiden," he breathed. "I'm just passing through. I—"

He tilted his head to the side, watching Tegan lift a floorboard covering an underground room.

"I don't want to cause an inconvenience," he said.

She threw her hand up. "I don't own the bar, Aiden. I work here to pay my rent. When I see a beautiful man like yourself looking for help, I give it. Now follow me."

They entered a small space below the tavern. The room carried the scent of perfume, masking the acrid smell of what Aiden believed to be mold. His eyes danced around the small space. There was nothing but a tiny bed, a pile of clothes in a bin in the corner by the washroom, and a tub.

"Well," she said, lighting two lanterns by the bed, "This is it." Loose spiral curls had escaped her braid and fell over her eyes as she bent down to pick up a white towel from the ground, then tossed it to him. "You smell like horse manure, Aiden. You'll clean up here." The merest hint of a smile brightened her already charming features.

Aiden opened his mouth to protest but found himself silent. Instead, he nodded. If he was going to have the strength needed to get to Newick, he needed both to bathe and rest his head—the journey up the mountain, though only taking a few hours, felt like an entire day.

She stopped at the stairs before climbing back up. "You're not going to kill me?" she asked, arching a brow. "You have kind eyes. Has anyone told you that?"

Aiden couldn't help but smile at her strange behavior. He hadn't met someone like her before. *It is refreshing*, he thought.

However, his attempt to smile faltered. "No, Tegan, I'm not going to kill you."

She let out a whistling sound. "Whew. That's good to hear. There's been a monster tearing through our village all week. I've survived so far, and I would hate to be taken out by a sword in my own room."

Aiden stilled. Suppose the creature had started in Newick and was already moving through every city and village in Myloria. Even heading down the trail of Whitestone Mountain, killing anyone that had magic. In that case, that thing was coming for everyone, not just the Newick witches.

"How many from your village?" he asked, waiting in eerie silence as she counted on her fingers.

"Six so far," she said. "It was only here for a day, but it murdered all the folks who carried magical gifts. It likes to disappear back into the forest rather quickly after it's eaten."

Aiden's memories of earlier that morning haunted his thoughts once more. The memory he hoped to drown out with bourbon came crawling back, making his stomach tighten and bile rise to his throat. He saw Valkanon's face again, a desperate plea in his eyes for Aiden to save himself.

She regarded his expression and held out a towel. "Anyways, let's get you cleaned up. You really do smell like horse shit." After Tegan winked, she moved past him, stopping at the doorway. "The water is warm, but it won't last. Probably best to make it a quick one. There's soap next to the tub."

As she turned to walk up the steps, Aiden called back, "What city are we in?" he said, holding back his pain with a stern stare and jaw set.

"Oh, um, you're in Heyerberg," she said.

Heyerberg—Elijah's birthplace. I'm in the country of Myloria but still too far from my destination. But he couldn't tell the stranger where he was going, he reminded himself. *Trust no one.*

"Aiden, I suggest once you clean up and get some food and rest, you be on your way."

Tegan left him down in the room, and he looked around. She was right. The more people knew about him, the harder it would be to make it to Kieran without being stopped and questioned. If Kieran knew he was coming, he would lose that element of surprise and get himself killed.

18

AIDEN

Aiden's eyes flickered open to the sound of coarse dirt falling through the crack of the floorboards. Awareness sprang to life about where he was and how long he'd been there.

Loud, boisterous shouts inside the tavern jolted him to sit upright. Aiden looked around the tiny room, adjusting to his cramped accommodations. He wondered how that woman slept down there, dust falling through the cracks and onto the bed sheets anytime the boots of patrons stomped overhead.

How long have I been asleep? he wondered.

There was only a crack near the washroom next to him that peeked over to the tavern entrance. From what he could see outside, the sun was setting again—he had slept all day.

"Fuck."

Before rolling off the bed, he rubbed his eyes a few times. He brushed off the dirt, picked up his sword, and moved quickly up the stairs to the hidden trapdoor. Aiden pressed his ear against the floorboard and listened.

It was difficult to make out what they were saying, but he did hear one word: elf.

Aiden used his heightened senses to home in on the sound, listening intently to their words. He recognized them as older men, maybe two to three of them, then heard Tegan's soft voice shouting back. They were arguing about sighting a black-haired elf coming into the tavern, causing a brawl, and where he might have disappeared. Tegan insisted that no elves had been there, and *did they not have more pressing matters to attend to*? She sounded viciously annoyed as her voice echoed loudly above the ceiling.

An authoritative voice shouted back right before wood shattered, as if someone had cracked a chair against the floor.

As Aiden shifted his weight on the ladder, it creaked loudly, bringing the sounds above to a stop.

"Get out!" Tegan's voice again, that time sounding more murderous than it was before. A gunshot blasted through the walls, causing Aiden to duck instinctively from the sound of the shot; his mind moved quickly.

He unsheathed his sword and held it out.

"Ah, fuck it!" Aiden said, opening the door and wielding his sword at the ready. There were more men than he had thought surrounding the tavern.

Aiden charged for the men, not caring that he was completely outnumbered.

He arched back, sliding across the wooden floor as magic left their hands—dark magic. *Sorcerers!*

Aiden jumped up as he reached the bar, his feet climbing the wall next to him and kicking off. His sword came down with him with one swift move to the right, slicing down on the arm of one of the men. It was severed along with the power of its owner.

All at once, the patrons scattered like roaches out of the tavern. They pushed the sorcerers out of their way—some fell, and many escaped.

For a fleeting moment, Aiden watched Tegan dash behind the bar and disappear behind a back wall. Aiden continued to fight off the men that were coming from every direction. His eyes widened when he saw her reemerge with a bow and a quiver of arrows in her hand. Tegan shot two arrows, splitting them into completely opposite directions.

Two men dropped to the ground, quickly replaced by three others charging for Aiden. He used his sword to fend them off, feeling the burn from his tired muscles and drawing deep upon the strength of his Elven powers. His hand came out, releasing his magic to create an impregnable shield, as Tegan shot two more arrows to stop the men charging him. They fell to the ground with loud cries that were cut short.

The room fell quiet as Aiden dropped his power. Aiden noticed that he and Tegan were the only ones still standing in the tavern—all was calm aside from a few moans and grunts from the bodies on the floor. He and the girl were unharmed.

"Thank you," Aiden said, turning to Tegan as she ran up to him. He placed his palm against her cheek. "You are a strange yet magnificent woman, Tegan. Do not change for anyone." She gave him a wink as he dropped his hand to his side and stepped toward the door. "Goodbye, Tegan."

There was a sparkle of hurt in her eyes, but he had to turn away. He had to leave her. As he found the will to command his feet to move, he hurried out of the tavern and into the blistering cold.

Nalla was still tied to the tree, but she had sunk onto her side, a massive gash on her flank. She was still alive, but barely; her body let out pulses of blood into the white snow as she whinnied in pain.

"Bastards!" Aiden shouted into the growing night. He knew it wouldn't solve anything, but he was so angry that he somehow felt like he had to let the rage build up in his heart. "Oh, Nalla. I'm sorry, girl," he said, placing his hand on her side. "I'm so sorry I left you out here." She let out a noise, kicking ineffectually at the dirt beneath her. The light in her large eyes grew dim, and her breathing became even more labored. He rested his hand against her neck and closed his eyes in fresh grief.

She won't make it, he thought, running his hand down her neck one last time before releasing his light magic. It blanketed her in a deep slumber so that she could pass in her sleep.

"Over here," Tegan said from behind him. When he turned, she had a black cloak on, a large bag draped over one shoulder, and she was carrying her bow.

He narrowed his eyes at her but walked swiftly to keep up. His eyebrows furrowed in confusion. "What are you doing?" he asked.

"Me? Oh, well, I just saved your life back there." She placed her hand on her hip and balanced on one heel. "You're welcome."

He scrunched up his face. "I could have handled—"

"Riiight!" she said, drawing out the word. "Now, shut up, and swallow that pride of yours. I'm not done helping you."

She opened a barn door next to the tavern, and they slipped inside. Tegan quickly shut and latched the doors behind them. She picked up a lantern off the ground and quickly lit it with some flint. The room was filled with a soft yellow glow as she turned to Aiden.

"Sorry," she said. "About your horse...I know you want to grieve, but you must keep moving." She waited for his response, and Aiden gave her a nod. She was right. Without a horse, getting out of the city wouldn't be easy. With a coven of sorcerers heading their way, he had to move quickly.

Tegan rushed to the end of the stalls, opening the gate to the last one. There stood a large black horse with golden eyes and a long, patterned black and white mane and tail.

As Tegan prepared the horse, Aiden looked over his shoulder at the barn doors, seeing lanterns beam through the crack of the door. There was a faint sound of movement and voices coming from the outskirts of the village.

"You've been here one day, and you've already drawn the Newick witches' attention to us."

"Well," he said, "there's a reason for that." He had no doubt Kieran had sent his men to find him. Janelle never returned, and Newick witches would have strung together the inevitable outcome that Aiden would come to gain his sister's freedom.

"Come on," she said. "You can share your story on the ride to the cabin—it's a safe place, so we'll be able to hide there for a few days. Get on."

He turned back to her. "I can't go with you."

She let out a jaded breath as she climbed onto the horse, settling into the saddle. "They will kill me because I helped you. I can't stay here anymore," she said.

Aiden shook his head. "And I appreciate everything you have sacrificed for me, but it's too dangerous."

Aiden knew Newick, a city filled with sorcerers, was even too dangerous for him, but a woman? He couldn't have her blood on his hands.

"Get on the horse, you buffoon," she said. "I can hear the others entering the tavern. You don't have a choice. They will check the stalls next. Then we're both dead."

Aiden let out a grunt. He sheathed his sword as she leaned forward, extending a beckoning hand. He gripped her tiny fingers and threw himself over the saddle, nestling behind Tegan. Once he settled her between his legs, his rough hands covered her exposed waist. Her muscles clenched beneath her taut, velvety skin. Aiden felt the curves of her body as he pulled her closer into a protective grip, her back flattening to his chest.

The fear of dying before he reached Newick had ebbed away, as if Tegan's presence blanketed him with power and strength. It was an aberrant response that was both foreign and intoxicating—the woman wasn't truly human. Since birth, he had been gifted with an intuitive sense of others' magic. The energy she radiated caused his own powers to seize.

As his thoughts slowly came together, he tilted his head, trying to read her aura and study her movements and the energy that trailed behind it. She let out a command for the horse to move forward and hurried them out of the barn.

The dark forest behind them was all they could see.

"What direction were you going?" she asked.

At that point, lying wouldn't help either of them. "Newick, the capital," he said, waiting for her reaction.

"Well, then," she said. "We will be going in the opposite direction. We'll be at the cabin within three hours." She looked over her shoulder. "Unless you have a death wish."

She clicked her heels, and they trotted forward, bringing her horse to a gallop as they disappeared into the forest, heading northwest.

19

JANELLE

The magical rope burned against Janelle's wrist, but she resisted the urge to wince at the pain. She wouldn't show Elijah any weakness. Not anymore. She had already shown him too much of herself; it made her feel vulnerable and exposed. Instead of worrying about the king and his vacillating ethical integrity, she needed to focus on getting out of the restraints. It was time to escape and find her brother on her own.

If she showed herself outside the gates of Kieran's property with King Elijah standing next to her—alive—Kieran wouldn't kill her. That would be too kind. Instead, she would become his property, more profoundly than she already was. She would become nothing but a prized broodmare, locked away—her only purpose: to be bred and birth more hybrid elves for their coven.

The man was wicked, fundamentally cruel, and unforgiving. Janelle wouldn't subject herself to a life as his puppet. She would rather die than let him touch her.

She wanted to marry for love.

That wasn't love.

After a few hours of traveling north, the coolness of the air dipped further. She shivered as the wind picked up—they were only a few miles from Whitestone Mountain. It was so dark they could barely see the path in front of them.

Once they reached the terrain, the snow was thick, at least eight inches high, and though they were on a horse, the breeze blew against the direction of their path, making it harder to move through.

"Do you need another blanket?" Elijah asked, leaning over Janelle's shoulder. His face was so close to her cheek that she felt his lips graze against her skin.

Her stomach did an involuntary flip before she looked away.

She didn't want to *need* anything from him.

"No, I'm fine," she said stubbornly. She would rather pretend to be unaffected by the bitter cold than give Elijah one more ounce of control over her.

He leaned back. "You're a terrible liar," he said, pointing to a tiny stream ahead. "We can at least get some fresh water."

The stream wasn't frozen over yet. Elijah and Janelle dismounted and opened the saddlebags. Elijah grabbed two canisters from his bag, walked to the stream, and filled each bottle. The metal containers felt ice cold against her fingers when he handed one off to her. She drank it slowly, feeling the coolness down her throat. Elijah reached down and untied the magically infused rope that bound her to him. Janelle subtly scratched the patch of skin around her wrist and sighed.

"Thank you," she said, not looking up to meet his eyes.

They both sat on a thick stump above the snowbank facing the brook. The moonlight peeked through the trees and cast light on the stream, the water rolling over each rock in its path with the heavy current.

Elijah reached for one of the bags and pulled out a blanket, covering her shoulders despite her earlier refusal. She tensed at first, her brain doing rapid-fire calculations to determine if this was an acceptable amount of weakness to show or not. Ultimately Janelle was too cold to come to a decision. The part that always wanted to fight went slack, and she pulled the blanket tight around her body. She could allow herself just a little comfort. As she lifted her head to the skies, a tiny snowflake hit her nose.

"Do you even like being king?" she asked, turning back to him. "You don't come off as someone who would do well behind closed gates."

He threw his head back, a hearty laugh escaping him.

Janelle frowned at him, not sure what to make of this response. "You're telling me you enjoy staying in one place your entire life? Having people constantly waiting on you?"

"As opposed to what?" he asked.

"Well, I don't know. Traveling from kingdom to kingdom. Meeting new people who aren't ogling over who you are?"

"Ogling?" he repeated with a small laugh.

She mirrored his smile. "I would hate the attention. And I most certainly wouldn't want the responsibility."

"Like making sure assassins don't break into your kingdom and slaughter your people?"

She scrunched up her face. "I think 'slaughter' is a little dramatic. But still, I'm sorry about that."

"I know," he said, turning to the water. "But if we don't start being civil to each other, fighting Kieran may be impossible, and then you will be just as much a prisoner as I am, I guess."

She shook her head. "I will kill myself before that happens." She regretted the words the moment she said them. Despite her bleak future and her love of hyperbole, she truly believed that life was always better than surrender. Thinking of Kieran as her husband caused her stomach to churn; she knew that life would be a fate worse than death.

Elijah reached out, startling her, and took her small hand in his. Despite the chill in the air, his skin was warm, and she didn't object as he gently moved her hand to face palm up.

He traced the lines on her skin with his finger and closed his eyes.

"What are you doing?" she asked, wanting to pull away, but a strange sensation entered her hand with every stroke of his finger. "What—"

"Shh," he said, gliding the tip of his nail gingerly until goose-bumps trailed the back of her arms—a tormenting touch she craved most wantonly. Her eyes shut, feeling the swarm of butter-flies reach her insides.

Before she could pull back, she felt a connection form between her powers and his. It was strange, a feeling she had never experienced before. Then, just as suddenly as it had begun, the moment was over. He released her hand and turned back to the river while she tried to convince herself she didn't miss his touch.

"What was that?" she asked.

He shrugged. "I was testing a theory that has been pressing on my mind since the moment you came into my palace. Even before you attacked me."

She lowered her brow.

"I thought it was the Newick gem at first, but then I questioned it the more we were around each other."

"What are you talking about?" she asked.

She knew what he meant; she felt it, too, but pretending it didn't happen felt less scary. Janelle didn't want to know.

"Do you not *feel* it?" he asked. "As if our magics are trying to link their elements together." He reached out, retaking her hand. "The first time I questioned it happened in the cell when I used the Voleric pendant on you. I didn't know what it meant at the time. I still don't. But right now, as you speak of becoming Kieran's, I can feel your energy. Your power is screaming inside you to release itself upon the world, if not at least on your enemy."

As he brushed his fingers along the lines of her palms, her stomach did a flip. She struggled desperately to mask the sensual sensation it gave her while every muscle in her body tensed.

"No," she lied, wriggling her hand from his. "I believe we both have intense magic, and we're feeling things that aren't real." It sounded so much like a lie. Even she didn't pretend to believe it.

The expression on his face grew distant as he turned to the river. The moon's radiance drew shadows over his face, making him look like some ancient marble statue. His jaw tightened.

"My magic may be dark and ominous, but I know when light touches it. I've been around Fae. I've felt the powers of an elf. But with you—" He continued to stare ahead. "With you, it feels as if my own powers are trying to surrender to yours."

Magic was only linked to the one born with it. Janelle didn't understand anything he was saying. She wasn't taking anything from him, at least not intentionally. Magic didn't surrender or reach out to one another. They were bound to the body.

"Well," he said, breaking the awkward silence and climbing to his feet, "perhaps it is all in my head." Elijah turned back to her; his smile turned somber. "I want you to know, though, your power is beautiful," he said. "Janelle, *you* are beautiful."

They didn't stay long at the stream. Janelle walked away from it, feeling unsettled. The week before, she and Elijah had done nothing but fight and spew venom at one another. Now, in the wake of that single, tender moment by the water, Janelle glimpsed something she had long given up on. Peace. She had felt peaceful, held in his soft gaze after he called her beautiful. If it hadn't been for Elijah's abrupt exit—as if the words had been physically torn from his chest—she could have basked in that moment for much longer.

They traveled for the next few hours in awkward silence, the magic rope reconnecting the pair. Janelle's treacherous brain reminded her to focus on her escape, not the warm and tingling feeling of being complimented by someone like him. It didn't matter if Elijah thought she was beautiful. Janelle berated herself for not taking advantage of that moment by knocking Elijah out and fleeing into the woods. She was still his prisoner. She was still bound to him, leashed like a dog.

"We won't make it, Elijah. It's too dark, and the wind will knock us right off the edge," she said. "We need to wait until morning."

He nodded and looked around. His eyes narrowed as he spotted something unusual at the bottom of Whitestone Mountain.

"Over there," he said, pointing to a fallen tree in the distance and what looked like a dead animal lying over it.

"What is that?" she asked, squinting her eyes to look through the falling snow.

"It's...it's a horse, I think. From the palace. The rider is also there."

Janelle's stomach dropped.

"Aiden!" she cried, pulling at the reins, but Elijah gripped his hands over her stomach, pulling her between his thighs.

"Stop, Janelle!" he said into her ear.

If Aiden were at the bottom of the mountain, nothing would stop her. She elbowed him hard against his stomach. After she heard him wince, she pulled their horse to a stop and jumped down, her knees growing weak as she sprinted toward the mountain. Elijah pulled on the rope, flinging her back until her backside hit the snow. She tugged at the rope, but even if she were to figure out how to break it physically, the magic he placed on it made it indestructible.

He jumped off the horse and moved through the slush until he stopped at her side.

She stayed on her knees and looked up. "I hate you!" She gave him a pointed look while ignoring his outstretched hand and clambered to her feet on her own.

"Oh, I'm aware," he said.

Janelle snarled at him and turned to the body. She covered her mouth in shock, stifling the hard sob that escaped. The hair on the body was white as the snow beneath their feet.

"Valkanon...oh no."

She ran her hand down her face, wiped the tears that fell, and drew in a shuddering breath. It wasn't Aiden, but that didn't ease the pain she felt tighten in her chest. Valkanon was someone she'd known since she was a child.

"Valkanon was a heroic warrior," he said. "He served the elves and fairies with honor." He straightened his coat and looked around. "He should be buried with honor."

<hr>

They both ignored the freezing temperature and punishing weather while digging a grave for the next hour. First, they scraped back the snow and ice using some sturdy tree bark as makeshift shovels. Then they dug into the hard, frozen dirt beneath it until a suitable hole had been made. Together, they lifted Valkanon's body and placed him carefully into the hole, piling the rest of the dirt and shrubs over him. His horse would be left for the animals to feed upon.

"I'm surprised the wolves haven't tracked down their scent," Janelle said, doing her best to push away the sadness. They hadn't seen one wolf or mountain lion since they left Zemira. It was winter, but still, there ought to be some heartier wildlife moving around. They hadn't seen any tracks or even heard the hoot of a winter owl.

"We need to look around for Aiden. He wouldn't have left Valkanon like this," she said. She shouted as the gust of wind picked up, making it harder to hear each other. "Aiden might still be out there!"

Elijah shook his head. "It's too dangerous, Janelle. He may already be up the mountain and has taken shelter. Survival. That is what the Elven teach their young before they even hand them a sword. He may not have had a choice. We need to get that tent up from your bag, or we will freeze to death out here," he said, and she knew Elijah was right. Her Elven constitution would give her some small protection from the cold, but powerful sorcerer or not, Elijah was still human.

Moving quickly, Janelle and Elijah pulled out the tent and set up camp. They moved easily together, both working quickly without needing instruction, and it felt bizarrely natural to be sharing a space. As they tucked their blankets safely inside the tent, they began to change their clothes for warmer items. It was below freezing, and Janelle could feel her teeth start to chatter. Still, there was this strange heat between them. It was indistinct, something Janelle couldn't put her finger on. A fluid warmth tugged at the two of them, drawing them together.

Janelle did everything she could to ignore it. The rush of blood in her ears, the swoop of her stomach as she glimpsed Elijah pulling off his shirt to change it, the prickle on the back of her neck as she wondered if he was also watching her. She ignored all of it. By the time they were both freshly dressed and wrapped in blankets, tucked away in the relative warmth of the tent, she felt sick with it. Her fingers twitched to reach out and touch Elijah, who was only a few inches away from her. She saw Elijah wringing his hands and wondered if he was suffering the same way. Instead, they settled into a tense silence.

Harsh winds rattled the trees around their tent, and icy raindrops hit the canvas top, keeping them alert. Janelle imagined it would be impossible to sleep, no matter how hard they tried. The silence seemed to drag on, with an unspoken tension mounting between them.

It was Elijah who spoke first. "Remember my friend, Nola, back at the castle? The siren?"

She nodded once.

"Two years ago, she and I had to take shelter in a cave shortly before facing off with my father."

Janelle cocked her head and gave him a quizzical look, unsure what his point was.

"She and I had to stay in a cave during a storm and—" The side of his mouth quirked upward.

"Why do you have a stupid grin on your face?" she asked, irritated by how sexy he looked when his lip turned up like that, creasing his dimples.

His grin evaporated instantly, raising an eyebrow as if lost in thought. "Well, it was cold that night. We had to come *together*...you know, her body flush against mine, to keep warm."

He has got to be joking, she thought.

"Well, it is a good thing I'm an elf. It's not below zero, and these blankets are rather warm."

Janelle smiled back until his features changed, his eyes narrowing, and his lips pressed dramatically tight together. She had annoyed him.

Good, she thought.

With her self-control suddenly renewed, Janelle laid down at the far end of the tent, away from Elijah. She wasn't the biggest fan of sleeping on hard, frozen earth, but it was still better than letting herself fall into the arms of an immoral, arrogant king.

Okay, maybe not, she thought. She found it almost painful to admit it.

Janelle kept her gaze focused on the top netting of the tent, noticing Elijah watching her out of the corner of her eye.

She reluctantly turned her head to face him, sweeping her thick, long locks into a braid over her shoulder before laying her head back down on a rolled-up blanket.

The expression in his deep blue eyes was unreadable. A hint of a smile danced on his lips as their gazes met. His hand came out from underneath the blanket, and his fingers opened, his palm up. Over his hand, some black smoke hovered and swirled quickly until it turned orange, and heat radiated from the aura. The light from the flames, or whatever she saw, warmed the space between them.

"Are you fucking kidding me?" Janelle said, agitated. "You've had the ability to keep us warm this entire time?"

A cocky smile claimed his features before he turned over. With his back on the ground and facing the top of the tent, he smirked. "It looks like I'll be much warmer than you are tonight."

Her nostrils flared, and heat reached her cheeks as she watched the orange ball of warm light leave his palm and hover above him. She had seen the kind of magic the Newick witches held, but this was the first time she had witnessed anything like that specifically. Janelle was fascinated, even as the rest of her brain reminded her to be furious at Elijah's deception. Regardless, she was still cold. She could only feel a small amount of the heat, but it was enough.

Janelle narrowed her eyes on Elijah. As he reached into his bag with the warm flame still floating over him, she followed his movements. He pulled out the pearl-colored gem hanging from a thin silver chain in his pocket and placed it over his chest.

She recognized the stone from when he used it on her in the cell. "What is that stone exactly?" she asked. Her eyes stayed on the gem, watching his thumb run gingerly over the smooth surface.

He cleared his throat. "It's called a Voleric pendant. It's not a Newick gem if that's what you're wondering." Elijah moved the pendant over his chest, lying back down.

"I've never seen anything like it," she said.

"It belonged to my mother—the mother who raised me," he explained. "My father never knew it existed, but she gave me one last piece of her several months before she died. The Fae king, Argon, had given it to her before their banishment. I didn't know it contained magic until I played around with it one night. My mind seemed to shoot through a portal; before I knew it, I saw inside my brother's dreams a few doors down the hall. I watched his desires and hopes play out before me. We caught eyes for a split second, and he and I both realized what was happening."

He gripped the stone, and she blinked, a smile growing on her lips. Whether it came from a Fae, an elf, or a sorcerer, magic was always so fascinating. Even her own powers still amazed her.

True, Janelle could manipulate light, and yes, her senses and speed were incredibly heightened...but magic, that was truly a wonder to her. It was most likely why she was drawn to the Newick coven and their gems in the first place.

Her brows knitted together. "Whose mind do you plan to invade now?" she asked.

Elijah grinned, moving back over, placing both shoulders against the ground until he faced upward. "I'm going to find your brother."

20

AIDEN

Tegan placed her bow and quiver on the oak table by the kitchen and turned to Aiden. "I'm not sure if they have running water anymore, but there's a well in the back of their yard if we need it. You can settle in the parents' room since you're much taller." She giggled a little, so quiet he hardly heard it. "I'll take the small bed where their child used to sleep."

Aiden watched her as he sat on the sofa, slowly placing his own bag down. It was strange to him how willing she was to help him—a stranger.

Exhaustion ran through him as he sat down in the nearest chair. He leaned forward, intending to rest his elbows on his knees, and shut his eyes for a moment. The world lurched out from under him before he could.

The room spun around him as he struggled to regain his equilibrium. His eyes clouded over, and he felt the blood drain from his face. "Ah, fuck," he said.

Tegan's footsteps hurried toward him as he slumped forward, trying to keep himself from falling over.

"Tegan," Aiden called out.

"What...what's happening? Are you ill?" Her voice sounded panicked. Aiden shook his head.

"Not to make this awkward between us, but I'm going to need you to catch me here in a min—"

And with that word, Aiden slipped into his dream state.

Aiden's eyes felt heavy and dry as he adjusted to the dark space surrounding him—objects of nature materialized until he found himself in a familiar place. It was the prison he lived in within the Eastland Forest. Enormous, half-dead trees blocked out the sun with their skeletal branches, casting deep shadows along the ground. Crooked trails were spider-webbed out in all directions. The gloom of it lay thick over everything he saw, and it was exactly how he remembered it.

Elijah emerged from behind a large, rotting tree trunk. "Well, this place is a bit scary," he said.

The feeling of being watched crept up Aiden's neck, making the hairs on his skin stand straight. Inconsistencies in that world made it obvious he was in a construct, not a memory. He moved to rest his hand on his father's sword, an instinctive comfort whenever he felt vulnerable, but his fingers found nothing but air.

"The Eastland Forest is one of the most beautiful places in this world," Aiden said, "but within that land is this place, the Whispering Woodlands, and it would make you have nightmares for years."

Elijah glanced around, looking nervous as if he felt like he, too, was being watched. "Where are you now, in the real world?" Elijah asked.

Aiden stood tall, looking up as if he would see Tegan peering down at him. "Northeast of Heyerberg. We had a complicated run-in with Kieran's men—"

"We?" Elijah asked.

"A girl is with me. She helped me escape and took me to a location hidden within the forest when it was no longer safe. We're in a cabin for the night."

"Good," Elijah said, and Aiden gave him a quizzical look. "I'm not far behind. Camped at the bottom of Whitestone Mountain." He paused, his eyes glossy with pain as if he struggled to get the next words out. "Aiden, I'm sorry about Valkanon. Rest assured, he's been buried with honor."

The memory of the Shadow Creature and Valkanon's fall had been ever-present in his mind since it happened. The sight of his oldest friend's face at the moment of his death. It was never far from his thoughts. But Elijah's words brought it screaming back to the forefront, and he felt the pain grip him just as tightly as it had the first time.

"Once the storm settles," Elijah continued, "we'll meet you where you're staying."

Aiden shut his eyes. *He cannot come here.*

"You should not have left Zemira, Aiden. What were you thinking? Why didn't you talk to me before you left?"

Aiden closed his eyes as anger contorted his features. He didn't want Elijah's help. He knew if Elijah had heard his reasoning, he would have stopped him from leaving. It was too late now. Elijah was miles behind him.

"Elijah," he started. "I believe I fought the Shadow Creature; it was drawn to my magic. I have felt its own power. It drew itself to me because that is what it feeds upon. It was ripping the very life from me." He stopped, trying to string his words together the best way he could to help Elijah understand. "If that is true, my sister, with whom I share that same magic, needs more protection than ever. I will give Kieran something he will want far more in exchange for her."

Elijah looked as if he was biting the inside of his cheek. "And what is that?" Elijah asked.

Aiden shook his head. "I can't tell you, but trust me when I say she'll be safe. Keep her protected in your palace. Tell her I love her and—"

"Don't be a fool!" Elijah fumed. "You honestly believe she's going to allow you to venture onto Newick land, knowing you're about to sacrifice yourself for her life."

Aiden held up his hand. "Right now, I'm more concerned about that creature out there. If you're at the bottom of that mountain, be wary. I don't know where that creature went after I stabbed it with my father's sword, but I didn't kill it."

He watched Elijah go still.

"We have bigger problems than a villainous sorcerer," Aiden added.

Elijah stepped forward, and the trails shifted, moving in different directions and altering the dreamscape. The shift seemed to have startled the king as he suddenly lifted his hands, guarding himself against something that might appear and attack.

He turned back to Aiden. "Aiden, your sister was willing to die at my hand to protect you from Kieran. I wouldn't be surprised if she's preparing to slit my throat as we speak. If you go to him, he'll capture you and use you to get her to come back. Whatever you're about to offer him for her life, please reconsider. I've prepared the pirates and my army to strike at my command. Come home!"

Aiden held up his hand, confusion, and shock radiating through him. "Wait. She's with you now?"

Elijah pressed his lips together. "Your vengeance will get her killed. Stop being a hero," Elijah said. "He'll take you both, and you're a fool to believe otherwise—"

"Take her back home, Elijah!"

"She's safe with me, but she won't be if you piss off Kieran. He's clearly obsessed with her." Elijah's tone stayed level, but Aiden noticed a tightness around his mouth as he said it.

Aiden's eye twitched.

"Come back to Zemira, and we'll send my army," Elijah said. "You cannot do this alone."

"How could you bring her?" he asked angrily, no longer listening to Elijah's words.

"She insisted," he said. "But don't worry; I have her trussed up nicely, right by my side."

He had to get Elijah out of his head.

Aiden closed his eyes, using his Elven gifts to shut out the king. He felt violated having Elijah inside his head to begin with. The less control he had, the more Elijah would be able to manipulate his thoughts from within his head. His mind reached out into the projection, trying to find a way to push Elijah back.

"Get out!" Aiden shouted.

A giant, lumbering troll appeared at the edge of the trees. It roared before rushing forward at full tilt, charging at them. Aiden shoved Elijah roughly out of harm's way, and then the world around him fell away. He opened his eyes to see Tegan looking down at him with wide, worried eyes. A warm rag was draped over his forehead, and his broad shoulders were cradled in her arms.

She breathed a sigh of relief. "Aiden! What the hell happened?" she asked him as he lifted himself slowly from her lap. "I thought you died."

A tiny smile flitted across his lips. "Not quite. More like dreaming."

"You simply passed out and started dreaming?"

He shook his head, unsure how to explain Elijah's little tricks to an average human. Not everyone knew the King of Zemira was half sorcerer. Perhaps there would be more assassination attempts if they did, as those who governed nearby lands would come to fear him.

"I need to keep moving tomorrow morning," he said. "To Newick."

Tegan backed up, practically dropping Aiden to the ground. "Do you have a death wish?" she said. "You think I risked my life for you for nothing so that you can—what? Trot my little horse to the Newick coven? Nobody sets foot on their grounds. Don't be a fool. You should go home."

Aiden stared at her. She was kind, certainly, but also seemed ruthlessly practical.

Why would she even care whether I lived or died? he wondered. *Let alone risk her life to help me.*

"Tegan, I appreciate that you're helping me, but this isn't your fight. The coven leader, Kieran, is going to hurt my sister," he explained. "I don't have a choice."

He hesitated to share the details of his mission. He didn't know the woman, but he wanted to trust her.

"I have a plan," he said, using his head to gesture to his sword laid across the table.

"You're going to ride into their village and kill him with your sword?" she said mockingly. "Yeah, that'll work." The sarcasm in her voice agitated him. He wasn't an idiot. That was far from his plan.

"No," he said. "But it's best that's all you know."

"I know Kieran," she said. "We all know what that coven has been doing the last twenty years with creatures like yourself, starting with Kieran's uncle. If an elf dares venture into their territory, they'll kill you or imprison you."

Aiden nodded. "I know," he said. "But my only concern is my sister right now. If she doesn't return to Kieran with King Elijah's head, which she won't, he will send another one of his people to find her. It's going to start a war. I don't trust Elijah not to trade her for the peace of his people if he runs out of options. I have something that the coven leader will want more than her."

Tegan's eyes went wide, glancing at the sword, then back to meet his eyes.

"Then good luck because this is a fool's errand," she said. They stared at each other. The unspoken weight of Aiden's imminent mortal peril filled the room. Tegan took a deep breath and looked up at him through her dark lashes. "This may be your last night of freedom." Her voice was quiet, just a whisper. It pulled him her way, and he wanted to reach out and touch her.

Aiden lifted his hand, gliding his fingers through the auburn lock of her hair that had fallen across her face and tucking it behind her ear. As soon as he realized what he was doing, he pulled back with a flinch. His hand hovered in the air between them like he had been burned. He felt suddenly and abjectly at a loss.

"You should go home," he said, voice soft, "or stay here; I don't care. Just wherever you'll be safe."

The fire in her eyes made him drop his hand to his side. Her voice was steely as she spoke, and its sound stoked the growing fire inside him. "I shot Kieran's men with my arrows and then helped you escape," she said as she stared at him. "Do you honestly believe I'll be safe if you send me back there?" It wasn't fury carried in her tone but disbelief, thinking he could do such a thing when she'd done so much for him.

She cannot come with me, he reminded himself.

Tegan had proven her worth a dozen times over that day, but he couldn't take her. He barely knew her, not much more than that she was a strange woman. She fought for him today, but who was to say that would last until tomorrow?

"I'm sorry, Tegan. You're only a human—" Her expression fell, and he felt like an ass, as if calling her human was an insult. "Right?" Aiden waited for her answer. He'd sensed she was different, but maybe he was wrong.

"Of course, I'm human," she said, standing up and pacing to the kitchen. She stopped abruptly, turning to look at him, her shoulders slumped. "Aiden…" Her lips parted as her words trailed off.

The room stilled for a fleeting moment before she walked to his side and placed her hand on his cheek, calming his thoughts.

"I'm trying to save your life." The desperation made her exquisite eyes darken. Devotion rolled off her in waves, and Aiden was drowning in it. He was the protector, not the protected. Aside from his own family, he had never known anyone to care for him with such fervent determination in all his life. He would never have expected it from a stranger.

What possible motivation could she have for this? he asked himself.

"How about—" he started, but his voice caught in his throat. "Does this family have anything to drink?"

She gave him a small smile, and the moment took an intimate turn. "I hope so," she said, looking almost relieved he had asked. "You're sad. I'm scared. I'd like to forget about it all for a night."

Tegan turned on her heel and strolled into the kitchen, opening each cabinet until she snagged a bottle of red wine with a triumphant cry.

"Will this do?" she asked, holding it up.

Aiden smiled. "One last drink before I die, I guess," he said, smiling with good humor despite everything.

She pulled out two glasses and filled them to the brim with the ruby liquid. "Here," she said, handing one to Aiden.

An hour passed, and while they had finished that bottle, Tegan was able to find a few more in the back cupboard. They drank those, too.

Aiden's head buzzed, and his mouth was dry, but he was warm, tingling, which made his pain and fear feel far away. It didn't hurt that every time Tegan leaned over to top off his glass, he was gifted with a view of her bosom, sending his blood flowing southwards. While it wasn't the most productive use of his energy, it did seem to put things in a rosier light.

He blinked the thought away, setting his empty glass on the table with a dull *clink*. He looked upwards, expecting to see Tegan readying herself for sleep, but instead, she stood in front of him, so close he could feel the warmth from her body buzzing along his skin.

She reached out to trail her fingertips over his collarbone, her touch not more than a whisper, but it left a trail of goosebumps in its wake. Aiden had almost forgotten what the slow, mounting heat within him felt like, how addictive it could be. His stomach fluttered as he watched her tongue flick out to lick her lips. Oh, how he suddenly understood the raw, primal urge to reach out and taste her.

"Tegan—"

"Shh," she said, laying a finger over his lips to silence him. "Just be quiet, will you?"

Aiden knew he should stop looking at her the way he was. His mission to protect his sister was all that mattered, not the woman before him. No good would come from giving in to his baser cravings. But it had been painfully long since someone had looked at him with desire, touched him so reverently, and he felt powerless under her hand.

His best friend faced death; his sister faced something worse; and Valkanon...He knew that was a gaping, festering wound inside of him that would never truly heal. All of that was barely contained inside his body, alongside the exhaustion and pain he had carried for days.

It was too much. *Tegan* was too much. That woman, the stranger, with her soft hands and easy smile. She made him feel warm and safe. Her very presence eased his burdens. It was as if she wanted to wrap him up in gauze, hold him tight, and protect him from the things that would hurt him. It was an undignified thing for a warrior to crave, but he desired it, nonetheless. No matter how reckless it was, he wanted to take this one thing for himself. He wanted *her*.

"Come on, we're drunk. We aren't thinking clearly," he said in a last-ditch effort to do the right thing as her fingers walked up his chest. "We can't do this."

He stood up and reached out, gripping her hand in his to stop her, but the smooth glide of Tegan's skin ignited heat between his thighs, and his resolve melted away.

She looked up, using her other hand to push his black hair out of his eyes. When she spoke, her voice was thick with arousal. "Why not?"

His only response was the quickening of his breath as her hand trailed down his body. "Don't you ever get lonely, Aiden?" she asked, her fingers coming to rest on the strap of his trousers. "Don't you ever want to let go of that burden of guilt and purpose for a little while? To give yourself over to someone, even if it's only a moment?" She huffed out a wry laugh. "You might be dead tomorrow and—"

She froze mid-sentence when Aiden cupped her cheek in his hand. He gripped her, just shy of too tight, watching the frantic look in her eyes. He could already feel himself coming apart, and they hadn't done more than touch. It was dangerous, so dangerous. But he still wasn't going to stop.

Tegan breathed harder, her shoulders pulling up and down faster as he watched her breasts steadily rise and fall. Her eyes were liquid dark as she looked at him. He wondered if she was as wet between her thighs as he was hard.

"You are stunningly beautiful. I won't deny that." He ran his fingers from her cheek down to her breast. Tegan closed her eyes and shivered at the touch, tilting her chin up to give him better access. "Are you sure?" he asked. "Because I'm not."

She answered by arching her back, pushing her chest into his hand, making the softest, most intoxicating moan Aiden had ever heard. He let his fingers roam and toyed with the bindings of her shirt, caressing the silky fabric as he released the strap. Her shirt fell, pooling around her waist, and her glorious skin was exposed to his sight but more to his touch. His mouth went dry, and his need was hot, molten.

If he had struggled to control himself before, he had no chance now that he was looking at her, half-naked with her tongue sliding across her lips, leaving a glistening path he wanted to taste. Never was a man more wretched with the need to taste a woman. The tattered remnants of his restraint abandoned him, and he wasn't turning back. He couldn't. To stop now would kill him. Although he'd still leave in the morning. It was just one night, just sex, a well-deserved release.

We'll never see each other again, he reminded himself as the heat of arousal drowned out the conflicting thoughts filling his head.

He straightened a little before stepping closer to her. The liquor buzzed in his mind as he looked at her with a stern gaze. "Let's not make this harder than it has to be," he said because he had to say it aloud. He had to speak the words, so he could hear them as much as she could. "We fuck, you sleep, and I'm gone by morning."

Her lips parted instinctually, and then he crashed into her. He kissed her deeply, hands in her hair, chest to chest, as he pulled every remaining inch of her against his body. Her mouth was soft and pliant beneath his. She tasted like the sweet, savory flavor of rich wine. Aiden reached out, taking her slender shoulders and wrapping his arms around them until she was enveloped. She moaned against his lips, making him squeeze her even tighter.

Aiden felt it, the moment when the atmosphere seemed to shift. Holding each other close wasn't enough; he wanted more. Still pressed together at the mouth, he lifted her, his hands under her thighs as he walked her backward. There was a slight *thud* as her back hit the wall, but neither of them noticed because her legs wound around his waist, exactly how they should be. He used his hips as leverage to hold them even closer together, deepening the kiss as his hips started to move in a slow, sensual grind.

She was weightless as he suddenly spun around and moved her to the sofa. As desperate as he was to get her undressed, he still took a moment to lose himself in her eyes. The heat there burned him, sending him right back to her mouth for a wet, open kiss.

Tegan tugged at his clothes, unfastening his buttons, so she could pull off his shirt. Aiden stopped touching her long enough to fling it to the floor, but she stopped him before he could claim her mouth again. Her hands explored his chest, keeping him at arm's length as she stared at him. Her gaze devoured every inch of his flesh until she snapped her head up, pulling him down and kissing him deeper than before.

Aiden couldn't think, almost couldn't breathe.

He was surprised by her strength as she took control of him, and he certainly didn't dislike the feeling. She pulled him closer and grabbed him, scraping her fingernails down his back. The pain and pleasure mingled, and he moaned. Nothing had ever been so exquisite. He bit his lip, trying to maintain some semblance of control as the pressure mounted. The scratches felt like liquid fire, pooling in him until that pressure threatened to erupt.

Leaning back just enough to move his arms, Aiden took both her wrists in one large, calloused hand, pinning them above her head. He bent his neck forward and nipped her exposed collarbone. She moaned and writhed, bucking her hips, pushing herself closer while he held on to his control with the most tenuous of threads. She was more than he'd imagined. Stronger. More sensual. The kind of woman he had only ever dreamed of being with.

He captured her mouth in another deep kiss, swallowing the moan that poured out of her.

With his other hand, Aiden fumbled with the clasp, desperate to undo her belt, to slide her pants down until she kicked them the rest of the way off. He let his hand roam, exploring the curves and dips of her body, making her gasp when he rolled a pert nipple between his fingers. Her body quivered, so he quickly replaced his fingers with his mouth, and when his teeth scraped ever-so-lightly over her breast before he sucked it, she threw her head back and cried out. Her hips rolled into him, uncoordinated, desperate, leaving him completely breathless. He'd been hard for some time now, but the way she was grinding into him made his cock throb with need. There wouldn't be time to do this well if he didn't slow down, but he needed more. So much more of her.

Aiden wanted everything.

He released her nipple and left a trail of biting kisses across her chest while she writhed. Her hands slid up and down his chest, around his back, into his hair, twisting and pulling.

"More," she sighed.

Aiden sucked a violent kiss into the soft skin of her breast, making Tegan cry out with pleasure. He felt himself drifting in a sea of ecstasy, losing himself in the feel and taste of her. His mind was pleasantly fuzzy, and the only thing he cared about at that moment was relieving the aching need to be inside her. Every breath and moan only spurred him on.

He leaned back to unbuckle his trousers, shoving them down, and clambered out of them as quickly as possible. Sighing with relief as they were finally naked, he pressed his skin to hers. Aiden took a moment to stare at her, taking in the vision of the woman on that sofa, and the only sound in the room was their gentle panting.

Aiden pushed her deeper into the couch, holding her in place. His memory etched every detail of her body into a picture his mind could call up later. After that moment passed into another, he nudged her thighs apart, leaning in to taste her or draw it out. Either way, he wanted it almost as badly as he wanted to sink inside her warmth.

Aiden trailed slow kisses down her chest and taut stomach, nipping at the tender skin on the inside of each thigh as he curled his fingers into the fleshy skin at her hips to keep her still. He briefly looked at Tegan to wink at her before lowering his head. He flicked his tongue out, licking from her slick opening to the top of her most sensitive spot. And when she twitched and bucked, he followed the path down. When she cried out, he sucked the nub into his mouth and milked her with every pull. Tegan tightened her thighs, and he stopped, waiting for her to loosen her hold before he resumed. She wound her fingers into his long hair and held him, but he could move, suck, lick, and slide a finger inside her wet heat.

The cabin was suddenly filled with the sounds of her pleasure echoing through the room. Her fingers scrambled for anything she could hold onto, one hand finding a cushion and the other sinking into the flesh of Aiden's back.

He moved his tongue in and out of her luxuriously, not working with any real purpose but relishing the feeling of her scratching him and gripping his hair. Her body was strung tight, muscles twitching, her legs trembling where they rested now on his shoulders. She screamed, just once, as her body found release and her hips bucked. That time, he let her move and followed the rhythm she set. Her slickness dripped down his face as he worked her through the waves.

Aiden moved higher up her body, replacing his tongue with two of his fingers and letting his own pleasure curl as he moved them in and out of her wet heat. His arousal wasn't going to wait much longer. His cock was hard, leaking against his stomach.

He needed her. Now.

Tegan whimpered, trembling, wrung-out but still pulling him in, desperate for more. She dug her fingers into his skin and moaned his name. For the space of one second, he thought it might be the sweetest sound he had ever heard, but then his need overwhelmed him, and he groaned at the sight of her like it was the first time he'd seen her.

"Aiden. I need you inside me right now!" she begged. "Please."

Aiden was nothing if not obliging. He pulled his fingers out and wrapped them around his cock. He slowly stroked it, preparing himself, so he could have a second before he plunged inside her.

Lining himself up with her entrance, he thrust inside, sharp, deep, enough to make her pitch and cry out. Whatever he'd done to deserve the exquisite agony, he would do a thousand times over for just the promise of another moment like that one.

Tegan bit her lower lip, humming her pleasure as he thrust deep into her. He had her legs spread, strong hands pushing her knees apart. Aiden's thumbs stroked the inside of her thighs, high enough that she trembled with every touch against her warmth. She was open to him, and never had he seen anything better. His blood rushed at a brutal pace, heart hammering with need.

Her body rocked each time he drove himself into her center, punching out gasps that made her breasts bounce. Aiden growled as he picked up the pace because he needed more. So much more. Tegan was as intoxicating as any drink he'd ever consumed. And she wound her hand in his hair, tugging. His cock was tighter and more swollen inside her.

Aiden moved relentlessly. Her inner walls were pulling at him as if desperate to drag him deeper. Every gyration and grind of her hips sent pulses of pleasure through his body. His hips began to stutter as desperation made his coordination fail, the flush of orgasm gripping his body. He was lost to every sensation, tethered only by their connection to the world.

Tegan's body quivered as her thighs clutched him tight. He felt the crest of her pleasure take over as she threw her head back and gasped. Aiden was a primal, feral thing on the edge himself, thrusting into her to capture his release. The column of her neck was long in front of him, soft and inviting, and he didn't think before he leaned in and bit down. His teeth sank into the tender flesh. The salty tang of blood erupted in his mouth right as he started to pulse hot inside her.

"Aiden!" she cried, but she didn't pull back from the pain he knew he had inflicted upon her. Their waves of ecstasy slowed into a tender beat, and he pulled his cock out and groaned as he lay on the sofa beside her. His breath came in heavy puffs, and he turned to watch her doing the same.

Tegan smiled as she moved toward him, one arm sliding over his chest. He held her closer and dropped kisses on her damp forehead as her eyes grew tired.

Aiden clenched his jaw, knowing he'd have to leave her in the morning. He cared deeply for this human stranger for some reason, as if he had known her longer than just one day and night.

Fear and worry grated his nerves. There would be no tomorrow for them. That was all they had, yet he worried. Not just for his own safety but for the woman in his arms.

He sighed and closed his eyes, savoring his last moments with her, wishing it could be more but knowing it couldn't.

One night he'd never forget, with the beautiful stranger from the tavern.

21

ELIJAH

When Elijah opened his eyes, an icy draft was moving through the tent. The magical fire above him was gone, and it felt as if more time had passed than when he last used the pendant. The sudden, painful pounding in his head caused him to wince. He lifted his hand and ran his finger over his forehead, feeling the thick warmth of liquid along his scalp. Elijah then brought his fingers together, rubbing them slowly—blood.

He turned quickly, seeing the empty blanket beside him, ash scattered over the bottom of the tent, and a shredded, burned rope sitting in the middle of it.

Did she use my fireball to burn through the rope? He didn't think that was possible, given the magic he used to fortify the rope. Then again, it appeared she had found a way—magic against magic.

Fuck me, he cursed in his mind.

Elijah quickly clambered to his feet, wiped the blood from his forehead, and gathered his things. Thankfully the snow had stopped falling, but the chill was still there.

He quickly dressed and wrapped as many blankets over him as possible and ran to where they tied off the horse. "Oh, that bitch."

He would have to go on foot.

Elijah looked around for hoof marks, catching a faded trail that wound up to the top of Whitestone Mountain. She was heading in the direction they had planned to go. The wiser choice for him would be to go back to the palace, where he would have better protection from his enemies. He could take the damn dragon over the mountain, despite Lincoln's protest over Anaru's safety.

Gods, I'm such a fool, he shouted in his mind. *Believing she'd not flee the moment that I wasn't watching her.*

Right then, in his anger and frustration, he decided that all that mattered was stopping Janelle before she reached Newick. He wouldn't go back to Zemira until he found both her and Aiden.

⎯⎯◆⎯⎯

Elijah's magic was many things, and every day he felt the strength of his power like his own heartbeat. Whether he used it to kill his enemies or step into someone's dream, it was *his* strength, *his* will. Using his black smoke to stay on the trail and transport himself to the top of Whitestone Mountain wouldn't come easily with the heavy wind and the snowy slope.

He had to muster the energy to harness his power, but once that energy drained from him, using his own physical strength would be nearly impossible. He was still human, after all.

It felt as if he had traveled for hours, taking as many stops as possible to gain strength. By the time he reached the top, the clouds had parted, and the sun began to rise.

The trail he had followed, showing which direction Janelle had gone, was now covered with snow as the wind scattered the flakes over the terrain. Unfortunately, he hadn't a clue which direction she had traveled.

He still held the Voleric pendant in his pocket—to find her now, he would have to use magic. However, Janelle would know the moment he tried and would push him out.

A slight worry hit him that perhaps she hadn't made it to the top—he barely had been able to while on foot.

He trudged forward, his limbs almost giving out with each trek through the snow. He felt frost blisters forming on his lips, and he cursed himself for being such a fool as to leave her alone in that tent while he floated away into Aiden's mind. As he reached the end of the trail, Elijah could see the faint outlines of small buildings and houses. He'd managed to reach a small village.

Movement in the distance caught his eye. He stepped back, his eyes narrowing on what looked to be a woman with long black hair, placing a basket of something next to a storefront.

Elijah straightened his back, combing his fingers through his tousled hair over his head. He then gingerly washed the dry blood from his forehead with the snow and felt the gash. It was more of a small cut, really, nothing too extreme that he couldn't explain away. No one could know he was the King of Zemira, but rather someone they could trust, like one of their own. Someone they'd be willing to feed and give shelter to until he could figure out where Janelle had gone. Perhaps she was in that town ahead, but was she foolish enough to be found in plain sight? If he had to, Elijah would search every home and business until he found her.

Elijah trudged through the snow until it thinned out on the road. It appeared that the townsfolk were up early, clearing the path. Businesses lined the main road, and up ahead, there were a few cottages.

The woman picked up a rug from in front of the door and shook it out, placing it back down. She then ran her hands down her dress to wipe them dry. The black-haired woman looked up as Elijah stood in front of her.

His stomach dropped. *Heyerberg Coffee* Co. was painted on the sign. He was in his birthplace. Being in the village he was born in yet never returned to, the same place his mother died...he felt solemn peace, yet the nerves wracked his body.

"Hello, miss," he said gently. "Are you open yet?" Elijah glanced through the window, seeing pastries in a glass case and a kettle on top of a small stove.

"Oh, dear. You startled me," the woman said. "I open in ten minutes, but you can come in to keep warm. Your cheeks are blood red."

"Thank you. I've been out all morning. My horse was injured, and I was thrown from her, hitting the rocks. I had to walk the remainder of the way."

She scratched her head. "Oh my. I'm so sorry. Where are you traveling from?" she asked, stepping in front of the door as if she questioned whether inviting a stranger inside was a good idea after all.

"Mayberry," he answered quickly. Elijah may have never traveled through the mountain range before. Still, he was familiar with the smaller villages between Zemira and Whitestone Mountain. They were not part of any kingdom. They governed themselves as either country had never claimed them.

"Mayberry?" She gasped. "You came all the way up the mountain from Mayberry? In the ill weather that we had last night?"

He nodded. "My home's wood stove was broken, and I was almost frozen to death last night. I could really use some shelter until I can find some fuel."

The woman held out her hand, gesturing to him to come inside the shop. "Of course."

The black-haired woman was short, with busty hips and a narrow nose. Her hair was scrunched up in a high bun, and she had a blue scarf wrapped tightly around her neck. Her dress reached her ankles, looking as though it had been worn and repaired numerous times.

"I'm Archer," he lied, giving her his middle name.

"Nice to meet you, Archer," she said, walking around the corner and lighting the stove to heat up the water for what he assumed would be the tea. "I'm Zelda." She pointed to a closed door in the back of the shop. "If you need to wash up, we're one of the few businesses in Heyerberg that has running water," she said. "I can make you some tea now. On the house."

Elijah smiled. "Tea would be pleasantly appreciated. Thank you, miss."

She gave him a warm smile, pulled out a tea leaf jar, and turned to the stove again, the kettle now emitting a steady column of steam.

Elijah looked around and then back to her. "I saw a woman on the trail on my way up here. She looked—" He paused and thought carefully about his next words. "She looked injured. By the time I rounded the corner to help her, she was gone. *I hope she's okay. I—"*

The woman handed him the hot tea in a blue ceramic mug. "A woman," she said. "Hmm, I haven't seen any woman. What does she look like?"

Elijah carefully sipped the steaming hot liquid and placed it back on the counter right as a bell chimed behind him, and the door opened. An older couple walked in, dusting off their shoes on the doormat.

Elijah moved aside from the counter, letting them approach to order their drinks.

"White hair, tall, skin the color of the fallen snow but lips as red as fine wine." He stopped, recounting more of her beauty. "Her eyes are the color of the most beautiful sapphire gem you will ever see, and her smile is like—"

He stopped again, shaking his head, thinking to himself. *But behind that beauty, she has the temper of a wild beast and a mouth like a peasant thief.*

Elijah hadn't realized he was staring off into the distance, no longer speaking with the woman.

"Hello?" Zelda said, handing off two coffees to the couple, who thanked her and stepped back, leaving him alone with the woman again. "Are you alright? You really look like you need to rest."

Elijah laughed, meeting her eyes again. "I'm sorry, you're right. Is there an inn around here?" he asked softly, giving her a charming smile until she mimicked his features, grinning back.

"Yes. The bright yellow building at the end of the town center. It's only a half-mile down the road. You can't miss it. Maybe that is where the little lost woman went." She winked and gestured for another couple to move forward. Elijah hadn't realized four other patrons stood in the line, waiting to order their morning brew.

"Thank you, Zelda," he said, stepping back and placing the now-empty mug on a table before leaving the shop.

Elijah removed his gloves and placed his hands over his cheeks. He felt the warmth and took in another breath of the crisp air.

"Where are you?" he said quietly to the wind.

He turned to see more of the village and began to walk. The sun was bright enough to shine over the city. The shops were now all open, and people were moving about from store to store. Some older, some children—they were all human, at least in appearance.

The yellow inn came into view as he approached the grove of trees that circled a glass gazebo at the end of the square. It was a two-story building with yellow siding, white shutters, and a picket fence. The outside sign read *Giselle's Inn*.

Elijah walked through the gate and up the steps, opening the unlocked door.

The warmth of the inn was inviting, the heat from the fireplace moving through the hallway. The walls were covered in cream-colored paper with dried purple lilies bordering the doorways. A straight stairwell led up to another hallway, and Elijah assumed that was where the rooms were.

"I'll be right there!" a man's gravelly voice called from the back.

A moment later, an older man poked his head around the corner, holding a bread basket, which he then placed on the console table by the stairs.

"I'm just doing my round for breakfast for my guest. How can I help you, sir?"

Elijah glanced around the room again, ignoring the old man. He spotted wet patches of water on the carpet leading to the backroom. Near the corner was the black scarf Janelle had been wearing.

"Sorry, I'm late to meet my wife. She should have our room ready. White hair, blue eyes?"

The man perked up. "Oh, not sure if she has white hair. She wore a head wrap around her head, but I can't forget those bright blue eyes and crimson lips."

Elijah placed his bag on the floor. "That's my love," he said. "Is she already settled in our room?"

The man's features dropped. "Um, she—" He scratched his head and swallowed. "She didn't say she had a husband coming. What...what did you say your name was—"

Elijah's hand came out, using his powers to grip the old man's throat. The black smoke thickened until it squeezed hard enough to make the man quickly pass out. Then Elijah checked to ensure he hadn't killed him once he lay on the floor—his heart was still beating.

He walked quickly to the front door and latched the bolt. His eyes moved up the stairs and waited. Silence.

Slowly, he continued up the stairs and then crept down the hall on his toes, placing an ear against each door, listening. When he reached the last door, he heard a slight creak of the floor, giving her away. Elijah placed his hand on the knob and turned it slowly, but it was locked.

A wry smile flitted across his face before he stepped back. Then he rammed his foot into the door, breaking off its hinges.

Janelle leapt for her sword, but Elijah kicked it away. Then he wrapped his strong arms around her waist and pulled her back into his chest, squeezing.

Placing his lips next to her ear, he whispered, "Little elf, why do you insist on being so difficult when I'm only trying to help you?"

Elijah waited for the answer, but her elbow came back instead, slamming into his stomach. He winced and released her. But it was only for a moment before his hand reached out and gripped her ankle as she attempted to flee again for her weapon. He pulled back, tossing her to the ground.

He straddled her thrashing body, pinning her to the ground and squeezing his knees tightly together. As she attempted to wrench herself free from his grip, he grabbed her wrists and pinned them above her head. "Are you enjoying this?" he teased, looking down at her with a grin on his lips. "You're not putting up much of a fight."

She flashed him a mocking, angry grin, but it only amused him. "I was going to ask you the same thing," she said. "Using your strength to gain power over a woman," she said. "I thought the King of Zemira was above taking a woman down against her will?"

He released one of his hands and placed it against her chest, pinning her down. Her eyes widened. "Careful, Janelle. I suggest you stop fighting this," he said, letting a dangerous edge creep into his voice. Genuine fear sparked in her eyes. A plague of guilt washed over him as her body went slack, no longer resisting.

Her lips parted.

"Are you going to hit me now? Kill me?" she said, a tear welling in her eye. "I dare you to try."

He squeezed her bound wrists. "Don't threaten my power, Janelle, unless you'd like to get intimately acquainted with the powers my mother gave me." His magic slowly left his fingers, clouding around them. "Are you done?" he asked, trying once again to keep her still, but he couldn't turn his gaze from her.

Even when his body was filled with rage, the sight of her stunned him.

"I don't want your help to save my brother. You'd be nothing if not completely useless." She snarled, and Elijah's lip twitched. He wanted to be angry and punish her for knocking him unconscious and leaving him at the bottom of the mountain all night. Show her how much he ached when she left him. All he could do was stare down at her, dumbfounded by how much she affected him. She made him grow mad with need—a feeling he hadn't expected.

"I cannot protect you when you're not near me," he said.

The room grew silent.

Elijah's lips parted as they stared into each other's eyes in agonizing stillness until her body went slack under his pressure. His gaze drew to the hollow at the base of her neck. He watched her chest rise and fall with just the barest flutter of her pulse visible. He felt his heart rate quicken the more he stared.

"Perhaps Kieran was right," she said in a soft voice. She sounded defeated, and Elijah briefly regretted the part he must have played in that. "You should have never been a king, and I will curse myself until my very last breath that I wasn't strong enough to kill you when—"

Elijah pulled her into him, crushing his mouth against her lips, tongues meeting in an aggressive assault of *taste* and *feel*. He released her wrists, bringing one hand to grip her jaw and direct the kiss, even while the other wound itself in her long, wild hair. He grabbed her thigh to arch her up into him and tugged hard, swallowing the gasp she let out as he kissed her. Every inch of him was strung tight with desire. Every inch of him was hungry. He pressed himself into her, letting Janelle's moans vibrate through his mouth as he kissed her with untamed desperation. The ache between his legs spurred him on further. All he could think about was his need to bury himself in every part of her lush, supple body.

Gods, he wanted her.

It felt as if his brain shut down for a moment, not able to think clearly about what he was doing. He needed to gulp for air to breathe, but he resisted the urge, not wanting to let Janelle go.

As swiftly as he had taken her, she pressed her hands to his chest and pushed him off. He released her, rolled off her body, and stood up. She let out a heavy sigh, placing her fingers on her red lips.

"Why to the stars did you do that?" she asked, taking heavy breaths as if he had kissed away all the air left in her.

Elijah looked down at her and stepped back until his back pressed against the broken door. His swollen lips tingled. Time seemed to stop as they stared at each other. All he could hear was the clock in the room.

Tick, tick, tick.

"Fuck!" he cursed, his lips parting ever so slightly.

Janelle stood, straightening her shirt. What looked like frustration flitted across her features.

"We are never to speak of this again," she said. "Not to anyone or each other. Understand?" She looked away, uncomfortable under his gaze.

Elijah gave her a bitter smile. "Don't worry," he said, ignoring the pang of hurt that tore through his chest. "I can think of a thousand humiliations that I'd prefer over letting anyone know I swapped saliva with a surly elf."

He placed his hand on the doorknob and looked over at her. His mind was washed out with bitterness and regret, but he refused to show it. His lie had sounded hollow, even to him.

"The innkeeper has been knocked out. Once he awakes, he will be running for help. We leave now."

Janelle snapped her head toward him and stared, and he fought the urge to wither under her stern gaze. He didn't regret kissing her. In fact, it was one of the most arousing experiences of his life to date. But it was foolish and even more ridiculous to assume whatever passions had driven him were reciprocated. He felt like a spurned schoolboy, not a king, which was a sharp sting to his ego.

Janelle closed her eyes and shook her head.

"The next town is miles from here, *Elijah*. Your damn horse got injured on the way up the hill, so we would have to go on foot. The one place where we could have stayed, at least a day to gain our strength, you assault the innkeeper. Gah, you're a bloody idiot!"

Oh, you infuriating woman, he screamed in his thoughts.

"Then we put up a no vacancy sign on the door and lock him up for the day until we find another horse," Elijah suggested. "We don't have a choice."

Janelle folded her arms across her chest and looked out the window as if half expecting someone to already come for her.

Another silence loomed between them, and Elijah scratched his head. "Stay here."

He left the room and came downstairs to find the man still lying on his back.

Elijah lifted the man and carried him upstairs, heading into one of the open rooms, and placed him on the bed.

The sudden movement jolted the man awake, and he gasped.

"Shhh," Elijah said. "It's okay. I won't hurt you...again."

The old man attempted to flee, but his frail body wasn't strong enough to withstand Elijah's power. The smoke crept up again, but he didn't touch the man that time. Instead, it circled him like he was sitting in the middle of a fog.

"Now," Elijah said to the man. "Where can I find some rope?"

22

AIDEN

The loud crowing from the roosters behind the cabin jolted Aiden awake, sitting bolt upright from his pillow. He had slept alone that night, leaving Tegan to her own space on the couch. He had thought about carrying her to the children's room and sleeping next to her. Her still, peaceful form curled up with a blanket made him reconsider. The truth was, he wanted to hold her until morning, but he was already wracked with guilt. He had to slip out before she awoke.

His head pounded relentlessly throughout the night—the after-effects of Elijah's intrusive mind sorcery—

Or possibly the wine, he considered.

The only thing that helped him sleep was the memory of Tegan's soft touches from the night before. He still felt the way her body had pressed against his as they moved together and how she clung to him through their release.

For the hour that followed, Tegan ran her fingertips over his chest. It was something delicate yet unforgiving. The sensation had lulled him into a peaceful sleep. Every inch of him screamed to reach out and grab her, clutch her body to his, and work her repeatedly until she screamed his name again and again. He briefly wondered if it were something he would ever tire of, given a chance. Instead, he woke up and slid out from her sleeping embrace, sneaking into the main bedroom.

Aiden had known it wouldn't be easy to walk away the next day. He had reminded himself of it more than once. His gratitude for how she had helped him would never fade, and he hoped that the memory of their night would stay with him forever as well. But it was time to leave.

He rubbed his temples and moved his thumbs to the crease of his eyes. He pressed down, trying to ease the throbbing pain in his head, grateful that his species healed easily.

A bright stream of light slowly filled the room, slats of it taking over the mattress as the sun rose higher. The brighter the room, the more conscious Aiden was that it was time for him to go. Eventually, he heaved his body enough to roll off the mattress. Still naked, he pushed his long, black hair out of his face and stretched. His muscles strained and protested as his shoulders cracked, but it felt good to stand tall. Aiden strode to the window, pulling aside the curtain. His movements were loose and unhurried, no matter what his mind urged him to do.

The day was clear and bright. Snowmelt was running off the roof, just as sluggish as he was, landing on the drainpipes underneath with a steady drip. The sound of the sun warming the land had always been soothing to Aiden. He rarely considered himself someone in need of being soothed, but there he was.

Aiden pulled on his clothes and let himself wander back into the space. He pulled his bag over his shoulder as he rounded the corner and was immediately caught in Tegan's gaze. She was standing in the kitchen's door frame with a mug of tea clasped in her hands.

Dammit, he cursed in his mind. He hadn't expected her to be awake so early.

She sucked in a breath, looking more defeated than upset. "I think you should listen to your friend and turn back," she said. "Go back to Zemira, Aiden."

Aiden blinked, feeling himself freeze up. Apparently, telling himself that leaving her would be difficult was nothing compared to truly experiencing the loss of her. He had known this fiery woman for less than a day, but something about her had taken hold of him. She had risked her own life to save his. She had sacrificed the comforts of her existence without a second thought. All for a stranger.

The only way he could think to repay her was to get as far away from her as possible. Anything else would only endanger her even more.

Aiden moved to the table, letting his hand fall and watching as his fingers drummed over its surface. He was taciturn at the best of times, but it wasn't usually that difficult to pull words from him. Something about it created a hollow feeling in his chest, and he didn't care for it.

"I'm sorry, Tegan," he said distantly. "I can't go back to Zemira. My sister will be forced to marry Kieran. She will not only lose her freedom, but she could also lose her life. You know I cannot allow that to happen." He paused, lifting his gaze from the table to look at her. "I hope you can understand."

Tegan huffed out a breath and put her tea down on the kitchen counter with a thump. Her movements were calm and controlled as she rested her hands and pressed her palms on the counter. Aiden realized after a moment that he was holding his breath.

"I'm not blind. I've seen what Kieran has done to elves," she said. "I understand the risk, and I know you must be a good man to care so deeply for your sister's safety." There was a pause as she straightened her back. She looked away from Aiden, her thoughts turning inwards, and ran her long fingers through her hair. "I just...I know you think you're doing the right thing, but no matter what weapons you bring or what bargaining chips you have in your pocket, there's no way it will be enough. You won't save her, Aiden. You can't save her."

Something twisted in Aiden's chest. He could feel anger bubbling up, even as a small part of him wondered if she was right. The bigger part of him was too focused on how sincere Tegan sounded and how much affection she held in her eyes when she looked at him. He gripped his bag tight, hitching it higher on his shoulder, and steeled himself to leave.

Tegan said nothing else. She crossed the space between them, taking a seat at the table in silence and resting her elbows in front of her. Aiden noticed the tremble in her hands as she clasped them together. A small tear formed in the corner of her eye, and she couldn't bring herself to look at him.

"Rising up against Kieran, or any of the Newick witches for that matter, is—" She shut her eyes, and a slow, exasperated breath left her lips. "Aiden, there's no way for you to make it through this alive. It's not possible."

A buzz of static filled Aiden's head as he looked at her. Without thinking, he reached out and touched her hair. It shone in the sunlight as he let the locks slip through his fingers. It was a strange movement, meaningless, but his body seemed to act on its own.

"If you're afraid of him, they would welcome you in Zemira," he said. "King Elijah will help you and anyone else who fears that man. Your country has no king. There's no one to protect you, and now I'm responsible for you losing your home. The least I can do is make sure you have one in Zemira. You'll be safe there, I promise you."

Tegan sucked her plump bottom lip into her mouth. Her eyes were still glued to the table. "Is there anything I can say to get you not to leave?" she asked, looking up.

Aiden didn't think before shaking his head no. It was an instinct. He could think of a hundred things she could say which would tug at him and make him want to stay with her. But none of that mattered.

Red hair fell over Tegan's eyes, and Aiden reached up to push it aside before he caught himself. Instead, he tucked the strand behind her ear and resisted the urge to kiss away the tear that rolled down her cheek. He wondered how long it had been since he had touched someone with that kind of softness instead of using his hands to fight.

"Go on, then," she said when he didn't answer. "We didn't have long together, but it's been nice. Thank you."

He leaned down from the chair, kissing her gently on the forehead before saying, "If I survive this, beautiful human, I will come to find you. Be sure of it."

"Two, I say. Give me two coins for tha' one there," a merchant bartered with a patron in front of his tent. Aiden couldn't tear his eyes away from how strange the people in Newick looked—much different than the Zemirans.

Each townsfolk's outfit was more vibrant and showier than the next. He tried to see it as merely a difference in convention but still found it pretentious. Thick makeup painted the women's faces, and their dresses were made of extravagant silk and cashmere. He had a hood drawn over his head to conceal his face. Aiden was ready to draw his sword if he attracted too much attention. He had to assume everyone he passed could wield magical gifts.

"You ripped me off, ye bastard!" the patron shouted, tossing the product on the floor. Then the patron placed his hands on the table, running his palms across it until everything was knocked to the ground. The merchant let out an angry bellow and launched himself over the table, tackling him.

A fight broke out quickly, giving Aiden a chance to slip through the market to a small alley without being seen. He ducked around the wall before the convenient distraction had ended.

Looking up from the alley, it was easy to see the spires of a tall, stone-walled mansion. It sat at the far end of the city, with each corner anchored by a tower that reached into the sky. Even the trees were not high enough to block the view. It loomed over the city like a shadow. Painted glass windows were scattered between the heavy gray stones, sparkling like jewels in the sunlight.

"I'm sorry. I'm sorry." His blood went cold when he heard a familiar voice. When he turned, Tegan stood in the alleyway, her arms laid still to her side. She looked exhausted as if she had been running all day to catch up.

Panic clutched his throat. He looked around, making sure no one was watching them. He was surprised but probably not as much as he should be. As if he hadn't secretly seen it coming.

"You're crazier than I thought, woman," he said. "You should have stayed in that home, Tegan. I'm expecting to die or spark a war here, and you—"

"I know," she said, chewing on the inside of her mouth nervously. "But I know this city more than you do. If you want to get even remotely close to Kieran without his men stopping or killing you with their magic, you'll need my help. I really am your only chance to do this right since you won't turn back."

Aiden mulled over what she said, but he still didn't like it. He was already taking a risk in not knowing the details of what Janelle was to Kieran. He didn't know what else had been planned for her. A bargain may not be enough.

"For one, you need to dress a bit differently than you are right now," she said, sizing him up. Her cheeky tone sounded a little forced. "You could not look more like an Elven warrior. Time to brighten you up a tad. Stay here."

Tegan strode toward the vendors, leaving Aiden behind a few barrels catching water from a draining pipe. He waited patiently with his back to the brick wall, his head resting against the rough surface. He wondered if Elijah had taken Janelle back to Zemira. Knowing the two of them, he doubted it.

His eyes turned right as a heap of clothes smacked him hard in his face.

"Put that on," she said, looking over her shoulder. "Quickly."

Aiden waited for Tegan to turn around, but she didn't.

"Are you serious? Aiden, I've seen you naked." She laughed, her eyes moving down his body with an appreciative smirk. "I need to make sure you can pass as a Newick resident."

There was still tension between them. Tegan was acting casual, but they both knew that joining him was tantamount to a death sentence. She could tease and flirt all she wanted. He knew she was just as scared of dying as he was. If they were marching toward certain death, he figured they might as well enjoy the time they had left.

Aiden felt himself smile, returning her smirk and eyeing her just as obviously as he undressed. He placed his weapons on the ground and removed his black clothes, putting on the new items she had offered him, piece by piece.

The pants were light gray, stitched in a fabric that shone in the light like rippling silver. They were snug on his long legs, clinging to every curve of his muscles and holding to some parts of his anatomy so tightly that Aiden felt they should be outlawed. The shirt was red silk, seemingly bland enough, but as he buttoned it, he quickly realized there was no way to fasten its top half. It splayed open, a deliberate design, leaving his chest exposed. He looked like he should pose for an oil painting eating grapes.

This is ridiculous, he thought.

Next, she tossed over a hat for him to tuck his hair into. The hat was bright red to match his shirt and wide enough to hide the most prominent Elven feature—the ears.

"Gods, you look hideous," she said bluntly, tossing out a giggle. "At least you no longer look like you're going into a battle."

It was on the tip of his tongue to tell her that was the problem, but he managed to restrain himself. Tegan bent down and gathered his clothes up. She lifted the lid on a nearby trash can and tossed them in with more pleasure than the situation called for.

"Is throwing away my things really necessary?" he asked.

"If they find your clothes here, they'll know an outsider is in the city," she said, holding out her hand. "Now, your sword."

Aiden shook his head, picking his sword up from the ground and pressing it against his chest, moving back. "You aren't taking my damn sword."

"Aiden," she said with a sigh, "if anyone sees you walk within a hundred miles of Kieran with *that* sword, you'll find yourself blasted out of existence before you can blink. You'll never make it through with the sword, so you might as well give it up now. You can always buy a new one later."

He shook his head again, eyes slightly wider than before.

She's bloody mad, he thought.

"This sword belonged to my father. I'm not parting with it."

She sucked in a heavy breath and looked over her shoulder again. "Fine. Here, we can hide it for now." She reached out toward Aiden, and he hesitantly handed it over. Tegan walked over to the barrel that was collecting water and pulled off the top. "They don't empty the barrels until spring."

She slid the sword inside and sealed off the top, keeping the little spout open for more water to enter.

Aiden kept his eyes on the barrel, realizing he would have to come back for that sooner rather than later. His hand twitched to take the sword back. It felt like he had to physically tear himself away from it as quickly as possible and keep moving before second-guessing himself.

"Let's go," she said. Her jaw was set as she reached out to take his hand. "This way."

Aiden tried to relax and let himself be led. They approached a tall gate at the base of the mansion he had noticed earlier. He could hear people gathered before he saw them, and a crowd came into view after a few more steps. They were talking amongst themselves in a gathering on the grass, and Aiden frowned as he tried to discern what they were doing.

"I cannot tell what is happening," he said to Tegan, looking down at her.

She didn't look back at him, but she squeezed his hand just a little as she watched the crowd in front of them. When she spoke, her voice was stiff. "It looks like they're doing some kind of ritual," she said.

Black smoke rose in a column from the center of the group, reaching high above their heads. Standing at the outer fringe of the crowd, a woman turned to cough and caught sight of them in the process. When the woman's eyes landed on Tegan, she smiled and waved at them.

He looked back at Tegan to get a read on the situation. How worried should he be that a citizen had just spotted them? Tegan kept her face forward, though. She waved back at the woman with a ghost of a smile before she dropped her head to stare at the grass.

"Do you know them?" Aiden asked. It felt like he was still missing an essential piece of the puzzle.

With her eyes locked on the ground, she said, "If I had let you keep that sword, you would already have been shot on sight," she said. "It's better this way."

Finally, she tilted her chin to look up at him. Though her face was dry, her eyes were bloodshot, and her skin was flushed. Aiden could see the wall of emotion held just underneath it, clear as day. It clicked in his mind what her strategy truly was at that moment.

"Oh," he said as Tegan brought her dagger to his throat. Their eyes met.

"I really am sorry, Aiden," she said. "I didn't want this for you." Now there were heavy tears rolling down her cheeks. The sight of those tears brought him that same sensation of pain from earlier that morning.

"Tegan!" Aiden heard a man call out as he ran to the gate. He had barely even noticed him until it was too late. He was too focused on the woman with a blade at his throat. Everything about it felt wrong. "Tegan?" the man called again when she didn't answer.

Aiden continued to look at her and she at him. The moment seemed to pause between them.

"Kieran is waiting for you, Tegan," the man said, and Aiden's heart sank.

The man signaled to the guards, who quickly opened the gate. He then walked toward the pair with a sword out to his side.

"He doesn't have any weapons on him," she said, stepping further back until the man could take hold of Aiden's elbow. He didn't even try to pull away as the man grabbed him. Aiden felt completely numb. His body moved slowly as it was pulled, clumsy like a wooden doll. He couldn't tear his eyes away from Tegan's face.

She closed her eyes for just a second, taking a deep breath, and when she looked at him again, her expression was made of stone. "See? I told you," she said, the sadness in her voice covered by steel. "You should have gone home."

Tegan closed her eyes again, and the man ushered them both inside.

23

JANELLE

The day flitted by; the innkeeper still bound to the chair Elijah had put him in that morning.

"I'm not opposed to tying someone up, but is this necessary? He's an old man," Janelle said, glaring at him. Elijah had not only tied and gagged the innkeeper, but he placed him facing a wall in a darkened room all day with the shades pulled shut.

Elijah pinched the bridge of his nose. "When will you ever address me as king?" he said.

Agitation ran through her veins. "When you stop standing around expecting it instead of doing something to earn that title," she bit back. "Elijah, you're not the first royal asshole I've encountered. Just because you wear a crown does not make you better than the people who wash your sheets."

She folded her arms and lifted her chin. "So, no. You're not my king. I'm not Zemiran. I was raised by a single mother until I was four. Then I spent the next years learning how to fight the very man who threw out my family from your blasted kingdom—your father." She took a breath as she watched Elijah's expression fall. "And you didn't answer *my* question." She gestured to the man who had stopped struggling hours ago. The way he had tied those knots was already pressing into the man's skin, turning the flesh red. "Have you no respect for him as a living, breathing human?"

He let out a sigh and tipped forward to stare at the old man. The man's eyes grew wider as Elijah moved closer to him. "I will remove your bonds, but if you leave this place, I will hunt you down," Elijah said imperiously.

"Not helping," Janelle said, pushing Elijah out of the way. She knelt in front of the shaking man. "Please don't flee, sir. I promise we're not going to hurt you."

"That's it," Elijah mocked. "Because kindness has always helped you during this rough life of yours, hasn't it?"

She gritted her teeth and flashed a snarl. Her irritation climbed to the surface, her cheeks turning bright red with hot rage. "I had planned to leave your unconscious ass in that tent and return alone. You ruined everything by following me."

"Return to a man who plans to take you like property? Force you to lay with him. An evil man who you don't love and will make you bear countless children you never wanted. Is that it? That's the life you're rushing to go back to?"

Janelle's stomach twisted. Yes, that would be the life she would return to, but she had nowhere else to go. No other home, and if returning to Kieran meant keeping her brother safe, then she would do it.

"Well, then. Let me cut off your head, so my doomed future with a demented sorcerer can all go away...." Her voice trailed, and then she stifled a laugh at her joke. She then sat slowly on the bed in the room and looked at the old man. A level of exhaustion sat deep in her bones, making every movement a little bit more difficult, but she did her best to ignore it. The world was still at risk, regardless of how tired she was. "What about a spell?" she suggested. "Maybe you can make him forget us?"

Elijah looked over to the man and tilted his head. Janelle wondered if there was kindness in the Zemiran king's heart and how willing he would be to find compassion where there may not have been any.

"I can try," he said optimistically, lowering his voice to almost a mere whisper. He walked around the old man and knelt, removing the gag.

The old man let out a hard sob, but he didn't speak or lash out. The man stared only at Janelle, pleading with his eyes for mercy.

"Are you okay?" he asked. The old man turned his eyes to him and nodded. "What's your name?"

"Uh, please don't kill me," the man said quickly. "Please don't—"

"Shh, I'm not going to kill you. What is your name?"

"Br...Bran," he said. "Bran Ophelia."

Elijah gave him a gentle smile and then placed his hand on his cheek. "I'm a sorcerer, Bran. I want to be civil and kind, but I sometimes have difficulty controlling my magic and seeing my victims' pain and suffering because of it."

Before Janelle had ever met Elijah in the flesh, she had been educated on the details of his upbringing. She knew he wasn't born into a family with magic, but rather, taken from one and denied the chance to learn how to control his powers or use them for good.

She also knew that his father hated Elijah, ordered the death of his oldest son, and murdered the two women he called "mother."

She had never seen these facts with an empathetic eye before. Her focus had always been on her own mission. But now that she had met him, the situation didn't seem so black and white any longer. Elijah had to rule a country that didn't trust him and still find the time, energy, and self-discipline to teach himself how to wield his own power.

The more Janelle pondered, she realized that he had no teachers to guide his way with magic. Every step must have been taken in the shadow of his father's contempt for it and exploited for purely cruel motives. No wonder he suppressed its potential for as long as he did. Janelle didn't understand how Elijah's magic worked. She had never seen how his father treated him before he died, but she knew a thing or two about learning to make it on her own from a young age.

Elijah's weaknesses were not his fault, necessarily. It was her shortsightedness that stopped her from taking that into account when she made the plan to kill him. Janelle just asked Elijah, a man who had fought for every ounce of control he had over his magic against terrible odds, to create a spell out of thin air. There was no way to predict how it would play out. She was inadvertently asking Elijah to put his own mind at risk, as well as the old man's.

"Wait," she said, walking over to him.

She looked into the eyes of the old man, who stared back at her intently. Then she removed her head wrap, revealing her ears. The man's jaw dropped, and his breath hitched.

"You're a—"

"Yes," she said softly. "My name is Janelle, and I'm an elf. I work for Kieran of the Newick Coven. Several weeks ago, I was ordered to kill this man standing right here. King Elijah of Zemira."

She searched Bran's expression for a reaction, trying to gauge where they stood.

Throughout Myloria and their surrounding villages, it was known what Kieran had been doing—capturing and imprisoning elves, as well as breeding them himself for almost a decade. The innkeeper would be aware of that. More importantly, he would know that no elf sent by Kieran would be standing around, playing allies with a Zemiran. Janelle was counting on that.

"We won't kill you, and we don't want to harm you, but we're hoping you might consider helping us hide."

"Sorry I knocked you out with magic," Elijah added.

"Kieran will kill you both," Bran said.

She nodded. "Do you want us dead?" she asked. "Or can we trust you to keep our secret and let us sleep here tonight? We'll be gone by morning, and you'll never see us again, I swear it."

The man adjusted himself in the chair and looked them in the eyes one more time before nodding.

Elijah's brows furrowed, and then he looked up at Janelle. "We're just going to trust him? Since when have you been the bearer of optimism in every situation?" he asked.

She nodded. "Elijah, you had me tortured in your dungeon, and I still agreed to travel with you up that mountain because I believed there was a small part of you to be trusted." A gasp left Bran's lips. "Trusting each other is better than the alternative. Perhaps we do that for him too. Unless you want to fry the old man's brain and your own, pulling a spell out of your ass that you don't know how to control."

She leaned forward, unbound Bran's wrists and ankles, and then placed her hand on his cheek. A bright light shone so vibrantly that he had to shut his eyes to block it out. He didn't move as the still, calming bliss rushed through his body.

After removing her hand, Bran rubbed his wrists and stood from the chair.

"It's getting late...would you both like some tea?" he asked, his voice no longer trembling.

Janelle smiled softly and looked at Elijah. "We'd love some."

Janelle and Elijah sat across from the old man, who ate his dinner roll quietly, then sipped his tea. The room was silent aside from the muffled sounds of the old man or the creaks of the inn.

Elijah leaned forward and whispered into her ear. "When are you going to tell me what you really did back there to get the old man on our side?" he asked.

She shrugged. "Not everything is a spell, Elijah. Hush and eat your dinner. You're being rude."

He gave her a quizzical look before turning back to Bran. "So, you are okay if we stay here a night, then?" he asked, cocking his head, trepidation clear on his face.

Janelle waited for the answer too. She had used light manipulation many times in the past. The old man was vulnerable; she had sensed that as soon as she saw him, and it was a prerequisite for that kind of enchantment. It wasn't a true spell. It didn't alter his memories or change the fabric of his mind. It merely gave him a push in the right direction. His emotions, stemming from his deepest, most instinctual level of consciousness, were something she could manipulate to her advantage. All she needed to do was ease his fear and allow his rational mind the freedom to make its choice and do the right thing by helping them.

"My wife created this place." He gestured to the corners of the room with his hand. "She hoped to help people like you, traveling through the city. To help them feel safe. I only have three beds here, though. One for me. The far-right room's been gutted for renovations. The two of you can take the one at the end of the hall." He placed his tea down and smiled at Elijah. "I don't see a ring on either of your fingers."

Janelle felt her spine snap straight. A jolt of adrenaline hit her at the words, despite it being a complete overreaction of her emotions. Blush colored her cheeks as she realized how foolish she looked. "Oh, Gods. I am far from his queen." Her voice was a little unsteady for her liking, so she smoothed a hand down her hips and tried to pull herself together. One look at Elijah, though, and the humiliation was replaced with irritation. He was sitting there, watching her with a smug smile, giving her just enough rope to hang herself with. She glared at him as fiercely as she could, but it only made him more amused.

"A single bed will be just fine, Bran," Elijah said, ignoring her protests. "Thank you. I will pay you generously for what you have done for us. In fact, I'll help cover the cost of that renovation to thank you for putting yourself at risk for our sake."

Bran smiled widely. Janelle could have sworn she saw tears in the man's eyes. It was easy for people who had money to forget how much of a difference a few coins could make to someone who was struggling. Not Elijah, though. For all his faults, he seemed to have a constant, focused awareness of how his actions were affecting the people around him.

"Oh, my. Thank you, sir," Bran said. "That is incredibly generous of you."

Elijah leaned back and tapped his fingers on the table. "It's the least I could do after the way I treated you today. I'm deeply sorry for that."

Janelle watched Elijah with a keen eye. As much as it was a comfort for her to always cast him as the villain, she couldn't convince herself he was being insincere whenever he talked like that. She had seen many sides of him, and she believed she could tell by now when he was speaking with genuine kindness.

Bran waved his hand in the air but paused, only briefly, as if contemplating whether he meant what he would say. "All is forgiven," he said. Janelle, taken aback, parted her lips.

She was shocked by the way the man forgave Elijah so easily. Janelle had been raised by the Fae, who were famous for their ability to hold a grudge, and it was clear to everyone who met her that it was a trait she held onto tightly. After the Fae, she was trained by the Newick witches, who were also not known for their soft temperament. They cared too much about training hybrids to start a war to concern themselves with trivial things like empathy or compassion.

After a lifetime spent learning how to hate and channel that hate into action, it was jarring to see someone choose forgiveness over revenge. The thought of holding that much love inside yourself, enough that you could bestow it on every stranger who crossed your path, was anathema to everything she knew.

"But it's getting late," Bran continued. "The two of you may be pretty and young, but I'm almost ninety, and my memory starts to fog over around dinner time." He gave them both a cheeky smile. "I'll lock up for the night, but I suggest drawing your shades. I don't need Kieran's men coming into our town and spotting the two of you in the bedroom. You don't exactly blend in."

The day had gotten away from Janelle, and she felt her fatigue set in. It was exhausting being angry and frightened all the time. Constantly being on guard against Elijah, Kieran, and every other man she encountered drained her mentally and physically. Janelle felt like she could sleep for a week and still be exhausted.

Still, if any of Kieran's men came through that door, she would slaughter them before they reached the hallway. She'd heed Bran's warning and protect the man who had put them above his own life.

24

J A N E L L E

J anelle had used the washroom to take a long bath. After the hot water had cooled off, she climbed out and dried her body. She looked around the room and realized she had no clean clothes in her bag, so she wrapped the damp towel tightly around her chest, looked at her reflection in the mirror, and grimaced.

Oh, Gods. How did I get here? she thought, cursing at herself.

Kieran had given her two jobs, both straightforward: break into the palace to kill the king and find the pirates' location to retrieve the Kroneon. It all seemed so simple at the time. She was more than proficient at accomplishing the tasks and escaping unnoticed. Annabelle would help her get inside through the tunnel after two weeks of memorizing every detail she gave her about the castle. Then Janelle would take care of the rest. She had the exact skill set for the mission. The last thing she had expected was to fail and be captured—taken alive, no less! To then be dragged everywhere with Elijah...forced to speak with him, walk with him, and share the same air. It was insufferable. Janelle had thought her training contained irrefutable facts about his villainous nature. Now she wasn't so sure. Still, sharing air was one thing; sharing a bed would be a step too far.

That's it, she thought. *I'm sleeping on the floor.*

Janelle retrieved the extra blanket from the closet, placed it on the wooden floor at the end of the bed, and threw down one of the pillows. She quickly wrapped herself in the blanket, ensuring no skin was exposed, and laid down, resting her head. Elijah turned to watch her wiggle around like a fish until she found a comfortable position to sleep.

"You're sleeping on the hard floor?" Elijah asked.

She kept her eyes closed, pretending to be too tired to speak.

"Janelle, get your ass on the bed," he fumed. "You're being ridiculous."

She cleared her throat. "I've already laid next to you on our little adventure. Once is enough for me."

The floor creaked next to her, and she opened one eye, looking up to see him standing over her, wearing nothing but a towel around his waist. He had bathed before her but remained undressed. "I had no clean clothes either," he said, but her mind didn't comprehend the words. The sight before her took all her concentration.

If the Gods were to craft a statue, chiseling every plane and curve to perfection, it would look like Elijah. He was flawless. All muscle and sinew; strong abs covered in soft, lightly tanned skin. Elijah was the most beautiful man she had ever seen, even if she refused to admit it. He was nearly naked, moving with the loose, effortless movements of someone in perfect physical shape, and his skin was still slightly damp from the bath. Janelle licked her lips on instinct.

I can almost taste his skin, she thought as his warm, masculine scent hit her nose.

Elijah radiated strength and confidence with every breath or twitch of a muscle, making her stomach flip. No matter how much she fought it physically, the feelings he inspired in her were nothing short of wanton.

Janelle let her eyes drop lower. She caught a glimpse of his slight erection, poorly concealed by the towel, and it took everything she had to look away and not choke on her own tongue. She shook her head, trying to banish the thoughts as she cursed herself for letting them in in the first place.

Fuck. I can't look, she cursed at her reckless brain, shutting her eyes for a moment before opening them again, forcing herself to look at Elijah's face instead.

"The bed is too small," she said and cast an appraising look of disdain. Quite honestly, it was of perfectly adequate size for sleeping...as well as anything else she might consider whether she wanted to or not.

"It's big enough." Somehow, when a smirk spread across his lips, she didn't think he was only talking about the bed, or maybe it was her mind taking it too far. Perhaps she was the only one thinking of something else. "Get up," he ordered her. Janelle scrunched her face, bristling at the tone of command in his voice as he reached out his hand to her. She reluctantly wrapped her fingers in his but quickly released them to grab her towel tighter to herself. A quick readjustment was needed, or Elijah would see a lot more of her than she cared for.

The bed was a bit bigger than the one she slept in at the palace but not by much. Going an entire night without brushing against each other would be nearly impossible.

For a moment, as she stared at the bed, she remembered the feeling of that kiss. She hadn't expected Elijah to barge through the door and grab her, taking possession with a kiss as if it were the only thing that mattered in the world to him. She would be a liar if she said she hated it. Elijah's lips were soft, his movements tender but passionate. The man had a mouth made to be kissed. Moves that made her tremble when she thought of them. He had sparked a feeling low in her belly that traveled down and settled between her legs—although she would die before she ever uttered those words and before she ever admitted it. She would never allow another kiss like that, never again. Cutting off her own lips would be extreme, but if she had to stop herself from wanting him, she would.

Probably.

Maybe.

Another thought pressed in on her mind. Would she still be willing to kill Elijah to gain her freedom? She still hated the man, loathed his smug behavior, and was trapped with him. But they'd been traveling together for long enough that it felt natural to have him stand next to her. Lying together was a whole other story, an untenable situation.

Of course, the tension and hatred in her eased when he wandered farther away than expected. But another feeling overshadowed it. Emptiness. It was as if he had taken a part of her with him and left her hollow where that part belonged. That hollowness infuriated her because she hated having little control of her own body. And she resented him for it.

"Which side would you like?" he asked softly, still standing next to her. She blinked, and seconds passed. She hadn't realized exactly how long she had been staring blankly at the bed, but it must've been a while because he was standing with his arms crossed, a smirk toying with the shape of his lips.

"Oh, um, right side," she answered shakily. There was no real reason other than that it was closer to the door if something happened, and she needed to bolt.

Janelle was the first to slip under the covers, the sheets feeling cool against her skin. She laid on her back for a second because a glimpse of him would satisfy whatever was going on inside her. That way, she could do it without being obvious. Then Elijah joined her, pulling his side of the sheets back. He moved slowly, as if he might spook her with any sudden movement. She rolled onto her side immediately, putting her back toward him, and curled protectively into herself. Janelle was lying on the edge of the mattress, but it was useless. She could still feel his presence. The only way she could have felt *more* of him was if she moved to lie on top of him.

The mattress dipped as he lowered himself onto it, and warmth radiated from his body against her back. Her skin tingled at the sensation. All she could do was screw her eyes shut and try to fall asleep. But her mind was restless. A pinch in her chest and a flutter in her stomach distracted her, no matter how much she tried to will them away. She was never, ever going to fall asleep with him next to her.

It was no surprise to Janelle that her body would betray her that way. Despite all her anger and frustrations, she had been powerfully attracted to him from the start. She felt the pull to him in her bones, in her stomach. So many flutters.

Her body didn't care that his father was evil or that his own sins were many and notable. All it recognized was his warmth, calm, coiled strength, and it wanted him in a way she couldn't understand. It wanted his body wrapped around her.

But her mind wasn't having it. She would never forget that Elijah was the son of King Matthias, the man who slaughtered her people for over twenty years. He could tell her how different he was until he ran out of breath, but she couldn't just forget that.

How could Aiden work for him? Janelle thought. Then again, it had been over six years since she and Aiden had seen each other. Perhaps Aiden had changed. He had to have changed, and not for the better, to work for *that* man.

"Janelle," Elijah said, pulling her from her thoughts.

She turned, and he was facing her, his head resting easily on the pillow.

"I'm tired, Elijah," she lied, her voice hoarse. "What do you want?"

His steely blue eyes sparkled in the faint moonlight that filtered through the window. Something about it made him look almost ethereal.

But the smirk on his lips told her he was about to say something snide and obnoxious.

"Are you going to kill me in my sleep?" he asked, his grin still pasted on his pretty face.

There was no doubt he believed she would and was capable of doing so, but he was willing to humor the challenge.

"I might," she said, the side of her lips quirking up. "I've been trained all my life to fight off a man. Even one as—"

Janelle stopped herself. She wanted to say, *Even one as intense and magically skilled as the one in front of me,* but it would only give Elijah more to tease her about.

"I'd like to suggest you not take my life," he said, his tone lighter with amusement. "I would hate to have to pin your arms over your head again and teach you a lesson about what happens to someone who threatens a king."

He was teasing her, acting playful, but there was an undeniable heat behind it, heat that built low in her belly, heat she didn't want to acknowledge but couldn't ignore. It was supposed to be a threat of violence, but the tone suggested it was a promise of something carnal.

Elijah's smile seemed forced, pained almost, and his pupils were large and dark as he watched her. His lips were parted just slightly, and his breath came faster than was normal. Janelle could see that he wanted her; that much was obvious.

Fuck. Close your eyes and go to bed, you idiot, she said in her mind, rolling her eyes closed.

"You're interesting," he said, and she reopened her eyes. "It's not a bad thing. When you aren't trying to kill me or run away, you are indeed unique."

"Unique?" she asked. It was a word that could be taken in many ways, and none were particularly complimentary. "Of course, *you* would be able to make a simple word sound like an insult."

"Well, most of the women I surrounded myself with have cared more about their image or wealth than they have about anyone or anything else."

"That's pathetic," she said. "In a world with so much destruction, that's all royals and nobles care for. People who only talk about their wealth and status waste oxygen for the rest of us. We should fight to survive this world while caring for those who can't care for themselves." Janelle was passionate about the state of the world and how it got so dark and violent. It would only change when people changed it. The type of women he *surrounded* himself with were vain and shallow little buckets of greed with perfect bodies and hair. It made her sick.

He paused briefly before gazing at her and saying, "I fight to survive, too, Janelle. And you almost took that from me."

She blinked as she turned his words over in her mind. She had truly been blind. That was becoming clear to her. Her only thought was to survive the worst fate she could possibly imagine, being wed to the evilest man she knew—so cruel, she couldn't help hating him. If it was possible, she hated even more that her fate was to serve as little more than breeding stock, expected to spawn hybrids for such a man. That hate and fear had clouded any consideration for others.

Murdering Elijah would make her no better than Kieran. That monster did whatever he could, destroying anything and anyone, just to protect himself. He was arrogant and selfish. Inherently, that was his game, not hers. As she realized what Kieran had done to her mind, it filled her with regret, more than she could ever overcome. After all this time she spent with Elijah, she now recognized he was nothing like what Kieran had told her. The truth was, at that moment, she knew she couldn't kill him. Not anymore.

Janelle wanted to tell Elijah all of this and see how it shifted their dynamic. Was it rational to expect the man she hunted to suddenly help her find her brother and protect her from Kieran? All because *she* asked him to? Would Elijah forgive her?

"Tell me more about Kieran and these hybrids," he asked, changing the subject.

Janelle felt her train of thought derail at the interruption, but she was grateful for it. She was grateful to talk about anything other than her own feelings of guilt and shame.

"After Kieran's parents died, Kieran's uncle led the coven. He created the first hybrid elf. A little over twenty years ago. She grew much faster than they expected. When I joined the coven, she was only a teenager like me but looked much older. A *woman* with Elven traits and magical abilities from coven blood. It became his responsibility once Kieran became old enough to lead the coven. He continued to breed the creatures as weapons only—an army at his disposal with heightened strength and power. They trained the hybrids from childhood to be obedient no matter the cost. I've watched these children train day after day. They know nothing of life except for fighting. He uses their strongest to fight anything that he deems a threat. Now he wants to use them to battle the Shadow Creature, and he doesn't care if they die in droves.

"All he cares about is killing the beast so that he can expand his power over the borders of Myloria to other countries. The Shadow Creature poses the perfect cover for Kieran to rise to power as a noble hero. It has created such an ominous imbalance that no one will question his tactics or motives. He can exploit all kingdoms and countries if he moves to strike it down. Kieran already fancies himself king of all the peoples and kingdoms he sees. He was just waiting for the perfect disaster to exploit."

She wrinkled her nose in disgust while watching Elijah's expression fall, as if he was processing what she had shared.

"My father always taught me that the different species should not breed with those outside their kind," Elijah said. "Elves have babies with elves and Fae with Fae. Humans with other humans. He didn't say it was impossible, just that we shouldn't. It was unnatural."

"Well," she said. "Your father was an ass." She smiled.

Elijah chuckled to himself. "Part of the reason I've always tried to distance myself from him and his memory."

That was something, at least, she thought.

Janelle's eyebrows pinched, moving closer toward the center of her forehead. "But you're king of the most powerful country in our world. It's expected that you'll find a queen to help carry on your royal bloodline."

He frowned. It was clear Elijah loathed being told what to do and what the expectations of him were.

"Do you not worry that you'll become more like your father the more you're forced to follow in his footsteps?" she asked.

He shrugged. "I haven't met the right woman. Not that I don't sleep with them." A wide grin broadened across his features. Elijah appeared proud of his conquests, not at all concerned about the trail of broken-hearted women who had lain with him. It made it difficult for her stomach not to lurch. *The trail of women who had been allowed to touch his body.* If that was jealousy, she didn't like it one bit. But then he continued. "It always leaves me feeling a lonely void, but it'll be for love if I marry. I don't believe in politics in marriage, Janelle. That's what happened to my father and my mother. They were miserable together, and it made my brother and me miserable as well. I don't want to continue that wheel of suffering."

Janelle shook her head. "I don't want children, either, but for different reasons," she said. Hers were reasons that a king probably wouldn't understand. The way they had lived was too different.

"And why's that?"

At least he's curious, she thought. *That's also something.*

"Our world is shit," she said instantly.

Elijah let out a laugh. "You're not wrong."

She shifted her body to face him. "I love fighting too much and desire to wear my armor and protect those who cannot defend themselves. I know little about my mother, but I do know that she couldn't defend herself even if she tried. If I brought a child into this world, they would have to watch me die because I'm willing to sacrifice myself for my people over being a parent. There is no way I could carry a child and expect to love them and keep them safe, all the while still willing to go to war." She turned on her back and stared at the ceiling. "Kieran will take me and force me to do everything I swore I wouldn't. I'm perfectly aware that these are the last few days of my freedom. After this, it's nothing but what Kieran wants to take from me in whatever way he wants to take it. Until I die, or he tires of me enough to kill me."

His expression was unreadable. She was desperate to know what he was thinking, but no flicker of movement was on his face. She could only see him studying her as he pieced together whatever he wanted to say next.

"I did a spell once to make sure I can't have children," he said quietly, almost in a whisper. "So, just ask if you ever want me to ensure it never happens to you."

She nodded slowly, but her mind tried to grasp the reality of it all. Having a child with Kieran would destroy her because then that child would be raised by a monster, and it would be her fault for not fighting harder to stop it.

Before she could respond, as if he sensed her discomfort, he said, "I'm sorry I kissed you earlier. I shouldn't have done that. It won't ever happen again."

His voice was soft, and something about his tone made Janelle feel a pang of sadness in her chest.

She could still feel the phantom press of his lips against hers, even as she opened her mouth to agree.

Elijah cleared his throat. "Are you going to fight Kieran or roll over and let him dictate what happens to you next?" he said.

How dare he? she thought, pressing her mouth into a thin line. It wasn't her choice, and he damned well knew it. It again sparked her irritation and did more to pull her mind away from that kiss's memory.

"I loathe Kieran," she said, her voice low and deadly. It was her battle voice. "At first, I felt obligated to him after he confessed his feelings toward me. I thought about how he and his family gave me a home. They helped me learn to fight better when I no longer had my brother. I was too afraid to go back to the Eastland Forest. Cassia would have thrown me to the trolls because I would have never stopped trying to rescue him from that prison or kill her as an act of revenge for what she did to him. Kieran knew my weakness—Aiden. Once he dangled my brother's life in front of me, I had to make a choice."

It wasn't really a choice, she thought. Anyone who thought otherwise had no idea. Aiden was all she had, and she had lost him.

"Kieran watched me closely, waiting for me to become a woman. He never made a secret of his feelings. I used to want it, too, until I saw how cruel he truly was. The older I got, the more I understood how wrong and frightening he was."

"Then why not kill him?" he asked.

"Because he has magic, and I don't. If I try and fail, Aiden is dead. No matter how much they trained me, I'm not strong enough to turn around and kill him. At least, not now. But I will be someday, and then he will get what's coming for him."

Elijah's brows drew together. "You're not giving yourself to that monster," he said.

"Yes, I am." Janelle turned away from him and looked up at the ceiling. If he thought there was another way, he would've said so already. This was posturing. This was asserting his authority because he could, but without the action to back it up, it meant nothing. "If he takes Aiden, it will only be to trade me, to put me under his thumb. So, yes, I'll play the doting wife and mother until the time is right. Then I'll rip his throat out, take whatever children he gave me, and find us a place we can live freely. A new place to call home."

Janelle realized she'd planned more of her future in her mind than she had thought.

"You probably did the same with your own father," she said. "Played along until you could fight back."

She glanced at him, watching his expression change.

The more time Janelle spent with Elijah, the more she realized they had a lot in common—both being raised under the thumb of a powerful, evil man. They had been brainwashed by dangerous ideologies and stripped of the freedoms that other children took for granted. And they both had to fight and still fought to untangle the poison planted in their minds.

"But you do this for your brother's safety," he said, and at first, she thought it was a compliment. "It's not noble, Janelle. It's stupid."

She grimaced at his tone; his words hurt. The pain and fear swelled suddenly, as it sometimes did, like a sharp punch to the chest. She felt a tear form at the corner of her eye, but she blinked it away. Elijah would never see her acting as weak as she truly felt sometimes.

"The children of Hagmar are too valuable to Kieran," she said. "Most likely, he'll keep us both," she continued. "Especially now that Aiden is going right to them."

Elijah said nothing in response. He was lying much closer to her than Janelle realized, and the urge to reach out and touch him was back with a vengeance.

Janelle could share a bed with her enemy. She could plunge a knife into his heart, end his life, and possibly have hers ended in return. Every fiber of her upbringing told her that vengeance mattered more than all the rest. But as she lay near him, quiet and content as she let his warmth sink into her skin, Janelle's desire to harm him faded to nothingness. A new passion took its place, as unwelcome as the last. She didn't know what to do with it. It was like a floodgate of new emotions broke open inside her heart, and Janelle truly saw Elijah for the first time.

Flicking her gaze up, she took in the deep blue eyes that watched her, the lean frame strung with muscle, and his steady, controlled breaths. He was waiting for her to make a choice. Every inch of him, every beautiful inch, was tense and ready, honed in entirely on her. Those consistent breaths felt like a rare treasure to her now. She couldn't believe she once considered ending them.

Janelle closed her eyes, letting herself sink into the sights and smells surrounding her. A chilly breeze blew in through a small crack in the window, the same draft that rustled the leaves gently, lulling her to a profound sense of peace. Her intuition was so sure now of what Elijah meant to her. She had no idea how she had missed it when she first attacked him.

Elijah sat up and rested his back against the headboard. She moved to sit beside him, her lower back settling into the pillow, their shoulders comfortably and uncomfortably touching.

The world felt still and silent around them as she leaned forward, pulling her arms around her knees and staring down at the throw blanket pooled at her feet. The only sound in the room was the rustling leaves from the trees and the howling of the winter wolves from the forest behind the inn.

"Elijah—" Janelle started but couldn't finish. His fingers were suddenly on her skin, featherlight touches that made her burn with want and need. She blocked it out or tried, but passion shuddered through her when his fingers found the scars on her back and traced over the patterns with an achingly soft touch. Janelle lowered her head and enjoyed the contact more than she should have. She hugged her knees closer, curling up under his touch. She felt small and delicate but in the most exhilarating way. It was such a foreign feeling that she could barely comprehend its novelty, and words completely escaped her.

She could count on one hand the number of people who had touched her with gentle affection in her life. It never bothered her to be left alone. She was fierce. There was no need to pull warmth from the people around her to keep herself fulfilled. But, strange as the feeling was, it was also delicious. Everything internal and physical shifted. She wasn't a warrior beside him. She was a woman who wanted to be touched. To be touched by *him*.

Janelle took a deep, shuddering breath as she let herself acclimate to the touch. He kept his fingers on her back and continued to trace her scars.

"Who did this to you?" Elijah's voice was soft, almost less than a whisper, but at the same time, more than a growl. So much more that she fell into its ferocity.

She glanced over her shoulder at him. Elijah sat with his jaw clenched in barely restrained anger. It sent a buzzing curl of plea-sure through her spine because he wanted to punish the person who'd done it to her. It was written in his dark, steely gaze, in his slow, unflinching breaths. He was protective, and the thrill of it washed through her. Her body wanted to grab onto the sensation with both hands and never let go, which confused her rational mind.

"What?" she asked. Her tongue felt thick as she pushed out the word. Her body was already adrift in the pleasure of Elijah's touch.

"These," he said. His voice was distant. He continued to look at her, drinking in every inch of the scarred flesh with rapture. It was as if the world were falling away around them as they walked through the same soft dream.

"Oh. Um. They're from Kieran's punishments," she said eventually. The words came easily because they were a truth Janelle had lived with. A life of pain and bloody wounds was all she knew. Her body's reaction didn't cause a waver in her voice because years of wearing her scars had left her well-practiced in discussing them, letting none of that pain and fear into her voice. However, Elijah was coming up against the memories for the first time. His face hardened again as she continued. "Five lashings for every time I disobeyed him. That was always the rule."

Janelle endured the pain of her decisions, and it was often. She defied Kieran repeatedly. She couldn't stop herself from rebelling, and she didn't want to. It was her way of taking a small piece of control away from that man. Those scars represented her strength and resilience, and she had no regrets about earning them.

Janelle closed her eyes, sinking back into his fingertips as they left tingling trails over her skin, as if he could remove the markings with his soft touch, with the warmth of his breath against the scars and the more delicate flesh of her back.

But Janelle had never been built for gentleness. Every square inch of her was created to fight, run, kill, decimate, and destroy. She didn't have the right foundations to process the warm, syrupy contentment that Elijah was trying to pour into her. She'd lived a hard, brittle life, and the sudden softness felt like it was eating at her from the inside out. It was terrifying.

"I know they're hideous," she said. The softness of her voice was as surprising as the deliciousness of his fingertip, but the words were sharp. "You don't have to touch them."

His fingers stopped suddenly, hovering over the ridge of her spine. She could feel the heat emanating, seeping into her even though Elijah was no longer touching her skin.

"Hideous?" he said, his scoff not much more than a semi-hard puff that blew the short hairs at her nape. "No, Janelle. These are not hideous. They're beautiful." He left a trail of warm air kissing across her shoulders as he spoke, sending a thrum of urgency through her. "These scars are a testament to your strength. How you survive what so many others couldn't have. That monster may have intended them to be your mark of shame, but all I see is you."

Janelle's lips parted, chest rising and falling quickly as a well of emotion rose behind her eyes. Her mind fought to want him, fought needing his touch. She shivered, and her very flesh ached to go back to being numb, cold, and hard. Allowing herself to sink into his words, to want him so badly, was a blight against the strength he'd only just complimented. The emotion his words exposed was too big for her to grasp, so she leaned away from it. Janelle's worth was always on the battlefield. The idea that someone saw her—truly saw her—beyond the sword...it was incomprehensible.

Janelle had talked herself in circles, trying to get around it, but it was too late. She could admit it now; her heart had given up the fight long ago. Since she met Elijah, every ounce of hatred she felt for him had been conflicted with the pull of attraction that was just as strong. His gentle touch had burned his devotion into her skin—a brand deeper than any of Kieran's scars—and she felt like he had somehow claimed her.

What was worse was how intensely she wanted to be claimed. It echoed through her mind and heart—her entire body.

"Mmm, that feels good, Elijah," she confessed. The words rolled out of her without a thought, and his name felt natural on her tongue. She finally let the pleasure of his touch sink in.

Janelle sensed the shift in the air between them. It was apparent in how his touch was more confident and less tentative. Each gentle caress against her skin left trails that shot spirals of heat between her legs. Janelle twisted to look at him even as his finger continued swirling on the scars. She watched as his lips parted, as his chest rose and fell with the subtle uptick of his breathing. As much as she'd doubted herself, forever it seemed, she had no doubts about how much Elijah wanted her.

Elijah's hand traveled over her flesh, stopping briefly at the edge of the towel. She arched her back in an invitation, and a shiver of pleasure rolled through her as he slipped the fabric away. He tugged her shoulder, pulled her down next to him, and she went willingly. Janelle held his gaze for a second before his eyes fell to her collarbone, then the swell of her breast. Oh, the heat. The beautiful heat of his stare wasn't lost on her. She was drowning in it.

The towel had only fallen a little. There was still a hint of modesty, although Janelle knew the sight she made before him was nothing short of obscene. The edge of the towel was held up only where it caught on her nipples, and at some point, her thighs had parted with need. She could hear her own heavy breath echo in the room.

She felt debauched, never wanting it to end.

Elijah's eyes, darkened with lust, devoured the sight of her like a starving man gazing at his last meal before he dove in.

With a slow, graceful stretch of his body, he moved over her. He could reach every part of her body, and some she wanted to be touched more than others. Some she wanted so badly she could taste it. Elijah moved again, burying his face in the crook of her neck, pressing his lips against the tender flesh below her ear. He trailed the kisses down her throat, moaning in appreciation as he let his hand drag from her collarbone to her shoulder and back. His teeth scraped every inch of her along the way.

That was it, the contact that broke through their walls. Their touch before had been sensual, undoubtedly, but with plausible deniability. Had one rebuffed the other, they could have spent the rest of their lives pretending nothing had happened.

But now Elijah kissed her neck, tugging at the flesh with his teeth, nothing gentle, nothing sweet. The heat coursed through her, made her want, and Janelle brought her legs up to wrap around his hips and pull him closer. They'd been on the edge of a cliff together, swaying in the wind, and now they were tumbling off it, hand in hand.

"Elijah," she breathed as his hands explored her body, "you know that if Kieran finds out another man has touched me, he'll kill us both, right?"

It was her last lingering doubt. She needed to say the words aloud, or she would never be able to truly let herself go. She needed to hear his acknowledgment.

But he froze. His eyes flicked up to meet hers, and that savage anger he usually kept so tightly chained lit him up. The sight of it made Janelle gasp, and she could feel her arousal growing stronger underneath that gaze.

"If Kieran ever touches what's mine again," he said through his teeth, "what I do to him will be so brutal he'll beg me to kill him before I'm finished." His voice was a low growl as he spoke. He reached up with one hand to stroke a thumb over her cheek. Even as his hands trembled with contained anger, his touch was gentle, and she pushed her face into his touch greedily.

Then his fingers trailed down. He wrapped them around the column of her throat, so slowly she felt his touch burn through her.

Elijah squeezed. It wasn't hard enough to hurt her or constrict her breath, just a possessive gesture. Just enough to make her feel taken in his hand. His eyes bore into her, and that was worth risking any punishment Kieran might conceive.

Janelle wanted Elijah to own her. She belonged to him then, and she loved it. She still had her pride, and no man would ever control her life as Kieran had again, but right there, at that moment…

"You're mine," he growled again. And it was true to the fibers of her being, to the core of her very life force.

"I'm yours."

The words escaped her like a sigh, long and drawn, a scream and a whisper. Squeezing her thighs tighter around his hips, she could feel Elijah's hard length, covered only in the flimsy towel, pressing against where she was throbbing and wet for him.

"Please, Elijah," she breathed. "I want you to fuck me until we're nothing but each other's only desires and needs." Janelle steadied her breath. "Because I've not stopped thinking about this moment since our eyes met for the first time in your hallway the night I tried to kill you."

She saw every fleck of color in his eyes that night when he had subdued her. That memory would never leave her.

The noise Elijah made in response was something feral. He grabbed her roughly, his hands everywhere at once, pulling the towels off them both and closing the last remaining inches of space between their bodies. His hips rolled into her, making the hot, hard shaft of his cock rub over the most sensitive part of her body.

Janelle gasped at the sensation. She'd never suffered such exquisite torture, never been so consumed. Elijah's mouth brushed against her neck, where he had just laid a path of gentle kisses, and bit down. Hard.

The pain of the bite, along with the pleasure of him rubbing against the delicate bundle of nerves between her legs, made Janelle feel as if someone had set her body on fire. She moaned deliciously, her body melting into his touch. She turned soft, writhing, and the pleasure threatened to tear her into pieces. Only he held her together with his large, firm hands where they gripped her.

Elijah reached between their bodies to wrap one of those hands around his cock. For a second, she watched him. He stroked once, twice, slowly, the same way he touched her, and he used her wetness, slick and hot. His cock glistened, and she wanted him inside her more than anything she'd ever wanted in her life. She tilted her hips, pushing against him as he glided over her effortlessly and positioned himself at her entrance.

Janelle arched her back, desperate for Elijah to fill her, but as soon as he pressed the very tip of his cock into her, he paused.

The hand holding his length moved to grip her hip fiercely while his other traveled up her body. He ran his fingers through her hair, taking hold, tugging, so a sharp pain stung her scalp.

Janelle was pinned between the two points, held utterly in the position he desired.

What would have been her worst nightmare on the battlefield was now her greatest desire, under her *lover's* hands. Her eyelids nearly fluttered shut, but she kept them open, not wanting to miss a single moment of what was happening.

Leaning down until their faces were close, Elijah's lips grazed hers as he spoke.

"I'm going to make you come so hard you scream for me, little elf." He punctuated this by nipping at her bottom lip. In one hard, firm stroke, he thrust and tore through the barrier and settled inside her. The entanglement of their bodies was complete.

All Janelle could do was moan. The initial pinch of the pain of a foreign intrusion faded quickly, replaced by a beautiful, indescribable feeling of fullness. He almost completely dragged his cock back out and then snapped his hips forward to fill her again.

Elijah's hands roamed, pinning her with his weight and pushing himself deeper inside.

Janelle lost herself in the building pleasure as Elijah thrust into her again and again. Their bodies found a rhythm immediately, like they were two halves of something that had finally been slotted back together. Everywhere they touched, their skin was hot, sweat-slick, sliding over one another. Janelle's arousal soaked into the sheets beneath them, and it only made her cling tighter, strengthened by the intense need to have him.

Elijah twisted his hand tighter into her hair and turned her face toward him. Then he captured her mouth with his, ravaging until she was quivering, half gasping. She opened for him, pliant, and they fell into a wet, hungry kiss as he continued to fuck her. Their tangle of limbs and breaths reached a fevered crescendo until he released her, grabbed her by the ass, and tilted her hips to get the best angle to keep their bodies flush. His open mouth trailed down her body, lighting all her cells on fire, making her body coil into a tight spiral. His fervent kisses burned from her throat to her breast, and he sucked a hard nipple into his mouth. Teeth grazed over the sensitive bud, and Janelle pulled her lower lip between her teeth to keep from screaming as the pleasure curled through her.

"Oh, fuck," she panted. "Gods, Elijah, please, please don't stop." She would beg. Plead. Do whatever he wanted so long as he never took his mouth away, never robbed her of the exquisite pleasure.

Elijah released her nipple with another growl and pulled their faces together so that they were looking into each other's eyes. His thrusts increased to a brutal pace. It seemed impossible to tell where she ended and he began; they were just a collection of slick, hot flesh, moving together as one single being, bent on pleasure.

They were both breathing too hard to kiss but kept their faces close together, sharing the air, panting, gasping, one as lost as the other.

"Come for me, darling," Elijah gasped. "I want to feel you clench around me as you scream." His fingers tightened, and his body tensed.

Elijah had moved one hand to the place where they were joined, and his thumb rubbed small circles against her wetness as he thrust in and out. A tautness spread over Janelle's body and her muscles, taking her in its grip. Janelle could only whimper. She had neither the will nor the desire to fight anything she was feeling.

"Elijah…" she said, her voice trembling. "Elijah, please…" She didn't know exactly what she was begging for, but she needed to appease him.

"That's it," he moaned, and the sound was pure ecstasy, husky and deep, sensual and so erotic she couldn't hold on any longer. "Let go for me, Janelle."

The soft call of her name from his lips was the final push she needed to throw herself over the edge. Every muscle in her body tensed, and her inner walls clenched around Elijah's cock where it speared into her. She was clinging to him inside and out. The tightness turned into a rush of pleasure as her orgasm washed through her.

A scream of euphoria escaped her. Elijah growled in response, and his cock throbbed inside her with his own release. One final hard thrust left him spilling into her, grinding their hips together as more of himself filled her up.

Her legs shook, and her body trembled as the wave of pleasure ebbed, leaving tiny sparks of itself behind. When the last of it faded away, their bodies relaxed into the mattress, and Elijah pulled out of her.

Janelle was jolted by the sudden emptiness, the loss of his weight on her, the missing warmth. Elijah collapsed next to her on the bed, breathless, but his hands were on her body again in a few seconds. He needed to keep touching her as badly as she needed to be touched. She told herself as much anyway. And she didn't mind it. Wanted it even more than she could find words to voice.

"Fuck, Janelle," he said. There was a shade of wonder in his voice. She thought she could hear how loudly their hearts were pounding at that moment, even without using her heightened Elven senses.

Janelle turned to him as he reached to caress her cheek. She stilled, gasping for air.

His lips pressed together, and she wanted to bask in that feeling, the wholesomeness of the moment. There would never be another like it, and she wanted to etch every detail into her memory.

"Janelle." Her name again from his lips was better than a symphony.

She let out a sudden exhale, wondering if he'd regret what they did in the morning.

A small smile spread across his features, but it faded when he looked at her. "Stop thinking about what we just did and whether we should've done it," he said, still catching his breath.

She let out a laugh because the moment demanded it. "And if I said we shouldn't have?" she asked, although she wasn't saying that. Would never say it.

"Then I would call you a liar, little elf." That tone he used for the endearment made something in her stomach flutter.

His thumb ran down her cheek slowly, caressing her soft skin. At that very moment, she was his, and she wasn't going to fight the need she felt for him any longer. Janelle wouldn't deny all the desire and longing ever again.

She was his.

***

The sun rose to the window, letting a small beam of light hit the bed through the curtains. Janelle was the first to get dressed. She ached in the best way between her legs, every muscle, a delicious reminder of what they had done last night.

Janelle watched Elijah sleep as she pulled her pants on and looked toward the door. Not so long ago, she'd felt his hands roam every inch of her body, and the feeling of him gliding in and out of her still throbbed between her legs.

"Are you contemplating running off again?" he asked, pulling her from her dirty thoughts about him. They locked gazes.

"I was, actually," she admitted, watching Elijah raise a brow of amusement. "But I changed my mind." She picked up her bag from the ground and pulled it over her shoulder. "We should eat, and I need to check on Bran. Thank him for what he has done for us."

Elijah smiled and threw off the blanket to roll out of bed.

He was still naked, and she didn't hide the fact she was staring, holding her gaze.

A slight chuckle erupted from his mouth as he walked past her and into the washroom, his shoulder brushing gently against hers.

"I'll meet you in the kitchen for breakfast," she said, thinking how domestic that sounded out of context.

He gave her a smile before shutting the door behind him, shooting her one last side smirk.

She walked down the hall quietly, just in case Bran was still sleeping, but his door was open.

Janelle tapped lightly against the wood. "Bran?" she called. "We're awake now. Can we help ourselves to coffee and food?"

The only sound was the wind tapping against the window.

A sudden rush of fear slammed into her. It was an intuitive force she hadn't felt since she was a young girl. The last time Janelle had felt that power was right before Queen Cassia's guards marched into their tent and tore Aiden from his bed. That was right before he was sentenced to the Whispering Woodlands.

She cracked the door further open to look inside. Bran was lying on his bed with his back to the door. "Bran?" she asked. Her voice shook.

Before she made it any further into the room, the scent of blood touched her senses; and then she saw it. Her heart filled with horror. The red-soaked sheets twisted around Bran, and a tiny dagger was lodged in his throat.

As she stepped forward, a large hand clapped over her mouth, and another gripped her waist, yanking her roughly against a man's broad chest. She moved swiftly, about to use all the moves she had learned for a close-contact escape, but the sharp tip of another dagger pressed into her spine.

"Easy, Janelle," a man's gravelly voice whispered as he pressed his dry, calloused palm firmly against her mouth, muffling her scream. She knew it was one of Kieran's men when she saw the dagger etched with the coven's crest along the hilt.

As she lifted her leg for an attack from behind, the blunt force of an object crashed hard against her skull. She fell to the floor, slipping into darkness.

25

AIDEN

Kieran's men had violently shoved Aiden into a dark, closed-off room right below the kitchen. The outside of the mansion was extravagantly beautiful, almost castle-like. But that room was different. The baseboards and shelves were heavily covered in dust and reeked of mold and decay—it felt like an ancient tomb.

His mouth tasted bitter and dry as bile rose to his throat from the acrid smell leeching out of the rug he sat on.

Aiden leaned back against the wall with his hands clasped together between his legs. Waiting. He was unsure how long he had been in there, but it felt like at least a day.

He thought of Tegan, despite his constant battle to forget her.

How had she betrayed him? Sure, he barely knew her, but for him not to see it? Not to see through her façade of deception? She tricked him easily, like a child, and he struggled to wrap his head around it. At what point had he let his lust for her overtake his common sense? It was even worse knowing that he craved her. Not only then, he still did—desperately. He hated her for what she did, but that did nothing to temper his hunger for the woman.

Perhaps Kieran had given her the pretense of a choice between loyalty to him or suffering the consequences—as he did with Janelle.

Or maybe she really was just a liar, he concluded in his thoughts.

He could hear the soothing torrent of flowing water that spilled into the river behind the mountain which stood outside the window. The mountain's peak towered over the city, its presence being the only peaceful thing about the area. Aiden looked out the window at the damp trees hovering over the river. A crack in the window would bring in the scent of the crystalline water, drowning out the grotesque odor. He took a deep breath, trying to cleanse his lungs of the foul air that polluted the room.

He clambered off the dirty, rough rug when he heard the creak of the door.

"Aiden," Tegan said, sticking her head through the crack.

He watched her expression change when their eyes met. She slid inside, shutting the door behind her.

Aiden was unsure if it was guilt or if she genuinely cared that they locked him up. She pressed her palms against the wall behind her and leaned back. Tegan's bright red hair lay messy around her face as if she hadn't slept for days. Her eyes looked distant, like a ship adrift in the sea.

"Tegan," he said calmly, but his jaw tightened.

"I want to explain," she said. "I need you to understand—"

"Understand?" he repeated with distaste falling on his tongue. "Understand that for the few short days since we met, I saw you as a kind, fierce woman willing to fight to protect someone she barely knew. One who—" He swallowed. "One who I gave myself to because I couldn't stand another moment without wrapping myself around your naked body. I wanted you so badly from the moment I saw you in the tavern, and I gave in to that temptation like a damn fool. How foolish I was to think humans were anything but selfish."

She blinked while he studied her expression, wondering if he was simply wasting his breath. *She is no different than the rest*, he thought. *A liar—my enemy.*

"You know what I don't understand," he continued. "Why would you fight Kieran's men at the bar? Clearly, you knew who I was. Why not simply have them take me?"

"Because," she said, her eyes glistening. "I changed my mind when I met you. Janelle is my friend. I saw something in you and me—" She paused. "But then you left me at the cabin, so determined to go on this suicide mission of yours. I...I realized it didn't matter what I did or how much I warned you to stay. You were going to Kieran anyway."

He looked down to the ground and shook his head. "Alright, fine," he said. "You had a guilty conscience. But you, you're—" His stomach tightened. "Tegan, what are you?"

He waited for her answer, but all she did was press her lips together.

Silence moved between them.

"I'm a creation that Kieran's uncle made twenty years ago before he died and gave control to his nephew. Something that will, in time, protect the people in this land." She stepped back. "A weapon."

A hybrid, he thought, remembering what Janelle had told him.

"I, um—" She fiddled with the bottom of her shirt. "I can speak with Kieran. I know if you don't threaten him, he might be willing to listen to you." She threw her hands up. "You were going to bargain for something! Right, you had something Kieran could want?"

Of course, his plan was always to get inside the mansion and make Kieran hear him out, but the circumstances were different now. He had no control over what happened next. He had no way of escaping if Kieran decided he didn't like what he had to say.

"I'll tell you what. You retrieve my sword from the barrel you stuck it in and bring it to me. *Not* to Kieran," Aiden said. "Then perhaps you can earn back that trust."

Tegan looked at him with her brows furrowed and nodded. "Okay," she said, not even questioning why. "I'll hide your sword under my mattress until you're ready."

"Thank you," he said. "Now, leave me alone." His lips set in a rugged, fierce line. "I cannot look at your face right now."

Her lips parted, and she stepped back. Her hands were balled into fists, but she said nothing, backing out and locking the door behind her.

Aiden leaned back against the wall and slid to the floor. His dark hair fell over his eyes, mangled and tousled. He buried his face in his palms, running his hands down his face, then combed his long hair through his fingers and out of his eyes.

A tinge of regret for his words burned inside him.

The stench from the room continued to assault his nostrils; he had to get out of there.

He clambered to his feet once more, catching himself on the wall before walking to the door. Then Aiden pounded hard against the wood three times. "Hello!" he shouted. "I need to speak to someone!"

Footsteps sounded in the hall before they stopped at the other end of the door. Someone's shadow moved under the door crack.

"What is it, elf?" a man with a gravelly voice asked.

"Please inform Kieran that I need to speak with him," he said. "Now."

"Fuck off!" the man growled, his feet shuffling back. Quickly, Aiden placed his hands on the door and drew a deep, steady breath. The movement of the man's feet stilled. Aiden focused his Elven magic, pressing it forward through the fibers of the wood, reaching for the man's energy.

A moment later, he heard, "Alright. Give me ten minutes."

Aiden let out a sigh of relief. His light ability had worked.

He rarely used that power, but it was the one magical trait he and Janelle had shared. Seeing his sister reminded him that he was more than just a warrior with a sword.

Aiden and Janelle had the power of light to fight against darkness. It was a delicate form of mind control that dealt with parts of their emotions. It forced their auras to leave their bodies for just a moment to touch another's soul, making them more compliant and at peace.

He waited minutes before he heard the stomping of boots descending the stairs. The man had returned and opened the door slowly, holding a sword in one hand.

There was no sense of power coming from the human man, just a slightly vacant look on his face. He had a razor-sharp beard, angular brown eyes, and a narrow jaw.

"This way," he said.

The man didn't bind Aiden's wrists or take hold of his arm as he escorted him to the living room.

It was opulent, far more than Aiden had expected. The rows of jewels and trinkets that lined the walls stood in stark contrast to the dust-filled coffin room where he had been held. The look of the people within the mansion was clean-cut, almost military in appearance. The room was dark gray, so it felt like he had never truly escaped the darkened room, but that dungeon had a chandelier. Crystal balls dangled from metal rings, casting light through the space in every direction. The entire place seemed to shine, despite its darkness.

It felt like a grim reminder of the palace that Aiden had left behind. It was as if the Newick coven lived like royalty but without the crown.

His eyes stayed on Kieran, who sat in a tall-backed chair and watched as Aiden slowly approached. Several men and women were also in the room, but many ignored what was happening. A few had looked over their shoulders to see the tall, black-haired elf standing before their coven leader, but it seemed like any other day.

Kieran cleared his throat before standing tall in front of his chair. "Aiden Patrov. Son of Hagmar and Mariella. We finally meet after years of hearing the tales of your brave and valiant history. A warrior with a colorful career, fighting for the Fae, the elves, and the humans. Your rebuilding efforts with the Elven people of Zemira and your loyalty to your kind have not gone unnoticed. Janelle had nothing but heroic things to say about—"

"Do not," Aiden started, his words cutting sharply through his teeth, "speak of my sister."

Kieran held a smile of amusement and clasped his hands behind his back. "Now, Aiden. We've always treated her like our own since she came here as a terrified teenage girl."

Aiden's expression hardened more than it had before. He didn't believe that for a second.

"Like your own people?" Aiden seethed. "How many do you plan to take by force? Let us not pretend like you're her ally or even someone who intends to take care of her. You sent Janelle to her death. If she had succeeded in your plan, you'd still be throwing her back into a world where she'd wish Elijah would've killed her."

Kieran faked a smile. "Janelle doesn't know what she wants."

"Oh, believe me, she does. If she opens her legs for you, it will be because you force her. She's never wanted children, even in her younger years. And she most certainly wouldn't want them with someone she doesn't love. You've brainwashed her since she was fifteen years old, twisting her into something you could control."

Kieran held up his hand. "Janelle is far from submitting to me. She's too stubborn for that. She just needed someone to *guide* her in the right direction." The sorcerer ran his hand slowly over his chin and pursed his lips. "She made a deal with me. I don't see King Elijah's head at my feet, which means she failed. My men are bringing her in now."

Aiden's eyes widened as a sudden chill swept through him.

"Yes," Kieran continued. "Word spread that a Newick witch and a white-haired Elven woman had visited an inn in Heyerberg. King Elijah was with her, but my men would stand no chance against his power. We shall use her as bait to reel him here. Then I will kill him and take Zemira, his guards, and your sister." Kieran's wicked grin caused Aiden's stomach to twist. He didn't have to be so close to the man to feel the dark magic swirling around him, trying to reach out and grab his own power. Challenging it. If what he said was true, Aiden hoped and prayed to the Gods that Elijah had his army ready at the borders for an attack. Otherwise, Zemira would never see them coming.

"Take Zemira?" Aiden asked. "Why?" He gestured to the window. "The Shadow Creature? Did it ever occur to you to simply *ask* Elijah for help in defeating that monster? It would be far better than going to war over a kingdom that doesn't belong to you."

"Oh, Aiden," he said, "there's so much you don't know." Kieran straightened his shoulders and snapped his fingers at a man near the back of the room, who opened the doors, escorting Tegan inside.

Aiden sharpened his gaze as she strolled past him. When their eyes locked, she nodded her head, and a slight smile reached her lips.

She retrieved the sword, he said in his mind. *But can I trust her to stay quiet about it?*

Tegan lowered her head, watching her feet and avoiding eye contact with Aiden as if to hide from Kieran their voiceless communication.

He was still unsure if he could trust her, but he was taking a leap of faith.

"Twenty-two years ago," Kieran started, "King Matthias went to war with your species and all magical creatures, slaughtering those who disobeyed his law. Matthias came here soon after removing magic when he discovered that not all Fae and elves had fled Zemira to the Eastland Forest. He learned my parents had given them homes and a safe haven. He slaughtered my mother and father right before my eyes as punishment. I was only seven years old. My uncle, Bastian, then assumed power over the coven. Bastian feared that the sorcerers on the land would not be strong enough if Matthias and his soldiers came back for the rest of us. So, he began to prepare. If power wasn't enough, *he* could make it enough."

"Hybrids," Aiden said, watching Kieran's wolfish grin flit across his lips.

"After Bastian died, the coven went to me. I was seventeen when all of this became mine. It scared me to keep making these forbidden creatures with such unpredictable magic. I grew alongside Tegan as she developed. Her command over her power and the way she executed brutal strength with such ease…It was magnificent, and it renewed my dedication to building up the hybrid armies. I was trying everything I could to pull this community back together and protect who was left of our kind. The hybrids are our only hope." He gestured around at the people. "I had to create more like her. No matter the cost." He reached up and brushed a hair away from Tegan's face. "They are the future of every battle that will soon be fought. We will train them for what's coming."

He held out his hand for Tegan, but instead of taking it, she shifted to the left, avoiding him. Kieran's face didn't grow hard at her defiance, only concerned, as if he hadn't understood why.

"The daunting battles ahead of us are more complicated than you and I can ever imagine. Kings or queens don't rule Myloria…but they can. With me as king, Janelle, my queen, and Elijah's—"

Kieran was cut off abruptly as Aiden spat on the floor. "I thought I told you not to speak about my sister," Aiden hissed.

A cold, humorless smile spread across Kieran's face as the room went silent. Then, lightning-quick, his arm shot out, and he wrapped one firm hand around Aiden's neck. Aiden was far from small-statured, but he still felt the breath explode from his lungs as Kieran shoved him back against the wall.

"As I was saying," the sorcerer continued, "with me as king, Janelle as my lovely, supple queen, and Elijah's soldiers..." There was a brief pause as he tightened his grip on Aiden's throat, slowly dragging his body upwards. He was pinned between nothing but the wall and Kieran's hand, choking out his breath. "We will have everything we need to defeat any attack on our people, even by creatures who cross through portals. Zemira is close enough that we'll form one country together, from one sea to the other. One union of all people: witch, monster, fairy, elf. You and I both know Elijah is not fit to lead. His own people hate him. And you, dear Aiden..." Kieran released his hold as he said Aiden's name, letting the elf fall and crumple as he hit the ground. "You can direct that army. You can join with the rest of our people who sought protection and strength after King Matthias banished magical folk. My parents gave the Fae and Elven a home. Loved them. Now it is my turn to *lead* them."

Aiden coughed, taking in enough deep breaths to clear his vision and find his voice again. His lips set in a grimace as he stood and addressed his captor. "You want to go to war with Elijah over his army?" He waved his hand at the door. "I've seen the Shadow Creature that has been attacking your coven. If you want to save your people from that *thing*, you need Elijah as your ally."

Kieran scoffed. "Ally? Elijah is the reason the Shadow Creature left its own world and entered ours. The pirates and Elijah must both be stopped. He might pretend to be on our side, but he's not." He waved his hand around the room. "These people here, both Newick witch and Elven, together, we can take what we want while creating our *own* species."

"But you're doing all of that by force!" Aiden added.

"*Not* by force. Every elf here chose this because they also believe it is the only way. Tegan here—" He gestured to her, but she still wouldn't look up. "She was the very first half-elf created on our land."

Kieran placed his hand near her hair and tucked her red strands back. Then he put his hand on her ear, and purple mist left his fingers. When he removed his hand, Aiden saw what magic had made him blind to—her pointed elf ears.

"Her mother offered her body to create this life with one of our own. We knew if Janelle failed to kill Elijah, you would come here to find a way to protect her. Tegan offered to assist in your journey and bring you in if you crossed Whitestone Mountain. I'm a bit surprised Tegan felt inclined to fight off my men, but she did the right thing in the end. You came right to our gates."

Anger grew inside Aiden's chest, but the wrath wasn't directed at Tegan. Seething anger replaced the pain that Aiden had initially felt at her betrayal. First, his sister, now Tegan. Kieran had made a career by giving young women impossible choices and then making them do his dirty work. He wanted to slit the man's throat with a rusty blade and watch him drown in his own blood.

Tegan was yet another victim. He thought of every plea she had given him since they met. She warned him to go home. He didn't listen. Because why would he?

"So," Aiden said, "no matter what I say, it will not make a difference?"

Kieran let out a hearty laugh. "Assuming you're here to trade your life for Janelle's, my answer is no. Especially when I can have both of you—the most powerful, magically gifted elves ever born."

Aiden reminded himself of the reason he was there. He knew the one thing Kieran would want more than Janelle. At least, he hoped that the sorcerer's greed would overtake his lust. He had to carefully choose his words, or his plan wouldn't work.

"What if I can give you something more powerful than Elven blood?" Aiden said, looking to Tegan, whose eyes grew wide. He was sure now she understood why that sword was so vital.

Kieran grinned. "What could you possibly offer me?"

Aiden looked to Tegan for only a pause before his eyes returned to Kieran's. "My father's sword," he said. "An *Elven* sword."

"A sword?" Kieran repeated with a slight chuckle. "I don't need a sword when I have magic."

A smile pulled at the side of Aiden's lips. "An *Elven* sword," he repeated, as if he should have known what that meant. Elven swords were not just any kind of weapon. The Fae gifted his people the weapons during the First Treaty. If the elves agreed to protect the Fae from the other lands, they would enchant their swords with power.

"Unless your sword is more powerful than Newick magic—"

"It is," he answered honestly.

If Kieran finds no value in my weapon, then I'm fucked, Aiden thought.

He truly believed anyone who desired the magic it wielded would be tempted to take it. It was known throughout their world what an Elven sword could do.

"It will destroy a Kraken with just the tip of its blade," Aiden started, hoping he would understand, "or even a monster from an unknown world." Kieran's expression looked more bored than intrigued.

The sorcerer's brow lifted. "Just like a Shadow Creature?" he asked.

Aiden nodded. "It's yours if you release my sister."

Kieran appeared to be pondering his offer, then he threw back his head and let out a hearty laugh.

"You honestly thought I would trade your sister's life for some Elven sword?" He stepped forward, his grin sending a shiver down Aiden's spine. "Oh, I have a better idea. One where I can have both your little magical sword and your loyalty." Kieran stepped closer to him and placed his hand on his shoulder.

The magical walls around the elf crumbled, sending him to his knees as blackness blanketed the back of his eyes. His pounding heart felt as if it were being ripped from his chest. The darkness. The darkness was inside him, leeching out of Kieran's eyes and into his own.

No, he screamed into the silence of his mind, his light succumbing to Kieran's power. *No!*

26

JANELLE

When Janelle opened her eyes, all she could see was the matted white hair of the horse they rode on.

Victor's calloused hands held her stomach in a vice-like grip. She didn't want to turn around to look at him and avoided his soulless eyes as best she could. She hated the man from the depths of her soul, so much that it burned, but Kieran used him for every mission because he always got the job done. The moment Victor's lips grazed against Janelle's cheek as he whispered into her ear, right before knocking her out, had caused every hair on her neck to stand straight.

Victor thrived on bringing pain and violence to anyone weaker than him, but he loved hurting young women most of all. Her body had suffered enough violence from his hand over the years that she was tuned to his presence purely on instinct. Whenever he was near her, Janelle would be on edge until she was free of him. He had been Kieran's first choice to enact her punishments every time she disobeyed an order as a teenage girl. And he didn't just deliver the disciplines; he relished in them.

Throbbing pain ripped at the back of her scalp so heavily she had to close her eyes, or she would vomit.

As her head spun, she tried to thread her fingers through the horse's mane, but her grip wouldn't be enough; she was going down.

"Fuck!" Victor cursed as Janelle slipped from his grip, hunched forward, then slid down the horse's side until she crashed to the rough ground. Twigs and rocks cut into her knees and back.

A cry tore from her lungs as she willed herself to sit up. It was a feeble attempt at best, but the rough ground still felt better than standing and even better than being on the horse with Victor.

Within moments, Victor stood over her, his shoe crushing into her fingers intentionally.

She raised her chin in defiance. "Come on, Victor," she said, clearing her throat. "You don't want to help a lady up?"

Pain exploded in her jaw as his fist cracked against it. It was as if he was punishing her for falling off the horse. She winced but shoved back the grimace on her face, so he'd not see how much he had hurt her. Not anymore.

After straightening his back and running his bloodied knuckles through his buttermilk-blond hair, painting it with streaks of red, he glanced back down. A sinister grin pulled at his lips. Then he quickly slid his boot forward, kicking dirt into her face.

"You are no lady," he grated. "Just an Elven bitch who tried to deceive our coven leader. Fraternizing with the enemy instead of cutting off his head like you were ordered to do?"

She held her tongue. It wouldn't matter what she said anyway. Victor got off on hurting women. Janelle knew he anxiously waited for the chance to unleash his wrath upon her at every moment he could. He hated how much attention Kieran gave to her over the rest of the coven, and he made sure she knew it.

His mother must've hated him, she thought in her head. *Now he takes his fury out on women. It's the only thing that makes sense.*

She blinked back tears from the blow. "What exactly do you think is going to happen when you return me to the mansion with bloody cuts and scrapes?" she asked. "Hmm?"

Victor began to undo his belt knot.

Lars, who watched nearby, stiffened. "Victor, think about what you're about to do," he warned. "Kieran will cut your head clean off if you touch her."

"Touch her?" Victor repeated, choking out a laugh. "I wouldn't touch that vile elf trash if it was the last thing I did." He spat on the floor beside her, tiny droplets splashing her cheeks. "I need to piss, and if she so happens to be in the way—"

Janelle quickly held up her hand. "Stop, you dickless scum. Do you really plan to assault your future queen?" she asked. "Because the first order I plan to execute is to have a knife driven through the center of your throat. In fact, I will insist Kieran allow me to do it myself."

All amusement disappeared from Victor's features.

"Oh, filthy elf, you think he's going to believe you after you betrayed him?" Victor said, tightening his belt loop before stepping back. "No, see, King Elijah caused those injuries after you tried to kill him. Right, Lars?" He snuck a glance at his friend. "We watched it happen before we rescued you."

Janelle gritted her teeth and bit the inside of her cheek. It wouldn't matter what she said. Those men were brutal, and anything that came from her lips, they'd punish her for it.

"It doesn't matter anyway, does it?" Victor said. "The moment Kieran takes you as his bride, he'll mold and shape you exactly how he wants you. One whip and laceration at a time."

Janelle felt heat behind her eyes, powering down everything she had not to fight back. Her will to unleash violence always overcame her self-preservation.

Janelle leapt from the ground, barreling into Victor's chest. He flew back, smacking his head against a jagged rock. Blood soaked the gravel and dirt beneath his lacerated scalp. Lars jumped off his horse, gripped her hair, and pulled Janelle back, slamming her hard once again against the ground. He kept her pinned under his boot, then spat on her face. She stayed down, wiping the disgust from her cheek before he kicked her three times in a row against her gut. Pain crashed into her body as her ribs cracked from the blows.

"Thought that you assholes weren't going to touch me," she spat, looking up. Her weak and injured body would heal, but every punishment was a reminder she had failed. Not that she failed Kieran's order, but she wouldn't be able to save her brother in her current state.

The men weren't human; they were sorcerers. She also knew if she tried to fight back, they'd use their magic and rip her apart from the inside out.

Lars picked her up by her hair. His face was up close to hers, close enough for her to be washed in the stench of his breath and see every ridge of the thick scar that stretched across his cheek. His expression was one of pure, vicious contempt. "I think we both changed our minds."

She tasted the metallic flavor of copper on her tongue and felt a trail of blood crawl from the corner of her mouth to her jawline.

"Now get up!" he said, pressing his mouth to her ear. He took a moment, just a moment, to run the flat of his tongue up the side of her face, licking up a part of her blood. Revulsion curled in her stomach, and she would have preferred that he punch her a dozen more times rather than mark her with his wet stench.

Bile rose in her throat, her stomach twisting, but she fought it back down. The only thing Janelle had left in her now wasn't letting him see the effect his little violation had on her.

"Enough of this bullshit. Let's go," Victor said, climbing back on the horse. He grabbed her arm roughly and yanked her up with him. Fighting was pointless, and she knew it. Their next stop would be the mansion in Newick, where there was no hope of surviving her fate.

27

ELIJAH

King Elijah ran his hands over the footprints in the snow. He rubbed his fingers together slowly, breaking a few ice clumps apart to fall back to the ground. The prints led through the forest that separated Heyerberg and the frozen river but stopped before meeting the clearing. The wind erased all traces of their direction, making it impossible to see anything.

Elijah tilted his head to the side, his eyes rolling back into dark shadows. When he opened them back up, his blue irises turned as black as a starless sky. Power warmed inside his chest; his anger grew like a mighty dragon. Vivid images paraded through his mind of what he wanted to do to whoever took her.

As the still moment loomed in the air, the sound of nature silenced itself. Darkness fell upon the path leading back to Heyerberg, just beyond the line of trees.

Ominous gray clouds formed overhead, rolling over the terrain. Cries and wails from those running from Elijah's power filled the air—their panic causing him to hesitate.

No innocents will die, he said in his mind. However, he continued to order the black mist to find and devour anyone who had Janelle—anyone with ill intentions in their heart.

To resist the dark power was no longer in his control. The sensation behind his eyes burned like fiery flames. The black smoke left his fingers again and trailed down the curvy path. The emptiness that came crashing into his entire body when he didn't feel *her* was unbearable. Janelle's presence was gone, and those who took her were going to feel his wrath when he found them, with one missing limb at a time.

What had transpired over the last week was unexpected. At first, all Elijah wanted to do was kill and punish the woman who broke into his palace. But something had changed. *He* had changed. Not being able to keep her out of his mind drove him mad. He couldn't stop thinking of her body flush against his, how she tasted when they kissed. Elijah had never felt like that about anyone in his entire life. The bond the two of them now had was beyond anything he had ever experienced.

It wasn't just the desire for her beauty but the desperate need to protect her at all costs.

When Elijah stepped out of the washroom and saw that she hadn't returned to the room, his stomach dropped. For a moment, he assumed she had fled again. Pain slammed hard against his chest, and he began to think of how he could punish her for betraying him after their night together. He wondered if it was all a lie.

He searched the rooms of the inn until he eyed Bran through the crack of the bedroom door, lying in his own blood. Elijah knew straight away that she wouldn't have done that to the old man.

Sorrow and panic choked his heart, drowning out that initial anger and leaving him with want. He was desperate to do everything he could to track down and kill whoever touched her.

Elijah had never felt so much rage as he felt right then. Janelle had been taken, and he was unable to save her.

When they first started their journey, his plan was simple: reach the country of Myloria. Then, once they arrived in Newick, he would use Janelle to trade her life for Aiden's, despite the fight Aiden would put up. He knew Aiden would never allow Janelle to be exchanged for his life. Elijah needed his strongest Elven warrior in their country, and he wouldn't risk him being taken by another ruler. He was valuable to Zemira, and his army needed their seasoned leader. Aiden was such a fool to go on his own. Once Aiden's freedom was secured, Elijah would either break the peace between their countries or outright kill Kieran and suffer the consequences of war.

Oh, bloody fucking hell, he cursed in his mind.

Elijah pictured her face to help calm the anger inside him. He thought about how her hair sometimes fell, covering her eyes in a way that made his fingers itch to push it back. He thought about her laugh, the soothing sound that made his stomach flip. The memories of their first kiss and how he felt like his heart might burst into flames as her tongue touched his. He thought about what it felt like to finally touch her the way he wanted to touch her—his long fingers smoothing over every marred and damaged inch of her skin with his affection. How soft and supple she had felt in his hands, responding to every touch like it was the first time.

Elijah pushed back his thoughts before the darkness erased what humanity he had left. He was too afraid to lose himself.

Somehow, Elijah cared about these two siblings more than he had cared for nearly anyone in his life. He wouldn't rest until he found them both.

He gripped the ground harder, digging his nails so deep into the snow he felt the mud beneath it. He slowly pulled back his magic, feeling it settle back inside him.

Janelle wasn't there or anywhere nearby. He would need to find a horse.

Elijah traveled for an hour on foot before he came upon another village. The town was desolate. There were only a few horses and cattle spread about between small stalls near the cottages. Smoke rose high from piles of wood in the town square. Barrels of wheat were strewn across each lawn. Large crates of produce sat in front of a few homes. He didn't see any open shops like in Heyerberg. The village was quaint, comprised of tiny huts with smoke rising from the chimneys.

Elijah spotted a short man with white hair and several wool blankets wrapped around his shoulders. The man looked up as Elijah drew closer.

"Eh, mate. You must be freezing," the man said after throwing a thick blanket over one of the horses.

Elijah shivered, careful not to use his magic. What he had done earlier had already taken a toll on his energy.

He didn't trust most people, especially those from a foreign country, who may or may not know what the King of Zemira was capable of. The cold finally reached his cheeks, causing his skin to go numb.

"Your lips are purple," the little man said.

A smile stretched over Elijah's face. "Sorry, sir. I've been traveling for days," he said as softly and kindly as he could fake. "I'd like your horse, please."

The man dropped his hand from the horse and blinked, his forehead creasing. "Oh, um. My horse is not for sale," he said. "There's another town not far from here—"

Oh, Gods, I don't have time for this, Elijah thought as his hand came up, sucking the air briefly from the man, causing him to stumble back. The man had his back pressed against his home and froze, his eyes glistening into a trance.

Elijah pulled off his gloves and approached the terrified man, pressing his hand firmly to his chest. He withdrew his magic. "I will not hurt you if you do as I ask," Elijah said.

"Sorcerer!" the man choked out.

"Oh," Elijah said softly. "I am so much more than that."

The man attempted to break away, but it was of no use. The magic had gripped so tightly to his mind that his body no longer obeyed. Elijah controlled every word and movement until he released him.

"I'll be taking your horse, a few blankets, and more fuel for my lantern," Elijah ordered. "Go now. Give me what I need."

Elijah worked hard to distance himself from his father's legacy. It was too easy to fall prey to forgetting the value of others. However, it was sometimes helpful to tap into the monster, so his guilt didn't suffocate him. Right then, he had to be the villain most believed he was.

"Yes, sir," the man said, turning into his home.

Elijah put his gloves back on and finished covering the horse with the blanket, securing it in place with a few straps around its chest. He then pulled himself onto the horse, gripping the reins back, and trotted to the front of the man's house.

After a few moments, the man came out, handing Elijah a blanket, a few bread rolls, and a canister of water.

"I'm sorry, I have little fuel. Only enough for the winter."

Elijah bit his bottom lip, and before he could demand the man turn it over, the door opened. A woman emerged with a tight braid over her shoulder, carrying a tiny, wailing baby in her arms.

A tired, barely noticeable smile touched her lips but went flat when she noticed the horse that he sat on was theirs. "Xander, what the hell is going on out here?" she said in a thick accent. "Who are you? That's our horse, Xander!"

The man placed his hand over his wife's shoulder to pull her back. "Get inside, Anna," he said.

The little voice Elijah often ignored pressed at the back of his mind. King or not, righteous mission or not, those people were innocent, and he knew it. What he was doing was wrong.

Elijah gritted his teeth. He couldn't take the last bit of fuel that the man had to keep his wife and child warm. He'd have to make do with what he had.

"Shit," Elijah uttered quietly before pulling an apologetic face. "Miss, listen to your husband, and go back inside," Elijah said, feeling the last of the magic he had fading off the man. Xander came to and leapt forward to stop Elijah when he realized what was happening. Elijah kicked his heels against the horse, taking off down the road, hearing the cries from the couple behind him fade into nothing.

28

JANELLE

Janelle saw the top of the mansion through the trees, but they were still at least a mile away. The forest was the only thing separating her from her imprisonment.

"I need to pee," Janelle said. "Please, I can't hold it."

"Pee inside the house when we get there!" Victor said.

Her blood turned to ice as he glared at her, but she continued. "I've been holding it for hours. Let me off before I pee all over your animal. Now!" she cried.

Victor mumbled vulgarities at her before pulling back on the reins. "Two minutes!" he ordered as she jumped off the horse.

She hurried, skipping behind a grove of trees. She relieved herself, and thankfully, the sick bastards weren't watching. A thrill bounced in her belly at the thought of taking off, even though she knew she'd not get far before they stopped her.

Janelle also realized she had nowhere to go. The streets ahead would be vacant, as it was almost dusk. The Shadow Creature came out at night to hunt and feed on the people caught unaware.

Kieran had ordered the Newick citizens to lock themselves behind closed doors after sundown, banning all magic until dawn.

Janelle's heart pounded in her chest at the thought of fleeing into the wilderness. However, one flick of her captors' wrists and they'd knock her to her knees with their magic. At least for now, she was alone for the first time in hours; that gave her a little peace.

After Janelle had sorted out her clothes and stood up, she looked around. The trees cast shadows along the grass, but a dark feeling came over her, as if they were being watched. A strange rustling sound came through the darkness of the forest floor.

She closed her eyes tightly to hone in on the sound getting louder every second.

Janelle looked up, turned around, and narrowed her eyes through the trees behind her. The pounding sound of her heart rang in her ears. They were exposed. That creature would find them, and they were too far from the gates to escape.

What is that?

As soon as the figure came into focus, Janelle felt her eyes grow wide. It wasn't the creature at all. It was someone on a horse, galloping at breakneck speed, leaning down over the horse's neck with his cloak dancing in the wind behind him.

"Elijah," she whispered into the air.

Janelle never thought the sight of the man she had hated for nearly two decades would fill her with that much happiness. She could feel the memory of his touches from the night before ghosting over her skin and leaving tingling trails behind.

She set off running for him without a second thought. Victor and Lars called after her, their angry voices chasing her as she ran, but she was undeterred. She'd make it to Elijah; she was sure of it.

Elijah's hands tightened on his horse's reins, bringing it into a turn as he prepared to make a leap for Janelle. As soon as he launched himself from the animal, magic sparked from his fingertips. The black smoke shot through the air, wrapping itself around Victor's throat like long, inky black fingers.

As Elijah's boots hit the ground, his other hand came out. His powers took hold of Lars next, cutting him short as he tried to throw his own dark power at Elijah. Janelle saw Victor raise his arm, and a black mist gathered at his fingertips. The bolt of magic aimed at Elijah's heart flew. She cried out so loudly that a burst of light from her body sprang out, toppling the brush around them and throwing Lars and Victor back. The blast broke Elijah's hold as she kept her power up to shield him from the attack. Janelle tried to push Victor back. However, she couldn't save herself as she, too, was flung back off her feet. Sharp pain stabbed at her back as she fell against the rough, thorny rocks.

She quickly rolled up and turned to Elijah, ensuring he was safe. Elijah stood tall, his arms still out as the men struggled to draw their swords, climbing to their feet.

The men's magic pooled out, ready to strike when Elijah's black mist took hold of Victor and Lars's waists, severing their attempt. He lifted the two men in the air as his magic crept over their skin, squeezing their life out, bit by bit. Elijah looked strong and confident as he watched them with his arms outstretched. Janelle could see every muscle in his body tense, and his face was a mask of total focus—the entire strength of his power crushing the men to death.

There was a moment, just a moment, where he looked like something utterly terrible. Janelle was powerless to do anything but look on in horror as Elijah snapped his wrists sharply. A sick crack rang through the air, and the two men's spines broke clean in half.

His work was done; Elijah's magic released their lifeless bodies to fall to the ground. They were nothing more than worthless sacks of meat now, wet with their own blood. The dull thud of them hitting the ground made Janelle's stomach churn even further than it had when their spines snapped.

A stillness settled over the two of them as Elijah slowly turned to look at Janelle.

The last time she had used her light magic was when Queen Cassia stole Aiden, the only family she had left, and banished him to the Woodlands. Several fairies and elves died that day from the blast, being taken by the light's force. She was afraid to fight with her abilities because Newick magic was far more powerful than hers. They would have killed her.

Janelle breathed heavily as her eyes locked on Elijah's. Shame filled her as she had promised never to unleash that kind of power, no matter the reason. But at that moment, she thought only of killing the two men before they hurt Elijah as they did her. It didn't matter what power he held. She wanted to save him, too.

But he had saved her first. He turned into something vicious to do it, but Janelle realized that even as he was choking the life out of those men, she never feared him. As wrathful as he became, she only felt safe.

Janelle had spent a lifetime being a tool for committing violence on behalf of others. She had been trained and molded into a warrior. She had immeasurable violence done to her in the process to keep her in line. Kieran had threatened to kill her more than once.

No one had ever killed *for* her. No one ever protected *her*.

Elijah dropped his power and ran toward her, cupping her cheeks in his palms.

"Janelle," he said, lifting her up to her feet. "Look at me."

Her eyes looked up, letting out a heavy breath. She placed her hand over Elijah's and leaned into his palm.

Elijah moved back a flyaway hair that spilled over her face. He froze as his eyes locked on the bruises on her cheek.

An uncomfortable silence settled between them before he ran his thumb along the wound caused by her captors. Elijah's eyes turned dark again, savage. He was so angry that she felt the energy flow through him and into her, taking in his own rage.

"I'm sorry," he said, his voice low and desperate. "I wish I could kill them all over again for what they did to you, just to watch them suffer."

A tear slipped from the corner of her eye, but she wiped it away before it fell down her cheek. Janelle knew she should feel guilty for what she had done or frightened of Elijah and his combined capacity for violence. But she didn't. All she felt was the depth of his feelings for her, his willingness to kill for her, wrapping around her like a warm blanket.

"We can unleash that anger on the one who sent them," she said.

Elijah's power dimmed slightly, his features softening before he nodded. But his hand still caressed her injured cheek.

"No one will ever hurt you again," he promised. "I give you my word, Janelle. If anyone ever touches you again, I will unleash the monster inside me to protect you. Do you understand?" Her eyes widened. Janelle didn't know if she should be afraid of him then. She could still feel that darkness leeching out of him.

In the last two weeks they had known each other, she had never seen that look in his eyes. The look that said Elijah would *kill* for her. He would protect her, even if it meant risking his own life.

He leaned in, pressing his forehead to hers, and whispered. "You're the only one who has ever made me feel light when consumed by darkness."

Elijah used his thumb to wipe away another tear falling down her cheek.

"Am I still your prisoner?" she asked, as a smile tugged at the side of his mouth.

He brushed the back of his fingers against her cheek. "Well, I don't want to let you go. So..." His smile dropped, his features taking on a more serious tone. "I want you to choose to be mine as I choose to be yours."

Janelle's stomach fluttered. The last six years had never been hers. No freedom, no choice, no hope. The ones who trapped her behind the sorcerer's walls dictated and molded her into something she wasn't. At least not the version of her she wanted to be. But with Elijah, it seemed as if he wanted her so profoundly that she would surrender her body and mind for him to consume; she wanted nothing more. It was overwhelming in the best possible way.

But her hatred for Kieran would always remain hers and hers alone.

"Let me kill him," she said. "I *need* to kill him myself—"

Her voice trailed off, interrupted by a loud hum that vibrated through their ears. They winced at the sound, looking around to find the source. Everything was as still as before. Except, as she looked toward the woods, Janelle caught sight of the same dark shadow she thought she'd seen earlier.

"Elijah, quick, we need to get inside the gates," she said, eyeing the shadow as it moved past the trees, a roiling, ominous darkness moving swiftly toward them.

"To the enemy?" he asked, watching her with a confused look on his face.

"We don't have a choice. Kieran's mansion is filled with defensive magic. We'll die out here!"

She saw Elijah's eyes narrow as he sensed the same thing she did. He put his hand on her back, pushing her behind him.

"I can feel it," he said with a nod.

Sudden, icy terror gripped Janelle's body. More fear than she had ever felt at the hands of Victor and Lars or even Kieran. This fear was something primal, housed in the basest parts of her mind.

She moved back a step as the creature glided along the grass. Within the shadow formed a silhouette, long limbs, and red, sunken eyes.

"Get on the horse. Now!" Elijah shouted as he turned to run, reaching out to catch her wrist and drag her after him.

They sprinted toward the horses, jumped on, and urged the animals quickly into a gallop. They headed away from the monster, toward the city. Not once did they look back as fear spurred them forward to the gates. That creature was far worse than the Newick coven, and if they didn't hurry behind the mansion gates, they were going to die.

29

ELIJAH

The locked gate exploded open as Elijah threw out his power, slamming the force into the wood and blowing the hinges apart.

"Through there!" Janelle shouted, pointing to an archway that led to the mansion's back garden.

They jumped from the horse, slamming into the ground and rolling onto their backs. It felt as if the air had been ripped from Elijah's lungs. He inhaled, jumping to his feet before grabbing Janelle's wrists and pulling her with him. They ducked low before slipping through the entryway, looking up as the dark shadow covered the property. They held their breaths as it completely blocked the light from the moon.

Elijah lifted his arm, but Janelle slapped her hand over his and pushed it down, stopping what magic he was trying to conjure.

"Don't lose your strength," she said. "We're protected, Elijah. There's a rune shield around and above the property. It can't touch or see us here."

They both looked up again, watching the shadow circle the property from above before swiftly disappearing as if the wind had blown it away.

Elijah listened intently, hearing the buzzing sound of the creature floating back into the forest. The eerie noise tickled his ears.

Janelle lifted her head to meet his gaze. "Elijah, we did it. We survived that thing," she said with a shaky voice as adrenaline coursed through her. Her gentle voice enveloped him like heat from the sun against his cheeks, helping him calm his raging heartbeat.

Elijah cradled Janelle against his chest. The feather-light touches of her fingers along his forearm made his chest swell. Her body felt warm against his as they kissed, melting into one.

He smoothed out her hair, trailing his finger down her collarbone and gliding across her skin. For a small moment, when they had raced to the mansion, he thought they would die. Seeing her in his arms, feeling her touch, and knowing she was safe was all he needed to breathe.

Elijah's ears opened to boisterous laughter coming from inside. "Are they having a party?" he asked. He wondered how they could not have sensed the creature coming toward the home. The music still played, and no sorcerer came charging through the door to stop them.

"Always parties," she said, sitting up. "If Kieran is drunk, perhaps he won't kill us right away." She let out a laugh, as if what she said was funny.

Elijah raised a brow. "Then let us not die today, shall we?" he said, holding out his hand.

Janelle placed her palm in his. "Kieran is a psychopath, but he can be reasoned with. We can only hope he's in a good mood."

A tiny branch cracked behind them before they could make their way inside. They froze at the sound and waited.

"Janelle?" a woman's voice whispered from around the corner. Elijah silenced Janelle with a finger, placing it over her lips. She swatted it away and stepped forward.

Their attention turned to the woman as she came around the corner. She stood in a warrior stance, holding a black sword at her side with practiced ease. She looked lean and toned, like a fighter waiting to be called to action. She stood taller than most women, contributing to her overall intimidating presence. Her medium brown skin looked young, with a light dusting of freckles across her nose. Her black hair was slicked back into a tightly wrapped bun, and she wore a floor-length blue evening gown with a slit that reached the top of her thigh.

"Kora," Janelle said with a broad smile. "It's okay, Elijah." She gently placed her hand on his to lower it, reassuring him not to attack. "Kora's been my trainer for the last five years—a friend."

"Is that the king?" Kora's voice was feminine but with an edge of steel. The look she cast Elijah was no less sharp.

She looks like she hates me as much as Janelle did when we first met; the wry thought came to him, unbidden.

Janelle nodded. "Yes. Not dead, as you can see." Her voice was soft, and without saying the words, Kora read her plea to keep silent on the issue.

"Kieran's had a bit of wine tonight," Kora said. "May I suggest you come in from the back to avoid the guards? I can speak with him first." She eyed Elijah up and down. "Unless you'd like one more chance to complete your mission. I can cut off his head right now if you'd like." The woman grinned and moved her sword out front.

Elijah turned to Janelle. "You're right. She's absolutely no threat at all. A harmless kitten in a ball gown," he mocked.

"It depends on the day," Janelle replied with a subtle smile. She turned back to Kora. "No need to use your weapon. I need to speak with Kieran, Kora, and with you by my side when I do it. Please."

The woman glanced at Elijah one last time, and her features softened. "Alright," she said, lowering the sword. "Follow me."

⸺◈⸺

Elijah had thrown dozens of parties at the royal palace.

It goes with the crown, unfortunately, he thought. That party appeared to be no different. The atmosphere was libidinous and indulgent.

Beautiful men and women sprawled around the room, most of them straddled by sorcerers in various stages of undress. Cups of wine were shared, along with hungry caresses. Dancers were spread out in front of a stage, moving their bodies with slow, sensual movements, lulling a heavy-lidded audience into the slow burn of arousal.

On stage sat the host, looking for all the world like a king on his throne. Kieran drummed his fingers on the arm of his seat. Despite the array of sights before him, his eyes were trained on only one person, and they were hawk-like in their intensity.

Kieran watched Janelle as she and Elijah moved toward him, but they stopped abruptly as the man stood. Janelle's shoulders stiffened as she stepped back, glued to Elijah's side. Elijah could see the moment Kieran noted the lack of distance between himself and Janelle. He was the person he trained her to fear, despite her utmost loyalty to the bastard giving her orders.

It wasn't Kieran that drew Elijah's attention, though. He'd never seen anyone change their demeanor the way Janelle had as soon as they had stepped into that man's presence. She seemed to shrink in on herself. Her shoulders were rigid, her eyes locked on the ground, and her chin hung low for the first time since he'd met her. His beautiful, fierce warrior, reduced to a trained attack dog, set to harm others but beaten into submission by its keeper.

The sight of it made Elijah's blood boil. Kieran had trained Janelle to be a warrior, a trained killer. She was one of the most intimidating and confident people Elijah had ever met. But, in front of Kieran, she was his submissive.

No more, he thought. *Janelle no longer belongs to him.*

The band played an obnoxious tune in the corner of the platform. The music was so deafening that Elijah couldn't hear Kora as she walked over and spoke into Kieran's ear. He wanted to trust that woman, but she hadn't earned it yet. Years of encountering betrayal by the people Elijah believed to be trustworthy taught him one thing: everyone lied. He could spot a backstabber a mile away, and Kora had no reason to protect Janelle, not when her own life would be at risk.

Kieran's eyes looked as hollow as Elijah's father's, void of human emotion. He was cloaked in power, and with every step he took in their direction, Elijah shifted with him, being careful if the man was to strike when he wasn't looking.

"Elijah," Kieran said soothingly, standing before them. He reached out his hand. "Welcome to Newick. I promise we are allies today." He dropped his hand, giving Elijah a playful smile when he didn't meet his greeting with a shake. "My men have informed me that your army left Zemira a few days ago. That's fantastic news. But don't worry. You've done the right thing by bringing them with you. We can play nice until our people unite."

Right, Elijah thought.

He knew if Kieran even attempted to kill the King of Zemira, he would start a war. By sending an assassin weeks ago, he could keep it all a secret. No one would have known who sent Janelle because she'd have taken her secrets to the grave. He made sure to train her that way. But now the stakes had changed. To kill Kieran in his own home while the Zemiran army stayed ready at the mountain on his order...no, he was safe for now.

Kieran turned to face Janelle. "And you, my love—"

"You'll say nothing to her," Elijah warned, gritting his teeth and powering down the magic stirring in his chest. "Nor will you address her as *love*."

Kieran threw his head back and cackled, his drunken eyes glazed over.

The old-world treaties of the early kingdoms had been adhered to by all lands for centuries. As the head of Zemira, he would be waging war by taking the life of the leader of an outlying province, which Kieran was. Elijah had to proceed with caution in killing a ruler. With his armies, the Elven battalion, and the aid of the pirates, there was no doubt of Zemiran victory if it became necessary. As a man, however, cutting off Kieran's head in an instant to save Janelle's life was worth any consequence.

Elijah took a steadying breath before saying, "I may be surrounded by your most powerful sorcerers, Kieran, but I promise you, I'll kill you before they can stop me. And once I'm dead by your people, my army will come crashing through those doors and take care of the rest of you." A smile grew on Elijah's lips, but it didn't meet his eyes. "I have more soldiers than you; let us not forget that."

Kieran cocked a brow. "I find this all too fascinating," he said, wrinkling his nose. "So much protection for a woman you barely know. You even brutally killed my men for her." His smile turned to a frown. "All for a woman who tried to assassinate you, nonetheless."

Elijah's fingers coiled into a tight fist.

He didn't have to know everything about Janelle to do the right thing. He felt utterly bound to keep her safe. His father was a monster who not only refused to protect him but sabotaged any relationships Elijah had tried to form with peers within the castle. Until the day he died, Elijah had cultivated a powerful system of protection, but he learned only to guard himself. At no time in his life had he cared for anyone other than his mother and Lincoln. He built a steady wall around him that not even a ferocious dragon could tear down.

"You know, Elijah, you have to wonder..." His voice trailed off.

Elijah narrowed his eyes.

"What it all means," Kieran continued. "Anyways. We're having a party, and you're safe now inside my home. I promise not to kill you or Janelle. I'm glad you both are here, actually. Water under the bridge. Right?" He pulled a wine glass from a servant's tray as they walked by. "As you can see, that creature out there won't be coming inside these walls any time soon. So, let us enjoy ourselves and handle the details once I'm sober. We'll have a little chat when I can think straight again."

Elijah gave him a quizzical look.

Two weeks ago, Kieran wanted him dead. He made sure no one would be able to tie Janelle to him. Then again, Kieran must know the repercussions of killing the King of Zemira. By sending an assassin, no one would be the wiser.

But now he claims to want peace? Elijah wondered. *I'm not buying it.*

Janelle inched closer to Elijah, and he did his best to pour every ounce of affection and reassurance into her through his touch. He could feel her relax, just a little, as their shoulders brushed together.

Kieran's eyes narrowed on her and then back to Elijah.

"Have some wine to relax," Kieran said. "Then you can visit the oracle. She saw the two of you coming here today, and she wants to speak with you specifically." He gestured to Elijah.

"The oracle?" Janelle asked, her eyes growing wide.

Kieran reached out to place his hand on her cheek, but black smoke trailed from Elijah's fingers. Though he didn't attack, he kept the magic growing between them—a warning.

Kieran smiled and pulled his hand back before he touched her skin. "Well, the tension here is killing the celebratory moment," Kieran said. "Have a drink or fuck something."

Janelle stepped forward, ignoring his crude order. "Where's Aiden? Did you hurt him?" Janelle asked before Kieran turned his back on them to walk away.

"Oh, Janelle, lighten up. He's getting dressed, but he'll join us soon." Kieran ushered over another servant with a snap of his fingers. A short man rushed over, handing both Janelle and Elijah a glass of champagne. Elijah held it at the tips of his fingers, not taking that first sip that Kieran had waited for. "I said I won't kill you. Relax," Kieran said. "I've thought a lot about ending this conflict, and I believe you'll like what I have to say."

"Then say it," Elijah seethed, agitated by Kieran's casual demeanor.

"Not right now. I've had way too much to drink, and a beautiful, naked woman is waiting for me in my room. If you'll excuse me. I'm going to step out for the next hour." He turned to Janelle. "Go visit the oracle, Janelle. It is *you* she is most eager to see. She's waited quite some time to read you."

Kieran walked away sluggishly, catching himself from falling at one of the columns before slipping out of the ballroom.

"What the fuck was that?" Janelle said, turning to Elijah. "Like, honestly, he doesn't seem the least bit angry. I thought for sure he'd have at least ordered for you to be locked up. As for me, he should've killed me for what I've done...or didn't do."

Elijah stayed silent, his eyes not leaving the door Kieran walked out of.

"Elijah?" she called, drawing his attention to finally look at her. He lifted the glass of champagne to his lips and gulped it down in one tilt.

"We'll need more alcohol for this shit," he said, walking past her and over to the bar.

Her feet shuffled over the runner behind him. Elijah helped himself to another glass when they reached the bar and then turned to Janelle.

"What's wrong with you?" she asked. "We're supposed to be having a discussion with Kieran on how to get my brother back and end this madness between you two. Not getting drunk while he fucks one of his doting followers."

He reached out, placed his hand on her cheek, and watched the fear and panic fade from her eyes from his gentle touch. "Janelle," he breathed. "Why has the oracle not given you a reading after the last six years?"

Janelle's brows knitted together. "That's what you're asking me? Why has an oracle not read my future?" she asked. "What a weird thing to ask."

Yes, it is a weird thing to ask, he said in his mind, *especially given how our lives are in the hands of a drunk sorcerer bent on destroying them*. But a question has been pressed on Elijah's mind for the last two weeks, and an oracle could answer it.

Janelle placed her glass on the table and turned to Elijah. "What now?" she asked. "Do we just wait? We traveled all this way to stand around until Kieran decides if he'll kill us?" She threw her hands up. "Aiden could be dead. Or maybe Kieran is screwing with us, and my brother never made it here after all."

Elijah shook his head. "He's not going to kill us," he said, watching Janelle's features change. After pouring himself another glass of champagne and downing that a lot quicker than he did the last, he sat his champagne glass on the table and turned to her. Her face fell, shaking her head as if she was stunned by his behavior.

"Stop drinking, Elijah. I need your head straight," she said. "You're acting as if you trust Kieran."

He let out a hard laugh. "Trust him? No, Janelle, I don't trust that man, but I believe you were never sent to kill me in the first place." Janelle's lips parted in confused shock. "And that oracle is going to tell us why."

30

Elijah

When Elijah and Janelle walked down to the garden, they saw that someone had already propped open the greenhouse door.

Bright green vines climbed the glass walls, with rose-colored petals blooming out. They slowly walked closer and felt the heat of the living walls radiate against their skin.

The oracle stood at the back, her body molded into a large tree trunk, whose branches dropped low, almost encasing her like a shield.

Elijah raised a brow. "It's a dryad," he said, turning to Janelle, who stood by the doorway, not entering the greenhouse. "What are you doing? Come inside," he ordered.

"No," she answered quickly. "I'm fine right here."

He gave her a quizzical look and turned his attention back to the dryad.

"Another one of my mother's tales," Elijah said. "A dryad can't always be trusted, but an oracle? They cannot lie or hurt you."

"Why do you want to know your future, Elijah?" Janelle asked. "Isn't your destiny yours to choose? What if she tells you something you don't like? Would or could you try to change it, anyway?"

He shrugged. "I was tempted to use the Kroneon to look into my future," he said. "I chose not to for that very purpose."

"Then why now?"

"Because," he said. "Everything has changed."

"What has changed?"

The oracle suddenly lit up as if she had just become aware of their presence, encasing Elijah in light so strong he could touch it.

The words rose in him, but he stumbled as he tried to get them out. His tongue felt thick in his mouth.

Surely Janelle knows the answer already, he thought, which ultimately freed his mind enough to let him speak.

"You," he finally said. "You're what has changed."

Everything he had questioned since the moment they locked eyes in his hallway would soon be answered, and as much as he wanted to know his fate, he was afraid. Janelle's confused expression didn't ease his discomfort. Her expression looked dark and distant.

"I feel something when I'm with you, Janelle," he confessed. "Not just the flutter in my stomach whenever you smile. Not the pain in my chest when you're hurt or the rage I feel when someone else touches you. My magic suddenly doesn't feel like it's dragging me down into the underworld. It doesn't feel like I can be lost because of my darkness. It's because your light brings me back. Your light fills my dark, and I don't understand it."

Janelle pressed her lips together, taking a few heavy breaths. She stayed silent, though, and Elijah wished so desperately he could read her thoughts.

The oracle cocked her head, and her branches moved, as if the wind had blown through the window. "King Elijah Delamere. Son of Matthias Delamere and Gal Castellan," she said softly. Her feminine voice carried an echo throughout the glass room.

"Yes," he said, swallowing before stepping forward.

The dryad's branches moved again.

"Can you see?" he asked. "Can you see *me*?" Elijah poked his chest.

The dryad extended her branch and coiled it around his body but didn't squeeze; the only light in the room twinkled brightly along her bark like yellow diamonds. "I know you don't want to be king," she said.

She's right, he thought, taken aback by having his heart read aloud. He craved the power, but being king reminded him too much of his father and what he had molded Elijah to become.

He took a deep breath, shook away his feelings, and asked the question he was standing there for. "Do you see *her*?"

"Elijah!" Janelle interrupted, sprinting forward, but the light shield was so strong it blasted her back before she could reach him.

He turned, watching her climb back to her feet, and a painful ache filled his heart as he watched her wince from the fall.

"Elijah, what are you doing?"

He looked back at the oracle, who nodded yes.

"Your powers are drawn to each other," she said. "The balance of light and dark."

The oracle reached out another branch and circled Janelle, helping her to her feet and encasing her in a shield of leaves and twigs.

His eyes looked up again at the creature. "Janelle is my destiny. Isn't she?" he asked.

"Yes," she said. The echo of her voice was low that time, shaking the walls around them. The oracle lit up even brighter.

Exhaustion hit Elijah like a brick wall, and he sighed out a breath. Since the moment his magic had latched onto hers without him even realizing, he had questioned it. A part of him had always known the answer, but having the oracle confirm it made everything seem to click into place.

They were linked cosmically. But a profound connection wasn't the same thing as love. Elijah had hated Janelle when he met her, truly and deeply hated her. And he had no doubt that her hatred for him had burned just as bright. Despite their hatred, neither of them had been able to resist the pull they felt to be in the other's presence.

Now that his feelings had morphed into the opposite of hatred, Elijah questioned himself. Were they destined to love each other, but that initial hatred had reflected their true feelings before the bond had taken them over? Or was Elijah destined to hate her, the one thing that opposed his own dark magic, but his love for Janelle had been too powerful to be kept locked up?

It was difficult to know how much of their feelings were their own and what was fate's design. Either way, their connection was undeniable. Elijah and Janelle would be drawn together forever as the sun rose and the tide came in.

His hair stood on end. "Heartmates?" he asked hesitantly.

The oracle slowly shook her head. "No," she replied. "Heart-mates do not exist in our world, Elijah. You still have your free will. You choose your mate. However—"

The dryad ripped her branches that had grown into the walls and moved with grace toward them. Her long limbs dragged across the floor until she stood by their side. She closed her eyes and let out a screech so loud they had to clap their hands over their ears to drown out the piercing cry.

A rush of heat flooded Elijah's body before his eyes turned white, and a vision blanketed his mind.

Elijah knelt beside Janelle. His hand pressed over a bloodied wound on her chest, with a dagger protruding at the center. She looked up at him and touched his cheek, but her palm slipped, her eyes shut, and her body went still. Then, suddenly, Elijah's mind pulled back from the brief image. The thought of Janelle dying made him feel as if his soul had been ripped from his body, even within the vision.

He looked up at the oracle. "What was that?" he asked. "What did you show me?"

"Her future if you do not kill Kieran," the oracle said, turning to Janelle. "Your magic is fated to be connected to Elijah's, but so is your life. It is only Elijah who can save you."

"I...I die?" Janelle asked, and then she looked at Elijah. "How? When—"

"It doesn't matter," he said softly, turning to her. "It won't happen."

"Elijah!"

"Your powers have created a balance between light and dark," the oracle continued, drawing their attention to look back at her.

"Just because you carry darkness, Elijah, does not mean you *are* darkness."

Janelle threw her hand out. "Show me more," she said. "I've changed my mind. I want to know everything."

The oracle shook her head. "I cannot see yours, Janelle. Because of the path you are both already on, you have no future for me to show you."

Janelle clutched her hands into fists. "Because I die?" she hissed. "Oh, that's rich. Fuck oracles. Don't you give us guidance on how to change our destinies?"

The oracle bowed her head, and the light around her dimmed. "Janelle—"

Janelle raised her hands, and her light magic blasted out of her fingertips, but the moment the light hit the bark of the dryad, it bounced back, hovering on the surface of the tree in circles. She dropped her magic and stepped back.

"You aren't going to die," Elijah fumed, raising his hand to calm her. "Is it Kieran who does this?" he asked, turning to the oracle. "Is that all I must do? Kill Kieran with my magic, and she lives?"

"No," the oracle said. "You must shut off your power when he uses his to kill you. Do not fight back."

"Not fight back?" he said distastefully.

Even the thought of cowering to that man made him nauseous.

"Why are you telling me this?" Elijah asked. "Why do you even care?"

"Because," the oracle said, "I have been a prisoner under Kieran and his family's control for over a decade. His death will set me free."

She closed her eyes, and her body went still. The light in the room dimmed, and the oracle stood unmoving, as if she were simply a tree at the center of the greenhouse.

Elijah reached out to Janelle, placed his hand on her cheek, and leaned forward, pressing his forehead against hers.

"I don't understand what just happened," she said. "I—"

The knowledge was burning inside Elijah's mind—everything was clear now.

"Kieran knew," he said. "Kieran was never going to kill me, Janelle."

She blinked. "What?"

"He knew we were bound by magic, by the Gods. He knew the two of us would grow to care for each other, and I would undoubtedly sacrifice everything I have to save your life."

She leaned back and shook her head. "What are you talking about—"

"The entire purpose for sending you was to ensure that we met. The oracle showed him this outcome far before it happened. He wants to bargain with your life for what he wants most." He stepped forward. "I'll give it to him for you." He reached out to touch her, but she stepped back. "I was always going to give it to him for you if I had to."

"Give him what?"

"Zemira."

Janelle looked at him as if he had grown a second head. "If you give up Zemira for me, you truly are an idiot!"

Turning to storm out, Janelle jerked to a stop as Elijah grabbed her by the back of the neck and pulled her back toward him. He didn't have it in him to be gentle; too much was at stake. The buzz of fear and confusion flushed through his veins. He stared down at Janelle as she slammed into his chest.

She shoved at him, but he didn't let go of her, snaking his other arm around her waist and holding her firmly against him. When her face grew fierce, he smirked.

"And I'm not sorry for this!" he said.

"For—"

He closed the space between them and crushed his lips into hers, silencing her words. His magic dimmed as her own power blanketed them.

His nostrils flared as he released her. "Don't ever walk away from me again," he ordered, watching her lips part.

"Excuse me?" she said, watching his mouth curl up. He still found her temper amusing.

"I said to stop walking away from me. I won't be the only one admitting that what the oracle just revealed to us doesn't feel real."

"I didn't say it wasn't real. I feel it, too, in every fiber of my bones. But it still doesn't mean I'm worth trading for Zemira. Stop playing with everyone's lives, Elijah! Your people depend on you."

"I know we haven't known each other long, Janelle," he said, "but surely you know me well enough by now to know I always have a plan. I need you to trust me. Do you?" He tried to keep the vulnerability out of his voice as he spoke, but there was still a slight waver in the words.

Janelle looked at him for a moment. It felt like she was looking into him. Like every inch of him was something she already owned. Every part of Elijah had been splayed out and nailed down on a board for her to examine.

She nodded.

"Good." Elijah tried to push past his brief moment of doubt and focus on the task at hand. "Firstly, how much do you trust Kora?"

Janelle smiled. "I trust her with my life."

Elijah nodded. "Once the sun sets tomorrow night, I need her to drop the rune shield around the property without Kieran knowing."

Janelle's eyes widened, but she nodded without asking why. "Done."

⸻⸻◆⸻⸻

For the next hour, Elijah made a series of mental notes about the home and people—how they behaved toward each other. What they wore, what they ate. Then he scanned the room and noted every door and window for an escape.

Kieran emerged through the doorway and strode toward them, his face taking on a more serious tone than when they first met.

"Alright. It's time we discuss a few things, shall we?" Kieran said casually.

Elijah stepped forward, blocking Kieran from being able to touch Janelle.

A smile tugged at Kieran's lips. "Hmm, interesting reaction—"

"Stop pretending you don't know," Elijah said.

Kieran smirked again. "The part where you love her," Kieran said. "And I know you'll do anything for her, won't you?"

Love? Elijah said the word in his mind. He cared for Janelle and would fight to keep her safe, but he was unsure what *love* truly meant. At the same time, he was uncertain if he could give Janelle what she needed from him. But what Elijah saw from the oracle made him realize there was more to his destiny than ruling a country.

"Do you care about anything other than power?" Elijah asked.

"Don't you?" Kieran said. "You're the king of the most powerful country in our world."

"Fuck power," Elijah bit out. "I'd give it all up for her."

He knew as he said it aloud that it was true. He would give up anything for Janelle without question or doubt. Perhaps that was love, after all.

"Then do it," Kieran said, his lip turning up. "Give it *all* up."

Elijah stilled, giving her a glance before saying, "Done."

"Don't be a fool, Elijah!" she said. "I'm not worth everything you've built to protect your people! Have you gone mad?"

Just a little bit, he thought.

Kieran raised a brow. "I didn't think it would be this easy," he said. "Sure, the oracle showed me everything, but you should have given a little bit of a fight."

Elijah held his tongue, trying to avoid ruining everything he had planned. He wanted to, though. He wanted to jump forward and suck out the life from the monster before him, but he steadied his breath, slowly releasing each exhale to calm his nerves.

"Understandably, you'd want to kill me," Kieran taunted. "But we all know what happens next."

Kieran snapped his fingers, and a medium-built blond man came forward holding a dagger and a silver chalice, as if they had had it all prepared for that very moment.

"Just follow my lead, and we can be done here within minutes," Kieran said, slapping his hands together. "I've seen it, Elijah. I've seen everything go as smoothly as it has so far. Let's keep this going, shall we?"

After Kieran sliced the middle of his palm, he let the welling blood drip inside the cup. Then he wiped the blade with his shirt and handed it to Elijah.

Elijah shook his head, watching each carefully planned movement from Kieran and his people.

Everything from the moment Janelle stepped into his palace was planned by Kieran and his people. The fury for not realizing it sooner burned deep inside him, wanting to unleash itself, but he wouldn't show it. It was too late.

"I was right," Elijah said. "That you knew I'd do this. Not just about me handing over my army for Janelle, but you knew she and I were fated. Didn't you?"

"You were not destined until your powers touched. Even from afar," Kieran replied. "Until you sensed each one's powers and the Gods pulled you together like a tightrope. At least, that's what my dryad showed me before I sent Janelle." Kieran frowned. "Did I enjoy watching my dryad's vision of the woman I loved being fated to another? No. But unlike you, my people's protection is far greater to me than love. So, yes, I sent her to you once I saw her fate because she was too afraid to ask the dryad herself. I saw you overpower her when she attempted to kill you, and then the two of you were drawn to each other's power like a moth to a flame. No matter how hard you tried to deny it. I saw each moment until *this*." Kieran glanced down at the dagger still held in Elijah's palm. "The moment you slice your own hand and make a blood oath with another of your kind."

Elijah turned to Janelle. "It was you," he said. "It wasn't the Newick gem I felt during the two weeks you hid in my city. It was *you*. Our magic touched far before you entered the palace gates."

Janelle's lips parted, and she shook her head. "Please, Elijah. Don't let this knowledge deter you from what's right. Don't make this oath with him. Please."

Elijah looked down and moved the dagger around in his hand. His stomach flipped; his heart pounded frantically in his chest. He had to do it. After one steady breath, he ran the dagger along his palm, slicing at the center until he drew blood. Then he squeezed his fist tightly over the cup until his blood dripped, mixing with Kieran's.

Black smoke rose from the cup while the two men chanted their oath. Their sacrifice. As King of Zemira, Elijah swore to hand over his soldiers. In return, Kieran would release Janelle from becoming his bride.

The oath was binding, and death would take either of them if they chose to break it.

Janelle looked at Elijah with horror in her eyes. "Why did you do that?" she asked. "Why would you do that for me?"

Elijah couldn't answer her question. How could he? She would fight him no matter what he said.

"Do I not have a say in any of this?" she fired back. Kieran wiped his hand with a cloth and tossed it on the floor.

Elijah swallowed hard before answering, "No. You have no say in any of this." His gaze locked on Janelle, causing his heart to falter a little. He didn't find joy in ordering her around. At that moment, he'd do anything to protect her, no matter how hard she tried to stop him; he had to.

"Where's Kora?" Kieran said, looking around. One of his men took the bloodied cup and shrugged.

"I'll go look for her," the blond man said.

"Wait," Kieran called before he walked away. "Please escort Janelle to her room and lock it behind you. Enchant the door while you're at it."

Elijah's teeth gnashed, pushing Janelle back behind him. "We made a deal in blood! She's no longer under your control!" he said as magic spilled from his fingertips.

Kieran replied with a lopsided grin, "And I've not broken it. But until your army arrives and swears their allegiance to me, she'll be locked in her room!"

Janelle stepped further back as the blond man reached out to take her arm. "Don't touch me, Erik," she warned.

Erik's shoulder slumped, and he turned to look at Kieran as if waiting for what he should do.

Pain clutched Elijah's chest as he turned, giving her a pleading look to comply. He was afraid Kieran would order Erik to kill her if she didn't. Kieran may no longer have had possession of her life, but killing Janelle wouldn't break the treaty. He gave her up as his future wife, but it didn't mean he'd not take her life if she disobeyed.

"Wait!" She stepped forward. "Where's my brother, Kieran?" she asked. "Is Aiden even here?"

Kieran's lip turned up. "Oh, I forgot to tell you. While you were on your little journey, he and I made a deal ourselves."

Elijah's attention snapped to Kieran when he heard Janelle let out a heavy gasp.

"What did you do?" Elijah asked, already feeling his magic pulse wildly at the tips of his fingers.

"Well, we didn't make an oath like you and me, but Aiden has become quite useful, I must say." He snapped his fingers at the guards by the door.

They swung it open, and Aiden came in, dressed in heavy armor. A smile flitted across his lips as he strode across the living room to stand next to Janelle.

"Sir," he addressed Kieran, bowing his head slightly. "It's good to see you, Nelle."

Her eyes grew wide, and she stepped back. "You son of a bitch!" she said, turning to Kieran and then back to her brother. "Oh, Aiden. I'm so sorry."

"What the fuck did you do, Aiden?!" Elijah shouted, feeling like cold ice was dripping down his spine.

Aiden moved closer to Elijah and cocked his head. "I didn't do anything. But Kieran did. He gave me more power," he said with a wry smile across his lips. "He made me feel more alive now than I've ever felt in my entire existence."

Elijah narrowed his eyes on Aiden's irises. The color was the same, but the movement inside looked like blue liquid swirling around erratically. Aiden cocked his head to the right, and his eyes flashed black for a split second.

The darkness, Elijah said in his mind. *Kieran released the darkness inside Aiden, suppressing his Elven light!*

Elijah slowly turned his head and glared at Kieran. "Release him from that power," he ordered. "Now."

Elijah may have been able to control the darkness inside his own body and mind, but Aiden wasn't made for that kind of magic.

That *darkness* wasn't power alone; it was also an entity the Newick coven made a deal with centuries ago to mix with their own magic. If they did its bidding, it gave them more power. If the darkness were inside Aiden, it wouldn't only destroy his free will, but it would also consume his light until there was nothing left.

A wicked smile touched Kieran's lips. "Release him?" he said. "The Zemiran army and your Elven warriors now belong to me, Elijah. That includes Aiden. I need the best to lead them. Aiden will make a fine Mylorian warrior, and together, we'll create the greatest kingdom our world has ever known. But first." Kieran pointed to the window behind him. "You'll call upon your soldiers with that little pendant Aiden told me about, and command them to come forth to my city. I will house them, feed them, and then use what little hybrids I have left to draw out that creature, so we can get rid of the problem once and for all. That magic out there will protect our property borders for the time. But it's not enough. We cannot simply hide inside any longer." He turned to Erik. "Now, get her in the room and lock the door!"

Elijah watched Aiden do nothing as Erik took Janelle by the arm, forcefully escorting her out of the room. Aiden even dared to smile.

"I'm surprised you're letting her go, Kieran," Aiden said, slightly chuckling under his breath. "You've loved her for so long."

Kieran shrugged. "Love will not win wars. If anything, it creates them."

Elijah's nostrils flared. Night had fallen; the Zemiran army would be far past the mountain, hiding in the caves and the pirate crew a mile off the coast.

Tomorrow, everything would change, Elijah thought. Without Aiden's help, he didn't believe his plan would play out exactly as it should.

Elijah turned back to Kieran, who linked his hands together behind his back and raised his chin. "My intentions were never to start a war with you or your people. I understand you're the child of a sorceress killed by your own father."

Elijah gritted his teeth as Kieran brought up his family, especially his mother.

"You know, my father knew Gal," Kieran continued, and Elijah found his mouth opening in surprise.

Elijah knew it was plausible that the witches were familiar with her, even though she was considered a peasant and lived outside Newick. She was still a sorceress. Still one of them.

"Gal was a magnificent woman, I've heard," Kieran continued. "You never had a chance to become something greater than Matthias was because you were not raised as I was, with magic. I know that taking your kingdom wouldn't align with Gal's wishes, but I'm doing this for the good of our countries. You made a choice that cost you your own people. You handed over a weapon to a crew of pirates. *Pirates*, Elijah?"

"Sorry, I don't have an oracle to see the future as you do," Elijah said. "I guess I could've seen what was coming."

Kieran lowered his brow. "This isn't a joking matter! That *thing* out there," Kieran continued, pointing toward the gates through the window, "is a result of their little adventure. What happened to you before you dashed inside property walls wasn't the first time it has attacked us at this mansion. Many of my men have already fallen, including my hybrids. Your actions cost the lives of my people. *Your* people. Now I must make oaths with kings to take their armies because I don't have enough men to protect us." Kieran scrunched his face in disgust. "You might have been raised in Zemira, but this land is where you were born, where your bloodline lies. *We're* your people. Perhaps we can put aside this feud between us and fight together. Or you can go back to your country and live like a little rich boy with no crown."

Elijah's nostrils flared. "You think I'd leave without her?"

"Of course not. But if I don't have your army, those pirates, and the Kroneon in my hands—and soon—it'll be you who will have broken our treaty, and I'll make sure Janelle dies with you."

As Elijah stepped forward, wanting to address the threat against the woman he cared for, several of Kieran's fighters gathered around the two men with both weapons and power, ready to attack.

"Why the Kroneon? It's not as if you can choose what portal you want to open. It sends you where it wants you to go," Elijah said. "Unless you plan to send the shadow to another world where it doesn't belong, why go to all this trouble?"

"I'm aware of what that Kroneon does, Elijah," he said. "My own people created it. Your great ancestor, to be exact. Once those portals close, that's it. It is up to us to kill whatever spills into our world. Do you think this is the first time in history this has happened? Haven't you ever seen creatures that didn't quite belong here? For example, the creatures who hunt in the Marsh Wetlands. The trolls. Even the dragons...and the Fae. They all came from somewhere else, let in by mistakenly using the Kroneon since it was created centuries ago. Always by other foolish and selfish people, like those pirates. We must *destroy* it before something of this nature happens yet again. At least we know what the shadow wants."

Elijah scowled. "Right. Magic. And you're going to use hybrids to bait it?"

"There are only a few who have survived this long. But yes. Because that's what a true king would do. Sacrifices must be made to save the world. Blood spilled for the greater good."

Kieran's hand came out, and black power sparked at his fingertips. "I'm more powerful than you, Elijah. Both my parents were sorcerers, unlike yours."

Elijah's lips twitched.

"Aren't you the least bit curious about your own people?" Kieran asked. "I've heard you have never even met another Newick witch?"

"Why would I give a fuck about any of you?" Elijah said. "You're monsters."

"True, although you might have a point. Fighting against us would be more courageous than running home like a coward. I guess that gives you two ...maybe three choices." Kieran turned to Aiden. "Aiden, please go check on Tegan. We need her ready too."

Aiden bowed once again to Kieran, ignoring Elijah entirely, and exited the room.

"Tomorrow night," Kieran said, "once you hand over your people, you'll make your choice: Head back to Zemira with Janelle, go against us and die trying, or fight alongside both armies, but as one of us."

31

ELIJAH

Kieran's incessant chatter caused Elijah's head to throb. "Gods, does he ever shut up?" Elijah whispered to Aiden.

An hour had passed, and the party had died down. Still, Kieran had insisted the two dine together one time before Liam and the Zemiran army arrived at the front gates by dusk the next day.

Aiden sipped the full-bodied wine served at dinner, attempting to stifle a laugh with his glass. "Never ends, I'm afraid." He leaned into Elijah's ear. "He doesn't think like us. Not like Zemirans. His plan to kill the Shadow Creature is reckless at best."

Elijah narrowed his eyes at his friend, hoping that the dark magic Kieran cursed him with hadn't wholly consumed him.

"Like us?" Elijah asked, raising a brow. "Do we still fight together, my friend?"

Aiden gave him a small smile. "I fight for Kieran now, so it depends on you, Elijah. Which side are you on?"

Not Kieran's, Elijah thought. *I plan to kill him before tomorrow night is over.*

"Right," Elijah said. "I guess I don't have a choice in the matter if I'm the only one trying to protect your sister."

He waited for Aiden's response but was only met with a shrug. Clearly, he felt obligated to serve Kieran, who gave him that power. The lustful kind of magic someone would crave more than the people they used to love.

"Ah, she made her choice," Aiden said, taking a bite of his food.

Elijah gripped the sides of the chair he sat upon, feeling his knuckles crack under strain.

Aiden was being consumed by darkness, and Elijah had no way of saving his friend from it. Elves were born with light magic, which meant the power flowing through Aiden's body would alter and eventually change him forever, pushing his light out until there was nothing left.

Elijah tried to reach Aiden at that moment, but his mind was constantly pulled back to Janelle.

He had to watch her be taken from him, forced to muster every bit of control not to unleash his wrath upon that room. He could've done it—could've slaughtered them all with one controlled, swift surge of his power. However, that creature was still out there. As much as Elijah didn't want to admit it, he needed the sorcerer's magic to help.

Fuck, he cursed. Elijah realized then that though he had a plan since he left his palace, nothing would ever be that easy.

Elijah cocked his head to the right, kept his gaze steady, and narrowed his eyes on Kieran, filling his wine glass again before sipping slowly.

"So, Aiden, are you really Kieran's puppet now?" Elijah added quietly. He pinched the hem of the tablecloth between his fingertips and rubbed it absently. The coarse feeling of the fabric helped Elijah ground himself, keeping his mind rooted to the reality of the situation, despite the surreal events around him.

Aiden let out a chuckle. "Puppet?" he whispered. "Elijah, I'm surprised you don't boast more about this power of ours. The moment the darkness touched my inner core, I—"

"Craved it like sex?" Elijah finished. "You wanted it more than the people you once cared about? It drives your every thought and urge?"

Aiden nodded. "Yes," he said coolly. "And now I can lead the warriors with more power and strength. You'll be grateful for what he's done for me, dear friend."

Dear friend? Had that really changed? Elijah wondered.

Elijah sat back and shook his head. "What a shame," he said. "To think, once upon a time, I believed you to be one of the good ones. The brave and powerful Aiden Patrov, son of the great Hagmar, Defender of the Elven folk. Now you dine with the same man who, before that blood oath I made with him, had planned to rape your sister and make her a broodmare." Aiden's lips twitched. "Think about that for a moment." Elijah leaned closer to his ear. "You kill him, and you'll still have the dark power and your warriors, but that bastard will be dead."

Aiden seemed to ponder what Elijah had said, his brows pulling together, narrowing his eyes. He wondered if his words were enough or if that darkness would control what Elven nature his friend had left.

"What was that?" Kieran said, leaning back in his chair.

Elijah turned from Aiden to look at him. Kieran was so far down the ridiculously long table that it surprised him he heard them at all.

"Have you not been listening to me this last hour?" Kieran asked, taking a bite of his roasted meat. "I was just discussing our plan and everyone's role in taking down the Shadow Creature. My plan will work, Elijah."

Elijah smirked. "No, Kieran. I've completely shut off my ears from your blabbering tongue. Your plan is still to sacrifice your hybrids. So, until it includes fighting like men—"

Kora cleared her throat. He hadn't even noticed her standing behind him at the door.

"Men *and women*," Elijah corrected. "Fight because you're strong enough to do it. Using just their power will only kill them, and then all those years of forced breeding will have been for nothing." He shot Kieran an accusatory glare. "If you want a plan on how to kill it, use Aiden, for fuck's sake. Use him, not because you can control him, but because he's the greatest warrior you'll ever have at your side."

The room had gone silent, and Elijah watched his friend's troubled gaze morph into something more distant. Aiden's eyes slid to a redheaded woman who had entered the dining hall and stood by the door. He couldn't quite decipher if Aiden was pleased or annoyed to see her. The woman gave him a sharp look and turned her head, breaking their locked gaze.

Kieran's voice muffled in the distance as Elijah shut him out again.

"Care to explain who she is to you?" Elijah asked Aiden.

Aiden turned his attention to him and shrugged. "Tegan. A one-night fuck. She means nothing."

Elijah raised a brow. "Interesting. Because I've never seen you look at a woman like that since we met. And you're most certainly not someone who would fuck a woman and walk away." He waited for Aiden to respond as he topped off his wine and took a long sip.

"We all know women are only good for one thing," Aiden said with a wicked grin. "Like I said. She means nothing."

Hearing Aiden talk about a woman like that shook Elijah to his core. He never spoke that cruelly about anyone. His mother taught him respect and honor above all else when regarding women.

Is he really gone? Elijah wondered.

Tegan's troubled stare told Elijah one thing: she disagreed with what Kieran was doing. If anything, she looked scared to be there.

I can use that, Elijah thought. He needed more allies.

"She's a hybrid," Kieran shouted that time, loud enough that Elijah could no longer pretend he didn't hear him. Kieran pointed to the redheaded woman, trying desperately to melt herself into the wall. "Tegan, here, is our first and finest hybrid to come into the coven. She'll be on the frontline with her kind when we attack the creature."

Elijah lowered his brow. "But she—?"

"Looks forty years old? Yes," Kieran said. "True, we started breeding them only two decades ago, but they age fast. She's a beautiful, strong woman now." He sipped his drink. "It's quite extraordinary. Isn't it? She possesses incredibly rare magic that can trap that shadow."

Extraordinary and soon to become another asset of mine in this fight, Elijah thought.

"Quite," Elijah said, giving his friend one last glance. Aiden suddenly lost interest in the woman and turned his attention back to his food.

Elijah dabbed his lips with a napkin before throwing it down on the table and standing, placing both hands on the surface.

"I think I'll turn in for the night," Elijah added before pushing back his chair. He turned to Kora. "Goodnight, Kora." She bowed her head with a smile, and he left without finishing his meal, no longer acknowledging Kieran. Elijah couldn't stand another moment without checking on Janelle. She was all he could think about since they had taken her away, and he didn't look back as he left the dining hall.

⸻

Elijah hunted for the room down the main hall, spotting a red-painted door frame lit up by a black, enchanted protection border. No one guarded it, but it didn't matter—it was bound by magic.

Elijah sat down and placed his palm and ear flush on the door. "Janelle," he called, waiting for movement on the other end.

Quiet shuffles moved along the carpet before the sound of her feet stopped. He closed his eyes and listened to the shuffling sound of her sitting on the other end, and the burning sensation of her magic coming through the door reached his skin. He drew in a breath and waited for the peace of her magic to fill his entire body, helping him relax.

Janelle severed the connection to her powers, but he still felt her presence against the door.

"What now?" she asked.

He dropped his hand and turned, leaning the back of his head to the door.

"I'm going to use the Voleric to reach both Lincoln and Liam, informing them of the plan. We'll do everything Kieran wants because it's the only way to keep you and my people safe. The crew will stay out in the water until morning, then hand over the Kroneon without a fight."

She sighed heavily. "And then what?"

He shrugged, even though she couldn't see it. "By tomorrow night, we will gather on the field and wait for that creature to come to attack us. Kieran has agreed to come for you once I line my army at the gates for us to make the trade—your life for them. Janelle, we have no choice but to fight alongside Kieran and his fighters. But mark my words. The moment that shadow monster is dead, I will be certain to end Kieran and save as many hybrids as possible." Elijah drew in a breath. "As far as the weapon, it doesn't matter what they do with the Kroneon. It never belonged to me or anyone on that ship. They made it for the royal sea folk. Nola gave up the crown, so it goes back to the Newick coven...unless Ara stakes her claim to it, which she didn't."

"Elijah—"

"It's not ours, Janelle. Kieran was right to blame me. As much as I hate that man, what I did was foolish, and he's the only one who can destroy it. What the pirates did was catastrophic." He drew in another exhausted breath. "Using the Voleric, I'll instruct Liam to lead the Zemiran army to the city and then wait for my order. The hybrids will line the shore and draw the creature to the docks. Once it's there, they'll drop their magic before it reaches them. Then the hybrids' leader, Tegan, will use her power to trap and kill it. The hybrids will only use their light until Tegan has conjured enough of her magic to be the creature's primary target." He pinched the bridge of his nose. Just thinking about the plan was giving him a headache. "Between the pirates coming in from the water with Nola's power and the two armies fighting as one, we can force the Shadow Creature to solidify along the field. At least enough for Tegan to plunge a sword through its chest."

Janelle let out a heavy sigh. "Except now they'll be led by someone who doesn't care if they live or die if the plan fails. If a few hybrids fall, Kieran will feel nothing."

Elijah wanted to tell her more. He wanted to share with her that there was more to his plan that didn't include sacrificing anyone's life, but it was too dangerous. It was better she be left in the dark.

"Stay alive," he said, rising to his feet. "Please, Janelle. All I ask is for you to stay alive."

32

AIDEN

Tegan placed a bag in the corner of the room where Aiden would sleep and slowly looked up to meet his eyes. "Clean clothes are hanging in the closet there, and I've washed everything you own. It's inside this bag—"

Aiden stepped forward but didn't come too close to Tegan. His lips pressed in a hard line, watching her shift uncomfortably. Her pale skin was luminescent in the darkened room. The memories of their night together flashed in his mind.

It wasn't that he was incapable of feeling empathy or lust now that the darkness had consumed his soul, but his desire for Tegan felt different now.

She was undoubtedly beautiful, but now she seemed afraid of him. Tegan was willing to hide the sword from Kieran and even resisted the guards when they forced her to hand it over after hiding it in her room. Now, she stood as far away from him as she could.

Tegan changed from the girl I met at the tavern, he thought. *I might have to break her.*

"You know what?" she started, turning to face him with her arms folded across her chest. Tegan had a glowering expression, and her lips were pressed in a hard, scolding line.

There she is, he thought, remembering the fire she had when they first met.

"You're being a prick, Aiden. Yes, I tricked you, but don't sit there and pretend to be perfect. You let one taste of that darkness seep so far into your bones that you've forgotten who you are. I tried to save your ass, and you didn't listen. And now, you're so far gone that you're giving me this meek, silent treatment—"

"Silent treatment?" he interjected, his expression fierce. "Really? I understand what happened between us was for only one night. We don't owe each other anything. You lied to me then, and now I must pretend to be your ally for the sake of my new leader." He sauntered to her until he had her pinned against the wall. "Though I must say, you did a fantastic job convincing me you liked me." His finger touched her belt loop at her waist, and then he ran his nail up her belly until he stopped between her breasts. He paused at the cleavage. "But I won't complain about one moment of our night together."

"Stop," Tegan said, but he noticed a hesitation in her tone. She turned her face to avoid his eyes. His hand continued up her chest until he reached her throat, pressing his palm against her neck.

Aiden only wanted to threaten her, making her fear of what he could do if she ever deceived him again. But something else stirred within him, the pulse in Tegan's throat quelling his urge to harm her.

"Control the darkness, Aiden. I can feel it eating away at you." She turned her head to face him again. "We don't have to be longtime friends for me to know this isn't you. Janelle is my friend, and what she's shared with me about your childhood together...you're not *this*."

His face hardened again as the tightness grew in his chest. "Maybe this has always been me." Aiden's lips brushed her cheek. "But I had to suppress my true self. All because an Elven warrior is expected to be strong and brave for the people they serve. Never to be selfish, always sacrificing."

Aiden's lips touched her neck. His tongue came out and caressed wet trails up to her ear. The soft kisses against Tegan's flesh caused her body to squirm. All the worry left her face as she gave a moan of approval.

"Good girl," he hummed.

"You're...you're drunk. I don't know if we should—"

Aiden wrapped her red hair around his fingers and gave a tug at the back of her scalp. "We were drunk last time," he reminded her.

He used his grip on her to crash their lips together, swallowing whatever words of protest she was about to utter. It felt raw and visceral, and he never wanted to release her. The idea of owning Tegan, possessing her in every possible way, was like a siren call that he couldn't resist. He was trapped by it.

Sharp nails clawed into his back as she dug her fingers in. He ran his free hand down the soft skin of her stomach before sliding it into the waistband of her pants. His hand slotted neatly between her legs, pushing them farther apart, and he dove for the wet, hot center of her. The feeling of her shuddering as he touched her filled him with an innate, carnal hunger. She was slick between her thighs, and a quiet, desperate moan escaped her lips as he slipped his fingers into her.

Aiden pulled back, breaking their kiss with her taste still lingering on his tongue.

"You're so wet for me," he said. He released Tegan's hair, grabbing her by the hip instead, so he could hold her tight as she rocked down onto his fingers. He pushed deep into her, engulfed by heat, and watched as she sank into the feeling of being filled. As soon as his thumb found her apex and applied pressure, her moans turned to gasps. Aiden moved relentlessly, filling her from the inside as he sparked continuous pleasure by rubbing her, watching the sensations build and Tegan get lost in it. It drove him mad. He wanted to look her in the eyes as she climaxed.

Tegan cried out, fingers scrabbling at his shoulders as she clenched down on his fingers, his wrist trapped between her trembling thighs as she rode out wave after wave of sensation.

Contentment washed over Aiden, even as his erection remained untouched. He let Tegan sag into him in a boneless slump. She was warm and soft, and he held her close. He was nuzzling his face into her hair, inhaling the aromatic scent before her hand came out, pressing against his chest to give them a little space.

Tucking her hair behind her ear with gentle fingers, he said, "I'm not done with you yet."

Tegan reached out to cup the edge of his jaw and pulled his head up to look into his eyes. "Kieran cannot know what we've done," she pleaded. "I'm nothing but a weapon to him. He'd never allow this."

A wicked grin flitted across his lips before brushing the back of his fingers against her cheek. "I can't make that promise," he whispered, his fingers closing around her chin, keeping her gaze locked on his.

Tegan returned his smile, although her face looked more drawn and tired than his. She moved under the arm he used to pin her to the wall and then quickly adjusted her clothes and hair before opening the door. She turned, casting one last glance at Aiden before disappearing down the hall.

33

ELIJAH

Elijah could see the Sybil Curse rocking a mile off the coast of the Mylorian Sea. According to the plan, they were not to set foot on the Newick shore—not yet anyway. Only Lincoln and Nola were to rendezvous with Elijah on the docks to discuss the next phase of the plan and hand over the Kroneon.

"I promised you I wouldn't kill them," Kieran said, walking up from behind.

Elijah glanced over his shoulder. "I know you promised. But I'd rather trust the loyalty of street thieves than your own word." He smiled to himself. "So, kindly fuck off."

Elijah stilled as a sharp point of metal pressed against his back.

The power in Elijah's hands trailed from his fingertips.

"Are you threatening me?" Elijah asked slowly, trying to refrain from releasing his magic. If they were to try and kill each other now, their armies would turn on each other, and he would then have a bloodbath on his hands. Not to mention, Elijah was sure

Kieran had given the order to his people to kill Janelle if anything were to happen to him.

However, Elijah had his own leverage.

"Let us not forget," Elijah said, "if you kill the crew or me, that massive dragon in the sky will swoop down and scorch that pretty face of yours."

Kieran twisted the sword, digging it into the fabric of his shirt, causing Elijah to wince.

"This sword once belonged to Hagmar," Kieran said. "And now it belongs to me. I will save us all from that monster in the woods, Your Majesty." He nearly spat the words. "And *I will be the one* to lead Zemira into the future—uniting our people."

Something about the tone of Kieran's voice sparked a new understanding of their situation. Elijah realized, at that moment, that Kieran truly believed he was the hero of it all. That this was his story, and he was the one that history would remember as the man who saved them all from destruction. Elijah would have laughed at how delusional it was if Kieran weren't so close to completing his plan.

Aiden had shared with him the night before that he had given his sword willingly to Kieran. It was the darkness that compelled Aiden to hand over that weapon. The real Aiden would never give that up without a cause. That sword was ancient, powerful, and all he had left of his father.

Elijah mumbled obscenities under his breath. "I'll get the Kroneon," he promised. "Don't forget—that is my family out there. If you so much as touch them, I'll slaughter every last one of your hybrids, including your precious Tegan. I'll leave you all to be devoured by that shadow."

The sword eased off his back, and Kieran chuckled quietly. "So touchy," Kieran mocked before clearing his throat. "What time tonight will your soldiers arrive?"

"Dusk. They've been ordered to stand down at the gates until nightfall," Elijah said. "Once they arrive, I expect you to follow through with your end of the deal and release Janelle from that room. Then and only then will they be ordered to follow you after you hand her over to me."

Elijah turned as Kieran sheathed the sword.

"I do like obedient King Elijah," Kieran said. Elijah felt his blood heat, resisting the urge to snap the sorcerer's neck. "You want to kill me right now, don't you?" Kieran added with a lopsided grin. "I've got to say, Elijah, having you in the palm of my hand, doing whatever I want, has been the highlight of my week."

Elijah never bowed to anyone, especially someone as pathetic and twisted as the man before him. He had no choice, and Kieran knew he'd do whatever was asked of him to keep Janelle alive.

"I expect you to hand over the Kroneon the moment you have it in your hands," Kieran commanded. "Those pathetic pirates can head back to their ship and get as far away from my shore as they can sail. Unless they're also willing to help, as we discussed last night. It will all be under my order. Understand?"

Elijah didn't answer or pay him any more attention. Instead, his eyes stayed on Anaru, circling the ship from afar.

Kieran huffed when he didn't reply, turning on his heel and heading back into the city. Once the sorcerer was out of sight, Elijah took one steady breath to calm his anger. As he walked toward the docks, Anaru powerfully descended from the skies.

A few moments later, the beautiful creature landed on the grass by the docks, and Lincoln helped Nola off the dragon. She roared loudly before extending her wings, strategically blocking the three of them in for protection.

Nola was the first to step forward with the Kroneon sitting at the center of her palm.

"We're taking a risk by handing this over, Elijah," she said, carefully placing the Kroneon in his hand. "I don't care if his people created this weapon. He'll use it against us the first chance he gets."

"It's only for a few hours, Nola, just to buy us some time. Tegan will wait until Kieran's too distracted to notice when we take it back." He smirked at the thought, but that smile turned to a frown. "He'll kill Janelle if I don't hand it over. So, until she's safe in my arms, we'll let him think he's won." He looked to Lincoln. "She's not to know about any of this. Understand?"

They both nodded.

"Let's get back to the ship," Nola said to Lincoln. "Mazie's preparing the weapons. One call, and we sail this way with cannons aimed at the city and dragon's fire to engulf your enemies. Just say the word."

Elijah stepped off the docks. "Be back here at nightfall."

Lincoln turned to look at Nola and then back to Elijah. "We'll have everything ready on our end. The Sybil Curse might not make it, but this is our fault. Everything after this," Lincoln paused, "falls to us."

Elijah gave them both a hopeful smile. "See you on deck, Captain."

Kieran held the Kroneon in his palm, running his fingers carefully over the smooth surface.

"I only know my father's stories," Kieran said to Elijah. "He told me that the merfolk were at war with the Fae once upon a time. That was before they found peace to co-exist without strife and bloodshed. The Newick witches always favored the sea. Wanting to protect the merfolk, they created this device, so they would always know what was coming." Kieran looked up. "It was a tool to protect our allies of the deep, not to be a toy for careless freebooters to play with in the middle of the sea." He scowled at Elijah with accusatory eyes.

"When do you plan to destroy it?" Elijah asked, biting back his tongue.

"Let *us* worry about that," he said.

Elijah carefully watched him as he placed the Kroneon in his back pocket.

"How do I know you won't use that to kill us until then or further abuse the already altered timeline?" Elijah asked.

Kieran smirked. "You don't," he said, looking toward the open gates over Elijah's shoulder. "Time is ticking now." The sorcerer gritted his teeth as if his patience had grown thin. "The sun will soon set, and if you don't deliver—"

"I said they'll be here," Elijah replied angrily. "What I need from you is your word that your people will hold back their magic until my soldiers are safely through. You're to assure my soldiers are protected from them and you despite this alliance. Until then, stay away from that ship and Janelle. If anything happens to either of them, I'll break that oath—consequences be damned!"

"If you go back on your end of the deal, I'll be sure to bury Aiden next to you. Not only will you die, but that'll be Janelle's last memory of you—the man who failed and killed her brother."

Elijah swallowed down a hard lump in his throat.

"I'll prepare the hybrids and my coven as I promised. I don't have many fighters after the havoc that thing wreaked across our land, but I will have Tegan and the remaining hybrids ready at the shore. If I don't see your army bowing to me by then, ready to take my order, I will stick my dagger into Janelle's chest and make you watch her bleed out."

Elijah's stomach dropped. Janelle's fate that the oracle had shown him played out in his mind.

"You must shut off your power when he uses his to kill you," the words from the oracle had hit him once again. *"Do not fight back."*

But what does it all mean? he wondered.

"They'll be in the city in four hours," Elijah promised. "Until you see my men, you're not to go near her room, or you'll see exactly how I punish my enemies."

⸻ ◈ ⸻

After Kieran left, Elijah slipped into the hall, heading back down to where Janelle was being kept.

He placed his hand on the door again and called for her with a pulse of his magic.

"Hey, you," she said from the other side. "Have you come to rescue me?"

A small smile slipped from his features. The hopeful plea to rescue her was only that, a plea. They both knew there was nothing he could do to help her then, and it drove a nail into his heart.

"You know I can't," he said. "The magic used on the door is impenetrable. And even if I could, he'll kill Aiden if he sees you missing."

It was quiet on the other end, and Janelle sighed. "I wish I could touch you," she said. "Not just your magic through the door but really *touch* you."

It was strange how quickly they had gone from pure hatred to this. Elijah felt like he wanted to tear off his own skin at the frustration of being away from Janelle. It was a pendulum swing of emotion that left him dizzy.

But it was undeniable, the connection they now shared in heart and soul. Her words made his stomach flutter, and he yearned for her.

Yearned.

King Elijah, the ruler of Zemira, leaning up against a door. He would give his entire heart to a woman who held more power over his emotions than anyone ever had in his entire existence. It was unexpected but also impossible to fight. All he wanted to do was touch her soft skin and trail kisses down her neck. To hold her and never let her go again.

His hands couldn't reach her, though. All he had was his magic.

"I—" He paused, trying to string his words together. "Lie down, darling," he ordered, but his tone was gentle. "I want to try something."

It was quiet for a moment before he heard movement.

"Lying down, Your Majesty," she said.

Elijah reached into his pocket and pulled out the Voleric pendant.

"I want you to picture a ship," he said quietly. "The deck of the Sybil Curse is beneath your feet, rocked gently by the waves. Feel the damp wood pressed on your heels. Focus on the rocking back and forth from the water below. Do you see it? Do you smell the ocean?"

Janelle let out a breath. "Yes."

Elijah closed his eyes, seeing the ship manifest around them, sinking deeper into Janelle's dream through the stone's power.

Janelle smiled when she spotted him walking toward her. Elijah was stunned by her beauty, even inside her dreams.

"It's so quiet on the ship," Janelle said as she walked to the balustrade, keeping her balance on deck as the waves crashed against the side. "It feels so real."

Janelle placed her hands over the ship's rail, curling her delicate, long fingers over the wooden railing.

Elijah watched her white hair dancing in the wind as if trying to reach out for him. To tease him toward her. He couldn't resist the urge to let his eyes roam over the curves of her body, wrapped in her leather corset. Elijah had taken many women in his life, but they had only ever been something convenient. A warm body to share the bed for the night, a wet mouth to share some pleasure with. Never had he felt something like what he had with Janelle. He had never wanted so desperately to keep someone safe or been so willing to risk everything in the process.

While Janelle continued to look out over the water and through the city in her dream, she manifested warriors gathering in preparation for the shadow creature's attack. Elijah stepped onto the deck, sauntering over to her. His hips felt loose, and his movements were easy.

Before, he had never been shy around women, but something about Janelle made him feel completely unrestrained. He wanted to bury himself in her and never come out, even if only in a dream. Janelle turned as she noticed him, unconsciously tilting her face up toward him, flicking out her tongue to leave her lips shining slightly in the moonlight. She let out a deep breath, leaning against him as soon as he stepped in behind her. He wrapped his hands around her shoulders, pulled her back tightly to his muscular chest, and buried his face in her hair to place a soft kiss there.

He inhaled deeply, letting her sweet scent curl through his lungs. It felt like they were melting into each other, and it caused something unidentifiable to tighten in his chest.

"Is the crew safe?" she asked.

He leaned back, tugging her with him to keep her body pressed flush to his chest. He let his arms slide down around her waist to squeeze her tight and raised his chin enough that she could tuck the back of her head into his neck. It felt like she belonged there.

"Lincoln and Nola went back to the ship with Anaru. The crew is ready; for now, they are safe. We might have some leverage if we can spot the creature before it reaches the field." His voice was low as he spoke, just a rumble in the dream's night air.

She turned her head, looking over her shoulder. "Is Tegan safe?"

He nodded. "For now, but Kieran keeps a watchful eye on everyone. I'll do everything I can to protect her and the rest of the hybrids. I promise you."

"She's going to try to fight, Elijah. It is in her nature to use her powers to protect others. I'm…I'm afraid for her. I'm afraid for Aiden."

Elijah nodded. He knew that feeling in his very core.

"Aiden might be controlled by darkness, but he's not lost to it. I can feel his light. It's dim, but it's there," he said. "In the end, I believe he'll do the right thing and fight with us. Tegan plans to attempt to reach him at least."

Janelle nodded and looked back to the sea. There was a hint of a haunted look in her eye, and he felt powerless being unable to make it disappear. He leaned down, nuzzling at the smooth curve of her neck until he placed a kiss right beneath her ear. It was a light, gentle thing, but it felt electric. His skin tingled everywhere he touched her, and she moaned into that touch. He kept her pressed tight as she arched her back, rolling her body against him. He knew she could feel the thickening of his cock against her as she slowly, deliberately rubbed against it.

Something primal and unconscious within him surged, and a growl tore its way out of his throat.

"I can feel you as if you are actually touching me," she said.

"I am," he whispered as he dragged his lips over the warm skin of her neck. "Our thoughts are just as strong as any physical sense when using magic. Hold on to that feeling for as long as we are here."

Her hand reached back to touch him, grazing her fingers over his thigh, moving closer until she cupped his erection with a tender grip. Even the light contact made him throb, and he felt the heat begin to curl low in his belly. His body screamed at him to claim her. Elijah growled again as his hands fell to her hips, gripping her tight and pushing her body into the balustrade. He wanted to wrap every part of himself around her and hold her close.

"I want you," she purred into the night air. "Elijah, I want you to take me right here."

Her invitation felt like a shot of adrenaline to his heart. He crowded into her, releasing one hip to reach up and tangle his fingers in her hair. She gasped when he gave a gentle tug, and her body melted into him as he moved his other hand to grip her breast. As soon as he dragged his thumb over the pert nub of her nipple, she was undone.

"Oh, Gods!" she cried out, voice hoarse with wanting.

He needed to hear that sound for eternity. Everything about her was all Elijah desired. She was intoxicating.

"Don't let go of the dream," he said. "Stay with me."

He used the long line of his body to press her harder into the wooden handrail, lining up his hard cock with the cleft of her ass and taking another deep breath of her scent. Elijah twisted his hand around her hair into a knot, something that he could pull harder on and drag more of those sweet, gasping noises out of her.

"Really?" she asked, but he could hear the smile in her voice.

"I need better leverage," he said with a cocky smile.

Elijah punctuated this by rolling his hips into her, feeling his stomach flutter as she moved with him. She was surrounded by him between his hand in her hair and his other hand holding her breast. He wanted to assault every one of her senses, just as she was attacking every one of his. Elijah relished the smooth curve of her neck. The feeling of her heart pounding in her chest and the warmth of her breath as it puffed out in gasps...it made him want to taste every part of her body.

"Please," Janelle moaned, leaning herself back into his hips, "please take me."

Elijah felt hot and heavy between his legs; he needed more. He needed to bury himself in her warmth. His hand released her breast and flew to her trousers, tugging and twisting until they were down around her knees. Her skin was exposed to the air, and he would have bent down to lick every inch of her had there been more time. The desperation was beginning to pulse between them.

He wasted no time pulling himself free of his own trousers. Fingers wrapped around the shaft, he guided the head of his cock to her wet slit and let it slide into her. The sharp gasp she made as he placed himself inside her made every inch of his skin pull tight with lust.

"Elijah!" she cried out, leaning over the edge. He dragged himself out slowly, a tease until she was almost empty, and then he slammed back in. Her hips rocked into the railing, and he moaned as she clenched around him. She was warm and tight, tugging him deeper into her with each thrust.

Our bodies had to be meant for each other, he thought as he buzzed with a combination of lust and fear. Death was looming over them, and he wanted to capture every drop of her until it came to take them both.

She moaned, loud and hoarse with every thrust.

"You can scream as loud as you want here," Elijah whispered. "But it's unfortunate Kieran can't hear how much I love fucking you."

Her breathing grew heavy. "Isn't that a shame," she said, a husky laugh in her throat.

That brought a wicked smile to his face.

Elijah could feel her body trembling, yet she kept pushing back; regardless of all, he was more eager now than ever to live in the moment. They may die this night, and he would rather feel the joy of love than anything else.

Love? he thought. *Fuck. Is this really what I'm feeling?*

That word was so difficult for him to acknowledge, especially saying it aloud. Janelle's very existence mangled his thoughts and made him question everything he thought he was meant to be.

He sucked in each heaving breath through his teeth, feeling his body tense as he moved inside her, her wetness spreading over their skin.

It was too much. Elijah could feel pleasure start to build in him, but he wasn't ready to end it yet. He slowed his pace, keeping a tight grip on her hair and pushing into her deeper and deeper. The way she opened to him was incomprehensible. Her body made itself belong to him. He took a few more moments to move slowly, enjoying every shuddering gasp that slipped from her mouth and every tremor of pleasure he felt running through her, and then he picked up the pace.

Elijah pounded into her, hard and unrelenting. She almost choked on her heady moan as she braced herself to be taken by him. Her wet slit was pulsing around him, and he was sure she was close. Her cries grew louder and louder as he pressed into her until something gave way. She opened her mouth in a silent scream as she orgasmed. It was as if she was too consumed by pleasure to make a sound. A slow wave of ecstasy rolled through his body while Janelle arched to press herself down further onto his cock as he throbbed and clenched around her.

It was irresistible, and with a final thrust, Elijah found his release. He pulsed into her, pulling them tighter as he filled her wetness up with his own, at least how they imagined it in their shared dream state.

"My Gods!" she cried out again as her body loosened and the dream fell apart. "Fuck!"

The Voleric dropped to the floor as Elijah's eyes opened to his release.

"Well," Janelle said through the door, still breathing heavily, "that was different." Her tiny giggle caused Elijah's smile to broaden.

"Mmm," he moaned. "I wish I could sit on this floor with you all day and night, but I need to clean up now." Elijah took a moment for his body to settle before climbing to his feet and looking down the hall. "My little elf, I don't know if I'll be back before my soldiers get here," he said. "I—" There was a long silence as Elijah let the words he wanted to say finally rise to the surface. "I think I love you, Janelle."

Elijah felt her light come through the door and touch the darkness inside him.

"I think I love you too, Elijah."

He smiled and leaned his forehead against the door, but before leaving her, he slipped his dagger under the door's crack and silently prayed to the Gods she could protect herself when he couldn't.

34

JANELLE

Several hours had passed as Janelle sat on the hard floor by the door.

Waiting.

She watched as the moon climbed above the trees through the window, but Elijah hadn't returned.

The memory of what he had done with her hadn't left her mind, but her crushing reality overshadowed all that pleasure she had felt. She may never touch him again.

The harrowing cries outside from the hybrids being forced into battle lines caused her stomach to churn. *Had Elijah's army finally arrived? How soon would Kieran make the trade for her?* She sat, wondering, saying a silent prayer to the Gods that the man she had grown to care for was alive.

The thought that the Shadow Creature had already come for them caused her heart to beat faster.

I need to get out of here, Janelle thought as she clambered to her feet and walked to the window to look out over the forest next to the mansion.

She thought about Tegan and what Erik had told her before throwing her into that room—she had helped bring Aiden there.

The betrayal didn't matter, though—she knew why she did it. Sure, it hurt, but she wasn't angry. Kieran's control was impossible to break. He had plans to use Tegan's magic to draw out the creature. He was going to use her and the others as bait, and that gnawing fear that she would lose her friend overcame her.

Janelle's eyes scanned the field behind the property. The brightly lit lanterns along the fence illuminated a glow through the trees, giving higher visibility to the grassy area behind them. She could hear the sound of horses' hooves coming through the forest, the echoes bouncing off the thin glass of the window.

It sounds like everyone is getting into position.

The door cracked open behind her, and Elijah stood at the door frame. "Janelle," he said softly, as if out of breath.

She bolted from the window and jumped into his arms. "You're alive," she said, drawing him in for a kiss, relishing the fact that she could truly touch him. His lips were soft, exotic, and there was a light sweetness; her stomach leapt at his mere touch. "What is happening out there? I...is that your army, I hear?"

Elijah wiped his lips with the hem of his sleeve as if he were erasing the moment they had just had between each other. Then he reached out to caress her cheek with the back of his fingers. "I've handed my warriors to Kieran as promised. You're free."

She let out a sigh and placed her hand on his cheek. Being in Elijah's arms warmed every part of her soul, but at what cost? Her hand stayed there for a moment, in silence, before she pulled back. The connection they had once before felt different, hollow.

"It's okay, though," he said. "He's using the army to fight that creature. I think he's on our side. I believe the hybrids, the coven, and Zemira will all be protected by the new king, serving the two countries with their best interests at heart."

Janelle cocked her head to the side and narrowed her eyes slightly. The words that left his lips sounded nothing like Elijah. An uncomfortable silence crept into the space between them, and the terror that suddenly filled her made her faint. She reached out, placing her hand on his chest, and summoned her magic to touch his, but nothing happened. They couldn't connect, no matter how hard she tried.

The room spun, her vision grew blurry, and she lifted a finger to her mouth, brushing her nail along her lips that were still wet.

Poison?

She looked down at the small amount of white liquid coating her finger. Janelle looked up, and her eyes went wide. "What did you do to me?" she asked, stepping back, but he caught her wrist, pulling her back into him, brushing out her smooth, white hair. The man before her sneered, and his face shifted to show its true form.

Kieran.

She panicked as the room began to spin faster.

"There, there, love. While both armies defend this home from a monster, the two of us will be creating my heirs." His hand came up and gripped her throat, holding her still as her eyes grew even wider. "That's right, Janelle. Elijah won't want you after this." He looked down at her belly. "Not after I put our little hybrid child inside you."

The smug smirk across his face made her skin crawl.

"If you want, I can still wear his face so—"

Her fist flashed up and punched him hard against his throat.

He coughed out, "Bitch!" before lunging at her. She quickly shifted to the side, then reached for Elijah's dagger she had hidden between her breasts.

Janelle used her right leg to kick him hard in the groin, causing him to wince and fall back. Before she could use the dagger against him, black smoke left his hands and trailed the floorboards until it reached her. She kept her feet planted on the floor, her hands outstretched as white light shot out through her body, exploding into the room, but it had no effect on him. His darkness was too powerful; it pushed back against her.

Kieran jumped to his feet, barreling toward her, but she dropped her magic and thrust her hand out. The dagger clenched in her fist sliced across his cheek, blood splattering against the wall.

The wound did nothing to stop him, though. Kieran wiped the blood from his cheek, smearing red across his jaw and chin. She tried to run for the door, but his hand lashed out and gripped her hair, pulling her back into his chest. Janelle's training kicked in, and she twirled around, feeling her hair rip at her scalp as she plunged the dagger straight into his left eye. Power and darkness shook the room, his magic filling every space around them as he screamed in pain.

There was a loud hum from right outside the window.

The Shadow Creature crashed through the glass, coming straight at Kieran.

The rune shield is down, she realized. *I have to run.*

The moment Kieran turned to the sound and faced the creature, his hand released the grip he had on her hair. She planted her feet, bolting toward the door. When she swung it open, Tegan stood with her sword drawn, her face a mask of horror as she spotted the creature inside the room. Her friend reached out and gripped Janelle's hand, and the two ran as fast as they could through the hallway toward the front door.

They didn't stop moving until they reached the courtyard. Janelle shivered in fear as she felt the creature approaching them from behind, but it was not coming for them. It moved quickly through the grassy field at the front of the property, and it fled toward the forest. It was gone in moments. As if it had melted into the trees.

"It'll be back," Tegan cried, almost out of breath. "We need to keep moving."

Tegan gripped Janelle to help her when she suddenly slumped forward, catching herself on a tree to keep from falling.

"Kieran poisoned me," Janelle said sluggishly. "It's starting to have more of an effect on me."

"Okay. Listen. Try to run. We must run," Tegan said. "I know Kieran hurt you, but you need to move your legs."

"I'm trying," Janelle moaned in a weak voice. "We don't know if he's dead. I need to get to Elijah and his people." She used all the willpower she had to put one foot in front of the other, and together, they kept moving.

35

LINCOLN

Elijah stood at the front lines with the Zemiran soldiers that had now entered the city, standing along the grassy field. The hybrids and a few of Kieran's guards lined the coastline, creating a barrier in front of the Sybil Curse.

Lincoln stood behind Elijah, keeping his eyes on the ship and Anaru hovering above. He heard someone shouting Elijah's name, and he felt a surge of panic run down his spine. He turned toward the sound and saw two figures crossing the field toward him. It was Janelle and Tegan.

Janelle ran to him, stumbling as she went. It appeared her limbs had grown weak as she struggled to walk. The second Elijah saw her, he dropped his sword and sprinted in her direction, Lincoln following closely behind.

"What's happening?" Janelle cried out as she fell into his arms, burying her head into his chest. She reached out to touch his face. "Is this really you?"

He knitted his brows together as she sagged into him like dead weight. "Yes, darling. Kieran was supposed to release you from that room so that we could trade you. I—" Lincoln watched Elijah's eyes turn dark as he observed blood splatter on her neck and bleeding scalp. "Is that your blood? What did that fucker do to you?"

"Kieran's blood," Tegan answered for her. "He attacked her wearing your face, but she fought back. The shadow came through the window, drawn by Kieran's burst of magic, and we were both able to escape. We have no idea if Kieran is still alive or not. I need to get on that ship. Now!" Tegan said, pulling the Kroneon out of her pocket and placing it in her hand with a firm grip. "It's time."

Janelle looked up in a haze as Lincoln stepped beside Elijah, handing him back his sword.

"Go, Tegan," Lincoln said. "We'll be right behind you."

Elijah looked down, cupping Janelle's jaw with his hands. "Did he—"

She shook her head, opening her mouth to answer, but something wrapped around her neck and squeezed before she got the words out.

It was a thick, black fog, like Elijah's power, but he wasn't the one wielding it. Kieran, still behind property lines, called the power back to him with a flick of his wrist, flinging Janelle to the ground and dragging her backward over the grass. She kicked and tugged at the magic around her neck, but he was too strong. He pulled her until she was back in his tight grasp.

Kieran's skin was covered in blood, and his injured eye was swollen shut. Red covered so much of his face he was almost unrecognizable. A large gash on his forehead oozed; it appeared that the shadow had clawed his face before it retreated into the forest.

"I'll fucking kill you," Elijah ground out through his teeth, taking a step toward the bloodied sorcerer. Lincoln reached out and put a hand on Elijah's chest, attempting to push him back. Elijah wasn't running toward Kieran yet, but dark magic dripped slowly from his fingertips as his body trembled with rage.

"Don't use your power, Elijah," Lincoln warned. "Calm your anger, or that thing will be drawn back here before we're ready."

Elijah's jaw hardened. "He has to die."

Lincoln nodded slightly and turned toward the coastline. He let out a sharp whistle, a signal for the soldiers of Zemira to move toward their position. It was time for the blood oath exchange.

Janelle struggled against Kieran's dark grip on her neck and reached out to Elijah. But it was too late. He watched as the poison worked quickly, taking hold of Janelle's body and paralyzing her limbs. She dropped to the ground and looked up as the Zemiran army advanced and formed a barrier around them, their weapons out and ready to attack. Then her eyes shut, and her body went still.

Liam, the head of Elijah's guards, stepped forward, his sword wielded in front of him.

"Kill your former king!" Kieran called to Liam and the Zemiran army, pressing his boot into Janelle's prone body, which lay on the ground. Lincoln saw her chest rise and fall slowly, but she didn't stir.

She's alive, he observed.

"What did you do to her?" Elijah asked again, power covering his eyes as the darkness consumed him.

"Elijah, drop your power," Lincoln warned again, looking over his shoulder to see the Shadow Creature leave the forest. It moved slowly along the grass toward them, the moonlight illuminating its vapor-like form. "Now, Elijah." He was deviating from the plan. All he could think about was getting Janelle away from the sorcerer.

"Just a paralytic poison to make sure she couldn't escape me," Kieran said. "It hasn't reached her lungs yet, so there's time for you to fulfill the oath properly. Now that everything is in place." He stomped down on Janelle's stomach with his heel, but she didn't move. She couldn't protect herself. Her body was alive and helpless, and Kieran's poison kept her completely immobilized.

Lincoln took in the scene and knew it would be impossible to stop Elijah from attacking once the Zemiran army was traded. All they could do now was protect themselves from the Shadow Creature and get back to the ship as quickly as possible, so they could kill it.

Lincoln drew his sword and kept it by his hip, tracking the creature's slow movements but not alerting the sorcerer to it.

"Let her go," Elijah said carefully, his power moving along the grass until it reached Kieran. "You're the only one threatening to sever the oath. My army is yours the moment you hand her back to me. Then we fight that creature out there together. Now! Before it comes back and kills us all. Release her from your poison's control, and the oath will be complete."

A wicked smile crossed Kieran's features. He bent his knee and placed his hand on Janelle's head. He reached into his pocket, pulled out a vial, and put it to her lips. Then he helped tilt her head back to drink the blue liquid inside. She coughed three times before rolling onto her hands and knees and looking up. Tears fell down her cheeks, and her chest heaved with the pain that wracked her stomach from Kieran's boot.

"Do it!" Kieran said, fisting her hair, making her cry out in agony.

"Alright!" Elijah said, his voice filled with panic. "As King of Zemira, my army is yours. I give you Zemira and my crown as the rightful heir to both."

Elijah dropped his power and reached out toward Janelle.

"Hurry," he said, extending his fingers out to coax her to hurry toward him. She clambered to her feet, stumbling over the grass before falling into his arms again, still weak from what Kieran's poison had done to her.

"That wasn't so hard now, was it?" Kieran said, reaching up to touch his gouged eye as if he was just now realizing what damage Janelle had done. "I was beginning to think you'd go back on your oath," Kieran said. "Now, I command you"—he gestured to the Zemiran soldiers again—"to kill your former king!"

The sorcerer glanced around at the Zemiran army, who stood like statues behind him.

"What are you doing?" Kieran screamed when they didn't move. Even his own army looked around, unsure of what should be done.

The Zemiran soldiers were stronger in numbers, and Kieran's coven knew it. They had magic, but the Zemiran army was ten times their strength in brute force. They would be foolish to attack without Kieran's power protecting them.

"You're to protect me now, your *new* king!" Kieran ordered again.

"Oh, sorry," Elijah said, his lip quirking upward in the corner. "Technicalities. You're not their new king."

Lincoln turned as light radiated behind them along the shore. Ten hybrids stood ready at the shoreline, but they kept their powers dimmed as the shadow drew closer to the mansion. They linked their light hand in hand to create a border near the Sybil Curse at the docks. By keeping the shield power low, the Shadow Creature wouldn't be able to detect the hybrids and would continue its path toward Kieran.

Both men on the grass were unaware that the Shadow Creature was almost upon them. Elijah was so blinded by his anger that he couldn't see the imminent threat looming closer behind them.

"You're breaking the oath then by not *making* them follow their new king?" Kieran's frown turned up into a smile. "I guess you're about to die anyway at the hands of the Oath Gods."

"Kieran," Elijah said amusedly, "I cannot make them do anything, as it wasn't *my* kingdom to give." Elijah glanced at Liam.

A smile flitted across Elijah's lips as Liam stepped forward again, opened his coat, pulled out the Zemiran crown, and placed it upon his own head.

"King Liam of Zemira," Elijah started, "respectfully declines your bargain."

Janelle looked up at him, her eyes growing wide with shock. She realized what was happening.

"Sorry, love. I had to keep this from you to protect you." He leaned in and kissed her on the lips with rough eagerness, and then he slowly moved her behind him.

Kieran scowled. "What the fuck is this?" His breathing was heavy as he reached to his side and gripped the bloodied dagger that took his left eye, his remaining eye growing so dark it turned pitch black.

"I realized before we left Zemira that you'd stop at nothing to take my people, even entering a blood oath to make sure I stood by my word. But my word is void when handing over something I don't hold a right to."

Kieran stepped forward, a mix of fury and confusion flitting across his features.

"You made an oath with a Zemiran who holds no title, Kieran," he continued. "I'm just a little rich boy with no crown, right?" Elijah smirked. "I gave up my crown to the head of my guard, Liam, before setting foot on your land. For he is the new King of Zemira now. The oath should have been done with *him*. Not me. What we agreed upon in blood is not binding. So, I have broken nothing; I was simply keeping the throne warm..." He turned to his friend. "For a much, much better man."

Liam held his sword in front of him and smiled back at Elijah, giving him a brief nod of assurance. He would protect his people and their country, ensuring that the sorcerer never hurt another soul again.

The Delamere bloodline to the Zemiran throne had ended. Lincoln and Elijah were finally free from their father's legacy.

"Elijah, it's here. We have to stick to the plan," Lincoln said more urgently, finally drawing Elijah's attention to look over at the grass, spotting the creature coming their way.

"As the King of Zemira," Liam shouted, "I command you to seize that man." He lowered the sword and pointed it at Kieran.

Kieran reached into his pocket frantically, fumbling around. When his hand felt nothing, he looked up.

"Where is it?" Kieran growled through his teeth.

Lincoln smirked. "Where's what?" He knew what he meant.

"The Kroneon," Kieran fumed. "Where the fuck is it?"

Before the Zemiran army could move forward, magic shot out of Kieran's fingers, surrounding him with darkness, forcing the soldiers to give him a wide berth.

Elijah dropped his own power, gripping Janelle's waist tightly before they all dove to the ground.

Lincoln looked up as the shadow moved over them, charging straight toward Kieran, homing in on the surging magic pouring out of him.

"Run!" Lincoln shouted, yanking on Elijah's cloak.

Elijah jumped to his feet, pulling Janelle with them. The Zemiran army split apart as they ran toward the ship, hearing Kieran's guttural screams. The shadow attacked him once again, completely consuming his flesh, blood, and darkness—the only one foolish enough to unleash his full power.

Lincoln looked up as Anaru flew overhead, following them through the marketplace between the mansion and the ship.

"Wait!" Janelle shouted. "We need to find Aiden!"

"He's on the ship," Lincoln called back, pointing his sword at the Sybil Curse. "Keep running."

As they reached the docks, a bright yellow light shone on the deck.

"Is that Tegan?!" Janelle asked as the men helped her climb up the Jacob's ladder. She was still weak from the poison; Lincoln could tell by the trembling of her limbs.

"Get ready to hold on," Elijah said as they climbed over the railing.

Lincoln looked around, spotting Mazie turning the helm at a sharp angle and moving the ship to the left. Bay flew from Mazie's shoulder and sprinkled pixie dust over Tegan, who then floated slightly above the wooden deck, halfway up the mast.

Aiden stood at the stern of the ship with his father's sword drawn. When he saw her floating, he tossed the sword her way. Tegan caught the hilt in one hand, pulling the Kroneon out with the other. Power grew around her, drawing the attention of the Shadow Creature, who was still on the grass fields near the mansion. It let out a buzzing shriek and made its way toward the shoreline, picking up speed as it spotted the ship.

Lincoln covered his ears as the buzzing sound grew louder before running to the cannon, pointing it at the creature coming their way in case their plan was to fail. "Steady, mates!" Lincoln called out from the cannon. "Steady. Nola, use your call now! Try to subdue it!"

Nola stepped forward, attempting to use her siren call to weaken the creature, but it pressed on, unaffected by her power. Its hunger was fixed on the brightly lit hybrid aboard the ship, and it wouldn't be deterred.

Tegan pushed down at the center of the Kroneon, magic still radiating around her as the portal opened above the sea at the bow of the ship.

Mazie turned the helm again, moving the ship to the center of the black, whirling portal.

The shadow sprang forward over the border of the grasses to the sandy banks close to the sea. Lincoln whistled toward the sky, alerting the great beast above to attack.

Anaru dove toward the land, extending her claws to seize the creature Lincoln had realized wasn't yet solidified. Her claws slipped through its back, and she swooped back up to the skies, waiting for the next signal to strike again. The captain watched Anaru position herself to dive and let out another whistle, two short bursts. As they lined the sand, the hybrids lit up their power at once, drawing the shadow toward them. The creature fed upon their free-flowing energy and became drunk with power. It began to solidify as it gorged itself upon them. When the creature was almost within touching distance, they severed their bond, falling to the ground, one by one. As the last hybrid suppressed their magic, all were rendered invisible to the monster at once.

The monster's black wings sprang out as it took a solid form, and its blood-red eyes burned with vicious, endless hunger. It turned away from the group of hybrids, re-focusing on the immense magic pouring from the ship. It jumped onto the docks and scrambled along the planks until it leapt up, flying over the railing of the ship. Before it crashed down onto Tegan, she cut out the pulsing light of her magic and channeled it into the form of long, smoke-like fingers. With a shout, she wrapped the magic around the creature's throat and slammed it down onto the ship's deck. It thrashed and shrieked, trying to absorb and break the magic's hold before Tegan plunged Hagmar's sword deep into its chest, piercing the core. Tegan held the hilt with all her strength, feeling the monstrous beast fight against her magic and the magic within the blade.

The creature cried out again, and Lincoln signaled to the skies for Anaru. The dragon flew back down toward the ship, finally able to latch her claws into its neck, keeping it still.

Anaru unleashed her fire upon it, scorching off parts of its blazing dark flesh. An earsplitting roar shook the ship's wood, and everyone nearly collapsed from the shock wave that followed.

Mazie gritted her teeth and held tight to the helm. The ship continued to move forward. The bow entered the portal with the shadow shrieking so loudly that the crew winced at the sound. The creature was trapped, finally unable to flee back to the forest.

"We're going in!" Lincoln shouted, wrapping his arm around Nola and pulling her close. "Keep holding it! Steady, Tegan! Anaru!"

Lincoln observed Elijah running to Janelle, holding tightly to her wrists and helping her stand on her feet.

"This way! Grab on, and don't let go, no matter what!" Elijah shouted, taking her to the railing and helping her to keep from falling as she wrapped her arms tightly in place.

As Mazie steered forward, the portal dragged the massive ship inside, and everyone held onto the Sybil Curse. They braced for the pressure of the Kroneon's power to rip them through time, ensuring that the creature couldn't flee into their land again. It was the first time the crew had steered the ship into one of the Kroneon's portals while moving. Every time before, they jumped through from dry land in fear the ship wouldn't make it. To rid the Shadow Creature of their world, they had no choice but to risk their very lives.

The mast bent as the pressure of the portal pulled them through, shattering the wood and splitting the ship apart into two pieces.

There was a heavy thud as the broken vessel hit solid ground, followed by the chaos of broken wood and debris crashing all around them. There were screams and then silence.

Lincoln opened his eyes to a different world they had never entered during their time with the Kroneon.

The land was desolate and barren. The sky was blood orange, with black clouds moving slowly through tall mountain ranges in the distance. It looked as though they had crashed into a large valley. Dry, cracked rock surrounded them, and tiny streams of silver water moved in and out of tall, black-barked trees.

Lincoln took Nola's hand and helped her climb to the ship's destroyed helm. The Sybil Curse was smashed into two large piles of splinters.

"Tegan!" Aiden shouted, drawing their attention as the elf climbed down the ladder to run across the barren ground—Tegan had been thrown from the ship during the crash.

They looked over the edge of the broken ship to see Tegan lying along the rock with the Shadow Creature behind her. Its eyes were closed, and burned pieces of flesh were still smoking beneath the sword that impaled it.

"Tegan," Aiden said again, shaking her as he reached her side.

Her eyes opened slowly, and he helped her up. Tegan rubbed the side of her jaw, shaking off the dizziness. She leaned down and gripped the sword, pulling it free of the creature's chest. When the sword came loose, the monster turned to dust, ash scattering the surrounding land.

Mazie let out a groan, threw a plank off her, and jumped down from the ship. She saw where Aiden stood and pulled out her cutlass, lifting it up until the blade touched Aiden's throat, ushering him to back away from Tegan. "Easy, elf boy," she warned. "Stay away from her."

Aiden held up his hands. "I'm not going to hurt her."

"No?" she said. "Is that darkness still inside you?"

They all waited for his answer.

"Yes," Aiden confessed. "I feel it inside me. It's not as strong as it once was, but it's there. I'm not a monster, Mazie." He turned to look at Lincoln. "I want to survive, just as any of you do."

Lincoln turned around at the sound of a large breath behind the rear of the ship. "Anaru! Anaru, are you alright?" he cried out, running around the corner of the ship debris.

They came up to his dragon lying against a large rock near a small stream. They rushed over to her body, Lincoln placing his hand over her red wing.

"Anara!" He shook her. "What happened back there? We were completely destroyed going through that damned portal!" Lincoln turned back to Nola. "And where the bloody hell are Elijah and Janelle?"

Nola shook her head. "We'll find them. I...I don't see them near the ship. I don't know; they may have been thrown off as well."

Lincoln turned back to Anaru. Relief swept over him as he watched her chest steadily rise and fall. Something, however, was happening to her.

"Tegan," Lincoln said, looking up at her as she approached. "Do you know where you sent us?"

Suddenly, Anaru's wings shot out and began to transform. As her rough scales smoothed out into human, light brown skin, it gleamed like the golden fire against the warm desert sand. They all stepped back as she shrank and changed, each part of her form twisting until it was that of a woman. The crew could do nothing but stand back and watch it happen in complete shock.

Anaru's jet-black hair spilled over the rocks, and her eyes sparkled like the color of the sun. She glanced up at Lincoln, and the two exchanged a look of understanding.

"She's home," Tegan said. "When she flew over me, she connected our minds, showing me this place in a vision. I held onto the image with all I had until it took us here." She gestured to the sky as three dragons appeared and flew through the clouds. "This planet is Dragão Terra." She turned to Lincoln again. "Land of the dragon shifters."

36

JANELLE

Janelle groaned and opened her eyes to an orange-hued sky. She blinked before sitting up, wincing at the pain shooting through her body. She realized where she was and whipped her head around, frantically searching the grounds for Elijah. Their hands had been tightly linked together, but between the power of the Kroneon's magic and the force of the portal opening, it ripped them apart.

She landed on a grassy field surrounded by purple-budded flowers and moss-covered rocks.

"Elijah!" she screamed, panicking. "Anyone?"

Janelle slowly stood; her legs were still shaky, and she caught herself on a fallen tree nearby. Twigs and dried leaves stuck to her hair, but she ignored them. It felt like her body was floating, as if it were made out of air from the fear rushing down her spine. Janelle straightened her legs and began to walk through the grass. The air was stifling, and there appeared to be no signs of life anywhere. Janelle bit her lip, forcing herself to stay calm and think rationally.

Where is he? she wondered. *Did Elijah get thrown close by?*

"Elijah!" she called again as she came closer to a clearing. Her body went rigid as she heard a noise from behind. Three tall, bare-chested men were standing behind her when she turned around. Their hair was thick, reaching down to the center of their muscular backs. Black tattoos lined their entire torsos, and their bodies below the waist were covered in brown, tattered cloth.

One of the men stepped toward her; Janelle took a step back, feeling her blood run cold. The strange men didn't look to be friendly.

"Don't move!" she warned. "Stay where you are!"

Janelle's fighting instincts kicked in, but she realized that not only was she weaponless, but the men were also twice her size—they would crush her before she could land a single blow.

An arrogant smile turned up on one of the men's lips before the color of his skin started to change into various shades of red. It almost appeared like his skin had shifted into scales. Janelle's eyes grew wide, and she felt her body numb from fear as the man's lips peeled back from his teeth.

"Well," the man spoke, his voice low and gravelly. "Our master will be quite pleased with his new little pet."

ABOUT THE AUTHOR

D.L. Blade has always been passionate about creative writing, focusing on poetry during her younger years. One night, after having a vivid dream, she was inspired to pick up her pen and write her debut novel, *The Dark Awakening*.

Initially, Blade had focused on writing young adult fiction, but she has since shifted her focus to adult fantasy, paranormal, and dark romance. Through her stories, she takes readers on a journey into a world of unconventional love, morally gray men, and deliciously handsome villains.

When she's not writing, Blade enjoys reading, spending time with her husband and two children, attending rock concerts, and exploring new restaurants in Denver. She dreams of continuing to create exciting novels for her readers and taking them on a journey through the magical realms that spill from the pages of her books.